A Promise of Home

A Hometown Harbor Novel

Tammy L. Grace

www.tammylgrace.com
Facebook: https://www.facebook.com/tammylgrace.books
Twitter: @TammyLGrace

Published in the United States by Lone Mountain Press, Nevada

ISBN 978-0-9912434-4-0 (paperback)
ISBN 978-0-9912434-5-7 (eBook)

FIRST EDITION

Cover design by Kari Ayasha, Cover to Cover Designs
Interior Formatting by Polgarus Studio
Author Photo by Cook's Photography

Printed in the United States of America

ALSO BY TAMMY L. GRACE

Below you will find links to the electronic version of all of Tammy's books available at Amazon

Cooper Harrington Detective Novels

Killer Music

Hometown Harbor Series

Hometown Harbor: The Beginning (FREE Prequel Novella)

Finding Home

Home Blooms

A Promise of Home

Pieces of Home

Tammy would love to connect with readers on social media. Remember to subscribe to her mailing list for another freebie, only available to readers on the mailing list. Follow this link to her webpage and provide your email address and she'll send you the exclusive interview she did with all the canine characters in her books. Follow Tammy on Facebook at this link, by liking her page. You may also follow Tammy on Amazon at this link, by using the follow button under her photo.

Dear Readers,

I had so much fun hosting Sam and Jeff's wedding at my nursery, especially with Max's help. They had a short, but relaxing honeymoon on Orcas Island, where they spent time bicycling. Everything was going great until the day after the wedding when I tripped on a power box and broke my ankle. I had to stay at Sam's with Max while I recovered.

When Sam and Jeff came home, they decided to continue biking. Their happiness was cut short by a tragic hit and run. Jeff suffered a severe head injury requiring him to be flown to Seattle. Jeff was in the hospital for months and had to work hard to regain his strength. Brenda was finally arrested for the hit and run and the arson at Sam's shop. After she bailed out she ran her car off the road and died in an apparent suicide.

Sam didn't leave Jeff's side while he was in the hospital, so Max took up the slack and helped run Harbor Coffee and Books. He also bought a beautiful house on the water, not far from Jeff's family resort on Mitchell Bay. After my injury, I decided to sell my house. It was too big and very inconvenient with an immobile leg, so I sold it to a couple who are opening a bed and breakfast. While cleaning out things, I found an old photo and letter that led me on a quest for some answers about my family. It turns out my parents fled to Friday Harbor to escape mobsters in Chicago. They changed their names and faked their deaths. I was angered and hurt when I learned that I had been deprived of knowing my relatives. The silver lining in all this is that I found my dad's only living brother, Uncle Mike, and his wife Diane.

With Sam gone, Max busy at the shop, and my injury, we were lucky Jen introduced us to Regi Brady. She's the new secretary at the high school and Max hired her to help at the coffee shop on weekends. Regi has quite the story of her own. She visited the island for high school graduation with her boyfriend, Cam. They were going their separate ways, but made a pact to return to Friday Harbor for their fortieth birthdays this year. During their time on the island, Regi got pregnant, but didn't tell Cam. She came back this summer with the hope of reuniting with Cam during their birthday week, which is right around Christmas. Regi's smart and pretty and we're all a bit worried that she's wasting her time waiting around for this guy from twenty years ago. Nate, our local delivery man, is clearly attracted to Regi, but she seems to have her heart set on Cam and doesn't give him the time of day. Her daughter, Molly, doesn't know the whole story and just started college this year.

Max and I took a trip to Victoria in late September. We had a wonderful time touring the gardens and relaxing at The Empress Hotel. It was a memorable trip for both of us. Things got serious for us and Max asked me to move in with him, which I did, much to my mother's dismay.

I love the holidays and have decked the halls at Max's new house. After the annual tree lighting at the harbor, we had a lovely dinner with Sam and Jeff and then Max surprised me with the most romantic gesture. He decorated the entire yard with lights and then proposed as we sat by the fire. My ring is drop dead gorgeous and the wedding is only a couple of months away.

Christmas is in a few weeks and we're all anxious to see if Cam returns to Friday Harbor to fulfill the promise he and Regi made. Grab a cup of cocoa and catch up with your friends from Friday Harbor during the holiday season.

Linda

ACKNOWLEDGMENTS

While writing A Promise of Home I've had the pleasure of meeting several new readers, both in person and online. It's fun and rewarding to hear from people who have enjoyed their escape to Friday Harbor and meeting the characters in the Hometown Harbor Series.

As always I'm thankful for my early readers, who are so faithful about reading my manuscripts and providing valuable improvements. Theresa, Linda, and Dana, are three of my most loyal evaluators and provide such helpful feedback.

My cover designer, Kari at Cover to Cover Designs, is so talented and worked her magic again to deliver a beautiful cover. Jason and Marina at Polgarus Studio deliver expert formatting with first-rate customer service. I appreciate the assistance of these professionals who help me deliver a quality product.

I'm grateful for the support and encouragement of my friends and family as I continue to pursue my dream of writing. I appreciate all of the readers who have taken the time to provide a review on Amazon or Goodreads. These reviews are especially important in promoting future books, so if you enjoy my novels, please consider leaving a positive review.

~For my son, Josh~

"Your son will hold your hand for a little while.
But he will hold your heart for a lifetime."
Author Unknown

One

Linda and Sam sipped from steaming hot drinks, captivated by the scene outside the window of Harbor Coffee and Books. Downy white flakes fell from the sky while reflections of red, green, gold, and blue polka dots danced across the soft mounds of snow along the sidewalks. Snowfall was rare on the island, but it was the perfect accompaniment for the season. Friday Harbor was dressed for Christmas, from the strings of lights threaded across the streets and draped around the trees, to the majestic pine adorned with a bright star, towering over the park.

Stacks of bridal magazines littered the table and a rumpled bag from Soup D'Jour was pushed to the side. It had only been a week since Max proposed, but Linda was already working on a wedding plan and Sam was making lists.

"A summer event is so much easier, but I think the Lakeside Resort will be a great venue, even in February," said Linda.

"It will be fabulous. The lodge is incredible and with that wall of windows looking out at the lake, we'll feel like we're outside, even if we're not," said Sam.

"I thought about waiting until April or May, but I really want to be married."

Sam smiled. "I know you do. It's going to be gorgeous, especially the classy black and white with a touch of lavender. A Valentine's Day wedding is so romantic."

"As a florist, I absolutely abhor the idea, but as a bride, I find it charming. Those Valentine brides used to drive me over the edge, but now I am one." She smirked as she took a sip of chai.

"Let's plan a trip into the city with Jen and go back to Rose's Bridal Boutique and find you the perfect dress. Becky can meet us and we'll have another fun girlie day," suggested Sam.

Linda eyes gleamed. "Sounds like a great idea." She paused and flipped through a magazine. "I honestly never thought I'd ever get married."

"You just had to wait for the right man and Max is the best."

Linda nodded and smiled. "He was definitely worth the wait."

Sam sipped her tea while she watched a couple traipse down the sidewalk, huddled together in scarves and hats. "I've been thinking we need to plan something for Regi's birthday," said Sam. "I'm concerned that Cam might not fulfill his promise and she'll need the fun."

Linda nodded. "Yeah, I can tell she's worried. She's looked tired and miserable when I've seen her. I know she's disappointed he hasn't arrived yet."

"And his birthday is only about ten days away. I think if he was planning to come he would've been here by now." Sam sighed and clutched the warm cup in her hands. "At least Molly will be here during her college break. She and Kyle both get here tomorrow."

"That'll be good for Regi. I bet you're excited to see Kyle, huh? You'll have to share him with his grandma."

Sam laughed. "Yeah, I know. I've missed him. We email and keep in touch, but it's not the same. He sent me some great photos of his Thanksgiving trip to New York City with Marty."

"Is Kyle's mom coming to the island for Christmas?"

"That's the plan. She won't be here until Christmas Day, so he and Rita are coming with us to your house for Christmas Eve."

"Great. Max is so excited to host Christmas Eve. We'll have the house in party mode, so let's plan on throwing Regi a birthday bash at our place on the twenty-sixth."

"Are you sure that wouldn't be too much?"

"Of course not. It'll be fun. Let's do a dinner. That way everyone from the coffee shop will be able to come, since you're closing at five now."

"Okay, but let me do the bulk of the food."

"We'll split things up and I think we should have Ellie do a special cake," suggested Linda.

Sam nodded her head and flipped her notebook over to a clean sheet. She began making a list. "Okay, how about we do something easy like a taco bar?"

"Sounds perfect. Let's include some of her friends from the high school and Nate, of course."

"Poor Nate. If Cam does come, he'll be devastated. I think he really cares for Regi and I'm not sure she's aware of his true feelings," said Sam.

"I know. Max thinks we should explain the whole thing about the promise she and Cam made to each other twenty years ago, but I told him we need to stay out of it," said Linda.

"It's definitely her story to tell, not ours, but I do feel for Nate. He stops by when she's working, just to visit and I know he sees her every day when he delivers to the school. He's clearly smitten with her and I get the feeling she just thinks of him as a buddy."

Linda shook her head. "I invited her and Molly for Christmas Eve and told her to bring Cam, if he's here." She took another sip of her hot drink. "If he doesn't come, maybe she'll stop fantasizing and move on instead of living in the past," said Linda, with a sigh. "But, then who am I to talk about living in the past?"

Sam smiled. "You had your reasons, but now you've got a bright future."

"Speaking of, Jen and I are going out to Lakeside tomorrow to meet with the event coordinator. Do you want to tag along?"

"Sure, sounds fun. Jen's so excited about your wedding. She already asked me about using our house for the bridal shower."

Linda's eyes sparkled. "She told me she booked out the day to do everyone's hair. She's all over it."

"Is your Uncle Mike going to be able to make it?"

Linda nodded. "He said wild horses couldn't keep him away. He's going to walk me down the aisle," she said, as tears filled her eyes.

Sam grasped her hand. "Oh, how wonderful. And your mom?"

"She's excited and happy to know I won't be living in sin much longer." Linda rolled her eyes. "She and David and his family will be here, but that's the extent of my relatives. Max's children and his parents are flying in. His parents are coming a few days early. They're thrilled and so happy for us."

"If you need rooms for family, let me know. I'm happy to have them."

"I'll talk to Max. We were thinking about having my mom and Max's parents stay with us. Maybe we'll see if Max's kids could stay with you. We were going to put the rest of them up at the Lakeside or at Ben and Sherrie's."

"I'd love to host the kids. It would be fun to see them," said Sam. "Count me in."

Linda glanced at her watch as they heard a tap on the glass door and looked up to see Jen. She was wrapped up in the colorful hat and scarf Linda had brought her from Victoria. Sam jumped up and unlocked the door.

"Come in. How are you?"

"A little tired, but the walk in the snow was refreshing. It's magical with the lights and the tree—like a Christmas card," Jen said, plucking off her hat to reveal her blond hair streaked with red and green highlights.

"How about something hot to drink?" offered Sam.

"Sure, tea is fine. Surprise me," smiled Jen. She stepped out of her boots, exposing fluffy red socks decorated with snowflakes. She tucked herself into a chair and Linda angled the list so Jen could read it.

"Sam decided we need a trip to the city to pick out the dress where she found hers. She's going to come with us to Lakeside tomorrow."

"Oh, fun. I worked late tonight so I could have tomorrow off. Lakeside should be able to take care of the ceremony, reception and dinner, as well as the rehearsal the night before. They're giving a discount on the rehearsal dinner and throwing in two rooms for your family, when you book the wedding, since it's their slow season. And it doesn't hurt that you've done so many events there."

Linda smiled. "Aubrey is being especially generous." She glanced at Sam's list. "Max and I are cake tasting on Sunday after Ellie closes. We're having Ryan do the photography, like he did for Sam and Jeff. Sara has the flowers under control. Max is in charge of the tuxedos and if we get my dress and your dress in the city, I think we'll have it whipped."

Sam turned on some music and returned with a steaming cup of tea for Jen and a plate of fresh brownies. She put the box of invitations on the table. "Okay, let's get the assembly line started and we'll get these invitations done tonight."

They hummed along to "White Christmas" as they labeled, stuffed, and sealed the crisp envelopes announcing the marriage of Linda Louise Graham to Dr. Max F. Sullivan.

Sam chuckled as she read the invitation. "I see Max didn't allow his real first name to be used."

Linda smiled, "I know. I tried to convince him to use Maximilian Francis Sullivan, but he made an ugly face and refused."

Jen laughed. "Maximilian Francis. Wow."

The three women snickered as they sang along to the holiday tunes, finishing the envelopes before they dared to eat a brownie and get a chocolate smudge on the pristine invitations. By the time they finished visiting and dissecting the pictures of the brides in the magazines, it was close to midnight and the streets were carpeted in fresh snow.

Linda offered Jen a ride to her car and the three hugged and bundled into their snowcapped vehicles to make their way home. As Linda reached for her door handle, she shouted back at Sam. "I'll pick you up in the morning and we'll head out to Lakeside."

Sam nodded and waved, encased in her hat and scarf.

As Linda waved goodbye to Jen in front of her salon, her cell phone rang. “Hi, Max,” she answered.

“Hey, sweetie. I was getting worried about you. Are you on your way home?”

“I just dropped Jen at her car and am on my way now. We just finished up.”

“Okay, be careful on the roads. Go slow. I’ll see you in a few minutes. Love you.”

Linda smiled. She had never had a man in her life worry about her and take care of her like Max. “I love you too.” She disconnected the call and put both of her gloved hands on the wheel of the SUV. *I’m one lucky gal to have met Max. He’s made the last thirty years of waiting for the right guy worth every minute.*

Two

Regi slogged through the last week of school. The only bright spot had been the arrival of Molly from college. She did her best to hide her anxiety about Cam, but when she was alone, the mask of happiness slid off her face. Her new friends on the island kept Molly occupied while Regi finished up her office duties at the high school. Molly's plans for the week included helping at the nursery and the flower shop, getting a pedicure and manicure at Jen's salon, and baking with Sam. Regi let Molly sleep in every morning as she left for work and met up with her daughter each night around dinner time.

The last day of school finally ended and Regi was working at the coffee shop all weekend. Sam was doing her best to convince Regi to take a few days off the week of Christmas to spend with Molly. She even let Regi know she was flexible and if Cam showed up for his birthday on the twenty-third she could take time off.

Regi opened the coffee shop on Saturday morning, with her game face on, ready to spread holiday cheer. Hayley had already left with Charlie for their Whistler vacation and Rachel was out of town for the entire break. Megan and Regi would be working the bulk of the shifts over the holidays, with help from Kyle and Sam.

Regi slipped her apron on and plopped the Santa hat on her head. The festive bells on the door clanged as the first customers of the day arrived. Regi greeted them with enthusiasm and hummed along to the Christmas carols playing in the background.

She whipped through the drink orders with ease, commenting on the bustle of the holidays. She served up pastries and warm beverages to the steady stream of customers without missing a beat. As soon as the morning rush was over, Nate appeared.

"Morning, Regi. How's it going?" he asked. "Love your hat."

She rolled her eyes. "Hey, Nate. Steady morning today. What can I get you—your usual?"

He smiled. "Sounds perfect." He waited while she made his mocha and warmed up a giant cinnamon roll with gooey frosting. The shop had cleared out and he was the only customer.

"How about you take a break and join me? I could use some help eating this monster."

She glanced at the door and nodded. "Okay, I'll be right there."

He sat at the same table nearest the counter he chose every day. She plopped down in the chair with her caramel macchiato and fingered a sliver of the cinnamon roll.

"How's Molly?" he asked.

"She's great. Sleeping in again," she smiled. "She's going to stop in later. She has plans to help at Buds and Blooms today."

"Linda invited me to your birthday bash on Friday—it should be fun."

She chewed the pastry, her eyes on the front windows and nodded. "Yeah, it's thoughtful of them to have a party." She cut another slice. "Do you have to work today?"

"I'm waiting for the load to come in. I'll probably work for a few hours. This time of year is crazy busy. Monday and Tuesday will be the two worst days."

"What are you doing for Christmas?"

"I'll be at my parents' house. The whole family will be on the island this year. My mom is jazzed. What about you and Molly?"

"We're going to Linda's for Christmas Eve and it'll just be the two of us on Christmas Day. We're going to watch movies and hang out. My parents aren't making the trip to the island this year. They'll be at my aunt's house."

"Where do your parents live?"

"In the house where I grew up, near Ellensburg. My aunt lives just a few miles away from them."

"I'd love to take you and Molly to lunch for your birthday on Friday. Are you free?"

"That's kind of you, but I'm not sure what we're doing yet. How about I call you?"

He nodded, "Sure, sure. No problem, just let me know." The tinkling of the bells announced a customer. "Well, I better go check on my deliveries. See ya later."

Regi swiped the plate and her cup from the table and hurried to the counter. "See ya, Nate." She deposited the dirty dishes and turned around to greet a woman she didn't recognize. "Welcome to Harbor Coffee."

The woman smiled and took off her stylish red cape, depositing it on a chair before she approached the counter. "Good morning. I think I'll splurge and have a hazelnut macchiato."

"Would you like a pastry to go with that?" asked Regi, admiring the woman's tasteful clothes. She wore slim black pants and a crisp white shirt, topped off with a supple red leather blazer.

The woman's whiskey colored eyes widened when she looked in the pastry case. "I don't think I can resist a chocolate croissant." She started to open her handbag.

"Go ahead and sit down. I'll bring it over along with the check," Regi said, as she plucked a flaky pastry from the display.

As Regi worked the wands on the espresso machine, she watched the sophisticated woman, noticing how her chunky antique silver jewelry coordinated with the buckles on her black boots. Her hair was dark with silvery strands woven throughout and although Regi guessed she was close to sixty, her skin was smooth, lacking noticeable wrinkles.

Regi carried the plate and cup to the table. "There you go, enjoy."

The woman smiled. "I know I will. This is such a cute shop, are you the owner?"

Regi shook her head. "Thanks, but no, I'm just part of the staff. I'm Regi, by the way. Are you a first time visitor to the island?"

"Pleasure to meet you. I'm Kate, Kate Alexander, and I haven't been here for decades. I'm actually meeting a realtor to finalize my purchase of a business property down the street and look for a house."

"How exciting for you. Sam, the owner of this shop, moved to the island earlier this year to buy this business. Are you buying the old Island Jewels building?"

Kate took a sip of her drink and nodded her head. "Mmm, delicious. Yes, I'm opening an art and antique shop. I've been partners in a business in the city for years and have been looking for an opportunity to have my own small shop. I'm tired of the city life."

"You'll like it here. I just moved here a few months ago and have met some wonderful people." The bells sounded again and Regi glanced at the door. "Let me know if you need anything else."

Kate thanked Regi and turned her attention back to the croissant and the screen on her phone.

Regi kept busy for the next half an hour and saw Kellie come through the door and join Kate at her table. Regi finished with her last customer and wandered over to their table. "Hi, Kellie. May I get you something?"

"Hey, Regi. I'll take a chai latte." She had her tablet out, scrolling through pictures of homes.

"Kate told me she's opening a shop in the old Island Jewels building."

Kellie nodded. "Yeah, it'll be a great addition to the harbor shops. I'm showing her a few houses today."

Kate added. "I'm staying at The Haven, a charming bed and breakfast, right now until I find something I want to buy."

Kellie looked up at Regi. "Regi knows Linda, the previous owner of the house, before it became a B&B."

"Oh, that's a gorgeous place," said Regi.

"Yes, they've got it decorated for the holidays. It's lovely," said Kate. "This whole town is festive with the trees and lights. It reminds me of those snow globes of a perfect Christmas village."

Regi visited while she made Kellie's drink and listened to them discuss homes for sale. She learned Kate was alone, but wanted to find something that had a guestroom to accommodate her son when he came to visit. Kellie settled the bill for both of them and they made for the door with a cheery wave, intending to tour several properties.

"Wonderful to meet you, Regi. I'm sure I'll be seeing more of you," said Kate, as she flipped her black scarf across her neck.

* * *

Linda, Jen, and Sam had finished the wedding arrangements at the Lakeside Resort and drove into town for a late lunch at Soup D'Jour. Sam ordered an extra soup in a sourdough bread bowl and a crisp salad to go, so they could take it to Regi and give her a break.

They bustled through the door and found Regi finishing an order for a group of tourists, who had stopped in to warm up on their walk through town. "Hey, how'd your day go?" asked Regi.

Linda beamed. "It was great. We got everything taken care of out at the resort. I want to run the music selections by Max, but other than that I think the ceremony is set."

"We'll need to find a day to make the trip to Seattle to pick out dresses and then we'll be done," said Sam. She held up a bag for Regi, "Here's your lunch. Take a break and I'll watch things."

"Oh, thanks. You didn't have to bring me lunch."

"It's the least I can do for having you work all day today. Speaking of, we're covered on Friday, so you can have your birthday off, plus the weekend. That way you can do something fun with Molly. No arguments."

"Only if you're sure. With everyone gone, I know you're short." Regi spooned some of the baked potato soup into her mouth. "This is delicious. Thanks again."

Sam nodded. "I'm positive. Megan and Kyle have it covered. You're working the first half of the week, so don't worry about it."

"Okay, thanks. Molly sure enjoyed her time baking with you last week. I'm practically useless in that department. My mom is the baker, not me. Those cookies you guys made are to die for."

Sam grinned. "We had fun and Jeff and Max got the benefit of eating our creations."

The door chimed and Sam saw Regi jerk her head to look and then noticed her shoulders slump as she turned around, her attention back on her soup. Sam moved to the counter to wait on the new customer while Regi ate her lunch.

Linda and Jen noticed the tension building in Regi, noting it was only three days until Cam's birthday. While they hoped he would arrive, for Regi's sake, none of them held out much hope.

Regi finished and took the discarded containers in the back. The bells jingled again and Linda saw Regi's head poke out of the back. "She's going to snap from the stress of waiting for this guy," Linda said to Jen.

"I hope she isn't too depressed on Christmas Eve. Maybe the party will be a helpful distraction for her," added Jen.

The bells continued to ring out, welcoming a steady stream of patrons until closing. Linda and Jen weren't in a hurry to leave and enjoyed hot drinks while discussing hair ideas for the wedding.

The bells clanged against the glass as Molly filled the door, balancing a large wreath. "If this keeps up much longer, Regi's going to need to see a chiropractor for whiplash," whispered Jen, as she noticed Regi twist her head to observe the door again.

"What a beauty. Did you make that with Sara?" asked Linda.

Molly's smiled widened. "Yeah, she helped me make it for our door." She relinquished her gloved hands from the rough twigs she had used in the wreath and placed it on the table. "It looks very Christmassy."

Sam finished up at the counter and hurried to the table to admire Molly's arrangement. "Great job, Molly. I love the red berries and the mini pinecones."

Sam checked her watch. "It's almost closing time, go get your mom and take her home. I'll clean up."

Molly's eyes brightened and she rushed over to the counter as the last customer picked up his drink. "Mom, Sam said she'll clean and we can take off. I made something at the flower shop for you."

A smile spread across Regi's tired face. "How exciting. Let me get my coat and I'll be right out."

Molly turned to Sam. "I worry about Mom. She looks so worn out and seems stressed. I think she works too hard."

"She'll be off for a few days at the end of the week, so make sure she does something fun and relaxing. Sometimes the holidays are stressful."

Molly nodded, gathered up the wreath and met Regi at the door. "Oh, Mol, I love it." Regi sniffed the fresh pine and cedar. "Smells heavenly." They waved goodbye and trudged to Regi's Jeep.

Jen wished Linda and Sam a goodnight and headed across the street to her salon. Linda wiped the tables and chairs while Sam completed the cleaning routine on the machines. Sam turned off the music and doused the lights in the kitchen.

She put her arms into her coat and retrieved her keys. "It would be hard to be in Regi's shoes right now. I wonder if it would be easier if she told Molly the story. I think she's old enough to understand."

"But it would be scary. It's easy to keep believing something and holding on to hope. I did that for years. I convinced myself that Walt would come back and things would work out. I worry that the hope she's been clinging to for twenty years will crack like an old branch. What will happen to her?"

Sam hit the lights, but left her cheerful twinkling lights on in the windows. She turned her key in the lock and they walked in silence to the car.

Three

Despite Regi's vigilant scrutiny of the passengers arriving by ferry and any new faces at the coffee shop, Cam did not appear. It was Christmas Eve and Regi was thankful for the distraction of work. They were closing early today, but she had worked all day yesterday—Cam's birthday. She didn't want to face a gathering tonight, but for Molly's sake she knew she had to keep up the pretense of being in the holiday spirit.

The steam wand shrieked as she swirled the milk, daydreaming about seeing Cam walk through the door, grab her into one of his strong hugs and tell her everything was going to be okay. She finished the drink on autopilot and turned to her customer. "Merry Christmas, Stan. Have a good one."

"You too, Regi," he said, depositing a healthy tip in the jar.

Regi started wiping down the tables, letting a small flicker of hope invade her thoughts. *Maybe he'll be here by Friday for my birthday.*

She checked her watch and saw it was two o'clock, time to close. She flipped the lock on the door and put the closed sign in the window, plus a note reminding customers they would be closed on Christmas Day.

Sam had insisted Regi box up the remaining cookies and pastries and take them home so Molly could enjoy them. She hit the stop button on the MP3 player, with more force than she intended. The cheerful holiday tunes had worn out their welcome and she needed to silence Mariah Carey singing "All I Want for Christmas is You."

When she arrived home, she found Molly decked out in an emerald green dress, sitting on the couch, watching a Christmas movie marathon. She had a bag full of wrapped presents ready and waiting by the door.

"Sam sent me home with all the leftovers," Regi said, raising the box above her head.

Molly hopped up and took the box. "Yum. I'm ready to go, so the bathroom is all yours."

Regi dumped her coat and purse and wandered into her bedroom to find a suitable outfit. She chose a pair of slim black pants and a red silk blouse. She placed them on the bed and lumbered into the bathroom. After a quick shower, she focused on her makeup. The dark circles under her eyes were getting more and more difficult to disguise. She patted the concealer under her eyes, and hoped some eye shadow on her lids would draw attention away from faint purple shadows under her eyes. She curled her hair and then swiped on some mascara and lip gloss. She surveyed her work in the mirror and shook her head, noticing the anxiety in her face.

She padded into the bedroom and got dressed, slipping on some jewelry and a pair of boots. She spritzed on her perfume, reserved for special occasions, and taking a look in the closet mirror, pronounced herself ready. She gave her bed a longing look, wishing she could crawl under the covers and go to sleep. She hadn't slept through the night in weeks. She had been excited and then disappointed, her mind reeling with thoughts she couldn't shut off. *I've got to stop this. I'm so tired of waiting, but each night I tell myself he'll be here.*

Her thoughts were interrupted by Molly yelling, "Mom, come on. We're going to be late."

She took one more look in the mirror and turned off the lights. "I'm ready. We've got time."

Molly toted the bag full of gifts and Regi carried the bottles of wine she had purchased. Linda was adamant that she and Max were throwing the party and there was no need for the guests to bring anything, but Regi knew they'd enjoy the wine, if not tonight, later.

Regi guided the Jeep through the empty streets of town. She couldn't resist the urge to scan the benches and sidewalks, but they were uninhabited. She maneuvered around the town Christmas tree and hit the gas, leaving the cheerful colored lights in the rearview mirror.

They turned off the road at Linda's and as they made their way down the long driveway, Molly gasped. "Oh, wow, it looks like they have their own festival of trees." She grinned, reminding Regi of how she smiled as a young girl. "I'm so glad we got invited."

Regi smiled, caught up in Molly's happiness. They gathered the gifts and wine and dashed to the door. Max greeted them, wearing a Santa hat.

"Merry Christmas," he shouted, gripping them both in a hug. "We're so happy you could come." He motioned them through to the great room, where a fire was roaring and the huge tree twinkled. Lucy was curled up in front of the fire.

Linda and Sam called out a greeting from the kitchen and Jeff and Kyle embraced them and invited them to share the couch, next to Rita. As soon as Max delivered their drinks, the doorbell rang again and the remaining guests joined the group.

Accompanying Megan and Jen was Dr. Sean. He and Jen had been spending a lot of their free time together. When Linda and Max were in the bakery tasting wedding cakes and discovered Ellie had no plans, they insisted she spend the evening with them and she followed Sean into the great room.

Max took their coats and drink orders, while Ellie bustled into the kitchen to deposit several of her bakery boxes. "Hey, girls, do you need any help?" she asked.

Linda looked up from preparing a plate of bruschetta, spying the stack of pink boxes on the counter. "Ellie, I told you not to bring anything." Then she laughed and lifted a conspiratorial eyebrow. "So, what's in the box?"

Ellie laughed. "Oh, nothing much. I know how much you all love my chocolate mousse cake, so I brought one of those, plus a few cupcakes, and threw together some pastries for you for tomorrow morning. I didn't think you should have to fuss with breakfast."

"You're a sweetie pie," said Linda, turning to embrace Ellie. "How about you follow Sam out with some plates for the appetizers? I've got to get the artichoke dip out of the oven and I'll be right behind you guys."

Ellie picked up the tray of plates and utensils and followed Sam, who carried a large plate of crusty baguette slices heaped with tomatoes and basil. They situated the food on the coffee table next to the platter of a large Christmas tree made of alternating rows of cheese cubes and colorful grapes. Linda followed with the fresh from the oven dip baked in a bread bowl, surrounded by pita chips.

"Wow, all of this looks delicious," said Jeff, taking a slice of bruschetta.

"Dinner will be at least a couple of hours, so eat up," said Linda.

They stacked appetizers on their plates and sat back to enjoy the time visiting and snacking while they waited for dinner. Kyle helped Molly place the gifts from her bag under the tree. They were only supposed to bring their two gifts for the exchange, but Regi had packages for Sam, Jeff, Linda, Max, and Jen. She wanted to thank them for welcoming her to town and taking her under their wings. "Put these in the back. They're not for tonight," she whispered.

"It's nice to have a break from school, huh?" said Kyle, as he squeezed packages between others.

"Yeah, I love sleeping in," smiled Molly. "What have you been doing this week?"

"Just helping my grandma with some Christmas stuff and fixing a few things around the theatre. She keeps a list of chores for me to do when I visit." He chuckled as he rearranged the gifts. "But I don't mind."

"You're working at the coffee shop for a few days, right?"

"Yeah, I start on Friday and am covering the whole weekend. Stop by and I'll make you a special drink."

Molly smiled, handing him the last of the boxes. "I heard your mom's coming for Christmas tomorrow."

"Yeah, she gets here on the early ferry. We're having dinner and then she goes back first thing on Friday."

"I can't believe how great Sam is to you. It would be hard to find out your husband had an affair and a son, especially you—someone she knew already. Talk about whacked out."

Kyle nodded. "I know. I'm so lucky to have Sam in my life. She's incredible and I'm having fun getting to know Marty, my real dad. That's weird too, after so many years of thinking he was gone."

"My mom never says much about my dad. Just that he left before I was born and that was it. Sometimes I'm curious, though. I'm afraid to ask her anything about him." She glanced back at Regi, holding a plate and staring at the fire. "Especially now. She's stressed about something."

They were interrupted by the distinct sound of a video call on Max's new Smart TV. "That will be my family calling," he beamed. He hit a button on the remote and the screen was filled with the smiling faces of Peter and Alex, with Alex's parents waving in the background.

"Merry Christmas, Dad," said Peter.

"Merry Christmas to all of you. I'm watching you on my new television." He turned to Regi and asked her to get Linda and Sam from the kitchen. "We're having a gathering with friends here tonight."

"That sounds fun. We're buried in snow here in Minnesota. It took us hours just to make the short drive up here. I've got to be back at work on Friday, so we'll need to leave early tomorrow."

Alex added, "We already put in for the time off next year and we'll be there with you. We can't wait."

Max smiled as Linda walked over and sat beside him on the arm of his chair. "Hi, Peter and Alex. I just heard you talking about next year. That will be so much fun."

"We'll see you in February for the wedding, of course," said Peter.

"Sam's going to put you two and your sister and Mark up at her house," said Max.

Sam stood on the other side of Max and waved at the screen. "Hi, guys. Merry Christmas."

They continued visiting and Max adjusted the television so they could see the beautiful Christmas tree. "Wow, that's gorgeous," said Alex.

"Brooke is going to call in tomorrow. Have you talked to her, Peter?" asked Max.

"She called early this morning, worried about the storm here. They were heading over to spend the next couple of days with Mark's mom and dad."

They talked for a few more minutes and then everyone waved goodbye and wished each other Merry Christmas again. Linda and Sam hurried back to the kitchen and Max started *White Christmas.*

As soon as the movie finished, Linda announced dinner was ready. Max ushered the guests into the dining room and the beautiful table Linda had prepared. She elected to use a white and silver theme. The table was covered in a white jacquard cloth with a silver paisley runner. She had designed elegant floral arrangements of snowy blooms in large glass vases, filled with cranberries for a touch of color. Candles flickered in glass and silver holders along the runner. Each place setting consisted of a brushed finish charger in silver with white plates, rimmed with silver. She made place cards out of miniature twigs she glued together and decorated with a sprig of pine and red berries. Gray napkins were held with tiny metallic brushed pinecones sprinkled with miniature pearls.

The table was covered with glass and silver platters and bowls, allowing the candles to reflect off their surfaces. Spinach salad, twice baked potatoes, vivid green beans dusted with lemon zest, cheesy garlic bread, and a huge prime rib were waiting to be devoured.

"Oh, Linda, the table is gorgeous. We need to snap a picture before we ruin it," said Sam. She used her phone to take several shots and then insisted on more as people sat down.

Max asked everyone to hold hands as he said a blessing. After giving thanks for the lovely meal and the friends gathered around he added, "This year I am most thankful for Linda, the woman who opened my heart."

The group responded with a resounding "Amen." Tears filled Linda's eyes and as she looked around the table she saw Sam's cheeks were wet and so were Regi's.

"Let's dig in," Linda suggested, passing the spinach salad to start the food rotating around the table. The food was consumed with gusto while everyone heaped their praises on Linda.

As with most holiday meals, it took much longer to prepare than eat. When they were all stuffed, Max suggested they move to the great room and distribute the gifts. Kyle and Molly volunteered to clear the table and start on the dishes.

Everyone had been asked to bring a gift for a casual exchange. Max's twist was to require that all gifts start with the letter "M". Regi volunteered to gather the presents from under the tree and stacked them on the coffee table. "Okay, we have twelve boxes and twelve people. So far so good," she announced.

Linda called Kyle and Molly from the kitchen so the game could begin. Max passed around a bowl full of numbers and everyone drew a slip of paper. They played the classic gift exchange game, involving stealing presents from each other. By the end of the game, they were all laughing at the creative M-word gifts. The coffee table was littered with mittens, mugs of M & M's, music gift cards, movie tickets, monkey socks, bottles of merlot, meal gift certificates, a mirror, macadamia nuts, a mouse for a computer, and several moose—stuffed, chocolate, and decorative.

Ellie offered to help Linda serve dessert and expertly cut slices of her cake and plated her cupcakes. Linda sliced the cheesecake she had prepared and added berries to each plate. They carried their trays and offered the decadent treats around the room. They laughed when Max and Jeff took a plate of each.

"I didn't think I could eat another thing, but this cheesecake is delish," said Jen, as she slid the fork from her mouth.

Kyle added, "I've missed your cakes, Ellie. This chocolate mousse is one of the best."

Ellie and Linda both glowed under the shower of compliments raining down on them. "Thank you all for coming and making this such a special Christmas Eve," said Linda. As the guests bundled into their coats, Linda made sure they took their gifts. She handed Regi the metal welcome sign featuring a moose. "I bet Jeff could hang that for you."

"Sure, I'm going to start back working at the hardware store after the first. I'll stop by and put it up. Just mark the spot for me," he offered.

"Thanks, it'll look cute by the door," said Regi. "I'll put a sticky note on the spot."

"Don't forget about our big birthday bash for Regi's fortieth on Friday," said Linda, as her guests filed out to their cars.

Jen snatched her monkey socks and Sean's bottle of merlot. "We'll be here." She hugged Linda goodbye. "Merry Christmas, my friend."

Linda embraced Sam and Jeff as they left. "Drive carefully," she yelled as they got in their cars.

Molly retrieved her gift card and joined with Regi in hugging Max and Linda. "Thanks again for tonight. It was great," said Regi. "You two have a wonderful Christmas together."

"We will and we'll see you on Friday," grinned Linda. "Thanks for bringing the wine. I think we'll put it to use on your birthday."

"See you then." Regi waved as they sat in the Jeep waiting for the defroster to do its job. She turned to Molly. "Did you have a fun time?"

"The best. They're all so nice and dinner was incredible," gushed Molly. "It's comforting to be surrounded by such good friends. I thought I'd miss Grandma and Grandpa, but this was more fun. You're lucky to be living here."

"I am," said Regi, as she swiped the wipers one more time and put the Jeep in gear. Regi's response didn't match the enthusiasm of Molly's comments, but she was so wrapped up in the festivities and excitement of the evening, she didn't notice the sadness in Regi's voice and the tears in her eyes were cloaked by the darkness of the drive home.

Four

Regi and Molly spent Christmas morning sleeping late. Linda had made sure they went home with a few pastries from Ellie's box of goodies, so they enjoyed those while they opened gifts. Regi was prepared for the day with a stack of chick flicks and after opening presents, they spent the entire day in their pajamas watching movies.

Regi called her parents to wish them a Merry Christmas. She got caught up on the status of the family, including all the medical ailments of her aunts and uncles, upcoming additions to the family, and divorces of cousins she couldn't remember meeting.

After nibbling on leftover cookies, brownies, slices of pie, and the sweet breakfast they had, Regi decided they better eat some real food and made cheese omelets. They took a break after their second movie and ate the steaming eggs with toasted bread from Ellie's bakery.

Regi's cell phone rang out in the middle of *The Holiday* and when she looked at the screen she saw Nate's name. She plucked up her phone and shouted "I'll be right back, just keep watching," to Molly.

She touched the screen and answered, "Merry Christmas, Nate."

"You too, Regi. How was your Christmas?"

"It was great. Molly and I have been watching movies all day, just hanging out."

"Sounds relaxing. I'm just leaving my parents' house and was going to drop off some leftovers for you guys."

"Oh, that's thoughtful, but we're fine."

"I'm pulling up to your condo now and my mom insisted I bring you some, so I won't take no for an answer."

Regi smiled. "Okay, but we're in our jammies."

"Fine by me. I'll be at your door in a minute."

Regi came out of her bedroom. "Mol, that was my friend, Nate. He's stopping by with some leftovers for us from dinner at his parents. He'll be here in a minute."

Molly paused the movie as the doorbell sounded. "I guess he's here," she smiled.

Regi took a quick look in the mirror on her way to the door and sighed. There wasn't much she could do. Her hair was a mess and her penguin pajamas didn't do much for creating a sense of style.

She opened the door to Nate, smiling and loaded down with two large shopping bags. "Merry Christmas," he said, lifting the bags up.

"Wow, that's a lot of leftovers."

"Yeah, my mom cooks for an army and even with all of us there, she had tons of leftovers. I can't eat everything she packed up, so thought I'd share."

"Come in and meet Molly." She held the door wide as he maneuvered by her.

"I saw her in the back of Buds and Blooms the other day when I dropped off their delivery, but didn't have time to chat."

Regi led the way upstairs to the living room and took the bags from Nate. "Molly, this is my friend, Nate."

"Nice to meet you Nate," said Molly, standing to shake his hand. She looked down at her pajamas and shrugged. "Sorry we're such a mess."

"Don't worry about it. Lounging around and watching movies sounds great to me. I was ready to get out of the house. I'm on family overload," he said.

Regi scuttled into the kitchen and started unpacking the bags. She stacked container after container in the fridge. Two towers of ham, turkey, potatoes, veggies, stuffing, salads, and applesauce stared back at her. There was even a container of appetizers, a bag of homemade rolls, and some cake.

She returned to the living room. "I won't have to cook for a week," she smiled.

"Would you like something to drink, Nate?" asked Molly. "You could watch a movie with us."

Regi started to speak then said, "Uh, yeah, sit down, Nate."

Nate took a seat and Molly brought him a citrus concoction she had made to go with their holiday breakfast. She topped off the mixture of orange, pineapple, and lemon with ginger ale and handed him the fizzy drink.

"We're watching the rest of *The Holiday* and next up is *27 Dresses*. Have you seen either of them?"

He shook his head. "I don't think so."

"Don't feel like you need to stay," said Regi. "We're only watching chick flicks."

"I'll risk my man card." He smiled and settled in. "Go ahead and hit play."

Molly laughed and hit the remote. They finished the movie and Molly offered to serve cake before they started the next one. "Linda slipped us a slab of her cheesecake last night. It's delicious."

When she returned with the plates, she overheard Nate asking about lunch tomorrow. She delivered Nate's dessert and Molly said, "We don't have any plans for tomorrow. That'll be fun, won't it, Mom?"

"I'm not working tomorrow, so you name the time that works best for you. I'm flexible," said Nate. "And the birthday girl picks the place."

Regi looked from Nate to Molly, seeing the excitement on both their faces, wishing she could let go and be happy. "Okay, lunch it is. Let's go to the Front Street Café around eleven-thirty."

"Perfect choice," said Nate, taking a bite of cheesecake. "Wow, this is yummy."

Molly nodded in agreement and started the movie. She glanced at Nate from time to time and smiled when she caught him watching her mom. *I can tell he likes her. He's a nice guy and he's into Mom. I can't remember her even dating anyone. I hope she'll give him a chance.*

* * *

Friday morning, Molly made sure her mom was sleeping and tiptoed through the house and out the door. She slipped her spare Jeep key in the ignition and let the window defrost. She made the trip to Harbor Coffee and Books and found Kyle working.

"Hi, Kyle," she said. "I need to get an order to go."

She visited while he made Regi's birthday coffee and a hot chocolate for Molly. Kyle insisted on treating them to the birthday drinks and sent her on her way.

Molly parked and sneaked back into the condo. She put her eye to the crack of the opening in Regi's door and saw she was still sleeping. She went to the kitchen and warmed up an almond croissant and poured a glass of juice. She put it on a tray with the coffee and padded down the hall to the bedroom.

She opened the door with her slipper and began singing "Happy Birthday" at the top of her lungs. She laughed as she watched Regi jerk awake and sit up.

"I brought you breakfast in bed. Happy Big 4-0, Mom."

Regi rolled her eyes. "Thanks for reminding me. I feel at least forty today." She laughed and spied the coffee. "I need coffee, thanks."

Molly sat the tray on the bed and ran around to the other side and climbed under the covers. "Kyle treated us to the coffees this morning."

Regi took a sip and swallowed. "Perfection." She looked at the croissant. "After today, I'm back to salads. I've eaten way too many carbs in the last couple of days." She broke off a corner and popped it in her mouth. "But they are irresistible."

Molly shoved her shoulder into Regi's. "You gotta have a little fun once in a while, Mom." Regi nodded as she ate another piece of the croissant. "Speaking of fun, we have pedicure appointments today, so you need to get your butt out of bed. We need to be at Jen's at nine."

Regi glanced at her alarm clock. "Okay, I'll get ready. That'll be fun. Thanks, Mol." She gobbled up the rest of the croissant and took a swallow of juice. She took her coffee into her bathroom to get ready.

They arrived at Jen's right on time and were treated like royalty, including a glass of champagne for Regi and sparkling cider for Molly. After two hours they emerged with smooth, soft feet, and colorful toes. "Too bad it's winter and we can't show them off," said Regi, admiring the deep plum color.

Molly wiggled her hot pink toes with black polka dots. "Yeah, back into socks they go."

The sun was fighting to peek through the layer of gray clouds lingering in the sky and the sidewalks were full of shoppers looking for after-Christmas sales. They decided to walk down to the café to meet Nate for lunch.

Nate was seated at a table when they arrived. He stood and pulled out chairs for Regi and Molly. "Happy Birthday," he said, giving her an awkward hug resulting in them hitting heads.

"Sorry," she said, taking a seat.

"My bad, sorry," he said, touching his temple. "So, what have you two been up to this morning?"

With enthusiasm Molly answered, "We got pedicures at Jen's salon."

"Nice," said Nate, passing each of them a menu. The waitress stopped by for drink orders and described the lunch specials. Nate and Regi selected the salmon in a butter sauce with shrimp, rice, and veggies. Molly decided on the five cheese panino.

Nate asked Molly for details about her first semester at school and quizzed her about her job and classes. She chatted like the two were old friends, highlighting her favorite professors and subjects. "I really like my job at the library. It's fun and helps me learn about the whole campus."

After the topic of college was exhausted Nate brought up New Year's Eve. "You two should plan to go to the celebration this year. The town holds a party every year and it's always fun."

"I saw a poster about that, but didn't pay much attention. It's at the firehouse right?" asked Regi.

"Yeah, they move out the trucks and put in a dance floor, plus there are games for kids and adults, lots of food, and fireworks over the harbor at midnight."

Molly's eyes brightened. "Can we go, Mom? It sounds fun."

"We'll see," said Regi, as her cell phone rang. She saw it was the coffee shop. "Hi, Kyle," she answered. She saw Nate take the check up to pay at the register.

"Hey, Regi. Hope you're having a good birthday. Sorry to disturb you, but there's a guy in the coffee shop looking for you. I thought I'd call and see if you can come by. He said it's a birthday surprise."

Regi's heart fluttered and then beat like the wings on a hummingbird. "Okay. I'll be there in a few minutes. We just finished lunch."

Molly looked at her as she disconnected. "What's all that about?"

"Oh, somebody was asking for me at the coffee shop." Nate returned to them and Regi asked him, "Would you mind giving Molly a ride home? I need to run a quick errand."

"Sure, no problem."

Regi tried to slow down, but still hurried out the door. She knew it was finally happening and couldn't believe it. Then she remembered she needed to thank Nate for lunch. "Thanks so much for the birthday lunch, Nate. It was delicious."

"You're welcome. It was my pleasure." He watched her as she walked backwards already heading to the coffee shop. "I'll see you tonight."

She waved, "Yeah, see you then. Thanks for taking Molly." She turned and it was all she could do not to run down the sidewalk. She covered the few blocks to the shop in record time.

She hit the door and the bells clanged on the glass. Everyone in the shop turned to look at her. She scanned the customers for Cam, knowing she would recognize him anywhere. She looked again, slowing down her gaze. She didn't see him.

Then her eyes rested on a face she hadn't seen in years. She hadn't expected to see it again for several more. "Leon?" she asked with a furrowed brow.

"Hey, Regi. Happy Birthday," said a blond haired man, moving to hug her.

"What are you doing here?"

"Well, that's a fine welcome from my sister."

"How'd you know I was here?"

"Mom and Dad told me you had moved here. I got out of prison early about ten days ago and stopped to visit them. I figured you'd be there for Christmas, but they said you were in Friday Harbor. I told them I wanted to surprise you and not to tell you."

"Clearly," she said, looking at his eyes, the same gray as hers, studying his speech patterns, looking for a hint of the drug and alcohol use that had been his hallmark for years. His eyes were bright and clear and he appeared to be clean.

"So, how about you show me where you live and I can see Molly?"

"Yeah, hang on just a minute. I'll be right back," she said, motioning him to a table as she moved to the counter and went through the door to the kitchen.

She looked up the number for The Haven, hoping Ben and Sherrie had a free room. She did not want Leon staying at her house since she'd been burned by him before, multiple times. She knew he wouldn't have any money and the thought of paying for his room out of her hard earned savings peeved her.

Sherrie answered, "Happy Holidays at the Haven. This is Sherrie."

"Hi, Sherrie. It's Regi, Linda's friend from the coffee shop."

"How are you, Regi? I hope you had a nice Christmas."

"I did, thanks. I'm calling because my brother is in town and I need to find him a room. I'm paying, so hoping for the smallest and least expensive you have available for the next few days, maybe a week."

"You're in luck. We are full, but had someone leave this morning, so I have one bedroom left. It runs ninety a night, but I'll give it to you for sixty. We'll be losing all our guests come Sunday, so it'll be slow."

Regi let out a breath. "Thanks, Sherrie. I owe you and appreciate the discount. I'll bring him out to get settled." She hung up the phone in the office and took a deep breath.

Kyle was talking to Leon when she returned to the table. "Cool surprise for you that your brother showed up, huh?"

"I was totally surprised," she said, raising her brows. "You ready to go, Leon?"

"Sure thing. Nice to meet you, Kyle. See ya around." He found his bag Kyle had stored behind the counter.

Kyle waved as they went on their way to Jen's salon to pick up her Jeep. She got in and cranked the engine. "So, I got you a room at a bed and breakfast. My place is too small with Molly there. How long do you think you'll be visiting?"

"Oh, I don't know. Seems like a nice place, I might decide to stay."

She glanced over at him. "Then you need to find a job, because I can't afford to foot your bills."

"I know. I know. I'll start looking for a job next week and see what's up. Do you know of any openings?"

"Not off the top of my head. It's slow around here in the winter. Summer is a better time to find a job here. With your record, it may be hard."

"Yeah, but I'm clean and I'm not going back to that life."

"Mmm mmm."

"I mean it Reg, I'm gonna stay clean. I just need some help getting started. Mom and Dad gave me some spending money, but I know I'll need a job."

She guided the Jeep down the driveway to Linda's old house. "My friend, Linda owns the nursery," she pointed, "and this is her old house that they've turned into a B&B."

"Cool. Hey, Kyle said you're having a birthday party tonight. Can I come?"

"Yeah, I just need to call Linda and let her know. You need to be on your best behavior. These people you'll meet tonight have been incredible and they're my friends. Please don't be a jerk."

He shook his head. "Same old Reg. You think I'm going to embarrass you."

"You have to admit it's not the best opener to introduce my brother, who by the way, just got out of prison early for selling drugs and stealing to support his drug and alcohol habit. Not to mention Ronnie."

"I'm reformed now. Really. You'll see. As for Ronnie, I have to live with that the rest of my life. I know you blame me for what happened."

"What happened is our brother is dead because of you." She stopped the Jeep, slamming her door as she hiked to the entrance, leaving Leon to get his bag. She gave Sherrie her credit card and asked her to leave the departure date open. "I'll let you know when we have it figured out. Leon surprised me for my birthday, so this is all a bit last minute."

"No problem. We're empty after Sunday, so we can make it work." Leon came through the door and Sherrie smiled. "You must be Leon. A pleasure to have you staying with us."

He shook her hand. "Nice to meet you ma'am."

"Call me Sherrie and my husband is Ben. You'll meet him later. We serve breakfast in the dining room every morning from seven to nine, so just come down when you're ready and help yourself. Here's your room key. You'll be in Number Six at the top of the stairs. If you need anything, just let me know."

"Thank you, Sherrie," he winked and took the key.

"I'll be back to pick you up for the party around five."

"Okay, see you then. Thanks, Reg," he said moving to hug her, but she was already out the door.

Regi got in the Jeep and pounded the steering wheel. "Why did Leon have to show up now?" she said through gritted teeth. "Why couldn't it have been Cam?" she whispered.

Five

Regi made a point of taking the long way home and called Linda to let her know Leon would be joining the festivities. She arrived home and found Molly waiting, watching a movie. As she went past the living room into the kitchen, she saw two large bouquets of flowers. "Wow, these are beautiful," she said.

Molly turned her head. "Yeah, they came about an hour ago. What took you so long?"

"Uncle Leon came to surprise me for my birthday. He was at the coffee shop and I got him a room out at The Haven and drove him out there."

"I thought he was in prison for five more years or something."

"So did I. I guess he got out early for some reason. Probably overcrowding. He's coming to my birthday party tonight. I feel like I need to explain him to Sam and Linda and everyone. It's sad, but I just don't trust Leon. He stole from me, Mom and Dad…anyone he could. I'm not sure he's as reformed as he thinks he is and I wish he wasn't here. I can't even begin to talk about poor Ronnie."

"Sorry, Mom. I know how sad you get about Ronnie and I know Uncle Leon's been a real loser, but maybe he's changed."

Regi opened the card on one arrangement and saw it was from Molly. "Thanks for the flowers, they're gorgeous. I love them." She turned and hugged Molly tight, squeezing her eyes tight to stem the sting of tears.

"Who are the other ones from?" asked Molly.

"No idea," said Regi, plucking out the card. She read it quickly. "Oh, Nate sent them. That was thoughtful."

"He seems like a sweet guy, Mom. How long have you guys been dating?"

Regi whipped her head around to stare at Molly. "What? We aren't dating."

Molly shrugged. "Well, lunch and now the flowers. He likes you, I can tell. I assumed you'd been going out with him."

"Well, you assumed wrong. I'm not dating anyone. Nate is just a friend I met from working at the coffee shop and through his deliveries at school. He's a nice guy, that's all," she snapped.

Molly raised her brows, "Oookay, got it." She went to the fridge and poured a glass of juice. "I'll be in my room. What time are we leaving?"

"Around four, so we have time to pick up Leon."

"Okay, I'll be ready," she said walking down the hall.

Regi read the card from Nate again. *For a special lady on her special day. Happy Birthday! Nate.*

She plopped on the couch and sighed. *Maybe I've been blind to Nate. Could Molly be right? I consider him a friend, like Linda and Max or Sam and Jeff. I haven't felt a romantic vibe from him. Then again, I haven't been looking for one, only worrying about Cam not being here. What a mess.*

Regi rested her head on the back of the couch and turned on the television for a distraction. They were still playing a few Christmas shows and she stared at the screen, feeling her eyes getting heavy. They closed completely as thoughts of Cam and Nate swirled in her head.

* * *

Regi wore jeans and her favorite black sweater. She slipped into her black ankle boots and added a silver bracelet, earrings, and a necklace. She added the magenta pashmina she had received at the gift exchange at school and retrieved her purse. "Ready, Mol?"

Molly hurried down the hall. "Yeah, I'm coming." She put on her coat and dashed out the door.

Molly looked over at Regi as she drove out of town. "Sorry if I upset you about Nate. I didn't mean to."

Regi squeezed her daughter's thigh. "You didn't. I just never considered Nate in that way."

"How come? I don't remember you dating anyone. I wouldn't mind if you did, you know?"

"It's a long story. Long ago there was someone, but it didn't work out. I think I've always had other priorities and haven't given it much thought."

Molly smiled. "You need to think about it. Nate's a nice person. He'd be good for you."

Regi turned and grinned at her daughter. "Okay, I'll think about it." Then she chuckled. "One semester in college and you're already giving me advice."

Regi turned down the driveway and pulled in front of The Haven. She introduced Molly to Ben and Sherrie, both of whom were sitting with Leon in the parlor. They chatted for a few minutes and then Regi said, "We better get going."

Leon put his arm around Molly as they made their way outside. "I can't believe how grown up you are. And so pretty."

"Thanks, Uncle Leon," she said climbing into the passenger seat, while he got in the back. Regi followed the circular drive back to the road and listened to Leon and Molly visit. He wanted to know all about school and living in Seattle.

Regi turned off the main road and her brother let out a whistle as the house came into view. "What a spread these people have. Reg, you've got some rich friends."

Regi parked the Jeep and turned around in her seat. "Listen, Leon, I'm warning you. You need to be on your best behavior. I like these people and they've been more than kind to me. You need to be respectful and stop with the comments."

He held up his hands in surrender. "Okay, jeez."

They got out, Regi slamming her door harder than necessary, and followed the walkway to the front door. Regi rang the bell and Max answered, with Lucy, who let out a deep bark when she saw Leon.

Max extended his hand, "You must be Regi's brother. I'm Max. Welcome, come in. Lucy won't hurt you; she just doesn't know you yet."

Leon shook his hand. Max took their coats and led them into the great room. You're the first to arrive, but everyone should be here soon. He took drink orders and returned with Linda and a tray of drinks. Regi was relieved when Leon asked for lemonade, rather than alcohol.

Linda handed Leon his glass. "I'm so happy you could join us tonight. How sweet of you to surprise Regi. Are there other siblings in your family?"

Regi beat Leon to the answer. "No," she snapped. In a quiet voice she added, "It's just the two of us."

Leon grasped Linda's hand. "Thanks for having me. I just returned to the area and wanted to surprise my big sister on her special day," he turned and glared at Regi.

The doorbell rang and Linda excused herself. She returned moments later with Sam and Jeff, plus Kyle, Jen, and Megan. Regi introduced Leon as she received hugs from all the new arrivals. "Sean will be here later, he had an emergency at the hospital," said Jen.

Nate arrived with Ellie and carried her large pink box to the door for her. Linda whisked the box away to the kitchen before Regi saw it. Two of Regi's friends from school, Laura and Stacy, came through the door and deposited colorful gift bags on the coffee table before they were introduced around the room.

Sam excused herself to help Linda finish dinner, while Max retrieved drinks for everyone. He had made margaritas and sangria in celebration of the taco themed dinner. They visited while they munched on chips and sampled a variety of salsas.

Sean arrived just as Linda announced dinner was ready. "Great timing, I guess," he joked. He hugged Linda and said, "Sorry, I'm late. Busy day."

Linda had the buffet set up on the bar adjacent to the kitchen. They made Regi go first and she marveled at the selection of goodies Linda and

Sam had prepared. Regi chose a corn and a flour tortilla and then moved on to carne asada, lime chili chicken, and the more traditional ground beef. There were bowls of freshly grated cheeses, shredded lettuce, pico de gallo, guacamole, tomatoes, and onions. Regi worked to pack in all the toppings and then scooped up some rice and black beans.

"This looks and smells so yummy," said Regi, as she made her way to the table. The group moved through the self-service line and eventually they were all seated at the dining room table. Max raised his glass and toasted Regi.

They dug into their tacos and the cacophony of chatter was replaced by the crunching of tortillas and groans of delight. "Excellent carne asada, Linda," said Jeff, getting up to make another taco.

Jeff was getting stronger and more like his old self each day. His limp wasn't as noticeable and his excitement to go back to work lit up his face whenever he talked about it. "Anybody need anything while I'm up?" he asked.

Sam asked for more rice and he brought back a small plate. Kyle and Leon opted for a full round of seconds, as did Sean. "I haven't eaten all day and this is delicious," he said.

Once they were done, Jen and Megan helped with the clean-up. Linda had used paper plates, so the mess didn't take long to discard. They stored the leftovers in the fridge and loaded the dishwasher with the serving dishes before joining the others.

Sam stood and directed her gaze at Regi. "We know this is a special birthday for you, Regi, and we got you something memorable. We're so happy you came to live here and thankful to call you a friend. Now before we give you our gift, I want you to know Jeff came up with the idea and he says if you don't want it, he'll take it." She nodded at Jeff who went through the kitchen and out to the garage.

Regi wrinkled her forehead and gave Sam a questioning look. "I have no idea what it could be, but I'm sure I'll love it."

A few minutes later, Lucy, Bailey, and Zoe paraded into the room, followed by Jeff, holding a golden retriever puppy, with an enormous pink bow around her body. "Happy Birthday, Regi," he said, as he placed the warm furry bundle on her lap.

"Oh, my, what a cute baby," she squealed.

"Do you like her?" asked Sam, eyebrows arched.

"Oh, she's a love. Of course I like her," said Regi, petting the soft fur. "I've just got to figure out how to take care of her and doggy proof my condo."

Jeff cleared his throat. "I thought I could take her to work with me and she could stay at the hardware store with us during the day or at the house if I'm home. I don't mind her tagging along with Zoe and Bailey. They've been making friends with her already."

"That would be terrific. I'd hate leaving her while I'm at work." She brought the puppy to her face and touched its nose. "Oh, man, I don't even know if I can have a dog at my condo," said Regi, with angst.

Linda nodded. "We already checked and you can. You just have to pay a pet deposit, which Max and I did as our birthday gift to you."

"You guys thought of everything. Thank you," said Regi.

Max gestured to the gifts on the coffee table. "You have a few more things to open."

Molly reached for the puppy. "I'll hold her, while you finish opening your presents." Regi placed the puppy in Molly's outstretched hands.

She opened a collar and leash set from Kyle and a large bag of homemade dog treats courtesy of Ellie. Nate reached behind a chair and produced a dog crate, with a bow on the handle, and Laura and Stacy gave her a water and food bowl, plus a whole array of dog toys. Sean presented her with a gift certificate from the vet for shots and spaying.

"Wow, you guys were all in on this together. It's wonderful," said Regi, as tears clouded her vision. She looked down and stroked the puppy.

Jen and Megan had already given Regi pedicures as their birthday gift, but they offered to dog sit anytime. Soon the three big dogs were snuggled up together and Regi stooped and placed the new puppy in their midst. She burrowed in and closed her eyes.

Molly asked, "What are you going to name her?"

"I'm not sure. I'll have to think on it. We'll make a list of some names and see what sounds good."

Regi was content to watch the dogs sleep with her new puppy. She listened to conversations around her and was reminded how charming Leon could be. He talked to everyone and had a way of drawing things out of people. While his charisma was delightful, it also aided him in taking advantage of people. She hoped he had changed and wouldn't do anything to harm her new friends. Tonight he was acting like the perfect brother, but the perfect one had died when Leon was only sixteen.

While the dogs slept by the fire, Ellie readied her cake and brought it out so Regi could see it before it was sliced. It resembled a giant cupcake, decorated in shades of blues and teals, with a hint of lavender. Shimmering pearls and discs were scattered throughout the frosting and it was topped with a glittery sugar dusted "40".

Everyone oohed and aahed at the cake and took pictures of Regi posing next to it. "I hate to cut it open, it's so elegant," said Regi, handing it back to Ellie.

Ellie laughed and said, "Wait until you taste it."

After several minutes, Ellie and Linda appeared with trays of plated cake and ice cream. The cake turned out to be vanilla with strawberries and cream filling—one of Regi's favorite flavors.

Despite being stuffed, they devoured the cake and ice cream. The party began to break up after Linda served hot beverages. Jeff explained the puppy's habits to Regi and told her he had been working with her on housebreaking and she was doing well. He suspected she could be trained in a few more days. He went over his methods and told Regi he had stashed the puppy's food in her Jeep.

Regi hugged Sam and Jeff before they left, whispering, "Thank you so much. I always wanted a dog and never had one."

Jeff hugged her tight and said, "Everyone needs a friend they can count on, no matter what."

Leon carried the dog crate and went and started Regi's Jeep to let it warm up. Molly gathered the rest of the dog-themed gifts while Regi thanked Max and Linda. “What a wonderful birthday you’ve given me. Thank you both so much. I had a terrific time.”

They waved from the front door as Regi bundled the new puppy into Molly’s lap and ran around to hop in the driver’s seat. Regi waved back and drove home with a lighter heart, knowing she had made the right decision to move to Friday Harbor, with or without Cam.

Six

Regi turned the Jeep towards Linda's old house. She let Leon know she was off the next two days, but starting Monday she had to work. "You're going to have to figure out what to do about transportation and if you're really serious about staying here, find a job."

"I know. I was talking to Jeff tonight and told him I wanted to find a job and a cheap place to live. He suggested I talk to his brother about staying in one of his cabins. He said they're almost empty during the winter, so I could probably get a good deal."

"His family has a resort on the water. It's a beautiful place. Are you sure you're up to this? It's going to require discipline and responsibility."

Regi looked in the rear view mirror and saw him nod his head. "Yeah, I am. We could go out there tomorrow and see what he says. I worked in food services when I was in prison, so I thought I'd visit the harbor restaurants and see what I could find."

"Like I said winter is slow, so don't expect much."

She pulled up to the front door and Leon hopped out. "If you need help with the puppy, let me know." He reached the door and waved. Then he sprung off the step and ran back to Regi's window. "Hey, remember the neighbor's dog that we loved so much? You should name her Murphy."

Regi saw her brother's face light up at the memory of their childhood. All three of them had played with the neighbor's retriever mix. A happy good-natured dog, she had loved, like her own. "Yeah, I remember. That's a good idea. See you tomorrow, Leon."

He waved again as he ran back to the door and Regi pulled away. She heard the puppy's soft whining. Molly stroked its tiny head and whispered, "I think Murphy's a good name, Mom."

Regi smiled, "Murphy it is." She glanced over at the furry parcel in Molly's lap. "Did you hear that sweet girl? You have a name—Murphy."

* * *

Regi enjoyed a relatively quiet first night as a dog owner. She moved the crate into her bedroom so she could hear Murphy. She searched online and learned she should give the puppy something that smelled like her. She rooted around and found an old pair of slippers that she had relegated to the back of her closet and put one of them on Murphy's furry little mattress. She outfitted the pan underneath the crate with newspapers to make clean up easier. Jeff had told her the puppy would whine to signal her need to go outside.

Regi and Molly spent the weekend at home with Murphy, keeping the house training consistent and getting the condo doggy proofed. They played with her and were amazed at her bursts of energy and excitement. She raced around the furniture, rolled across the floor, and jumped to be held. They quickly learned about her tiny, but razor sharp teeth, thankful for the many chew toys in the bag of dog gifts. Murphy was especially fond of a fuzzy green frog that she carried around with her.

The puppy wasn't a fan of the stairs, so she confined herself to the main level. Molly spent hours trying to coax her down the stairs and the puppy would go so far as to put her foot out, but retreated. "In a few weeks, I probably won't be able to keep her from running up and down the stairs," said Regi, watching the lesson.

Saturday afternoon, Regi stopped by Sam's house on her way to pick up Leon. She was greeted by Bailey and Zoe when Jeff opened the door. "How's the puppy?" asked Jeff.

"She's terrific and she has a name—Murphy."

Jeff grinned. "I like it. Come on in and sit down." He led her into the great room and called Sam from the kitchen.

Sam came around the corner and joined them. "So, what's up?" she asked Regi.

"Well, I'm on my way to pick up my brother. He said Jeff suggested he talk to Jeremy about renting a cabin out at the resort."

Jeff nodded. "That's right. He said he was strapped for money and needed to find an inexpensive place. Jeremy's flexible on rates during the winter, especially a long-term rental."

Regi took a breath. "Well, here's the thing. I want you both to know that Leon has had a troubled past. In fact, I was shocked when he showed up here. I didn't expect to see him for several years. He's been in prison." She paused, and took a breath, seeing the questions in their furrowed brows. "He's been in and out of trouble since he was a teenager. Mostly for drugs, drinking, and stealing to support both those habits. He finally resorted to selling and that's when he got in real trouble. He's out early and supposedly he's ready to change."

"Sounds like you don't have much faith in him," said Jeff.

Regi shrugged as tears filled her eyes. "It's worse than prison. When Leon was sixteen, our older brother, Ronnie, tried to intervene and went to his drug dealer to tell him to stay away. Ronnie ended up getting killed by the dealer. He ran him down like an animal and left him for dead in the road. So, I guess I don't have much faith in Leon. He's said the same thing hundreds of times before. My mom and dad spent thousands of dollars trying to help him get clean. Over the years they've tended to make excuses for him and baby him. He's stolen from them, from me, and from our friends. I just wanted to warn you guys." Her voice became strained, almost a whisper. "I've found wonderful friends here and I don't want to lose you guys or Max and Linda when Leon decides to do something stupid."

Sam reached for Regi's hand. "I'm so sorry about your brother. I can see why Leon being here is so difficult. I'm sure it dredges up all those old memories." Regi nodded, tears streaming down her face. "Don't worry, Regi. You're not going to lose any of us. You aren't responsible for your brother."

She nodded and sniffed, taking the tissue box Jeff handed her. "Part of me thinks maybe it would be beneficial for him here on the island away from the derelicts from his past. It's just he always seems to find trouble, no matter what. I'm paying for him to stay at The Haven because I don't want him at my place and it's too small with Molly there. But, I can't afford to pay his way and told him he needs to find a job and his own place."

"Which it seems he's trying to do. Maybe he needs a totally fresh start," said Jeff. He paused and saw the concern etched in Regi's face. "I'll head over to Jeremy's now and explain the situation, so he knows the history about the prison record. It'll be up to him to decide."

Regi's shoulders relaxed. "That would be great. It's not that I don't want Leon to get a clean start and help, but he's always let me down and I don't want to disappoint all of you. And, I've never forgiven him for Ronnie."

Sam gripped her hand tighter. "It's okay, Regi. You've done all you can do. You can't control what happens or what Leon decides to do."

"Leon said he worked in food services in prison, so he's going to be going around to the restaurants to see about work."

"Lou would probably give him a shot. He starts everyone out as a dishwasher and then promotes them if they prove themselves. He's usually there and if not his manager keeps a close eye on things," said Jeff.

"I'll tell him to talk to Lou and see what happens."

Jeff got up, followed by Bailey and Zoe. "I'll run over to the resort and see you when you get there."

"You're okay to drive?" quizzed Sam.

He rolled his eyes. "Yes, sweetie. I got cleared at my last appointment, remember. Only day driving, no night time driving yet."

"Okay, be careful," she said, kissing him on the cheek.

Regi blotted her face with another tissue. She heard the door close and said, "He looks great and seems to be doing well."

"Yeah, he's made so much progress since he's been home. He's excited to go to work next week and get back to normal." She paused. "If you look closely, you can see he still limps a bit and he tires more easily, but outside of that things are looking good."

Regi gathered the tissues and put a few more fresh ones in her hand. "Well, I better get going. I'll see you Monday, if not before." She slipped on her coat and made for the door.

"I meant to tell you we're closing early on New Year's Eve in honor of the party at the firehouse. I hope you and Molly are planning to go. It sounds like fun and Jeff's super excited about it."

Regi smiled. "Nate asked us to go." She sighed, "Molly wants to go, so we'll probably be there. I won't be able to leave Murphy too long, though."

"Oh, I love the name. You can always run home and check on her. The firehouse is only a couple of blocks from your condo."

"That's true." She nodded. "We'll be there, for sure."

"Wonderful. You need to have some fun. If Leon comes he'll get to meet more people and see if he'll like living here among them."

"My life would be less stressful if he decided to forego the slow pace of Friday Harbor and move to Seattle or even back near my parents."

"I know how hard it is to let go of the past. You may want to consider talking to someone about it. Try not to worry too much about him. He's not your responsibility," Sam said, hugging her goodbye.

* * *

With her face lacking the red blotches she had when she left Sam's, Regi arrived with Leon and found Jeff outside talking with Jeremy. Jeff introduced Leon to Jeremy and gave Regi a knowing nod. Jeremy extended his hand and said, "Nice to meet you, Leon. Jeff explained you're looking for a rental."

Leon returned the handshake and said, "Yes, great to meet you. I'd like to stay here on the island at least for several months. I need to find a job and something with reasonable rent." He paused and looked at Regi. "I'm not sure if Regi told you, but I've been in prison for the past several years and just got out. I'm trying to start over on a new path, away from my old life. I'm clean and sober and plan to stay that way."

Jeremy nodded. "No, Regi didn't tell me anything. I'm glad to hear you're committed to making a positive change." Jeremy voice became stern,

"I can tell you right now I won't put up with any drugs or parties or other illegal activity. This is our home and if you don't intend to stay on the right path, I'll kick your sorry ass out without a warning. You won't get a second chance from me. Are we clear?"

Leon stood stunned, but managed to say, "Yes, sir. Crystal clear."

Jeremy motioned them to follow him to one of the small cabins. He opened the door and turned on the light. Inside they found a small, but neat space consisting of a living area with a gas fireplace, a small kitchen, and a separate bedroom and bathroom. It was basic, but charming, with a stunning view of the harbor.

Leon's smile widened as he walked through the cabin. "This is great. What are you thinking for rent?"

Jeremy said, "I'll make you a deal and throw in a moped for transportation. We have a few we rent out to guests and since we'll be almost empty from now until May, I can let you have both for three hundred a month. Once we get to May first, it will be a different story. This rents for a hundred a night during our busy season."

Leon's eyes widened. "That's more than generous. Let me pay you for the first month now and I'll plan to move in tomorrow, if that works for you?"

"That works for us. Come on down to the office and I'll have you sign a rental agreement." Jeremy followed them out and locked the door. He led the way to the office and filled out the paperwork for the cabin and the moped, giving Leon a receipt for the cash he provided. "Rent is due on the first. You can have these last few days of December on the house, so this will get you paid through the end of January. If you're late, even a day, you're out. Got it?"

Leon nodded his head as he signed the papers. "Yes, sir. Thanks, Mr. Cooper."

Jeremy gave him the key and shook his hand. "If you need anything, just let me know. We live in the large cabin," he pointed to the side of the office. "I'll leave your moped outside your cabin and put the key inside.

Laundry facilities are across the way by the gym and your cabin key unlocks both. You'll be on your own for cleaning and laundry."

Leon shook his hand again and thanked Jeff before he and Regi took off. "That's a great deal he's giving me. Thanks, Regi."

"Don't thank me. Like I said, these people are the real deal."

"Yeah and he made it very clear he's not going to put up with anything." Leon paused. "That's cool."

"Jeff thought Lou might you give you a job. He owns the crab place right by the harbor. You did the right thing by telling Jeremy about your past. You need to do the same with anyone who offers you a job, so they know everything."

He nodded. "I know. It's easier to tell them than have them find out and think I'm hiding it. I'll work hard."

"There are only two banks in town. You should pick one and open an account and get rid of that cash."

"Okay, I'll do that Monday."

"Since I'm saving a few days on your room at The Haven, I'll take you grocery shopping tomorrow when I pick you up and help you get settled in the cabin."

"Thanks, Regi, that would be great. If I can find a job, everything will work out."

She pulled up to The Haven and went in to let Sherrie know the departure date and thank her for the discount. She took her receipt and promised to see Leon in the morning to help him get moved.

* * *

Regi steeled herself for spending the day with Leon. She knew Sam was right about letting go of the past. Her parents had seemed to move on, but she had a hard time letting Leon off the hook. Molly was glad to stay home with Murphy while Regi spent the day helping Leon at the cabin. They went shopping and got him enough food to last at least a week, plus laundry and cleaning supplies. She showed him the gas stations, the banks, and drove past Lou's.

Leon offered to treat them to pizza for all the help. "I'll call in the order and have it delivered. I'll be at your place around six, okay?"

"We'll see you then," said Regi, waving as she left the Harbor Resort.

When she got home, Molly had cleaned the house and she and Murphy were playing on the floor, while another movie played in the background. "Everything looks great. Thanks, Mol."

"You're welcome. We've been playing and napping. What do you want to do for dinner tonight?"

"Leon's treating us to pizza. He's coming over at six."

They watched *Breakfast at Tiffany's* until it was time for dinner. Leon arrived minutes before the delivery. He paid the driver and balanced the boxes of pizza and salads as he made his way upstairs.

Murphy bounced across the floor to sniff Leon's pants. "Let's feed her and put her in the crate while we eat," said Regi, plucking her off the floor and taking her to the kitchen.

Molly set the table and they enjoyed one of Big Tony's creations along with fresh salads. Leon, full of enthusiasm, described the cabin to Molly as they ate slices of warm dough topped with pepperoni.

"When do you head back to school, Molly?"

"I'm going back on Saturday. Classes start on Monday, but I want to get organized."

"Smart girl, like your mom. How about you, Regi? Do you go back to school on the same day?"

"Yeah, I'm working at the coffee shop this week and have next weekend off before I start back."

"Hey, Mom, are we going to the New Year's Eve party?" asked Molly.

"Oh, yeah, that's right. I meant to tell Leon about it. There's a community New Year's Eve bash on Wednesday night at the firehouse. Everyone is invited and it's free. Sam and Jeff thought you might want to go."

"Sounds good, unless I have a job by then."

With Leon's help, they finished off the rest of the cake and after he played with Murphy, sent him home with some of the leftovers from Nate's parents. Leon hugged them both and whispered to Regi as he was leaving, "You've done good Reg, real good. What you have here is nice."

"Keep me posted on your job hunt. I'll be at the coffee shop all day tomorrow," she said, waving goodbye as he rode away on the yellow and black moped, which looked and sounded like an angry bumble bee.

* * *

Regi's mood was lighter when she arrived at the coffee shop Monday. Murphy was part of the reason for the change in her spirits, but so was the fact that there was an absence of anticipation and worry hanging over her head. Cam's birthday, like hers, had come and gone. There was nothing to agonize over. He wasn't coming. She couldn't tell herself he would be here soon. It was over. She'd carried through on her pledge, but it was obvious Cam was in a different place in his life and it was a place that didn't have room for past promises or her.

As had been his habit for several months, Nate stopped in with a delivery during a quiet time. She fixed him a mocha while he put the boxes in the back. "Thanks, Regi," he said, taking the paper cup. "Did you give any more thought to New Year's Eve?"

She smiled and noticed his vibrant eyes flicker with anticipation. "We'll be there. Molly's excited…and so am I."

"Terrific. You'll have fun. How about I stop by and we could walk over from your condo? With the whole town going, parking can be a bear."

"Sounds like a plan. I get off early Wednesday, so we'll be ready. I'll just have to check on Murphy every few hours. I don't want to leave her alone the whole time."

"No problem. I'll stop by around five."

She boxed up a fresh bear claw and handed it to him on his way out. "Here's a snack. On the house."

Nate grinned. He reached up to brush a strand of hair from the side of her face. His eyes locked on hers and he edged toward her. Instead of kissing her, he said, "I never refuse food from a pretty girl." Then he clutched the bag with the pastry and waved as he went out the door.

Regi shook her head, laughing as he left and began wiping the counter. With most of the Christmas visitors gone, the morning passed by at a slower pace. Close to noon, Leon came through the door, all smiles.

"Hey, Reg. I talked to Lou and he's willing to give me a chance. It's only dishwashing, but I should make enough to cover my expenses. I start Wednesday."

"Good for you. You told him about your past, right?"

"Yeah. His reaction was a lot like Jeremy's. Told me if I meant what I said, we'd get along fine, but the first time I screwed up, I was gone."

"It's a tight-knit community and for the most part crime free. I'm sure they'd like to keep it that way and while they're caring, they aren't stupid or pushovers. It's kind of them to give you a chance."

"I know. I'm grateful and I'm not gonna mess it up. I promise."

"What are your hours?"

"I'll be working noon to eight and my days off will be Monday and Tuesday. Plus I get a free meal while I'm working, so that helps. I'm heading to the bank now."

Regi saw a few people come through the door. "Great news, congratulations. I'm happy for you. I've got customers, so we'll talk later."

Regi turned her attention to the drink orders and while she poured the lattes into warm cups, she felt a small flicker of hope for Leon. *Maybe the island will be the answer for both of us.*

Seven

Regi closed the coffee shop at two on New Year's Eve. Her day had been steady, but nothing one person couldn't handle. There was a buzz of excitement with everyone getting ready for the party and several firefighters on the decorating committee had stopped in for a hot drink. She locked the door and headed down the sidewalk to her neighborhood. Molly had the Jeep and offered to pick her up, but Regi needed the fresh air. She hadn't thought about what to wear and mulled through a few outfits as she meandered home.

She looked into the window of the old Island Jewels building and saw Kate working. Kate glanced up as Regi peered in and the new owner motioned her inside. "Hi, Regi," she said, her hair swept up in a ponytail, wearing a denim shirt covered in blotches of paint.

Regi surveyed the room and turned back to Kate. "It looks great. You've made a lot of progress."

"I've been doing some cosmetic work. Sort of making it mine," she smiled. "And trying to organize my office." She glanced up at the loft area above the main floor. "I decided to perch myself upstairs."

"When are you opening?"

"I'm hoping by the end of January. I need to get it ready and then work on stocking it. I think I have enough pieces in storage, but want to get them placed in here and see how it all looks." She motioned to the wall she had just finished painting. "I don't like stark white, so I'm doing a few walls in neutrals for displaying paintings and photographs."

"It's a large space, now that it's all empty."

Kate nodded. "I think it will work out well."

"Did you find a house?"

The gold flecks in Kate's eyes shimmered. "I did. Kellie helped me and I fell in love with a home that's only about a half a mile from town. I could walk to work if I want and it's all one level, plus it's immaculate. It should close around the end of January. I'm at The Haven until then."

"That sounds like a great find for you."

"Are you going to the New Year's Eve bash tonight?"

Regi nodded. "Yes, my daughter wants to go and a friend of mine asked, so we're going. How about you?"

"It depends how much more I can get done. I'd like to go, just to meet some people, but I'm torn between fun and work."

"My daughter, Molly, could help you for a couple of days. She's here on her break from college and goes back on Saturday. If I'd thought of it sooner, she could have helped you all week."

"Oh, that's kind of you. I thought I could do all this myself, but it's a job. I was at Cooper Hardware and met Jeff. He told me normally he'd be available to help me, but he explained about his accident and recovery. He gave me the name of a guy he knows. I plan to call him for some of the more complicated things I need done. Check with Molly and if she's interested I could use some help cleaning and painting, plus getting my office set up."

Regi took out her phone and punched in a text to Molly. "Her phone's permanently attached, so we'll have an answer in moments." She and Kate both laughed and then chuckled again when they heard the ping of a new message. Regi scrolled the screen and nodded. "She's in. I'm working the next two days anyway, so it will be good for her. She'll just need to check on my new puppy every few hours."

"Wonderful and how exciting that you have a new puppy. Dogs are excellent companions." Kate gathered her painting tools and made for the back room. Regi followed.

"I hope you'll join us tonight," said Regi. "Now that you have some help, you could take a few hours off."

Kate smiled. "I agree. I'll get this stuff put away and get back to my room and clean up. I'll see you there."

"We're planning to be there around five. I'll look for you and save you a seat."

"Sounds great. Thanks for stopping in and hooking me up with a helper." She waved a wet hand and went back to cleaning her brushes as Regi left.

Regi strolled home and found Murphy sacked out on Molly's lap. "Is she tuckered out?"

"Yeah, we've been playing a lot today. I wanted to tire her out so she'd sleep."

"I'm going to relax for a bit. Go ahead and use the bathroom and get ready. I'll hold Murphy."

Molly poured the sleeping dog onto Regi's lap and when she returned from getting ready, she found both of them fast asleep. Molly slinked back down the hallway to let them rest. She decided to set out some clothes for her mom to save her time. She flicked through the hangers, looking for something other than Regi's signature jeans and a turtleneck.

She tossed several possibilities on the bed and then moved to hold them up and scrutinize them further. Molly knew this was a date with Nate, even if her mom didn't. She finally settled on a pair of slim black ankle pants, a sleeveless purple blouse with a hint of metallic detail at the neckline, and an elbow length black sweater. After tossing aside her clogs, tennis shoes, and flats, she finally unearthed a cute pair of black sandals with a heel.

Just as Molly was admiring her fashion choices, Regi walked in. "You let me fall asleep," she said, eyeing the bed. "What's all this?"

"I thought I'd pick an outfit and let you take a nap. This will look great on you," beamed Molly.

"It's a little chilly for sandals and a sleeveless shirt, don't you think? I've got a turtleneck I could wear."

Molly shook her head. "No, it's New Year's Eve. They'll have heat in the building and we could have Nate drive us, if it's too cold to walk." Molly twirled around in her dress and informed Regi she would also be wearing sandals.

"I don't have time to debate. Murphy's eating her dinner, so please take her out while I get ready," said Regi, taking off her jewelry.

Regi emerged from her bedroom, dressed in Molly's picks. She stopped in the bathroom to check herself one more time and moved a stray hair. She popped some dangly earrings in her ears and added a bracelet.

Molly was putting Murphy in her crate and telling her they would be back soon, in a soothing voice. She glanced up as Regi walked by. "Wow, you look gorgeous, Mom."

"I haven't worn heels in years, I'll probably fall down on the way," laughed Regi. "I need a coat and so do you," she said, plucking them from the closet. When she heard the doorbell she bent down and told Murphy goodbye.

Molly beat her to the door and found Nate waiting, looking very handsome in a jacket and tie. "Wow, you look nice, Nate."

"So do you. Are you guys ready?"

Molly nodded. "I talked Mom into wearing heels so you may have to drive us after all," she whispered.

He winked at her when he saw Regi walk up behind her, noticing she was almost taller than he was in her heels. "Hi, Regi. You look lovely. I thought I'd drive us tonight and if the parking is too bad, I'll drop you girls off and come back here and park."

Regi handed Molly her coat and turned to lock the door as she slipped into her own jacket. After helping Regi with her coat, Nate opened the door of his pickup and Molly made sure Regi slid in first to sit next to Nate.

He smirked as he ran around the truck and took his seat. "I ran into Kate today and talked her into coming. We need to save her a seat at our table," said Regi, as Nate maneuvered the streets to the firehouse. The parking lot was packed, but there were a few spots left on the street a couple blocks away, so he dropped them at the door and sped away.

Molly and Regi walked in and stood in awe at the transformation of the firehouse. White twinkle lights were everywhere and trees and plants had been positioned to hide the fire gear that lined the walls. A wooden dance floor was set up in front of the band and round tables draped in white cloths, with black napkins, covered the rest of the huge garage-like space. Metallic streamers, tissue flowers, and shimmering beads hung from the tall ceiling, as if floating. The tables were adorned with candles, flowers, and gold and silver decorations.

Molly and Regi both said, "Wow," as they moved into the room. As Regi glanced around, she saw Sam waving at her. She waved back and turned to look for Nate. "Mol, you wait for Nate, I'm going to go see Sam and make sure there's enough room for Kate."

Regi made her way through the maze of tables and found Sam and Jeff. "Hi, Molly's waiting for Nate to come back from parking. Do you have room for us and Kate?"

"We do. We had one extra chair, so it can be Kate's," said Sam. "Max and Linda should be here in a few minutes and Jen's coming with Sean when he gets off."

Regi turned to look and saw Molly and Nate coming up behind her. "Hey, everyone. I'll go check our coats and get us something to drink," he offered. Regi and Molly sat down and visited for a few minutes and then Linda and Max arrived.

Nate returned with drinks and Kate. "Look who I found on my way," he smiled.

Kate was naturally glamorous, wearing a black knee length dress, with bandage seams and a sheer chiffon overlay with an asymmetrical hem. She topped it off with sparkling strappy sandals and silver jewelry. "Wonderful to see all of you," she said, greeting all of them. She knew Linda from the flower shop and had met Max at the coffee shop on her morning caffeine run.

Nate offered to take her red cape she had folded over her arm. He walked to the coat room and Kate said, "He's such a thoughtful young man. I've gotten to know him since he's been delivering items almost daily. He's a keeper." She winked at Regi. "You're a lucky gal."

Regi stammered, "Uh, we're uh, not really together. I mean we're here together, but we're you know, not a real couple."

"Well, that's a shame. You're a lovely match," said Kate, taking a sip of her drink.

Linda raised her brows at Max over the rim of her glass as Nate returned to the table. "Are you all starving, or shall we wait for Jen and Sean before we get in line for the buffet?" asked Linda.

Jeff said, "I'll grab us some appetizers for the table and then we'll be able to wait it out." He got up, gave Sam a quick kiss, and headed across the sea of tables.

The group busied themselves visiting and snacking on the two trays of finger foods Jeff delivered to the table. Kate entertained them with stories of her travels around the globe buying antiques and art for her business.

Max and Linda talked about their upcoming wedding and told Kate she was welcome to attend. "I've convinced Linda to take a trip to Ireland for our honeymoon," said Max. "We're going to delay it a bit and go in late March rather than right after the wedding. I think the weather will be better."

"How wonderful. I know you've always wanted to take a trip there," said Sam. "How long will you get to stay?"

Max winked at Linda. "I talked her into a month in Ireland, with some time in New York on our way." Then he turned to Regi. "That's contingent on you being able to house and dog sit for us. You can bring Murphy. She'll have fun with Lucy."

Regi smiled. "I'd be happy to stay. I love your place."

"Wonderful. Thanks, Regi," said Linda, glancing up to see Jen and Sean joining the table.

Jen introduced Sean to Kate and then suggested they get in the food line. As they stood in the line Jeff explained that the firefighters held fundraisers throughout the year and with the help of several local businesses were able to put on the event at no cost. He pointed out the gold fire boots around the room. "Those are for donations for next year. We always collect a large amount at the party to help pay for next year's."

They filled their plates with yummy selections from several local restaurants, including Lou's. When Regi presented her plate for one of his famous crab cakes, she said, "Thanks for giving my brother a chance, Lou. I hope he won't disappoint you."

"I'll keep an eye on him, Regi. In my book everyone deserves a second chance. I hope it works out for him. He did a good job today and will be busy when I get back with all these dishes."

They left loaded down with food and the men offered to retrieve desserts for the table early to make sure they had the best selection. Jeff, of course, returned with slices of Sam's pies, and the others juggled plates of cakes slices, cookies, and fruit and cream filled crepes.

Half way through their dinner, the lights dimmed, and the band began playing. Jeff urged Sam to hurry so they could dance. She rolled her eyes at him, but gave in and followed him to the dance floor. Max and Linda decided to join them and work off their dinner before dessert.

Nate glanced at Molly and she nodded towards her mother and mouthed, "Ask her."

"Regi, would you like to dance?" he asked.

Her eyes widened, "Um, I'm not much of a dancer."

Kate patted her hand. "Oh, go on, it's fun and nobody is grading you."

"Go, Mom. It'll be fun," urged Molly.

Sean and Jen both got up. "Come on," Jen motioned. "We're going now, you can follow us."

Regi was outnumbered and hesitated as she gave her hand to Nate and felt herself being pulled to dance floor. Once there, Nate expertly turned her around and took her hand in his as "Brown Eyed Girl" began to play. Although Nate didn't look light on his feet, being less than six feet tall and solid through the shoulders and chest, he danced with ease and grace. Regi struggled to follow and he could see the tension in her stiff neck and shoulders. “Just relax and move with the music. Don’t think about it,” he whispered in her ear.

Through the next few songs she tried to loosen up and by the time “Sweet Home Alabama” had ended, she was laughing and moving with ease. Nate kept the momentum going as they continued through “The Time of My Life” and then he led her off the floor.

She took her sweater off when they sat down. “Whew, that definitely warmed me up. We better check on the puppy,” she said, looking at Molly.

“Jeff and I already walked home and she was sleeping. We took her outside and she went right back to sleep. I’ll make sure and check her again in a couple of hours.”

Sam and Jeff had danced to a couple of songs and returned to the table to finish off dessert. “You guys looked like you were having a good time,” said Sam.

Nate looked at Regi and smiled. “It was lots of fun. We just need a break and then we’ll go back.” He took a drink of lemonade. “Maybe I could talk Molly into a dance.”

Molly nodded her head. “I’ll go.”

He gobbled down a piece of pie and took Molly’s hand. “Okay, let’s go.”

Molly laughed at Nate’s old moves as the band played “Shake It Up” and Nate entertained her with his version of “Y.M.C.A.” Molly took a break and Regi rejoined Nate for a medley of country hits and the crowd line danced to “The Fireman.”

Regi spent the rest of the night dancing, only taking a break when the band took one. It was the first time in months that her thoughts hadn’t been consumed with Cam and his return. Tonight she was living in the moment, enjoying laughs with friends, and surprising herself on the dance floor.

The last dance before midnight was “Wonderful Tonight,” and Nate held Regi close as they swayed to the classic tune. She was reluctant to pull away from him when the song ended. He was content to let her head rest on his shoulder and feel the softness of her cheek on his. The band leader announced they had ten minutes to walk to the harbor and view the fireworks at midnight.

Nate finally broke the spell as couples around them cleared the dance floor. "Let's get Molly and go watch the fireworks. We need to retrieve our coats." He took her hand and led her to their table.

Molly greeted them with their jackets. "The others took off for the harbor."

They hurried into their coats and rushed out the door, arriving in time to hear, "Three, two, one," and the crowd erupt into cheers and whistles as the first burst of color lit up the sky.

Nate turned to look at Regi and said, "Happy New Year." Then he bent down and kissed her. She closed her eyes and felt his hand on the back of her neck as she returned his kiss. A tiny charge rippled through her with Nate's kiss. Everyone kissed on New Year's Eve, but the flutter of her heart told her this one was more than a token.

"Happy New Year, Nate," she said and took his hand in hers while they watched the explosions of color paint the endless sky and reflect in the inky water of the harbor. Regi reached for her daughter's hand and squeezed it tight as she smiled and hoped for a new start and the strength to let go of the promise tethering her to the past.

Eight

After spending a long weekend relaxing, playing with Murphy, and letting her feet heal from hours of dancing in high heels, Regi was back to work on Monday. Saturday had been quiet and gloomy after Molly's departure. Regi was relieved when she learned Kyle would be going back on the same ferry. She was thankful Molly had a friend near her at the university.

She worked out a schedule with Jeff, who was more than willing to look after Murphy. He stopped by the condo on his way to the hardware store and picked her up. He snuggled her in his coat and deposited her on the seat next to Zoe and Bailey and waved as Regi watched him drive away. Regi would pick her up each day as soon as she got off work.

Her vacation had been filled with rich calorie-laden food, so she made sure she packed a healthy salad for lunch and got rid of all the tempting delicious foods in the house. She was back to working weekends at the coffee shop now that school was back in session and Hayley had returned from her trip.

Nate made a point of stopping by her office when he delivered at the school. She hadn't seen him since Saturday when they ran into him at Sweet Treats before Molly caught her ferry. She felt her pulse quicken when he walked through her door and straddled a chair. "Hey, Nate, how are you?"

"Busy, but doing well. You doing okay without Molly?"

She nodded. "Yeah, she made it back without a problem." She turned away from her computer screen to face Nate. "Murphy's kept me busy and

I spent the weekend cleaning and getting organized. The fun's over until the next break."

"Speaking of fun, I wondered if you'd like to go to a concert Saturday night. It's at the community theatre. They'll have music and dessert, but we could stop for dinner before we go."

Out of habit, Regi started to say she couldn't go, but then remembered she wasn't waiting for Cam and had enjoyed her evening with Nate on New Year's Eve. The more she got to know him, the more she liked him. "Sure, that sounds fun. I have to work, but I get off at two."

"The concert starts at seven, so how about we eat around five-thirty? I'll pick you up."

"Perfect, I'll be ready," she smiled. "What's the dress code?"

"Nothing fancy. People wear everything from jeans to suits." He chuckled and then said, "I'm not wearing a suit. I'm more of a jeans guy."

She smiled. "Even better, I love my jeans and no more high heels."

He chuckled. "I gotta get moving, but just wanted to say hi and see how you were doing. See you Saturday, if not before," he said, leaning against her doorjamb.

She gave him a wave and watched as he said goodbye to the other secretaries in the office and ran to his truck. *He's a great guy and I have fun when I'm with him. I have to move on and leave Cam in the past.*

* * *

Saturday morning Linda, Sam, and Jen stopped by the shop for coffees on their way to the ferry. They were making the trip to meet Becky and help Linda pick out her wedding dress. They were giddy with excitement as they carried a box of treats and their coffees to Sam's SUV. "Text me some pictures," said Regi, as she waved goodbye.

She kept busy until she was relieved by Rachel and drove out to Sam and Jeff's house to pick up Murphy. She found Jeff on the deck watching Zoe and Bailey herd the puppy around the yard. The big dogs were rolling on the grass, letting Murphy jump over and on top of them, while the puppy yipped with delight.

"Sit down and watch for a few minutes. They're entertaining," said Jeff, when he saw Regi walking up the steps to the deck.

She glanced at her watch. "I can't stay long. I'm meeting Nate for dinner tonight and we're going to a concert."

Jeff smiled, "He's a great guy, Regi. I'm glad you're giving him a chance."

She nodded. "I really had my heart set on Cam coming back here, so I wasn't focused on meeting someone. But, I had more fun than I've had in years at the dance. I'm not sure about it, but I enjoy Nate's company."

Jeff eyed her serious face. "But he's no Cam, right?"

She looked at him and gave a slow nod. "Yeah," she whispered. "I don't know who Cam is now though. I just have my perfect memories of him."

"How about a cup of tea?" he asked, getting up to get it.

"I don't want to trouble you—"she began.

"I'm getting one for me anyway. Just sit tight."

He returned with two steaming mugs and the canine circus act continued below. She wrapped her hands around the warm ceramic.

"I'm no expert in relationships…far from it. But, I know what it's like to wish for the past and hope for things that may not exist anymore." He paused and sipped his tea. "My wife left me with my kids when they were young and for years I thought she'd come back and we would be a family, but it never happened. Then I gave up on anything to do with romance or finding a true partner. I was divorced for over twenty years before I met Sam and I knew almost instantly she was the one I'd been waiting for all those years. I was never truly happy until Sam showed me what I was missing."

"So, you're saying I need to stop beating a dead horse?"

He chuckled. "Yeah, that's what I'm saying. Live your life, Regi. Be happy. Maybe Nate's the one, maybe not, but stop waiting for something that isn't coming back. Maybe you're supposed to be on the island for you, not for Cam."

Sam saw Murphy's head reach the top step of the deck. "Looks like they taught her to climb stairs. She wouldn't do it at the condo with Molly."

Jeff scooped up the puppy. "She's a good girl, huh?" He pressed his nose to hers and she licked him.

"We better get home. Thanks again for watching her. I couldn't do it without you."

"Trust me, I love it. What's one more dog?" He followed her to her Jeep. "Take care. I'll see you tomorrow."

She settled Murphy into a blanket on the passenger seat and waved to Jeff. "Your dog sitter is one smart guy."

Murphy gave a yip, voicing her total agreement.

* * *

Nate picked up Regi and they drove to the Beach Club for dinner. Despite the cloud cover and grayness of the water, the view was impressive. While eating a delicious dinner, Regi learned more about Nate. He was the oldest of four in his family. His parents were in their early sixties and he would turn forty in the summer. His dad owned a real estate company—the one where Kellie worked. His mom had stayed home raising the kids and now spent her time volunteering. One of her favorite organizations was the community theatre.

"So your mom and dad will be at the concert tonight?" asked Regi.

Nate nodded his head, "Yeah, she's the one who recommended it. They have season tickets. Tonight's performance features local artists."

"That should be fun," said Regi. "I know the high school drama class is putting on a play there in a few months."

"That's an annual event. They do a great job. I've been yammering on all night about my family. How's Leon doing?"

"He's doing well at Lou's. I haven't heard about any problems, have you?"

"No, not at all. I've seen him a few times when I've been making deliveries and he's always working."

"I keep hoping this time he means it and stays on the right path."

"There are some meetings for recovering addicts here at one of the churches. Do you think he would go?"

"I'm not sure, but I'll tell him about it. I think it would be useful."

They declined the offer of dessert and Nate paid the tab and helped Regi with her coat. Nate parked and led Regi up the steps of an old school building. The building had been remodeled and featured a three hundred seat theatre. There was also space in the annex for costume storage, musical instruments, workshops and classes, and set construction. The old classrooms had been converted into galleries for showcasing artwork and it even sported a bar and gift shop.

Nate gave her a tour of the facility and ran into his mom, manning the cash register when they ventured in to see what treasures were for sale. Nate approached the counter and called out to a woman with short, but stylish gray hair and cheerful clear blue eyes. "Mom, this is Regi."

She took Regi's hand in both of hers. "Lovely to meet you. I'm Louise, but everyone calls me Lulu."

Regi placed her hand on top of Lulu's. "It's a pleasure, Lulu. Nate has been showing me around. What a lovely building."

"It's been a work in progress, but we finally raised enough money to complete the annex last year." She touched her hand to her chest. "It's a cause that's close to my heart. I enjoy volunteering and attending all the performances."

"I told Regi she'll appreciate tonight's concert," said Nate.

"Yes, it's one of our more popular events. Jack, Nate's dad, is already seated. You should sneak by and say hi before you find your own seats," said Lulu, eyeing a woman behind them ready to pay.

"Okay, Mom. We'll see you at intermission," said Nate, guiding Regi to the door.

Nate pulled the tickets out of his pocket and checked the seats. "We're not too far away from them, but they're in a box." He held his hand behind hers as he guided her up the steps to the box seats.

He poked his head around the corner and said, "Hey, Dad. I saw Mom and she said you'd be here." He turned and looked at Regi. "This is my friend, Regi."

Jack stood and shook her hand. "Great to meet you, Regi. I'm Jack Martin."

She looked into the aquamarine eyes and saw the same vivid color as Nate's. They reminded her of the tropical waters in beach vacation ads. "Pleasure to meet you, Jack."

"Our box is full tonight, otherwise you two could sit with us."

"No problem, Dad. We've got great seats," Nate gestured to the section below the box. "We should probably get down there. We'll meet up with you at the break for dessert."

Regi gave Jack a wave as they left and found their own seats. People began wandering in from the lobby and soon the theatre was filled and the lights were dimmed. They were treated to a variety of performances, including a wonderful pianist and a young violinist. After an hour, the lights were brought back up and Nate's mom appeared on stage announcing an intermission. "Enjoy the yummy desserts available in the lobby and remember the bar is open. See you back here in forty-five minutes."

Nate took Regi's hand and led her out of their row while his mom was still on stage. He guided her on the plush red carpet path and up the stairs to the lobby area where he found his dad. They eyed large tables filled with plates of decadent confections. Nate chose a piece of cheesecake smothered with berries and wedge of chocolate mousse cake. Regi opted for a pumpkin cupcake with cream cheese frosting.

Jack took a piece of lemon cake and a piece of cheesecake and led the way to the tables near the bar. "Would you two like anything to drink?" he asked, as he set the plates down.

"I'll take a coffee," said Regi.

"I'll come with you, Dad," offered Nate. He left his plates and said, "Mom should be here in a minute. We'll be right back."

Regi watched the two men walk away and saw Jack put his hand across Nate's back as they made their way to the bar. Lulu breezed up to the table as soon as they disappeared in a line of people waiting for drinks.

"The boys must have gone to get our drinks," she said, sitting next to Regi. "Oh, and Jack left me a piece of cheesecake."

Regi nodded. "Yes, they just left. All these goodies look so yummy. I'm trying to cut back after all the junk I ate at Christmas."

"I know," said Lulu. "This stuff is hard to resist." She took a bite of the creamy cheesecake. "Delicious. Are you enjoying the performances?"

Regi nodded, swallowing a bite of the moist cupcake. "Yes, especially the pianist and the young boy with the violin."

"He's one of the favorites. Nate tells me you work at the high school and at the coffee shop. Sounds like you don't get much rest with all that work."

"I keep busy, but I enjoy my work and with my daughter going to college, I like the distraction."

"I remember when my last one left and the house was empty," she said, lost in thought as she reflected. "I cried for weeks and was so lost. A job would've been a useful diversion. That's when I started volunteering."

Jack and Nate appeared with their drinks and joined them. "Here's your coffee, Regi," said Nate, as he set two steaming cups down on the table.

Jack handed his wife one of the glasses of red wine he was carrying. "Here you go, sweetheart."

Nate offered Regi half of his chocolate mousse cake. "I just told your mom I was trying to behave, but I can't resist Ellie's cakes," she said, as she dug a fork into the slice.

While they finished dessert they asked Regi more about her family and she shared that her father had worked at the post office and was now retired and her mom worked at the university, but was only part-time now. "They still live in my hometown of Ellensburg and stay busy with friends. They're planning to visit this summer when I'm off from school and Molly will be home."

Lulu finished her wine and said, "We'll have to plan a get-together at the house when they're here. I'd love to meet them."

The lights flashed, signaling the end of intermission. "It was wonderful to meet you both. Thanks for recommending the concert, I've enjoyed it," said Regi, as Nate stood.

"We probably won't see you after. Regi has to work early tomorrow, so we're going to bug out as soon as it's over," said Nate.

"I'm glad you came and it was a pleasure to visit with you Regi," said Lulu.

"Yes, I hope we see you again soon," said Jack, putting his hand on his wife's back and moving her along.

Lulu kissed Nate on the cheek, "See you later, sweetie."

Nate guided Regi through the crowd and back to their seats in time for the curtain to rise on a new performer. They spent the next hour listening to entertaining performances, including a solo by one of the singers in the band that played at the firehouse on New Year's Eve.

Regi caught herself yawning during the last performance. Nate whispered, "Do you want to sneak out now?"

She nodded and he gripped her hand and led her through the dark to the exit. "Sorry, the week has caught up with me and I've got to open tomorrow."

"Don't worry, I'll have you home in a few minutes," he said, helping her with the arm of her coat as he reached for the door.

He drove the few blocks to Regi's condo and left the truck running while he walked her to the door. "Thanks for coming. I had a great time," he said, as she worked her key in the lock.

"Thank you for inviting me and for dinner. I had a wonderful time, Nate." She popped the lock and opened the door.

He leaned in and kissed her on the cheek and held her in a strong hug. "I'll see you tomorrow."

Regi shut the door, savoring the warmth of Nate's embrace and the woodsy scent with a hint of lemon he left on her jacket. She checked on Murphy and sniffed her coat one more time before slipping into bed.

Nine

Linda's shower was scheduled for Saturday night at Sam's and Max was hosting the men and the dogs at his house. Since it was a holiday weekend, Kyle and Molly had both come home on Friday. Kyle volunteered to handle the late shift at the coffee shop, so everyone could attend the shower.

Since Molly would be turning twenty-one at the end of the month, Regi decided to celebrate with dinner and a cake on Sunday night. She knew Molly wouldn't be able to come home for her birthday and wanted to take advantage of the holiday weekend.

Molly had gone out to Sam's early in the day to help get things ready. Regi offered to pick up Max's pizza order on her way to drop Murphy before heading out to the shower. She pulled in the driveway and saw Nate waiting. "Let me give you a hand with all this," he offered, taking the stack of pizza boxes from her backseat. "After all, I'm a professional when it comes to deliveries," he grinned.

She laughed, grabbing Murphy's crate. "Are you ready for a manly night of celebrating?"

He gave a caveman grunt and laughed. "I have a feeling it'll be a tame evening. Max and Jeff have some card games planned and from the looks of the food, we'll be spending most of our time eating. Ellie just dropped off some great looking desserts."

She opened the door wide to let Nate slip through with his tower of boxes. She followed with Murphy, who voiced a greeting to the three dogs.

She set the crate in the entry and three dog noses wedged in as she opened the door and Murphy sprang out. The puppy scuttled down the step and dashed through the great room, with all four dogs ending up in a heap.

Regi laughed as she watched and Max came up behind her and gave her a hug. "Thanks for bringing the pizzas."

"You guys look like you'll have your hands full," she gestured to the dogs.

"We outnumber them," he laughed. "And Kyle will be here soon."

She saw Sean, Jeff, Charlie, and Jeremy plus a couple of firemen she recognized, all sitting on the couch engrossed in something on Max's enormous television. "Hi Regi," they all said without moving their eyes from the screen.

Nate came from the kitchen and put his hand on Regi's shoulder. "I can bring Murphy by your place when we're done."

"Are you sure?"

"Yeah, it's no trouble. I drive by there on my way home."

"I'm not sure what time we'll be done. I've got a spare key in the Jeep. I'll get it for you and you can leave her if we're not home."

Regi said her goodbyes and wished them a fun night. "Don't be too crazy, Max. No strippers, okay?" she smiled.

Max laughed and raised his hand. "I promise."

Nate opened the door for Regi and followed her to the driveway. She rummaged in the console and extricated a Minnie Mouse key ring. She blew a chunk of hair out of her eyes and handed Nate the key. "Here it is. This will get you in and you'll have to use it to relock the deadbolt when you leave." She rested against the open door, her hands perched on the window frame.

He leaned against the fender of the Jeep. "Got it. How have you been this week? I haven't seen much of you."

"I know. I've been stuck in meetings all week when you've been there with our deliveries."

"How about we do breakfast tomorrow and catch up? My treat."

She found herself nodding before she spoke. "I'm off tomorrow, so that would be fun, but Molly's home. We're going to celebrate her birthday tomorrow night."

"Bring her if she wants to join us. Let's say Front Street Café at ten. We could make it a birthday breakfast."

"Okay, I'll see you then. Thanks for taking Murphy home."

"No problem." He moved off the fender as she started to get in the Jeep. He shut the door after she pulled her legs inside. She rolled the window down and he leaned in, placing his head even with hers. "Have fun tonight," he said, and with a slight tip of his head inched closer.

Regi caught sight of the desire in Nate's eyes and smelled the same woodsy scent he had left on her jacket. She felt something for him, but she wasn't sure what. She sensed the heat travel up her neck to her face. His hand was still resting on her door. She patted his hand, "Have a fun time with the guys. I'll see you in the morning."

Before she could remove her hand, he covered it with his and nodded as he heard the engine turn over. "See ya, Regi."

* * *

Sam's house was teeming with what looked like the entire female population of Friday Harbor. Jen and Sam had outdone themselves with the food and decorations. Sam's dining table was covered in a delicate lavender cloth and amid gorgeous lilac, white, and violet flowers, votive candles flickered. A huge platter of veggies looked more like a piece of art, with red and green cabbages serving as bowls for dip, surrounded by cauliflower and Romanesco, looking more like a green fractal from space than a variety of broccoli. Colorful julienned peppers, carrots, and cucumbers were lined up like new pencils amid sliced baguettes and crackers. Savory meatballs bubbled in a slow cooker and a warm pan of bacon wrapped dates beckoned guests to the table. A tiered tray of sliced fruits and berries surrounded by puffs of whipped cream was stationed next to a bowl of marshmallow cream cheese dip. Barbeque chicken sliders and chicken salad croissants were stacked in mounds among bowls of salads.

The dessert table held beautiful cupcakes decorated to look like miniature wedding cakes with purple and lavender ribbons and roses. Lemon tarts, mini cheesecakes topped with berries, and salted caramel brownies covered another tray. Pitchers of iced tea, lemonade, and a punchbowl of pink sherbet punch completed the impressive buffet.

Jen took several photos before she and Sam herded the guests to the dining room and made Linda start the line. She loaded a plate and made her way to the throne of honor, decorated with flowers and ribbons. Sam and Jen helped the guests with food and delivered drinks and finally were able to fill their own plates and sit down next to Linda. Everyone raved about the food, commenting not only that it was impressively displayed, but delicious. Sam and Jen graciously accepted the praise and then Sam added, "We couldn't have done it without our sous chefs, Molly and Megan. You all know Regi and this is her lovely daughter who volunteered to help us on her holiday weekend from college, along with Megan." The girls' faces reddened as the women applauded.

Soon the feast was over and at Linda's insistence, bridal shower games were forbidden. Instead she asked everyone to bring a special recipe or piece of advice to share. Megan and Molly passed out scrapbook pages and asked the guests to write their recipes or words of wisdom with the colorful markers they provided.

Once the pages were collected, Linda opened her gifts. Since they all knew she would be touring Ireland for her honeymoon, many of the gifts reflected the theme of travel. Several of the women went together and purchased a gift credit card for Linda to use on the trip. She also received a set of new lightweight luggage and Annie knitted her a gorgeous ivory afghan. Kate presented her with a sparkly vintage crystal and silver hairpin. Linda's staff at the nursery and flower shop researched the gardens in Ireland and purchased tickets for the happy couple to visit dozens of them. Sam and Jeff gave them the gift of a suite at the Sherry-Netherland Hotel to use while they were in New York City.

When all the gifts had been opened, Sam and Jen served dessert. Ellie's creations were consumed with delight and the guests were overjoyed to learn the mini wedding cakes came in red velvet and white almond. When they were settled in the great room around the fire, Sam started a movie she had picked out, *The Wedding Date.*

Regi caught herself nodding off after the movie started. She was tired and wanted to go home, but knew Molly was having fun and had bonded with Megan. They were on the floor whispering and giggling. Regi slipped into the kitchen to get a cup of coffee. She found Sam tidying the kitchen.

"Hey, I just came to sneak a cup of coffee. I can't stay awake," said Regi. "If Molly wasn't having so much fun, I'd head home."

"Megan already decided she wanted to sleep over tonight. Molly could stay, if you want." She reached for a cup and handed it to Regi. "They wouldn't be any trouble."

"They seem to have connected this weekend. If you're sure, she'd probably like it. I'll get her attention and find out," said Regi, poking her head around the corner. She caught Molly's eye and motioned her over. They whispered and Molly nodded her head with enthusiasm and hugged Regi.

"Well, that looked like a yes," said Sam.

Regi smiled. "They were already cooking up a plan to ask me if she could stay, so you'll have another guest tonight."

"We love having Megan around, so one more will just be double the fun. We have plenty of room and they can help me clean up in the morning," she grinned.

"Thanks, Sam. I'm going to tell Linda goodbye and get home. Thanks for having us."

Regi crept to Linda's chair and whispered, "I'm going to get home. Molly's having a slumber party tonight with Megan. It was a lovely shower, thanks for having us."

Linda got up and walked Regi to the door. "I'm so happy you and Molly came. I had a great time. See you soon." She hugged Regi and held the door, watching as she wove her way through the maze of cars to her Jeep.

When Regi pulled up to her condo it was close to midnight and she noticed Nate's pickup out front. She used her key to open the door and when she walked into the living room found Nate on the couch with Murphy on his chest, both sound asleep.

Not having the heart to disturb him, she pulled a quilt over him and turned off the television before she went down the hall to her bedroom. She sloughed off her clothes, slipped on her nightshirt and fell into bed.

As her eyelids gave up their battle to stay open, she realized for the first time in her life she had a man sleeping in her house. She knew she should care about the perception created by Nate's truck parked outside, but was too tired to consider the repercussions.

* * *

Sleep came quickly and heavy for Regi and she didn't wake at her normal time. Her sheets were tangled around her leaving her legs completely uncovered. She felt a hand shake her shoulder and pried an eye open, and squinted in surprise as the light of morning drilled into her still sleeping pupil. "Mol—" she started then gasped. "Nate, oh, no, what time is it?"

"Sorry to startle you. It's almost nine. I hated to leave without saying so and wanted to apologize for falling asleep here." He ran a hand through his rumpled hair and sighed looking behind him at the door. "I'm sorry. I came in and started playing with Murphy and I fell asleep," he whispered.

Regi eased her head and shoulders up, trying to sneak a hand to her hair to gauge the level of dishevel she was showcasing. When she glanced down she forgot about her tousled hair, conscious only of her bare legs and her old grey shirt, thin and threadbare, insufficient to disguise what was underneath. She tugged the sheets to her chin, but they were too tangled to cover her legs. "It's no big deal. I was so tired and hated to disturb you, so just covered you up and came to bed."

"What about Molly? I don't want to give her the wrong impression."

"She stayed over at Sam's with Megan. Sam was showing a movie and I was tired and left before it was over."

She heard his breath escape and saw his arms relax. "Oh, good. I, uh, you know, just didn't want to cause a problem."

"No problem. I need to get up and get ready. We're meeting for breakfast, right?"

He grinned. "Yeah. I need to get home and take a shower. I fed Murphy and took her out. Are you still able to make ten o'clock?"

She nodded, still holding the sheet under her chin. "Yeah, I can be there, especially since you took care of the puppy."

"Okay, then, I'll meet you there." He stood staring at her.

She looked at him, expecting him to leave. "See ya there." She swung her calf over the side of the bed.

His gaze followed her movement.

She cleared her throat, "Uh, Nate?" She raised her eyebrows.

"Yeah," he moved his eyes away from her leg. "Oh, yeah, I'll get out of your hair." He backed up and ran into the open door, turned and waved and then shut the door. She heard him tell Murphy goodbye and then she heard the front door shut.

She shook her head and freed herself from the twisted sheet, gathered her clothes, and made for the shower. One cup of coffee and forty minutes later she felt human again. Appalled when she looked in the mirror before her shower and saw makeup streaked across her face, black smudges of mascara under her eyes, and hair that stuck out only on one side of her head, she now looked presentable. She smoothed her turtleneck, which she noticed was the color of Nate's eyes, and pulled on her boots.

She took Murphy out and decided fresh air would revive her and set out for the harbor. She waved at Hayley when she walked by the coffee shop and returned Annie's greeting as she was opening Knitwits. As she reached for the door of the Front Street Café, it opened and she saw Nate holding it for her.

"Saw you coming. I just got here myself. Did you walk?"

"Yeah, it's a beautiful morning." She led the way to a table and draped her coat over the back of her chair.

Their waitress arrived with fresh coffee and took their orders. Nate talked her into splitting an order of cinnamon roll French toast, in addition to each of their selections. Regi's phone chirped with a text from Molly. She smiled and tapped out a response.

She put the phone down and said, "That was Molly. Sam's invited us for dinner and Molly wants to stay out there until I come out this evening." Her phone pinged again and she looked at the screen. "Correction, we've both been invited to dinner at Sam's," she smiled. "She knows we had birthday plans tonight, but she says Sam thinks rather than just the two of us going out to dinner, we should come to her house."

"Sounds fun. I'd be a fool to turn down a free dinner with two pretty ladies," said Nate, his eyes twinkling with amusement.

The waitress delivered the cinnamon roll concoction along with an omelet for Nate and a veggie scramble for Regi. Their coffees were refilled and they were left to indulge. After he took several bites, Nate said, "I should warn you I ran into a couple people when I was leaving your place this morning."

Regi swallowed, "What do you mean?"

"I've lived here long enough to know gossip spreads like a wildfire on a windy day. Anyway, as I was getting in my truck, two of the teachers from your school were out running—Crystal and Robin."

"Ugh, two of the biggest mouths in the school. They're always yapping about someone." She took a sip of coffee. "Well, there's not much we can do about it."

He placed his hand over hers. "I'm sorry."

She shook her head. "It's not a problem. Those two bobble heads aren't known for their credibility—just their dramatic sensationalism. We didn't do anything wrong and we're adults."

He smiled. "I like you Regi, you must know that?"

She noticed the intensity of his gaze. "Yes, I like you too."

"I mean, uh, I like you as more than a friend. I'm attracted to you. I have been ever since the first day I saw you. I get the feeling that you're fine being friends, but nothing more. Almost like you're distracted."

She nodded. "That's my fault and it's a long story." She paused. "I'm sorry and I do like spending time with you."

"I've got all day. Tell me your story."

"It's not easy and it's embarrassing," she lowered her eyes to study the potatoes on her plate.

"Hey," he said, as he reached across the table for her hand. "You can let me in. I won't hurt you, I promise."

"I know, Nate. I don't want to hurt you."

* * *

Nate suggested Regi visit his house and after picking up Murphy, drove her through town and pulled up to a cheerful looking cream colored home with a huge deck. He gave her a tour outside, beaming when he pointed out his large barbeque and fire pit area, surrounded by plants. He led her to an enormous shop, where he kept his boat, kayaks, off road vehicles, and fishing supplies.

"Ah, your toy box," she joked. "Every guy needs a place to store his prized possessions."

"Truth is that's why I bought this place. Dad was going to list it and called me, knowing it would be perfect. I like the outdoors and this has great features. The inside is plain, but doesn't bother me."

"It's great and you're close to town, but it seems secluded."

He grinned. "Another plus. Come on, I'll show you the house."

After a quick trip around the living space, he started a fire and Regi went to work making hot cocoa. He looked across the living room to the open kitchen and gave directions as to which cupboards contained the ingredients she needed. He found an old pillow and set it on the floor for Murphy, who sniffed it and finding it acceptable, curled up on it.

Regi stirred the cocoa, surprised at how neat he kept his house, for a single guy. She carried two mugs into the living room and sat on the couch, next to Nate. He took a sip. "Okay, time for your story."

She held his gaze and said, "It all started during my senior year of high school." He let her talk, never interrupting her, only nodding to urge her on. It took two more cups of cocoa to get through the chronicle of her life, including Ronnie, Leon, Cam, and Molly. She sighed and ended with, "So, that's why I'm here and the cause of the distraction you noticed." She set her mug on the coffee table. "I wouldn't blame you if you took off running right now."

"I'm not going anywhere." He put his mug down and took her hand. "I'm so very sorry about your brother, Ronnie. And I'm sorry Cam didn't show up. It had to be a big letdown when you've been waiting as long as you have."

Regi nodded her head, willing the tears she felt pooling in her eyes to stay put.

"You're an incredible person with a wonderful daughter. I'd like to be part of your life and spend time with you."

Regi was quiet. "I haven't had a man in my life for a long time. I made a mistake when Molly was a baby and trusted a guy and it went horribly wrong. After that I decided I'm horrible when it comes to men and vowed to make it on my own."

"You did make it on your own. I don't want to be with you to rescue you; I want to be with you because you're you." He paused and then asked, "Do you like being alone?"

The tears she was desperate to contain surged over the rims of her eyes and down her face. "No, I don't." She took a breath and he retrieved a box of tissues. "With Molly it was easier, I didn't notice, but now it's so quiet and I'm truly alone."

He put his arm around her and leaned his head against hers. "But you don't have to be. I'm right here."

* * *

Sam had done a great job of throwing together an impromptu party for Molly. Jen and Megan were there, along with Kyle. Linda and Max came and brought Lucy. Nate and Regi picked up the decadent chocolate cake with fudge frosting she had ordered from Ellie. As they were leaving the bakery, they saw Kate locking up and persuaded her to join the party.

Sam used some of the fabulous leftovers from the shower and after learning hamburgers were one of Molly's favorites, Jeff fired up the grill and barbequed enough burgers to feed the whole island. Max made strawberry daiquiris and since it was Molly's special day, she chose one with alcohol.

They showered Molly with gifts, toasted her, and sang to her. Regi watched as Molly beamed, partially from the splash of rum in her drink, but mostly from the warmth of their newfound friends. Regi had planned to take Molly to dinner and splurge on the cake, but their new friends had taken it upon themselves to make her feel special and a part of something. She smiled, grateful for the friendship she felt for everyone around the table.

They finished the evening huddled around the fire, sharing memories of their twenty-first birthdays with Molly. Nate drove them home after the party and helped them carry Molly's gifts and the leftover cake.

As he was getting in his truck, they stood outside waving. He heard Molly say, "I'm so glad you moved here, Mom. I don't remember you ever looking so happy and having so many friends."

Ten

Regi had to endure a handful of disapproving looks at school the following week and when Nate stopped by with his deliveries, a few eyebrows rose higher, but she ignored them all. She had enjoyed a perfect weekend, highlighted by the party at Sam's. Molly left for Seattle Monday morning and Regi spent the rest of the holiday at Nate's.

She felt closer to Nate after telling him about Cam. Rather than passing judgment, he'd been warm and understanding. She and Murphy had spent the day exploring his property and sitting in an old chair in Nate's shop, watching him work on his boat. Soon tinkling of rain reverberated off the metal roof. The three ran from the shop and huddled in the house around a fire. They watched television and made soup and grilled cheese sandwiches. It had been a relaxing day.

In her effort to be a better sister to Leon she had suggested they meet for lunch on Tuesdays. She met him at Dottie's Deli and over sandwiches, they got caught up. "I like working at Lou's," he said.

"How's the cabin?"

"Great. It's quiet, but peaceful. I usually run into Jeremy or Heather, but haven't seen any other guests."

"How are you doing on finances?"

He finished chewing his bite of Dottie's famous turkey gobbler sandwich and said, "I can make it work. I'm not sure what I'll do when summer comes, but I'm okay now."

Regi noticed Kate at the counter and waved hello. She stopped by their table on her way out. "Nice to see you, Regi."

"Hi, Kate. I don't think you've met my brother, Leon," she said, turning to him. "Kate's opening an antique and art gallery." Leon stood to greet her.

"How's the store coming along?" asked Regi.

"Terrific. You'll have to pop in and take a look. I'm moving into my house at the end of the week and hoping to open February first." She shook her head. "Not sure if I can pull it off, but that's my plan."

"I'm always looking for extra work, I could help you with the move or anything else," offered Leon.

Regi gnawed on her lip and curled her fingers around her glass. "I'm sure Kate has it under control."

"Actually, I'd love some extra help. I'll be at the shop all day, stop by when you're done with lunch."

Regi stared at Leon and squeezed her eyebrows together. "Sounds great," he said, ignoring Regi's hardened gaze. "I'll see you in a few minutes."

They said their goodbyes and Kate left, toting her bag of food. "What's with the evil stare?" he asked.

"You need to tell her your history before she commits to having you around her store. Come on, Leon, you have a record of burglary and she's got a store full of expensive things." She shook her head. "You need to realize you're a risk."

"You'll never let me forget it, will ya?" He flung the rest of his sandwich down, stood, and snatched his coat off the chair. He tore out of the deli before Regi could say a word.

* * *

After a quick trip to the market and popping by the hardware store to check on Murphy, Regi parked in front of Kate's shop. She pulled on the door, but it was locked. She cupped her hands to peer through the glass and saw Kate waving with the key in her hand.

"Sorry to barge in," said Regi, when Kate opened the door.

"Come in, I could use a break," she said smiling.

"Is Leon here?"

She shook her head. "No, he was here earlier, but left about an hour ago."

Regi's let out a breath she didn't realize she was holding. "Oh, well, I wanted to talk to you for a few minutes."

"Sure, come on up to my office and see what you think. I've got it set up," she said, as she led the way up the stairs.

Regi marveled at the tasteful space Kate had created for herself. A large ornate desk dominated the room, and although every corner was filled with treasures, it wasn't cluttered. Bookshelves lined one wall, filled with leather bound volumes. Glass globes littered every surface, bouncing light around the room. A skylight above revealed a stained glass window and small tables and boxes held baubles of all kinds. Kate had chosen some beautiful paintings for her walls. The room evoked a vintage elegance and invited conversation.

Regi slipped into one of the cream chairs in front of Kate's desk. "It's gorgeous, Kate." She turned to take it in. "If I tried to put all of this different stuff together, it would look like a garage sale, but you've made it perfect and classy."

Kate's eyes sparkled. "I'm glad you like it. It's actually quite large, so I was able to add all of my favorite things. It makes it more like working from home."

"I can only imagine what your home must look like."

Kate's eyes widened. "That's a whole different project. Jeff and Charlie arranged for some help for me, so I think I'm set. It'll just be getting things organized after the heavy work is done."

"If I have some free time, I'll help, which leads me to why I'm here. I, uh, wanted to talk to you about my brother."

"Are you here to warn me about his past?"

A tentative smile touched Regi's lips as she nodded. "Yes. We got into it at lunch when I told him he needed to reveal his past to you before offering to work here. I feel responsible for him and I don't want him to do something to hurt the people I think so much of here in Friday Harbor."

"Leon told me he'd been in prison and about his past. He seems sincere in wanting to change. I'm going to have him helping me for a few hours here and there."

Regi nodded. "That's great. I was worried, that's all."

"I'll keep an eye on him." She heard the bells tinkle and turned to look over the railing. "Darn, I forgot to lock the door." She squinted and then smiled and waved. "Up here, Alec."

Regi angled her neck to see over the railing and watched a man with dark wavy hair, carrying a large leather portfolio, make his way across the store and up the staircase. Kate was waiting at the top of the stairs. "Alec, please come and sit down. Meet my friend, Regi."

He took her hand and kissed the back of it. "A pleasure, Regi." He made her name sound foreign and mysterious, making it rhyme with Faberge.

Kate added, "I met Alec at the B&B and he's an artist. He's here to relax and do some painting. I'm hoping to display some of his work." She smiled and her eyes crinkled in delight.

"I'll leave you to it. I need to get home. Nice to meet you Alec. I'll see you later, Kate," said Regi, starting down the stairs.

"Don't leave on my account," said Alec, his dark eyes riveted to hers.

Regi waved, "Not to worry, I was leaving anyway."

Kate waved goodbye and motioned Alec to her desk. "Stop by again, Regi," she hollered as Regi hightailed it down the stairs and across the store.

* * *

Saturday Regi was back to work at Harbor Coffee and Books. Nate stopped in for coffee and a pastry as soon as she opened. "Hey, what brings you by so early?" she asked.

"I promised Kate I would help her this weekend. She's got quite the job ahead of her with her store and her house."

"That's sweet of you. Leon has been helping her at the store, but I haven't talked to him since Tuesday." She explained their argument while he ate his apple turnover.

He took a sip of coffee. "I'm going to work on the house and see what I can get done. She warned me she has a lot of boxes."

"Have you seen her office in the shop?"

He nodded as he chewed. "Yeah, I think that's a preview of coming attractions at her house. She's a collector." They continued to discuss the home she was buying and Nate explained how to get to it.

Regi waited on a customer and returned to Nate. "I'll stop by when I get off and see if I can help do anything."

"I look forward to it," said Nate, taking his cup and checking his watch. "I gotta run."

The day wasn't busy and Regi was thankful when her shift ended at two and she went across the street to retrieve Murphy. She ran by her condo and made sure the dog was situated, brushed her hair, and put on some lip gloss. She hand fed the puppy a treat and promised to be back soon.

She made the turn onto Kate's street and saw Nate's pickup. She went through the open garage, filled with boxes, and shouted, "Nate, are you here?"

She heard scuffling and he appeared from the master bedroom. "Hey, Regi."

"What should I do to help?"

"You could help me finish unpacking the master bedroom and bath and then if we have time we could move some more boxes in from the garage. There's a shed out back and there are a few things we'll transfer to it."

They worked together for the next three hours, unpacking and staging boxes in the other rooms. Regi was on her way back in the house from taking the flattened boxes to Nate's truck, when Kate pulled in the driveway.

"Hello," she waved. "I just finished up at the store. I'd love to take you both to dinner to repay you for your help."

Nate came out of the garage, "Did I hear free dinner?"

"Yes, and many more in the future. I appreciate the help so much."

"Dinner sounds great, but I need to run and check on Murphy first," said Regi. "I'll meet you guys."

"I should clean up a bit," said Nate, brushing off his jeans. "Unless we go for pizza or something casual."

"Pizza would be wonderful," said Kate. "Let me go in and take a look and I'll find some towels and you can wash up."

Regi retrieved her keys from her pocket. "I'll meet you guys at Big Tony's in about a half an hour. Will that work?"

"Perfect, we'll see you there," said Kate.

Regi hurried home, took Murphy out and fed her and tossed her dirty clothes in the laundry room. She put on fresh jeans and a turtleneck. She surveyed her face in the mirror and dabbed on a bit of mascara and lip gloss, fluffed her hair, and rushed out the door.

Regi scouted the tables and found them sitting in the back. Nate waved his hand and she slipped into the booth next to him. "I'm starving," said Regi.

"Good, we ordered a huge pizza and some wedges, plus salads." Nate poured her a glass of iced tea from the pitcher.

Kate glanced at Regi. "Leon's doing a great job for me. He's helped me get the entire sales floor organized and set up. He's a hard worker."

Regi nodded. "I'm glad it's working out for both of you. I hope he's serious about changing his life. Like I told Sam and Jeff, I've just heard it too many times and haven't seen him follow through, so I'm cautiously optimistic."

"I understand. Family can be difficult…and heartbreaking," said Kate, with a trace of sadness in her eyes.

"Add stressful, overwhelming, and disappointing and I'm with you."

Kate was engrossed in the flicker of the small candle in the red glass holder on their table. She stared at it, captivated by the dancing flame, and finally looked up. "I lost a daughter a long time ago. She was about Molly's age. It was the most devastating event of my life."

"Oh, I'm so sorry. I had no idea," said Regi, bringing her hand to her chest.

"Of course you didn't," smiled Kate. "It's been twenty years ago, but there are still days when I feel like it just happened." She paused when the waitress arrived with salads and wedges of warm dough smothered in garlic and parmesan. "My daughter, Karen, killed herself."

Nate and Regi gasped. "What a horrible tragedy," said Regi, tears shining in her eyes. "I'm not sure I could survive it."

Kate nodded. "I didn't think I would. My marriage didn't, but my son needed me, so I kept going for him. He's thirty-five now."

Nate dropped a wedge onto his plate, unable to eat it. "I'm sorry seems so inadequate, Kate, but it's all I can think to say."

She reached across the table and patted his hand. "Thank you. I'm okay now." She picked up her fork and speared a bite of salad. "I'm sorry I mentioned it. We need to eat."

Nate and Regi both looked at each other, stunned. Regi twirled salad around on her plate and took a small bite of the wedge. She looked at Kate and took a deep breath. "I lost my older brother, Ronnie, when I was young. He was trying to help Leon get away from drugs and the horrible people he insisted were his friends. The drug dealer ended up running him over and killing him."

Nate put his hand on top of hers and squeezed.

Kate looked into Regi's eyes, both of them staring into fresh tears glistening in the candlelight. "I'm so sorry for you and your poor parents."

Regi nodded. "What you said about your son needing you, I think that's why my parents have overlooked so much with Leon. I still blame him for Ronnie's death, but they didn't. They were too easy on Leon, especially after Ronnie died. I think they were just thankful he was alive."

"Parenting isn't for sissies," Kate said, trying to laugh despite her dry throat and heavy heart. "Part of my memory is a complete blank after Karen died. I'm sure Mitch, that's my son, didn't get the best of either of his parents for quite some time. Eventually, I pulled it together, but it wasn't easy. I had a wonderful friend who helped me through it. My husband left a couple of years after Karen's death."

"Looking at you, I wouldn't have guessed you had been through such a devastating time. You seem so totally together," said Regi, as their pizza arrived and was placed on a stand.

Nate began dishing up slices for the ladies. "I guess it's proof there's more to most people than meets the eye," he said.

Kate nodded. "Most everyone has gone through some kind of hardship or tragic event. I know I need to keep busy, so I don't dwell on things I've lost. I try to focus on what I have and the future, but some days are harder than others."

Nate steered the conversation to the house and what he planned to work on tomorrow. Kate talked about the upcoming wedding and how happy she was to be included among the guests. At Kate's insistence, Nate took the leftover pizza.

Kate checked her watch and yawned. "I'm tired. I bet you two are exhausted."

"I'm ready to call it a night," said Nate. "I'll be back in the morning."

"I've got the shop under control, so I'll meet you at the house tomorrow and see if we can get the rest of it organized."

"I've got a short day tomorrow. I get off at eleven, so I'll stop by and help when I'm done," offered Regi.

"Ah, sweetie, you don't need to spend your only time off working," said Kate.

"I don't mind. I don't have anything better to do," she smiled. She slid out of the booth and plucked her coat from the hook. Nate hurried out of his seat to hold it for her. She shrugged into it and he straightened her collar, his hand lingering at the back of her neck.

"Thanks for dinner, Kate. It was a perfect ending to the day," he said. He held her cape while she slipped into the red bundle.

"You're most welcome. I loved the company. When I get settled, you're both coming over for dinner," she laughed. "My tab should be settled with you after a few years of dinners."

Nate had parked next to Kate to the right of Big Tony's and Regi was further down to the left. She hugged Kate goodbye and squeezed her tight. "See you tomorrow."

Regi moved to Nate and said, "I'll see you in the morning."

He closed the space between them and engulfed her in his arms. After a long embrace he said, "I'll be by early for coffee," and kissed her on the cheek.

As Regi started the Jeep she watched Nate open Kate's door for her and wave as she motored away. "He's a good guy," she whispered as she engaged the transmission and steered for home.

* * *

Sunday Jeff surprised them all with an invitation to dinner and football, while the three of them were busy unpacking at Kate's house. On his way home, he stopped by to drop Murphy off, since he had kept her at the hardware store. He put her in the backyard and she ran around exploring the yard, while Jeff gave Nate a hand with some of the heavier items and transferred a few boxes to the shed.

"Are you sure you should be lifting things?" asked Regi.

He rolled his eyes. "You sound like Sam. I'm fine, honest. I'm feeling great and I won't overdo it. I'll just help Nate move some of this furniture around."

"What can we bring to dinner?" asked Kate.

"Absolutely nothing. It's casual tonight—chili, salad, cornbread, and of course Sam's making dessert."

"It sounds lovely," said Kate. "I'm glad I'll be moved in by the end of the week. I've been eating out way too much."

The men made quick work of the furniture while Regi and Kate worked in the kitchen. By the time they were ready to call it a day, the kitchen was totally organized and all the large pieces of furniture had been placed. The only boxes left consisted of decorative collectibles, according to Kate.

The evening ended with a fun time of visiting at Sam and Jeff's. Max and Linda were also included. While the men watched football, the four women gathered around the granite island and visited while they nibbled on dinner. Kate invited them all to attend the grand opening of Alexander's, planned for the weekend.

"You've got a lot going on with your new house and the opening," remarked Sam.

Kate nodded. "It keeps me out of mischief," she grinned, taking a bite of warm cornbread smothered in butter. "Luckily, I've had some great help." She glanced at Regi. "Nate and Regi have put my house together. Jeff even helped us yesterday. I'm going to work on the small items left this week, but I should be able to sleep there in a day or two."

"Leon's been helping her at the store," volunteered Regi.

"Are things going okay with him?" asked Sam.

Regi nodded. "I think so. Kate said he's done a great job. I got into it with him at lunch last week and we haven't talked since." She glanced at Linda. "I'm not sure you know the whole story."

Linda nodded. "We do, Sam and Jeff told us." She placed her hand on Regi's arm. "We were saddened to hear about the loss of your older brother. And you don't need to worry about losing us as friends. We know you're not responsible for Leon, plus it sounds like he's making progress."

"Yeah," she said softly.

"Everyone makes mistakes and some people take longer to figure things out," Kate said, smiling at Regi from across the island. "From what I've seen, Leon is focused on staying on the right path."

"And if he makes another mistake, you don't need to feel responsible," said Sam. "He's going to make his own choices and all you can do is be supportive."

Regi nodded her head. "I know you guys are right. It's just hard to be positive when it comes to Leon. I'm going to do my best to move forward and keep the past in the past."

"You'll never forget, but perhaps you can find a new beginning with Leon and focus your efforts on your future. It's hard, I know," said Kate, tears brimming in her eyes.

Sam and Linda glanced at each other and shrugged as they looked back at Kate. She caught the movement. "I shared a bit of my past with Nate and Regi last night." She commenced telling them the story of her life two decades ago and the loss of her cherished daughter and ultimately her marriage. "I had a wonderful friend, Spence, and he helped me overcome all of it. Sadly, my husband withdrew from me and everything else and saw Spence as a threat. We just couldn't put the pieces back together. Spence and I have been friends since high school and I think my husband saw him as more than a friend for years before Karen's death. After, Spence was the one who was there for me and for my son."

Linda and Sam were both speechless, stunned into silence. Sam finally found her voice, "I'm so sorry. I'm just in shock to hear you had to go through such heartbreak and loss."

Kate's gaze was fixated on a bowl of glass globes and as she flicked her eyes away, the misery of the past drifted across them. She sniffed and blotted her eyes with a tissue. "I'm sorry to darken the mood. I haven't talked about this with anyone in a long time."

"What happened to Spence?" asked Linda.

Kate smiled. "I miss him. He lives in Seattle. He divorced a couple of years ago. He was in a horrible marriage and waiting for his kids to get old enough so he could leave. I'm hoping he'll come for a visit. I'm used to getting together with him each week for dinner or him stopping by for lunch. That was the hardest part about moving, but I was ready for a change."

"And where is your son?"

"Mitch lives in Olympia. He's single and works horrendous hours, but he's planning a visit to see my new house and the shop."

Max came around the corner, "Hey, what's for dessert?" Then he stopped when he noticed the rumpled tissues and tear streaked faces of all four of the women. "Are you guys okay?"

Linda nodded to him. "Everything's fine."

Sam added, "I'll bring dessert out in a few minutes."

Max nodded, but not before giving Linda a hug and a kiss on the forehead. He turned to leave and added, "No rush on dessert, take your time."

The four laughed. "You've got a good man, Linda," said Kate.

"Spence sounds like a good one, too," said Linda, with a smile.

"He's one of the best," said Kate, as she got up and offered to help Sam serve the lemon meringue and chocolate cream pies.

Eleven

Kate was busy putting the final touches on her grand opening early Saturday morning. Ellie delivered beautiful trays of cookies and pastries Kate had ordered and Sam sent Regi to handle the hot beverage bar she was supplying. Kate was stirring the foamy sherbet punch she had made and making sure everything was in order.

Kate hurried over to the mirrored walnut bonnetiere and checked her reflection. She wore slim grey tweed trousers, with a tailored white shirt, topped with a soft oversized cardigan in bright fuchsia. Her stylish gray streaked hair, chunky black boots, and silver jewelry topped it off. Regi saw her adjusting her necklace. "You look terrific, Kate."

Kate smiled back at herself. "Thank you. Just a last minute tweak." She turned from the mirror and popped a wedge of almond croissant in her mouth on her way to open the door. The deep green she had chosen to paint the front, along with the crisp black awning looked perfect. *Alexander's* was written in gold script across the awning and the front door.

The day was a bit dreary and overcast, but inside the store was bright and inviting. Soft music welcomed browsing customers and Kate stood near the door greeting guests. "Welcome to Alexander's," she said, offering treats and pointing out the beverage station on the other side of the display floor.

Regi recognized lots of her regular customers from Harbor Coffee and several people from school. She looked up after making a hot tea and found Leon at the bar. "Hey, Regi. How's it going?"

"Great, how about you?"

"I told Kate I'd stop in on my way to Lou's."

"You did a great job helping her with the store. It looks terrific."

Leon smiled. "Thanks. She's a nice lady." He glanced over at Kate, smiling as she showed off some paintings. "Very particular, but nice."

Regi chuckled and fixed Leon a coffee to go with his handful of cookies. "I wouldn't argue with her style. She has a knack for arranging things and displaying items. Most antique stores look like overpriced rummage sales to me, but not this one. She's got a calling for this."

"About our lunch. I'm sorry I stormed out," said Leon.

"I shouldn't have been so bossy and negative. I'm sorry. I'm going to do my best to let the past stay behind and concentrate on the future and the positive steps you're making."

He smiled, shoving a cookie in his mouth. "So, lunch on Tuesday?"

She nodded. "Yeah, see you then."

"I'm going to say goodbye and head over to work. Have a fun day."

She waved as he left and went to work ladling punch for two young girls who were waiting behind him. She had a steady stream of customers for a couple of hours and the shop was brimming with activity. Kate rang up a few sales, but mostly visited and answered questions.

Shortly after noon Nate arrived with bags of take out from Dottie's Deli. He winked at Regi when he walked by and said he'd put lunch in the back room. Soon, there were only a couple of browsers left in the store and Kate perched on a stool by the bar. "Nate brought us some lunch. He put it in the back room," said Regi, handing Kate a glass of punch.

"You go ahead. I'll watch the front and you eat and then I'll sneak back when you're done."

Regi frowned. "I don't mind waiting, are you sure?"

Kate waved her away while she took a gulp of the refreshing drink. Regi smiled and dashed across the floor to the back. She found Nate arranging the sandwiches and salads on a table.

"Thanks for dropping by with lunch," she said, pulling out a chair. "Kate said she'll come back when I'm done."

"Have you guys been busy?"

She took a half a sandwich and a spoonful of potato salad. "A steady flow. I don't think she's sold much, but lots of people in and out."

"I saw her yesterday and she was so excited to be in her house and sleeping in her own bed. She was a bit nervous about today."

"Yeah, it's a big venture and she's on her own."

Nate nodded as he finished the last bite of his sandwich. The front door chimed and they heard Kate let out a squeal. He jumped from his chair and ran to the front of the store. He found Kate in the arms of a handsome older man, with short gray hair, who at first glance reminded him of Mark Harmon, especially with those intelligent blue eyes.

Kate saw Nate and pulled away, holding the man's hand. "Oh, Nate, I'd like you to meet my friend, Spence."

Nate extended his hand, "Hi, I'm Nate Martin. Pleased to meet you."

Spence gripped his hand. "I'm Spence Chandler."

Kate's face glowed with happiness. "He surprised me and didn't tell me he was coming for the opening."

He put his arm around her. "I thought you could use an old friend to help celebrate your new adventure."

Regi had been standing behind them and came forward. "Hi, Spence. I'm Regi."

He shook her hand. "I feel like I know you two already. Kate emails to tell me about all the fantastic people she's met."

"We were just finishing up lunch. There's plenty left. You two go on back and eat and we'll watch the front for you," offered Nate.

"Sounds good to me," said Spence.

Kate kept her arm linked in his and called over her shoulder, "Come get me if you need help."

"Wow," Nate whispered. "Kate looks so happy. He must be a special guy in her life, maybe a boyfriend?"

Regi shook her head and led him over to the bar. "He's *the* old friend. She told us about him the night we had chili at Sam's. He's been her friend since they were kids and helped her get through the death of her daughter. Sounds like Kate's husband wasn't there for her and Spence was, and ultimately Kate's marriage collapsed." She glanced at the doorway to the back. "They do seem like they're made for each other."

The bells on the door sounded again and a few more shoppers trickled through the store. Nate played host and offered edibles to the newcomers and invited them to browse. By the time Kate and Spence emerged, the store had filled up and Nate was at the register attempting to ring up a sale. Kate stepped in and expertly rang up a lamp, wrapped it in tissue and placed it in a black bag, with the shop's signature in gold, and tied it with a green ribbon. "Thank you for coming in today," she said, as she handed the bag to the woman.

Spence wandered the store and made conversation with the patrons, nibbling on a few cookies while he checked out the merchandise. The afternoon kept all four of them occupied until closing time. She flipped the closed sign over and let out a sigh. "Whew, that was a busy afternoon. I didn't expect to make many sales, but I wasn't able to leave the register."

"That's a great start," said Spence. "How about we clean up and I'll treat all of us to dinner."

"Dinner sounds wonderful, but I insist on picking up the tab. You all helped me out today."

Nate looked at Regi. "All I heard is we're going to dinner and neither of us has to buy," he laughed. He picked up the pots from behind Regi and offered to transport them back to the coffee shop.

Kate supplied Spence with some bags and he stashed the leftover cookies and pastries in the back room, while she rang out the register and got her deposit ready. Regi cleaned up the bar area and scanned the shop for stray napkins and cups.

Kate hollered from her office and told them she made reservations at the Beach Club for seven-thirty. "Spence and I can finish up here. We'll meet you two at the restaurant."

Regi rode with Nate to return Sam's pots and once they had cleaned them and made sure the shop was locked, he dropped her back at her Jeep. "I'll swing by and pick you up on my way to the Beach Club," he said, as she hopped out of his pickup.

Jeff had dropped Murphy back at Regi's condo at five, so she didn't have to worry about her all day. She let her out of her crate so she could run around while Regi changed clothes. She vacillated between jeans and something a bit dressier. She thought about Kate's outfit, and decided to wear black pants, topped with a black shirt and a suede jacket in a cheery peacock color. She slipped into her black boots, took Murphy outside for a quick bathroom break and then gave her a through belly rub before putting her back in the crate.

She reached for her jacket when she heard the doorbell and met Nate at the front door. She was glad she'd made an effort with her clothes. Nate was wearing a button down shirt and jacket with khakis.

"So, about Kate and Spence," he said, pulling away from the curb. "Is he unattached?"

"I think so. She said he divorced a couple of years ago. It would be neat if they got together."

"Yeah, she lights up like a Christmas tree around him. She's had a tough go." He pulled into the parking lot and rushed around to open Regi's door before she could.

They walked in and were taken to one of the prime tables overlooking the harbor. Kate and Spence were already seated, enjoying a glass of wine. Spence saw them approach and got up as Regi slid in beside Kate.

After ordering, the conversation focused on Kate's new house and her new undertaking at Alexander's. "Katie's outdone herself," said Spence. "I told her she needed to slow down and take some time for herself and the next thing I know she's decided to move to the island and downsize with a small shop for herself."

"Spence is retired, but I'm not ready to stop working yet," said Kate.

"What did you do?" asked Nate.

"I was a detective in the city. I retired last year and have been doing some consulting work."

"That would be an exciting career. I bet it's hard to fill your time with something equally stimulating," said Regi.

Spence grinned. "I'm ready to be less stimulated. It was hard for the first few months, but I'm enjoying myself. I divorced a couple of years ago and moved to a small place I'm renting, so I've got a lot less responsibilities now. Plus the freedom to travel and visit friends is wonderful," he said, gripping Kate's hand and meeting her eyes.

"Yes, it is," she said.

As dinner progressed, they discussed hobbies and Nate found out Spence was an avid fisherman. They entertained each other with fishing stories and secret spots for angling. Nate extended an open invitation to Spence to join him on his boat whenever he was visiting.

"The other hobby I've always enjoyed is woodworking. I've tinkered a bit and when I divorced I had to give up my shop and now I've crammed all my tools into my garage and don't really have room to work. Plus my car has to live outside," said Spence.

Nate smiled. "I told Regi the whole reason I bought my house was based on the shop space. I've got lots of space for everything I enjoy."

"I need to work on a long term plan so I can get back to woodworking. My kids can't really come and stay with me now, because it's only a one bedroom."

"How many kids do you have?" asked Regi.

"I've got three. My youngest is twenty-two and still in college. She may be a professional student," he grinned. "The other two are boys, twenty-seven and thirty-one."

"No grandchildren yet?" asked Regi.

"Not yet. My oldest is serious about his girlfriend, so I suspect they'll be getting married soon and the middle one doesn't have anyone he's attached to yet. My two boys are close to me, but my daughter is much closer to her mom. Seems like I'm there to provide financial support, but we don't have much of a relationship anymore."

Kate inched closer to Spence. "She'll come around eventually."

"So, how long are you planning to visit?" asked Nate. "Maybe we can squeeze in some fishing."

Spence glanced at Kate. "I'm here as long as she'll put up with me. I don't have any set schedule."

Kate laughed. "Ah, the words of a retiree. I'll put up with you as long as you want to stay."

"That settles it. Let's plan a fishing trip," said Nate.

After finishing their meal, the foursome shared a dessert sampler and coffee. "Are you off tomorrow, Regi?" asked Nate.

"Thankfully, yes. The girls are covering tomorrow."

"This is one hard working gal, Spence. She works all week at the high school and usually every weekend at the coffee shop. Even with all that, she and Nate volunteered to help me move in. She's a gem," said Kate.

"I like being busy," said Regi. "I have to admit, I'm looking forward to sleeping in tomorrow and lounging around."

Nate noticed the restaurant was closing and was surprised to see it was almost eleven o'clock. "Wow, it's later than I thought. We better get a move on."

They said their goodbyes with Nate giving Spence his business card. "Maybe we could plan an outing next weekend. The weekend after that we have a wedding to attend. Give me a ring and you can stop by after work one night or sometime tomorrow."

Spence took the card. "Sounds like a plan. Great to visit with both of you tonight."

Regi hugged Kate and Spence and wished them a good night as they walked to Spence's SUV. They waved as they backed out and Nate settled Regi in his pickup.

"He's a great guy. I'm glad he likes to fish," said Nate.

"I hope he sticks around for Kate's sake," said Regi.

Twelve

Linda awoke disoriented on the morning of her wedding, until she remembered she was in the honeymoon suite at the Lakeside Resort. She slipped on her robe, padded over to the sliding glass doors, and pulled open the heavy blackout drapes to gain access to the deck overlooking the lake. Cheerful sunshine from a clear blue sky reflected off the smooth surface of the water. Linda's smile grew wider as she scanned the area across the lake, where the lodge stood.

Last night had been a wonderful evening gathered with friends and family. Max's parents had arrived earlier in the week and she and Max spent the days driving them around the island to show them the sights. They had spent each evening huddled around the fire pit on the patio, enjoying the stories told by Maggie and Sully. Max's children and his brother Frank had arrived yesterday and added to the fun and entertainment.

Linda's mom was doing well after her cardiac scare and since she was staying at Max's, spent time getting to know Max's parents. Uncle Mike and Aunt Diane had arrived earlier in the week and melded with Max's family as if they'd known them forever. David and his family got to spend some time with their aunt and uncle, since they were all staying at the resort.

As Linda reflected on last night's dinner, happy tears moistened her eyes. Uncle Mike had toasted them with a moving tribute about how inadequate he felt to stand in for his brother, but how very honored he was to reconnect with his family and walk Linda down the aisle. There wasn't a dry eye around the table when he finished.

The soft ringtone of wind chimes from her cellphone interrupted her memories of the week. She hurried from the railing and reached for her phone on the night table. She saw Max's picture on the screen. "Good morning," she answered.

"Are you awake?" he asked.

"I was out on the deck enjoying the morning. It's going to be a gorgeous day."

"I know. I was so glad to see the sunshine when I woke up. Your aunt and my mom are making breakfast for everyone. I just called to say I can't wait to see you."

"You're a sweetie. I can't believe it's our wedding day. All the planning and work and now it's here."

"It's going to be perfect. I just missed you and wanted to say hi and I love you."

"I love you, Max. I'll see you this afternoon. I'll be the one in the white dress," she laughed.

There was a knock on her door as she disconnected from Max. She was surprised to find a waiter with a room service cart. "Good morning, Ms. Graham. I have your breakfast and a delivery from Mr. Sullivan."

She opened the door and he wheeled in a tray and presented her with a small purple box, adorned with black ribbon. "Enjoy," he said, before disappearing through the door.

She lifted the lid off the platter and found heart-shaped waffles and fresh berries with whipped cream. She held the steaming chai latte and picked up an envelope with her name on it, resting on a vase of roses. She opened it and read the note from Max. *My dearest Linda-I never thought I'd love again, until I met you. You've given me such a gift. I'll love you forever, Max.*

Fresh tears blurred her vision as she set the card aside and opened the purple package. Inside she found a pair of sparkling diamond earrings, almost a perfect match for her ring. "Oh, oh, oh," she squealed as she undid the backs and rushed to the mirror to put them on. The dangly earrings peaked out from the dark strands around her face. She piled her hair in a messy blob on top of her head and smiled as she took in the full effect of the glittering stones. She admired them for several minutes before remembering her breakfast.

She took off the earrings and tucked them away in their velvet box and took her breakfast tray out on the deck. It was chilly, but wrapped in her robe, she didn't notice. Her phone chirped as she stuffed the last bite of crisp waffle in her mouth. Aubrey had texted letting her know they would set up on the deck at the lodge, since the forecast was clear. Linda texted back her thanks and a smiley face. She had opted for an early afternoon ceremony, hoping the weather would cooperate and allow them to complete the ceremony outdoors. The contingency plan had been inside the lodge, but her desire had been for a lakeside wedding.

She sent Max a text to thank him for the gorgeous earrings and tell him the good news about the ceremony. She hurried to shower, skipping fixing her hair and face, since she'd soon be on her way to Jen's salon for her wedding day treatment.

* * *

Regi had to open the coffee shop early, but Rachel was coming in at nine o'clock to relieve her and finish out the day. Jeff had offered to let Murphy stay with all the other dogs at their house during the ceremony, and had picked her up from Regi early in the morning. She needed to be ready by noon when Nate would arrive to drive them to the Lakeside Resort. As soon as Rachel came through the door, Regi hurried down the street to get her hair done at Jen's.

Jen had already worked on Becky, Sam, Linda's mom, and her aunt. She still had to do Max's daughter and daughter-in-law and her own hair, not to mention the bride's. She chatted while she worked and asked Regi, "Did you find a dress you like?"

Regi eyes widened and she smiled. "I mentioned I didn't have anything fancy to wear and Kate insisted I come over and raid her closet. Let me say the woman doesn't just collect antiques. She has marvelous clothes. She spent hours helping me try on and weed out different outfits. I finally found a perfect dress. It's floor length, black, on the plain side, but totally elegant."

"Oh, I can't wait to see it," said Jen, as she used her wand to make large loose curls. "I'm going to give you a messy twist."

"I can relate to messy," laughed Regi.

"Kate even let me borrow some jewelry she says is perfect. The dress is a fluid crepe silk and has a V-neck, but it's softened by a draping cowl and Kate pointed out it made the perfect frame for a necklace. She sent me home with matching earrings and several bracelets, plus a gorgeous sheer silk scarf in deep amethyst. I'll probably need her help to tie it. She's quite the fashionista."

"She always looks like a million bucks, so I'd take her advice."

"I'll never be that sophisticated or classy. I tend to find what I like and buy one in every color. It makes it easier to get dressed in the morning."

Jen laughed as she twisted and pinned Regi's hair. She twirled her around and pronounced her done. "What do you think?"

Regi checked it out from every angle and smiled. "I love it. How'd you do that so fast?"

"Professional secret," said Jen, putting her fingers to her lips.

As Regi left the salon, Linda was coming through the door. "Oh, Regi, your hair looks fabulous."

"All the praise goes to Jen. She's a magician."

Linda tugged at her still wet hair. "I hope so."

"You'll be gorgeous. We'll see you in a few hours," Regi said, hugging her.

Regi hopped in her Jeep and texted Kate to see if she would mind if she stopped by for help with the shawl. She received a reply by the time she had pulled in front of the condo and smiled as she read it. *We're not leaving until noon, so stop by anytime, K.* Regi texted Nate as she hurried to her room, asking him to pick her up from Kate's.

She opened a new package of nylons and pulled them on, instantly remembering why she loathed pantyhose. She pulled on her slip and plodded to the bathroom to do her makeup. She added a swipe of eye shadow she didn't normally wear and put on two coats of mascara. After applying a berry lipstick, she topped it with her usual minty gloss and popped in the earrings and fastened the necklace. She went back in her room and unzipped the plastic covering on Kate's dress. She slipped it on over her head and felt the soft silk flow over her skin. She adjusted her strappy black sandals and glided the stack of bangle bracelets over her wrist.

She looked in the mirror, surprised to see the transformation. She rarely wore anything but jeans and her attractive figure was usually hidden under turtlenecks or loose shirts. The designer dress hugged her curves in all the right places. She started to fumble with the purple scarf and decided to head to Kate's and let the expert finish dressing her.

She spritzed on some perfume before pulling an old evening bag from the top of her closet and transferred a few essentials into the small space. She dug her dressy coat from the back of the closet and flung it over her arm, balancing the wrapped gift, and locked the door.

When she arrived at Kate's, Spence answered the door, decked out in a beautiful charcoal suit with a lavender shirt and tie. "Regi, you look magnificent."

"Right back at ya, Spence." She stepped into the entry. "I need Kate's help with my outfit." She placed the gift on the floor by the door and he took her coat.

"She's back in her room getting ready. Go on back, she's expecting you."

Regi peeked around the open door and saw Kate sitting on a velvet stool in front of her vintage dressing table, putting on her jewelry. "Hey, Kate. Spence told me to come on back."

Kate smiled in the mirror. "You look lovely, Regi. That dress becomes you."

Regi's eyes glinted with delight. "Thank you for letting me borrow it. I do love it."

Kate stood, wearing a layered lavender chiffon dress with a sheer jacket floating over it. The necklace she had just fastened was an array of freshwater pearls, seed pearls, beads, and crystals forming a subtle V-shape. Dangling pearl and crystal earrings and pearl sandals completed the look.

Kate took the scarf and with practiced expertise tossed it across Regi's shoulders and arranged it in a soft cascade. "There, you're beautiful."

"The color of your dress is perfect and that necklace is stunning."

"It's fun to dress up. I haven't worn the necklace in years and worried the dress might look a tad too much like an Easter egg, but since we're all trying to wear a bit of purple in honor of Linda, I thought what the heck."

"It's gorgeous." Regi saw the clock on the nightstand. "I asked Nate to pick me up here, so I'll leave my Jeep, if you don't mind."

"Not at all. Let me just find a handbag and we'll be ready. I'm sure Spence is dressed and waiting."

Regi nodded. "I'll go visit with him while we wait for Nate." She wandered down the hall and found Spence at the island, reading the newspaper.

"She's almost ready and Nate's picking me up here. He should be here in a few minutes."

He folded the paper closed. "We had so much fun fishing last weekend. Nate has a great boat."

"He told me it was a terrific trip."

"I see why Katie likes it here. It's relaxing and unhurried; a welcome change of pace."

"You could always move here," winked Regi.

"Don't think I'm not considering it," he whispered. "I could use a change myself." The doorbell sounded and he moved to the entryway.

"Hello, Spence. You're looking dapper this afternoon," said Nate, trying to emulate a British accent.

He grasped Nate in a hug. "There you go you cheeky boy. See what I get for telling you I spent most of my youth in England."

Nate closed the door and his eyes locked on Regi. "Holy...wow, you're stunning, Regi." He moved to her side and took her hand, twirling her around. "Where have you been hiding all of this?" He waved his hand through the air outlining an hourglass shape.

"It's the dress," she said, her cheeks reddened.

He smiled and shook his head. "No, I'm pretty sure it's what's under the dress."

She looked down and felt the heat rise up her neck to her forehead. He moved closer and she felt his lips on the side of her cheek and then he whispered, "I can't wait to dance with you all night." He rubbed a gentle kiss over her cheek and stood back.

Nate wore a black suit with a purple tie and handkerchief square that matched Regi's scarf. She tugged his tie and said, "We're a perfect match tonight."

His eyes met hers. "That we are." He touched her hair. "I confess I had some guidance from Kate. She helped me with a tie and suggested this color."

"You look very handsome." With her heels, they stood eye to eye and she saw the flicker of desire. "Shall we get going?" she asked. Looking around, she noticed Spence had disappeared.

"Sure, I borrowed my mom's fancy car, so you don't have to ride in my pickup."

Kate came down the hall and Spence appeared from the other direction. "Are we ready?" she asked.

Spence asked, "Do you need a coat, Katie?"

"I don't think so. I'd rather not lug it around."

"I'll stash one in the car, just in case."

"Oh, but we need the gift," she called out as he was opening the closet. "I bought them a hot air balloon ride in Ireland. I just need to take the box I wrapped with the voucher."

She flicked on the outside lights as she locked the door and gave a whistle when she spotted the car to which Nate was guiding Regi. "Classy ride, Nate," she yelled, admiring the shiny charcoal Mercedes sedan.

"I borrowed my mom's car. I feel like I'm going to the prom." He chuckled as he made sure Regi's dress was inside the car before he shut her door.

Kate waved as Spence held the door for her on his SUV. Nate led the way to the Lakeside Resort and they entered the lodge and found the ceremony set up on the wooden deck area outside the huge glass doors. Jeff and Max's doctor friend, Sean, were serving as ushers and led them to their seats.

While they were waiting, Kate suggested they take some pictures overlooking the lake. She made Nate and Regi stand together and aimed her phone and took several shots. Nate handed her his phone and she took a few for him. Then they traded spots and Nate took some photos of Spence and Kate with the lake and trees for a backdrop.

More people were filling up the chairs, so they meandered back to their seats. Soon Jeff escorted Max's mother and father to their seats and Sean held Linda's mom on one arm and her aunt on the other. Jeff slipped into his seat next to Sam and Max's family.

Max stood smiling, between the judge and his son, Peter. He wore a black tuxedo with a white tie and vest and a lavender boutonniere. Peter matched his father, but for a lavender vest and tie.

The band began playing the song Linda and Max had chosen, an instrumental piano and cello rendition of "A Thousand Years." White satin covered in lavender petals lined the aisle Jen walked down in her flirty black chiffon dress, carrying a beautiful spray of white tulips, accented with purple and lavender lisianthus and stock. Her hair was restored back to its natural deep auburn luster and she had it secured in a tasteful chignon at the base of her neck. She smiled and winked as she passed Jeff and Sam and made her way to the front.

Linda got a squeeze from Uncle Mike as they set off down the aisle, with friends and family standing to gaze upon her. The sweetheart style dress was covered by a sheer fabric of a bateau illusion neckline and the bodice was covered with shimmering pearl and crystal beads. Linda's slim back was showcased in a dramatic keyhole design, formed by the sheer fabric adorned with beads. Jen had worked her magic with Linda's dark hair, resulting in a beautiful twisted updo accented with the gorgeous crystal hairpin Kate had given her. Sara had outdone herself on Linda's bouquet. Lavish full white peonies were paired with lavender hydrangeas, shiny greens, and purple lisianthus. It was the center of attention against the simple lines of her white satin trumpet skirt.

Max regarded Linda as a smile rivaling the sunny day shone upon his face. She met his eyes and her grin widened. As she approached, the reflection from the sun and water danced off the diamonds hanging from her ears. When the judge asked who was giving Linda away, Uncle Mike proudly declared, "In honor of her father and my brother, Ed, and her mother, Peggy, I do." He hugged Linda and placed her hand in Max's, embracing him.

The ceremony didn't last long and soon Linda and Max strolled arm in arm down the aisle to meet Ryan for pictures. No setting could compete with Linda's nursery for a wedding, but Lakeside was a close second. Ryan took pictures on a grassy point with the lake in the background and Lucas and Sara had worked to bring in pots of flowers to add color to the setting. Photos were captured along the water, in the trees, on the dock, and even in a rowboat.

When they finished, lunch was waiting in the lodge and Linda gasped when saw the white tablecloths sparkling with glassware, candles, and beautiful centerpieces made from elements of her bouquet. Ellie's cake dominated center stage, perched on a table for all to admire. The table was lit underneath with twinkle lights and sheer purple fabric draped over the snowy cloth. The four square tiers were decorated with pearls and icing resembling ruffled bands of ribbon. Ellie incorporated a lavender hydrangea on the side of one layer to give it a soft pop of color. She dusted it with glittery sugar and provided trays of cupcakes, frosted with lilac and soft blue petals making them look like hydrangea blossoms.

Linda and Max took their seats at the head table, surrounded by family. The buffet consisted of a variety of finger food and appetizers, including chicken skewers, crab cakes courtesy of Lou, small sandwiches, and sliders. Fruit and cheese platters, veggies and dip, and mini quiches rounded out the selection.

Regi and Nate followed Kate and Spence through the buffet line and visited as they nibbled on the delicious array of food. Soon it was time to cut the cake and Max and Linda posed for more photos with the elegant cake. Nate and Spence volunteered to wade through the guests and secure dessert. "Such a romantic day and on Valentine's Day," commented Kate.

"With all the festivities, I'd forgotten it was Valentine's Day. It's not a day of celebration in my life," said Regi.

"Years ago it used to be for me, but things change." Kate glanced at the front of the room and saw Nate and Spence still in line. "Were you ever married?"

Regi shook her head. "No." She paused. "It's a long story."

"Tell me, the guys are tied up for a bit."

"It all began in high school, after Ronnie died. I had a boyfriend, Cam, and things got serious. I spent less and less time at home and more time with him. We actually came here to celebrate graduating from high school. Looking back, I can't believe my parents didn't have a fit, but with all the drama with Leon and Ronnie, they didn't notice much of what I did. Anyway, we spent a romantic week here on the island. Cam's family was wealthy and had big plans for him to go to college and marry the right girl. I wasn't even a consideration in their eyes. Cam and I knew we would be apart as soon as the summer was over and vowed to meet back here on our fortieth birthdays, provided we were still available. I got pregnant with Molly on that trip. I never told him and she doesn't know about him either."

Kate's eyes widened. "That's a very significant and romantic gesture at eighteen and so much for you to deal with in your life."

Regi nodded. "Our birthdays are right around Christmas. So, the long and short of it is I moved back here this past summer and waited for Cam. He didn't come, so now I'm trying to move on."

"Well, a lot can change in twenty years. Does Nate know all this?"

Regi nodded. "Yeah, I told him the story. Plus Sam and Jeff and Linda and Max know everything."

"Perhaps Cam is married or something changed in his life that wouldn't allow him to be here." She patted her hand. "You're doing the right thing to move on with your life. From what I can see you've made a great life for yourself. Plus Nate's a wonderful man. I think you're good for each other."

Regi glanced behind her and saw him meandering around the tables. "Yeah, he's a terrific guy and the more time I spend with him, the less I think about Cam. It's hard to break the habit. I've been counting on reuniting with him for years."

Nate slid a plate of cake and a cupcake in front of Regi and Spence did the same for Kate. "This looks yummy," he said, sitting down to his own plate.

Max signaled the band and took Linda's hand to lead her in their first dance to "Me and You." Regi watched as the two glided across the floor, smiling and laughing, absorbed in each other. When the song ended, Regi swiped a tear from her eye, caught up in the magic of the lyrics.

Max and Linda waved everyone to join them and Nate tapped her shoulder and led Regi to the dance floor. The band played "The Way You Look Tonight," and Nate held her close, as they joined the other couples. They danced to a set of classic tunes and noticed Spence drag Kate to the floor. When the set ended, the band leader asked Max's mom, Maggie, and Uncle Mike to join Max and Linda. They danced to "Unforgettable" as the guests all stood to capture the moment on their phones.

Regi and Nate stayed until the last song played, "Never Alone," and when it ended he didn't release her. He finally moved his hands to the side of her face and held it while he kissed her. It was a kiss that reached all the way to Regi's toes. She felt the electricity and thrill of desire. "I think I'm falling for you, Regi," he whispered.

Thirteen

Sunday morning Regi was up early to open the coffee shop. Murphy had slept at Sam's house, so she wouldn't need to pick her up until she got off work. Last night after the dancing ended, she and Nate had stopped by the Jade Garden before returning to Kate's house. The foursome enjoyed Chinese while Spence regaled them with stories from his decades as a detective. She was sad to learn that he would be heading back to Seattle later in the week.

Trying to stifle a yawn while she steamed milk for a latte, she knew she was paying the price for staying out so late. As she worked the wand, her mind drifted to the Valentine's card she had found stuck on her dash when she got in the Jeep last night. Nate had walked her out and given her another sizzling kiss before she left and found his surprise. The sweet card contained tickets to another event at the community theatre next month.

She finished the latte and rang up the sale. The morning crowd was steady and in the midst of a continual stream of customers, Max and Linda arrived with Max's children. They were boarding the ferry and stopped in for a drink on their way.

"I had a wonderful time at the wedding yesterday. It was a magnificent setting and so much fun," said Regi, as she began preparing their order.

"We had the best day," said Linda. "We stayed up too late visiting and dancing, but outside of that, it was perfect."

"I only wish my kids weren't leaving so soon, but they all have to get back to work," said Max. "Tomorrow morning my parents and brother are leaving."

"Oh, too bad they can't stay the week," said Regi, placing two cups on the counter.

"And my family leaves with them," said Linda, gripping Max's hand in hers.

"Then we'll be all alone. What will we do?" he wiggled his eyebrows and kissed her square on the mouth.

Linda laughed. "You'd think we were twenty-something."

He wrapped his arms around her from behind and kissed her cheek. "We're even better now."

Regi gathered the other drinks and rang them up. "I'm looking forward to your honeymoon trip, so I can camp out at your place."

"We can't wait. It should be fabulous," said Max, peeling off some bills to pay for the drinks. Regi waved goodbye as the group left and were replaced by a foursome waiting for the ferry.

The thirsty people of Friday Harbor ambled through the door at a relentless pace until Regi's shift ended at noon. She pocketed her tips, took off her apron, and wished Rachel a good week, as she flew out the door. She hadn't checked her phone all day and noticed she had missed a text from Nate. *Cooking dinner tonight, please join me. My house at six and bring Murphy.*

She grinned as she put the Jeep in gear and steered it to Sam's house. She found Sam and Jeff relaxing in front of the television with the dogs sprawled around the floor, including Murphy, who was resting on top of Zoe.

"They've been playing nonstop and now they're all tuckered out," said Jeff, petting Bailey's ears with his foot.

She visited for a few minutes and then Sam twisted her arm into sharing their lunch of homemade soup and bread. "You and Nate looked like you were having a great time dancing last night," said Sam, clearing the island of dishes.

"We did have fun. Then we took Chinese over to Kate's and visited with her and Spence." She caught herself yawning again. "I stayed out too late."

"I'm glad you're hitting it off with Nate. He's a great guy and always so friendly and kind." She turned from the sink to look at Regi. "You sure look a lot happier than you did a couple of months ago."

Regi nodded. "I've been coming to terms with my feelings for Leon. Kate gave me some sound advice about focusing on what I have and the future instead of what I've lost in the past."

"Amen," said Sam. "She's a smart woman."

Regi stood up. "Thanks for taking care of the Murphster. I'm going to get home and take a nap before we head over to Nate's for dinner."

"Sounds like the perfect way to end the weekend.

* * *

Molly was getting more independent and her calls and texts to Regi were becoming less frequent. Regi found herself worrying when she didn't hear from her and as hard as she tried, she couldn't keep from texting her each night. It was easy to hear the distraction in Molly's voice when they chatted on the phone. Regi knew she was being selfish and that Molly was busy with work and school, but she sometimes didn't feel secure until she heard her voice.

When she pulled up to Nate's, she was surprised to hear Molly's ringtone on her phone. She fished the phone out of her purse, almost dropping it, and punched the green button. "Hi, Mol."

"I just wanted to check in with you and find out about the wedding."

"Oh, it was beautiful. Linda was gorgeous and the day was fun."

"You'll have to send me some pictures. I'd love to see you in Kate's dress you described."

"I'll do that. I have some pictures on my phone."

"What are you up to tonight?"

"Just pulled into Nate's. He invited us for dinner."

"Nice, I assume you mean you and Murphy."

Regi laughed. "Yeah. She spent the night at Sam and Jeff's last night and is tired. So, I think it will be a short night for her."

"You sound happy, Mom. I'm glad you're doing stuff. Tell Nate hi from me and I'll talk to you next week."

"Okay, sweetie. Have a good night and be careful."

"Always, Mom. Love you."

Regi stowed her phone in her purse and lugged it and Murphy out of the Jeep. Nate met her on the porch, greeting her with a kiss and taking Murphy's crate. "Dinner's almost ready."

He opened the door for her and when she stepped in she saw flames dancing in the fireplace and an appetizing scent wafted through the air. "Smells delicious," she said, hanging her coat and purse on a hook by the door.

"It's glazed salmon." He set Murphy's crate down next to a new dog bed and chew toy.

"Did you buy those for her?"

He smiled as he opened the crate. "Yeah, I thought she'd like having her own spot."

Regi bent down and ruffled the puppy's ears. "Did you see what Nate got you?" She picked up the chew toy and Murphy pounced on it, snuggling into the soft bed. "That was kind of you, but you didn't have to buy her anything."

He was taking a dish out of the oven. "It's not a big deal." He poured a pan of rice into a serving bowl and carried it and the salmon to the table. "Come and get it," he said, going back for sautéed veggies. "What would you like to drink? I've got wine, beer, water, and tea."

"I'll take water and a glass of wine." She settled into a chair at the table, noticing the vase of fresh flowers.

He returned with two glasses of water followed by a glass of wine and a beer he placed at his plate. He sat down and raised his bottle, "Here's to a great weekend," he said, tapping his beer against her wine glass.

She took a sip of the cold white wine and then took a bite of the salmon, tasting the soy sauce and sweet brown sugar glaze. "Yum," she said.

He grinned. "Glad you like it." He took a few bites of his dinner and then said, "I had a fun time at the wedding and visiting with Kate and Spence. He's so interesting."

She nodded and her eyes widened. "I know and he has such fascinating stories from his career. I was really hoping he would decide to stay here. He seemed like he was considering it."

"I think he's giving it some thought. When we were fishing he told me he could get used to living on the island and fishing every day. I think he'd like to be closer to Kate."

"Do you think they were ever romantically involved?"

He shrugged. "I don't know. I don't think so based on what Kate has shared with us, but when they're together they both radiate happiness."

"They're both single and available and Kate deserves something happy in her life."

"That she does. She's a strong lady, but I bet she misses him when he leaves."

"We should take them to dinner one night this week before Spence leaves."

"Count me in. I'm free except for tomorrow." His plate was empty and he sat back in his chair, sipping his beer. "I picked up dessert from Ellie's today, so save some room."

Regi put her hand on her stomach. "Oh, man. What'd you get?"

"I bought a few pieces of cake. Chocolate mousse, lemon, cheesecake, and red velvet.

"Ahh, you're not doing much for my dieting plan."

"You don't need to diet; you're perfect." He winked and stood to clear the dishes, giving her a peck on the forehead. "We should call Kate and see if they want to stop by for dessert and then we could mention dinner."

"I'll give her a call." She retrieved her phone and scrolled to Kate's name, while Nate started on the dishes. After a quick conversation she disconnected and remembered her promise to Molly about photos. She scrutinized the photos she had taken at the wedding and selected a few and sent them off to her daughter.

She returned to the kitchen and said, "Kate says they'll be here in a few minutes. They just finished dinner, so our timing was great." She grabbed a wet cloth and began cleaning up the counters.

After they tidied the kitchen, she hooked up Murphy's leash and took her outside. Nate came out after her, holding a small flashlight. "It's dark, I'll come with you."

As soon as they left the cover of the porch, they felt the sprinkling of rain. Murphy was on a mission to investigate every inch of the property and led them on a meandering excursion. After she finally did her business, they trotted back to the house. Nate found a towel and helped Regi dry the dog before she bounded into the house.

Murphy went over to her new bed and flopped down in contentment. As soon as they hung up their wet coats, lights in the driveway announced the arrival of Kate and Spence. Regi borrowed a towel to blot her hair while Nate stood on the porch to welcome them.

Kate took off her hooded raincoat and Spence handed it along with his, to Nate. Regi emerged from the bathroom, "Hi, guys. I'm glad you could join us."

Nate led them to the living room and Murphy rose to investigate the newcomers, parking herself in front of Spence who gave her a thorough petting. She eventually became bored and returned to burrow back into the dent she had left in the bed.

Nate made coffee while Regi chatted with their two guests. She brought up the idea for dinner. "What evening would be best for the two of you?" she asked.

Spence looked at Kate. "I'm free," he laughed. "Let Katie pick the best day, since she'll be working. I'm leaving on Friday morning."

"How about Wednesday night?" suggested Kate. "Where shall we go?"

"Spence should pick," said Regi.

"I like Lou's crab place. Does that work for everyone?" he asked.

Both the women nodded and Nate hollered from the kitchen, "Perfect, Lou's one of my favorites."

Regi helped Nate bring out the selection of cake slices and coffee. "Ladies first," insisted Spence. When Kate saw the red velvet she seized it from the tray. Regi opted for the lemon and Spence took the cheesecake, leaving Nate with the chocolate mousse.

"Oh, I almost took the chocolate," said Regi.

"I might be persuaded to share a few bites," said Nate, wiggling his brows at her.

Kate talked about her store and remarked how busy it had been during her first two weeks in business. "I hope it keeps up," she said, offering Spence the last quarter of her red velvet cake.

He didn't hesitate to take it from her and shrugged when she studied his own empty plate, wiped clean of any trace of the decadent cheesecake. "I told Katie she's going to have to hire a helper so she gets a break."

"I'm not used to being stuck in the store all day, or for that matter, working all day. I only had to work three days a week at the store in the city and we had help, so I could pop out if I needed to run an errand."

"Once summer hits you'll be swamped with tourists. They descend on the island starting in May and don't leave until September. You'll have to hire someone by then," added Nate.

"During the summer, I'd have more time to help out. I'll be working at the coffee shop, but not every day. I know Kyle is planning to come home for the summer, so he'll be here, plus the others," said Regi, eyeing Nate's cake. "I bet Molly would love to help out."

Nate offered to switch her plates, handing her the chocolate and taking her lemon. "You know my mom may be interested in some part-time work," said Nate. "She loves decorating and all that stuff you have in the store."

"I'd love to meet her. If she's interested, please have her call me," said Kate.

"I do dinner with them every Monday, so I'll ask her tomorrow."

"If Spence decides to move here, maybe he could work for you," said Regi with a wink.

"I'm thinking about a move. I've got some things to wrap up back in the city, but I told Katie I could surprise her one day and show up to stay." Spence's blue eyes flashed as he turned to Kate.

She patted his knee. "That would be wonderful. What could be better than having my best friend here?"

He placed his hand over hers. "We'll see what happens."

Spence and Kate wanted to know more about Nate's family and growing up on the island. "I'm fairly boring," he began. He recapped his family and his life growing up with three younger sisters. He was the only one who had stayed on the island and had started working for the delivery service in high school. He serviced the whole island every day and made weekly trips to neighboring islands. "I didn't intend for it to be my career, but as it turned out I like it and I make enough money to keep me happy."

"It's a plus to work for a company that offers a retirement," said Spence. "You'll be thankful when you get to be my age."

Nate nodded. "That is a definite benefit. Dad offered me a job selling real estate, but that didn't interest me, so I took this job right after college while I figured out what I really wanted to do. Now I'm the manager."

Regi heard her phone chirp and excused herself to check it. She found a text from Molly. *You look gorgeous in that dress! Nate's a cutie all dressed up. Looks like you had fun. Is that Mark Harmon with Kate? Love, Molly.*

She rejoined the group and Nate asked, "Everything okay?"

"Just Molly. I texted her a few pictures from the wedding. She wanted to see me in your dress, Kate. And she asked if Spence was Mark Harmon."

Kate smiled and Spence gave a hearty laugh. "Don't let that go to your head," she said, poking him in the shoulder.

Nate chuckled. "I have to agree with Molly. When I first saw him in your store I thought he resembled Mark Harmon. Are you sure you aren't related?"

"I wish," said Spence with a smile.

Kate glanced at her watch and announced, "We better get going. I've got an early day tomorrow."

"I wish we could squeeze in another fishing trip before you head back," said Nate.

"I'm not leaving forever," said Spence, giving Nate a firm pat on the back. "I'll be back soon and we'll set something up."

"I'll hold you to it," said Nate, retrieving their coats.

"You let me know what your mom thinks about a job," said Kate, as she stepped onto the porch.

"Will do. See you guys Wednesday night at Lou's."

"Let's make it seven, okay?" asked Kate.

"Seven it is. See you then," said Regi, as she waved from the porch.

Nate put another log on the fire and gave Murphy's head a soft ruffle. Regi was picking up the plates and cups from dessert and taking them to the sink. "I can do those in the morning, just leave them," said Nate, sneaking up behind her and moving her hair to gain access to her neck. He kissed her gently. "Come sit down."

"I should get going." He turned her around to face him and kissed the spot between her collarbone and neck. She sucked in a breath and her pulse quickened with delight. "It's getting late," she whispered.

"You could always stay here," he said, moving from her neck to her mouth, depositing soft kisses until he reached her lips.

She felt a familiar charge move through her when he hungrily explored her mouth. She reached for his shoulders, eager to steady herself against the rush of excitement.

Both of them were breathless when he ended the kiss and their eyes met. "Stay," he said, moving his forehead to touch hers and massaging her back with his strong thumbs.

She hadn't felt this way for longer than she cared to remember. The thrill of anticipation was bubbling under the surface and although her mind was telling her to go her body was shouting at her to surrender.

She whispered, "I want to, but I can't. Not tonight."

He brought his hands down to meet hers and squeezed them, brushing one more kiss on her lips. "If I told you I'd be a perfect gentleman and not take advantage of you, would you stay?"

A nervous giggle escaped her throat. "I'm not sure I believe you. Another night, just not tonight."

His intense eyes locked on hers. "I'll hold you to it," he said and then kissed her once more before she gathered her coat and Murphy.

He helped her to the Jeep and stood and waved as she backed up. As soon as she turned the corner the flood of tears she had been holding at bay let go and coursed down her cheeks.

She banged her palms on the old steering wheel. *What am I doing? I really like Nate but each time we get close, I'm thinking only of Cam.*

Fourteen

Nate was wide awake and finished the dishes for something to do. He stuffed everything in the dishwasher and started it. He shook his head at his reflection in the window above the sink. He was too wound up to sleep. He jammed his feet into shoes and took off across the porch for his shop.

He hadn't dated seriously in years and was beginning to understand why. He'd always thought he'd settle down and get married and have a family. Time had been on his side, but he was going to be forty soon, with nothing serious on the horizon. Then he'd met Regi and felt differently. He had been attracted to her when he met her, but after spending time with her, the attraction had grown into something much more.

He was falling in love with her, but he wasn't sure what she felt. After she shared her story about Cam, he understood more about why she seemed distant. She was a terrific friend and companion, but Nate was looking for more. As he busied himself tinkering with his boat he realized he wasn't sure if she was capable of giving more.

While his hands were busy, his mind was replaying scenes from their times together and he wondered if he'd misread things. They'd always had fun, especially lately, dancing for hours and hanging out with Kate and Spence. He could tell there was chemistry between them, especially when they kissed.

"What's the problem?" he yelled. His hand slipped with the screwdriver and slammed into his finger. "Ouch, dammit," he hollered and threw the tool across the concrete floor. He found a clean rag and held it against the gash and sat down. "Maybe she's not as ready to let go of the past as she thinks she is," he whispered.

* * *

Regi knew she had hurt Nate's feelings when she saw him bring in a load of boxes and leave without stopping by her office. She watched him walk to his truck, shoulders slumped, eyes on the ground. He heaved the dolly into the truck and motored away, without even a glance at her window.

"Crap," she muttered, as she turned back to her computer. *I've got to get it together and be done with Cam. Nate deserves better.*

She toiled through the day and after lunch decided to send Kate a text to see if she could visit with her. Regi hadn't had a healthy relationship with her mom since her unplanned pregnancy. That, coupled with Regi's lack of effort to find a husband to care for her and Molly, didn't make it easy to talk to her mom about anything resembling a relationship. She hadn't known Kate long, but felt an instant rapport with her and right now she needed a good listener and some advice.

Kate invited Regi to stop by for dinner at her house. Regi took a breath after replying to the text, feeling some of the tension in her neck ease. She hurried through the rest of the afternoon, eager to get to Kate's.

She stopped by the market and picked up a couple bottles of wine and rang Kate's bell at seven. Kate greeted her with a hug and led her to the kitchen. Spence was busy at the cooktop and the scent of lemons filled the air, making Regi's mouth water.

"Spence is spoiling me while he's here. He's made dinner for us each night. Come in the living room while he finishes up," said Kate, setting the wine on the counter.

"It'll be ready in about half an hour, ladies," said Spence, waving his spoon at them.

Regi snuggled into the soft couch and let out a sigh. "I'm trying to figure out what's wrong with me. I told you my past history with Cam and how I've accepted he's not coming and I need to move on."

Kate nodded, urging her to continue.

"Nate and I have been spending a lot of time together and I really like him. So, last night after you left, Nate asked me to stay over." She paused and looked down, fumbling with the tassels on a pillow. "I told him I couldn't stay, even though a part of me wanted to. I do have feelings for Nate, but I also feel like I'm betraying Cam." She shook her head. "I know it doesn't make sense."

Kate patted her hand. "The other night you told me you were trying to move on, but you had counted on reuniting with Cam for years. Feelings like that are hard to turn off."

Regi nodded as a silent tear slid down her face.

"Have you thought about trying to contact Cam?"

"Not really. I'm afraid."

"Because if you find out he's moved on or forgotten about you, it will end your fantasy, right?"

Regi nodded, ashamed at her transparency.

"Let me ask you a couple of questions and you don't have to answer them right now if you don't want to, but think about them, okay?"

Regi nodded and took the tissue Kate offered her.

"Number one—what would happen if Cam showed up here tomorrow? Number two—What would happen if you found out Cam was married or moved to Africa or was otherwise not going to be part of your future? Number three—are you willing to risk a meaningful relationship right now for the slim chance that Cam will show up sometime in the future?"

Regi plucked another tissue from the box and held it to her eyes. "I understand the logic; I just don't know what to do."

"I know sweetie," said Kate. "Feelings, love, relationships— sometimes have very little to do with logic." She paused as she rubbed Regi's knee. "If you would like me to look into Cam and find out more about his current situation, I could do that for you."

"Thanks, I'll give it some thought. I think I have my answer, I'm just afraid to leave him. I've lived with the thought of him for the last twenty years and it scares me to be without him."

"I've never been in your situation, but I've been scared to move on from the past. I was petrified when my husband left. After losing Karen, a part of me didn't want to go on without her. Luckily, I had Spence and he helped me by reminding me I was strong and could get through it. I had to rely on my friends. I don't think I could have done it alone."

"I've been so unfair to Nate. He knows about Cam and told me how sorry he was that I had been let down after so many years of waiting. I know I hurt him. He wouldn't even look my way today on his delivery route."

"You've got some choices to make. You can go on as you have been for the last twenty years, waiting and hoping for someone or you can let him go and work on the possibility of a real relationship you could have right now. Remember to answer those questions I asked you."

"I've been letting Cam, or the illusion of him, guide my life and choices for so long."

Kate nodded. "That's why you feel you're betraying him. He's not here and he hasn't been here. You've given him a lot of power in your life."

Regi nodded, wiping at fresh tears. "I'm sure it seems crazy to you. It sounds ridiculous when we talk about it out loud. It's always made perfect sense in my head, but now, I don't know."

Spence hollered out from the kitchen. "Dinner is served."

Regi excused herself to freshen up in the bathroom and Kate gave Spence a condensed version of their conversation while he plated up chicken piccata, garlic parmesan orzo, crusty garlic bread, and a crisp salad. Kate helped him carry the plates to the dining room and added water to the glasses and wine to the table.

Regi came in, looking less frazzled. "Dinner looks delicious."

Both Kate and Regi heaped on the praise when they tasted the chicken. Spence beamed with pride as they complimented his orzo dish. As they finished dinner Spence asked Kate about her day at the shop.

"It was a slow day, which was good. Alec, the artist I met at The Haven, stopped by with a few more paintings and he wanted a tour of the place. I sold some small items and greeting cards, but nothing exciting. I put in a call to Ryan who took the wedding photos. I'd like to carry some local photos or cards and thought he may be interested."

"What did you do today, Spence?" asked Regi.

"I worked on a case I've been consulting on, so spent some time on the phone and the computer. I'll finish it up when I get back on Friday." He looked at their empty dinner plates. "If you saved some room, we've got a little something from Sweet Treats."

Regi offered to clear the table and do the dishes and insisted Kate and Spence relax in the living room. She loaded the dishwasher and washed a few of the cooking pans by hand. She used a towel to dry them and her thoughts drifted to Nate and Cam while she wiped away the water.

While she was busy in the kitchen, Kate elaborated on their conversation and suggested Spence try to meet Nate for lunch and see what Nate had to say. He agreed and sent Nate a text asking about lunch on Tuesday, since he knew they were all planning to go to dinner on Wednesday and was hoping for a resolution to the issue between Regi and Nate. As Regi came in from the kitchen his phone beeped and he scanned the message and gave Kate a wink.

"Are you two ready for some dessert?" he asked, getting up from the chair.

Regi looked at her watch. "I should probably get home and check on Murphy."

"Oh, take one to go then," suggested Kate. "Spence picked up some s'mores cupcakes today."

Spence returned with a small plate of the delightful looking treats and gave her hug. "You take care and we'll see you Wednesday night for dinner."

Kate embraced Regi in a tight squeeze. "Call me if you need to talk, sweetie."

Regi nodded and said, "I will. Thanks for letting me come over."

"Anytime, you're always welcome."

She waved from the driveway and made sure the plate of treats was balanced before she backed out and drove the few blocks to her condo. She skipped television and stashed her cupcakes in the refrigerator. After taking Murphy out and playing ball, she put her in the crate and wandered down the hall to find her own bed.

The questions Kate had posed saturated her thoughts as she stared at the ceiling. Hoping to find the answers in her dreams, she drifted to sleep.

* * *

Tuesday Regi met Leon for lunch at Soup D'Jour. He looked good, clear eyed and smiling. "What's new?" asked Regi.

Her brother grinned. "I found a used car that I'm buying. Jim over at Island Automotive has an old Suburban sitting in his yard and is making me a deal. I'm making payments to him and he's fixing it. I used the extra money I earned from Kate and should have it paid off next month."

"That's great news. That'll be more practical than Jeremy's scooter. Jim has a reputation for quality work."

"Yeah, Lou hooked me up with him," said Leon, as the waitress delivered their plates. "How about you?"

"Work is busy and I went to Linda's wedding this weekend. I had a good time," she said, but her eyes had a sad look.

"Are you sure you're okay? You look down."

She nodded as she slipped a spoonful of potato soup into her mouth. "I'm okay, just tired." She had never confided in Leon and wasn't about to start now.

He told her Lou was letting him do some prep work in the kitchen at the beginning of his shift and he was hoping to move up soon. "I need to figure something out before summer and find an affordable place."

"You think you want to stay on the island?"

He nodded, chewing his sandwich. "Yeah, I like it here and I like working with Lou. I just need to make more money. Places here aren't cheap. I was thinking about asking your friend Linda about working at the nursery in the mornings to try to earn a little more dough."

"I don't know much about how many people she hires or if she has a crew, but you could ask her. She's at the flower shop today."

"I'll swing by there and see what she says."

Regi took the check and paid for lunch. "See ya next week," she said.

Her brother moved to hug her and said, "Thanks, Regi, for giving me another chance. I won't let you down."

* * *

While Leon and Regi were having lunch, Spence and Nate were enjoying pizza at Big Tony's. Spence asked Nate about Regi, as they returned from picking up slabs of pizza from the lunch buffet.

"I haven't talked to her since Sunday night."

Spence kept eating, hoping the silence he used interrogating suspects would prompt Nate to talk.

Nate continued, "I don't know what's going on. Everything seems right with her and we have fun together." He shook his head and took a drink of iced tea. "I pushed her too hard Sunday night. After you guys left, things started getting heated up and I asked her to stay over."

"I take it she said no?"

He pursed his lips and nodded. "Yep, told me she wanted to, but it needed to be another night and left." Nate held up his bandaged finger. "That's when I went out in the shop and did this."

"What do you think is wrong?"

"I think it has to do with this old boyfriend, Cam. It's hard to believe she's still stuck on a guy she hasn't even talked to in twenty years." Nate wiped his mouth with a napkin. "I know one thing, I'm sick of him. He's probably married with six kids while Regi's waiting around for him."

"When you've lived with an idea of something for that long, it's not easy to let it go. She could feel like she's betraying Cam by being with you. She doesn't strike me as the type of woman who takes relationships for granted. From what I know, she hasn't had a serious relationship since Cam."

Nate nodded, pushing the rest of his pizza aside. "Yeah, she hasn't been involved with anyone. I know everything was wrapped up in his return at

Christmas. I was glad she told me about him, because I couldn't figure out why she seemed so discouraged."

"Sometimes it helps to put yourself in the other person's shoes."

Nate thought for a moment and then said, "I get it. It's hard for me, because I don't think I would've ever given up twenty years to wait for someone. She's obviously loyal, but I don't think he deserves it. Not when I'm right here and I told her I'm falling for her."

"She's distraught over it. She called Katie last night and came over to visit with her about it. She knows she hurt you and doesn't know what to do." He took a gulp of his drink. "Actually, I do think she knows what to do, she's just having a hard time letting go of the past and her dream."

Nate's eyes widened. "So, you think she does care for me?"

"I know she does," Spence smiled. "She just needs more time."

"And less pressure from me, I'm sure." He lowered his head and looked at his hands. "I shouldn't have pushed so hard. I let the excitement get to me. I haven't dated anyone seriously in years and I think Regi could be the one for me."

"I've found women are slower to move in that department. At least any woman worth having. I think she's worth waiting for, Nate. My best advice would be talk with her and give her some room."

"You sound as if you have a little experience with this stuff."

Spence smiled and his blue eyes twinkled. "I have quite a bit of experience waiting for the right woman."

Fifteen

On Wednesday when Nate stopped by the school with his deliveries, he deposited the stacks of boxes and then made a beeline for Regi's office. "Hey," he called out when he came through the door.

"Hi, Nate," she said, turning around in her chair.

"I just need you to sign for these," he said, holding the electronic pad out for her. "I also wanted to make sure we were still on for dinner with Kate and Spence."

She scribbled her name and said, "Yeah, we're set for seven at Lou's."

"Could I come by your place early so we can talk?"

She nodded, seeing the flash of panic in his eyes. "Sure, I'd like that. I'm going right home when I get off, so come by whenever you want."

He grinned. "Great, my day isn't too bad, so I'll plan to stop in before six." She handed him the pad and when he took it from her, he held her hand in his and squeezed it. "I'll see you then."

She waved as he left and watched him get in his truck. This time he glanced at her window and gave a nod and a quick wave as he hopped up in the seat. She let out a breath and smiled as she went back to the document on her screen.

* * *

Regi took Murphy to the park after she picked her up from the hardware store and ran with her on the grass for almost an hour. Murphy rolled and played, chasing her ball around and jumping over the plants and bushes.

After feeding Murphy, she jumped in the shower and got dressed, so she'd be ready when Nate arrived. Murphy sacked out on the living room floor while she waited for Regi to emerge from the bedroom.

Regi turned on the television and the puppy, resembling a wet noodle, didn't stir from her prone position, her back legs extended out behind her. Regi flipped the channels, trying to distract herself from the impending conversation with Nate. She knew they needed to talk, but dreaded the topic.

The bell rang and Murphy raised her head and opened one eye, watching Regi get up to answer the door. Nate, handing her a colorful spray of flowers wrapped in tissue, kissed her cheek as he came through the door.

"Oh, how pretty," said Regi. "Thank you." She led him to the living room. "Take a seat and I'll put these in a vase."

Murphy rushed to Nate and wagged her tail, thumping it against his jeans. He picked her up and cuddled her on his lap. Regi returned and shook her finger at Murphy. "You're not supposed to be on the furniture."

"Technically, she's not touching the furniture," smiled Nate.

"You're both incorrigible." Regi sat down next to him and petted the dog.

"I feel bad about how our Sunday ended," said Nate. "I realize now I pushed you and I shouldn't have. I'm sorry, Regi."

She shook her head as she continued to stare at Murphy. "It's not you. It's me," she said, in a hoarse whisper.

He put his hand on top of hers as she stroked the soft fur. "I got caught up in the moment and let my hormones override my brain. It won't happen again."

She laughed and looked at his eyes, remembering why she chose the deep turquoise turtleneck tonight. "I was this close," she held her fingers only a quarter of an inch apart, "from letting my hormones win. Really,

Nate, I'm more than attracted to you. If I'd had a normal life, none of this would be happening. It would be much easier."

"Like I told you, I'm falling for you and I'd like nothing more than to take this to the next level, but I'm going to leave it up to you. I'm pretty sure you're still hung up on the idea of Cam and until you're truly ready to close that chapter, I don't think we can go there."

She was determined not to cry tonight. She felt the sting of tears and opened her eyes wide, hoping to contain them. She took a deep breath and eased her hand over Murphy's ears. "You're right. I thought I could move forward and I felt like I was until the prospect of true intimacy was staring me in the face." She stopped petting Murphy and looked up. "Part of the problem is this screwed up devotion I feel for Cam and then there's a part of me that's just plain scared. I haven't been with a man since Molly was a baby." Her face reddened and she began twisting her fingers in new feathers sprouting from Murphy's tail.

Nate reached for her and tilted her chin up, drilling his intense eyes into hers. "Don't be afraid. I'm not some Don Juan of the island," he chuckled. "I haven't dated seriously for several years. I want to make this work, Regi. I don't want to scare you or cause you stress. When you're ready, you let me know and until then, we'll keep doing what we've been doing. I think you're worth waiting for."

A tear slid down her cheek and he let her chin go and engulfed her in a long hug. Murphy stirred between them and wiggled until she was free and jumped to the floor. "You're a good man, Nate. Thanks for understanding," she whispered in his ear.

Nate took Murphy outside while she made a trip to the bathroom to repair the damage from the tears. She chided the face in the mirror as she blotted her skin. "You're a big chicken, Regina Brady." *I was all set to commit to Nate and leave Cam behind, because I didn't want to lose Nate. Then he took all the pressure away and I caved and couldn't do it. Why can't I let go of Cam?*

* * *

Nate and Regi secured a booth at Lou's and nibbled on an appetizer sampler while they waited for their dinner companions. Spence and Kate arrived in time to help finish off the starter.

As Spence waited for Kate to slide into the booth, he gave Nate a questioning look and with the hand he had behind Regi, Nate gave him a thumbs up. Spence smiled and scooted next to Kate, filching a jalapeño popper from the platter.

Lou himself came to the table to take their order. While he waited for them to make their selections he said, "Regi, just wanted you to know your brother has been great. He's been doing a bang up job in the kitchen."

Regi smiled. "We had lunch yesterday and he told me how excited he was to be helping with the prep work."

"Hopefully, he'll stick around for the summer when we'll need all the help we can get." He pulled the pencil from behind his ear and looked at Kate, "What can we get you tonight?" They made their selections and Lou promised he'd have their meals out in no time.

While they feasted on a variety of crab concoctions, plus Lou's famous lobster macaroni and cheese, Nate tried to entice Spence to stay longer. "Dad and I are taking the boat out this weekend for some fishing. You sure you can't stay the weekend?"

"I would love to, but I've got a meeting Friday afternoon downtown at headquarters and I can't miss it."

"What are you working on?" asked Regi.

"I'm looking at some cold cases for them…homicides."

"I bet that's a difficult task," said Nate.

Spence nodded. "It isn't easy. I always hope I'll find something that was overlooked or some evidence that can be analyzed further with today's technology. The families who lost a loved one deserve justice."

Regi smiled at Spence. "You're right to be so dedicated. I can't imagine not knowing or worrying about a murderer on the loose."

"I'm also working on a string of burglaries with the art theft unit. That one is a bit more fun, since it only involves the loss of property."

Lou came to check on them and offer dessert. They shook their heads and groaned about how full they were. Spence looked at the tray of sweets with yearning in his eye, but Kate reminded him they still had cupcakes at the house.

They lingered over coffee, finally calling it a night when Lou turned off the neon sign that lit up the outdoor deck. Once they were outside, Regi hugged Spence. "I'm going to miss you. Please tell me you're coming back soon."

He gave her a hug and chuckled as he held her tight. "I'll be back before you know it." He whispered as he pulled away, "You take care of Katie while I'm gone."

Regi winked and nodded as Nate stepped in to shake Spence's hand. "We've got some fishing to do when you get back here," he said.

Spence grinned and wrapped one arm around Nate's shoulders. "That we do. I'll email you when I know my schedule and we'll set up some trips."

"I'm looking forward to it," said Nate. "You have a safe trip home."

Regi put her arm through Nate's as they walked to his truck. "I bet Kate's going to really miss him. What a great guy."

As they pulled away, they saw Kate and Spence standing arm in arm at the harbor's edge, gazing at the water. "Yeah, they're definitely perfect for each other. I wonder what they're waiting for," said Nate.

* * *

The next weeks went by in a blur. Work was hectic, requiring Regi to work late several nights and she was scheduled at the coffee shop every weekend. She was looking forward to having Molly on the island during her break from school in late March. She and Nate went to lunch once a week and slid into a routine of having dinner together on Friday and Saturday nights. They usually went out on Friday and Nate cooked for her on Saturday. Nate's mom had agreed to work one day a week in Kate's shop, so she had some time away from it.

Nate took Regi to dinner at his parents' house a few times. She marveled at the house and the décor, seeing why Nate thought his mom would be a good fit for Kate's shop. She was also an excellent cook and both his parents were great conversationalists. She learned about real estate on the island from Jack and all about cultural events from Lulu. They had been married for over forty years and she could tell they were still in love by the private smiles and touches they gave each other. They also teased each other and were sharp witted. It was easy to see where Nate got his sense of humor and kindness.

Nate's sisters all had several children and Lulu dragged out photo albums to show Regi pictures from all their family events. Jack and Nate mostly talked about fishing, real estate, and Nate's business. Nate and Regi always brought dessert from Ellie's when they were invited to dinner. Jack and Lulu taught them to play cards and they usually stayed up too late, engrossed in a competitive game of pinochle or euchre.

There had been no more requests from Nate to stay the night. They spent time watching movies, going to events at the community theatre, taking walks, and lots of canoodling.

Nate always stopped by on weekend mornings and visited with Regi while having a drink and pastry at Harbor Coffee and Books. On a breezy Sunday in March, Linda and Max stopped in for hot drinks. She toted her sketch pad, hoping to finalize her design for Cooper Gardens. She had been working nonstop to finish her plan and get the plant list to Lucas so she could get things planted when she returned from Ireland in April.

"Good morning to you both," said Regi, as they came in and joined Nate at the table closest to the register.

"We stopped in to warm up and take one more look at the space for Jeff's community garden project. I need to finish it up this week," said Linda, ordering her chai and a cappuccino for Max.

"I bet it's going to be gorgeous, like everything else you design," said Regi.

Linda smiled. "I hope so. It's such a special project."

Max added, "She stole some ideas from the magnificent gardens we visited on our trip to Victoria."

"I fell in love with the concept of different types of gardens within a larger garden and tried to select plants and flowers to make sure it's beautiful all year. I can't wait until I get to plant it," she beamed. "Lucas is going to handle getting the area prepped while we're gone and then I'll help plant when we get home in May."

"How're the honeymoon plans coming?" asked Nate.

Max grinned. "It's only two weeks away. We'll be in New York for five days and then fly to Ireland for a month long trip and back to New York for a few days before we fly home." He took a sip of his drink. "We're staying in a small village and taking day trips from there. Then we move on to two more places for the other two weeks, so we can take in the whole country."

He gripped Linda's hand and she smiled. "I've never been anywhere, so I can't wait to see all these places. If it's half as pretty as what I've seen online, I'm going to love it. We're staying in a castle for part of the trip. How cool is that?"

Regi and Nate both laughed. "Totally cool," said Nate.

"I'm looking forward to staying in your castle," said Regi with a smirk. "Murphy and I won't know what to do with all that space and the huge yard. She's going to love it."

"Molly arrives next weekend, right?" asked Linda.

Regi nodded, her eyes full of excitement. "Yeah, I can't wait. She's coming home Saturday morning. I have to work at school that week, but will be off both weekends."

"That will be fun for you. We leave early on the twenty-eighth, so that will give you the weekend you're off to get settled at our place," said Linda.

"We'll leave you a list of where we'll be and my cell phone will work over there for emergencies. For non-emergency stuff, just email and we'll check it each day," said Max. He took a set of keys out of his pocket, "Here are the keys to the house and all the cars, just in case you need to move any of them." He pointed to two other colored keys, "These are to the nursery and the flower shop. You shouldn't need them, but you'll have them."

"Sara and Lucas will take care of everything, so you shouldn't have to be bothered with either place," said Linda, sipping her chai. "We left you their numbers though and gave them your cell number."

"I'm sure everything will be fine while you're away. You need to enjoy your time and bring back thousands of pictures for all of us to drool over," said Regi, getting up to wait on the couple arriving.

Nate continued to visit with Max and Linda and looked at her drawings and sketches of the garden. A spurt of customers kept Regi busy and by the time she rang up the last sale, Max and Linda were gathering their things.

"We'll talk to you before we leave and if you want to bring anything over early, just let us know. We can't thank you enough for taking care of Lucy and the house," said Linda.

"Believe me, I should be thanking you. Molly and I don't have any plans, just hanging out, so we'll see you before you take off."

They waved goodbye and set out for the future location of Cooper Gardens. Nate watched them leave and turned back to Regi. "They're excited, huh?"

"Yeah, it sounds like a trip of a lifetime. They deserve it."

"I better get going. I have things to do today. I'll call you later," said Nate, leaning to kiss Regi.

* * *

Regi's work week crawled by, while she urged it to hurry so she could reconnect with Molly. She spent her evenings cleaning the condo and making sure Molly's room was spic and span. As she cleaned she thought about Nate, reflecting on the fun they'd had over the last month.

Cam hadn't been dominating her thoughts and she found the routines she and Nate had comforting. Whenever they kissed or cuddled on his couch, as they did every Saturday night, she felt something deep inside her feminine self spring to life. Without Cam hovering in her thoughts and clouding her judgment, she could focus on Nate. She thought back to the talk Kate had with her and over the last month the answers had crystalized. She knew if she found out Cam was married and not going to be part of her life, she was going to be fine. Nate was attentive, patient, kind, thoughtful, and enamored with her. She couldn't come up with any strong negatives in his column. The only thing against him was Cam and he wasn't here; he was in her past and that's where she was going to keep him. She knew it was unlikely Cam would show up and if he did, she could talk and reminisce, but their chance at happily ever after was gone. She smiled when she realized she hadn't been obsessing about Cam. She felt stronger and sure of herself and Nate.

She went shopping Thursday after work and gathered all of Molly's favorites, plus lots of snacks. As she wandered the market, her thoughts drifted to Nate. She decided to surprise him with dinner at her house on Friday and stopped at the butcher counter to get some steaks. She picked out a bottle of wine and a six-pack of Blue Moon for Nate. She giggled as she pushed her cart through the market and splurged on a new candle. When she got home she made a note to stop by Sweet Treats and pick up dessert for her surprise evening with Nate. *I think I'll text him tomorrow and invite him to dinner and a sleepover.* She snickered at the thought of his reaction when he read the message. A loud snort of laughter sprang from her lips, earning her a scowl from the matronly cashier. "Sorry," she said, "I just thought of something funny.

Sixteen

Friday morning, Regi overslept and had to rush to get to work. She zipped through her morning routine, hurrying to drop Murphy at the hardware store, parking the Jeep in the lot with only a minute to spare. Luckily, it was Friday so she could wear jeans and a school logo shirt.

She sprinted to the building and flew into her office, poking the button for her computer as she removed her coat. Being late frazzled her and she hated starting the day stressed. She had intended to text Nate early in the morning, before work, but there had been no time for shenanigans. She checked her voicemail, jotted down her messages, and snagged a cup of coffee while she waited for the programs to load on her computer.

The bell rang for school and the morning chaos began. Once the office settled down, she used her phone and composed a short, but suggestive text to Nate. She reddened when she hit the button and squeezed her eyes shut, hoping for the best. She had just taken a sip of coffee and clicked on her first email when her phone chirped.

It was a reply from Nate. She grinned as she read his large *YES* and several hearts and kissing lips. She punched in a quick reply and put her phone aside to concentrate on work. She finished up a complicated project she had been working on and then treated herself to a donut from the pink box in the lounge. When Nate dropped off their delivery he dashed into her office, sporting a grin that wouldn't stop. "Can't wait to see you tonight. Do you need me to bring anything?" he asked.

She shook her head. "No, I think I have everything we'll need." He was in a hurry but after looking over his shoulder through her open door, he dove across the top of her desk and kissed her and then he winked and dashed out her door.

After Nate's visit the morning raced by and she realized she hadn't packed a lunch. She called in an order to Dottie's and stopped by Ellie's and picked up a loaf of fresh bread and a variety of cake slices for the weekend. She ate at her desk and fueled with the excitement of tonight's romantic adventure and Molly's arrival tomorrow, she pounded through the rest of the work in her baskets.

When it was time to leave, she carried her coat and the bread and detoured to the break room to collect the box of treats from the fridge. She had a spring in her step as she walked to her car, smiling when she opened the door and situated the bakery box on the passenger seat. *It's going to be a great weekend,* she thought, pulling away from the school.

After she picked up Murphy she marinated the steaks, put the potatoes in the oven, and slathered the bread with garlic and butter. She put together a salad and stashed it to chill in the fridge. It wouldn't be a fancy dinner, but it would be tasty. Once the kitchen was cleaned up, she tackled her bedroom and bathroom. She changed her sheets and put her new candle on the dresser. She tidied the bathroom and then went to work on choosing an outfit. As she surveyed her closet she wished she had Kate's surplus of choices. She finally went with a pair of jeans and a soft pink blouse.

She set the table and checked the potatoes. They needed to cook a bit more, so she took Murphy outside to play and then fed her. She slipped on an apron and went to work scooping out the potatoes to mix them with butter and cream, plus some bacon and cheese to create twice-baked potatoes. She got them in the oven and thought the living room seemed chilly, so she started a fire. Just as the flames licked over the logs, the bell rang, announcing Nate.

She greeted him at the door, noticing first the flowers he held and then his duffle bag. "Come in," she said, taking the flowers. "These are pretty," she sniffed them and led him to the living room. Murphy was bouncing under their feet, begging to be petted.

She put the flowers in a vase and set them on the table and picked up the duffle and carried it into her bedroom. When she returned, Nate was on the floor and Murphy was jumping over the top of him and back, like a circus act. "I've got steaks ready to grill," she said.

Nate laughed as he roughhoused with the dog. "I'll be right there and get them started."

While he manned the grill, she finished the potatoes and put the bread in the oven. She tossed the salad and put everything on the table as he came in from the balcony with sizzling steaks. "Smells delicious," she said.

They filled their plates and talked about their week at work. "Would you and Molly like to come out on the boat while she's here?" asked Nate.

"That would be fun, maybe this Sunday or next weekend."

"These potatoes are the bomb," he said, taking a huge bite of the fluffy, cheesy mixture. "I'm so glad you invited me tonight." He was wearing dark jeans and a white polo shirt, his intense eyes staring at Regi.

"Me too. I did a lot of thinking this week and realized I haven't been dwelling on Cam this last month. I know it can't have been fun for you, dealing with a girl trapped in the past with memories of a man she hasn't seen in twenty years. I haven't been fair to you and I'm truly sorry. You're all I could hope for and without meaning to, I've relegated you to the bench, while I've been obsessing about what I could have had with Cam. I know what I want now and it isn't a fantasy in my mind with a man I may never see again. It's you." She let out a nervous laugh and smiled.

He put down his fork and leaned close, giving her a firm kiss on the lips. "You made the right choice. I won't let you down."

They finished dinner and worked together doing the dishes and cleaning up the kitchen. "I stopped by Ellie's and picked up dessert today," said Regi.

"I can't eat anything right now. I'm stuffed," he said, checking to make sure the grill was turned off. "Later, okay?"

She nodded, putting the last of the dishes away. "How about a movie?"

"Sure, you pick," he said, locking the balcony door.

She made her way to the couch and curled into the corner of it, flicking through the channel guide. She found an old John Cusack film, *Gross Pointe Blank.* He joined her and slid his arm around her, resting her head on his chest. She pulled an afghan over her and twisted the fringe in her fingers as she watched the screen.

Murphy begged and whined to join them on the couch and Nate let her snuggle on the other side of him, making sure she was on a blanket. She rested her head on his knee, content.

Half way through the movie, Regi hurried to the kitchen during a commercial and plated up some cake. Nate held the afghan for her and she scurried back into their nest, offering him first choice. He took the carrot cake and left her with vanilla with strawberries. They traded bites and kisses as the movie progressed.

Minutes before the end, Regi's doorbell sounded. "Who could that be?" she asked.

"I'll get it," offered Nate, disentangling himself from Regi, Murphy, and the blankets. He bounded to the front door, surprised to see Jeff and Sam standing there.

"Oh, Nate, we're glad you're here," said Jeff. "We just got a call from Kyle and it's about Molly."

"Come in, come in," said Nate, seeing the worry etched in their faces.

Nate led them to the living room and when Regi saw them, she turned on a lamp and Murphy bounded over to Jeff. "Hey, you two. What brings you by tonight?"

Sam sat down on the couch and said, "Sit down, Regi. We've just received a phone call from Kyle." She saw Regi's smile fade as the realization hit her.

"Molly?" she said, with a lump in her throat.

Sam nodded. "Kyle's with Molly at the hospital. She went to a party tonight to celebrate the end of finals and he's not sure what happened while she was there, but he discovered her in some bushes and went with her by ambulance to the hospital."

Regi's hands covered her mouth and tears fell down her face. "Is she okay?"

"They're doing tests on her. He didn't want to tell you over the phone so he called us to come and get you. Jeff can take Murphy to our house and he's already called Steve to give you a ride to Seattle tonight. I'm happy to come with you."

Nate held Regi as she trembled with shock. "I'll go," he said. He stood Regi up and said, "Go put some things in a bag and we'll stay until she can come home." Sam took her hand and led her down the hall to the bedroom.

Jeff petted the dog's head. "I know where Murphy's stuff is, so we'll gather it up and can take care of her for however long is necessary."

Nate put his hands to his cheeks. "This is going to devastate Regi. Did Kyle say if she was raped?"

Jeff shook his head. "He didn't say, but I got the feeling it was a possibility. I think she was badly beaten and was barely conscious when he found her. She was near the library where they both work."

Nate let out a sigh. "I'll call you once we know more and how long we'll be. Thanks for getting in touch with Steve. There's no way she could have waited until tomorrow."

Jeff nodded as he saw the women come around the corner. Regi handed Nate his duffle bag and Sam held another small bag. "Let's get your coat on and your purse," said Sam.

Nate found his coat and checked the fire, which had almost burned out. He took Regi by the arm, after she got a hug from Jeff and Sam, and led her to the door. "Call when you can," said Jeff. "I've got a key, so we'll lock up as soon as we get Murphy's things."

"If you need help when you get there, call us and we'll have Max or Sean get in touch with the hospital," offered Sam.

Regi only nodded, staring at Nate's truck as he guided her to the passenger side. He shut her door and tossed their bags in the back and then hurried to the driver's side. Sam and Jeff stood watching as his taillights disappeared around the corner.

* * *

It was almost midnight by the time they arrived at the hospital and Nate gave Molly's name to the nurse at the emergency room desk. Regi's body trembled with the fear, feeling like a cold hand on the back of her neck. Nate held her close as the nurse led them to a waiting room where they found Kyle pacing. She explained Molly was still having tests performed and as soon as she was done, a nurse would be out to get Regi.

Nate shook Kyle's hand. "Thanks so much for getting her to the hospital, Kyle." Nate heard his phone and looked at a text message from Sam. She told him Becky was ready for them to stay over, and left her number to call when they were ready to turn in for the night.

Regi nodded and embraced Kyle whispering a quiet, "Thank you."

Kyle offered to get them coffee, but they both declined. After several minutes of silence, a nurse came into the room. "Mrs. Brady?" she said, staring at Regi.

"Yes," said Regi, standing.

"Molly's back, would you like to see her?"

Regi nodded frantically. "Yes, yes, please." She gripped Nate's arm. "Can we both go back?"

"Of course, follow me," she said, leading through a hallway and a swinging door. They stepped into a darkened room and saw Molly, looking very tiny in the hospital bed. Her face was almost unrecognizable beneath the mask of cuts and bruises and bandages. One arm was in a sling and the other held a collection of scrapes and cuts. An ice pack rested over her right eye and her left one was closed. A machine next to the bed tracked her vital signs.

Regi rushed to the chair by the bed and held the hand that wasn't encased in the sling. "Molly, it's Mom. I'm right here, honey."

Molly's eyelashes fluttered, but she didn't say anything.

The nurse said, "We've given her something for the pain and a muscle relaxant for her shoulder, but we need to keep her awake. She has a concussion." She looked at the monitor and then continued, "Dr. Wilson will be in as soon as she has the test results back and speak with you." She handed Nate some forms and asked that he get them filled out.

He took a seat and began asking Regi all the questions on the form and inking in the information. Regi continued to hold Molly's hand, caressing it with her thumb and talking softly to her.

After several minutes, the nurse returned and said Dr. Wilson would like to speak with them in the conference room. She pointed to a room a few doors down and assured Regi she would stay with Molly and keep her awake.

Nate held Regi's hand as they walked down the corridor and were greeted by a tall woman with dark hair. She held out a hand, "I'm Dr. Wilson, please have a seat."

They sat at a small round table and listened as she explained Molly's injuries. She had many cuts and abrasions, a dislocated shoulder, a concussion, and bruised ribs. "She didn't break anything, but she's going to be very sore for at least a week." She glanced at the chart. "I'm also sorry to say there is evidence of sexual assault."

Tears, like the hope she had been holding onto, fell from her eyes. Regi sobbed as Nate held her. "Have the police been notified?"

The doctor nodded. "Yes, they've been involved every step of the way. The young man who called for an ambulance also called the police. There's a detective and a victim's advocate who will want to speak with you and with Molly when she's more coherent." The doctor glanced at Regi, "I know this isn't easy and I'm so very sorry. Molly spoke with the police when she arrived, but they'll follow up with her tomorrow."

"How long do you think she'll stay in the hospital?" asked Nate.

"I think we'll probably be able to let her go tomorrow. I want to check her over and shoot for releasing her in the afternoon. In a few hours we'll be able to let her sleep. She needs the rest."

"We live on San Juan Island, do you think we can take her home or should we stay close?"

"You can take her home. She'll be more comfortable there and they have an excellent hospital if she needs it. I'll make an appointment for her to follow up in about a week."

"What about her risk for diseases or pregnancy?" asked Regi, in a weak voice.

"We've given her antibiotics as a precaution and also a dose of a hormone that reduces the risk of pregnancy. She'll need a follow-up test in a month and should also be tested for HIV over the coming months. She'll get all this information again at her appointment next week and beyond."

"So, physically, she needs to heal and rest. Her arm will be okay?" asked Nate.

The doctor nodded. "Yes, she shouldn't have any lasting physical issues. The more pressing issue is the emotional damage done when a young girl is raped. She'll need counseling and support for those injuries." Dr. Wilson looked at Regi again. "Are you doing okay?"

Regi nodded, her eyes glazed and angry. "I'm just so mad right now. I want to catch the bastard who did this."

"I'm with you. This part of my job is never easy and I hate that this happens to girls like Molly. I can tell you the detectives that handle these cases are vigilant. They don't rest until they catch the person responsible. I've got their business cards here for the detective in charge and the advocate." She handed the cards to Nate. "You're welcome to stay with Molly for a few hours, until we let her sleep and then you can come back in the morning after ten."

Nate nodded his head. "Thank you, doctor. We appreciate the help."

Dr. Wilson clasped Regi's hand in hers as she stood to leave. "She's a strong girl and she's going to get through this." She handed Nate another sheet of paper. "Here's my information and the numbers you need if you want to call and check on Molly after you leave. I'll see you both tomorrow."

Regi's head slumped forward on the table and her body shuddered as she wept. Nate massaged her back and dragged a box of tissues over to her. He didn't say anything, just held her as she moaned.

* * *

Becky picked them up around four in the morning and settled them into a bedroom at her house. Nate held Regi for hours, letting her soft sobs come and go. They finally fell asleep as the first hint of dawn filtered through the blinds. They slept until eleven, when Regi jerked awake.

She was disoriented when she woke curled around Nate's back. Then the horrible dream she thought she was having came rushing back as reality. She gently moved away from Nate and bundled into her robe. She closed their door and crept downstairs, finding Becky in the kitchen.

"Oh, Regi, how are you feeling today?" asked Becky.

"Numb, would be the best word."

"How about some coffee?" she said, moving to the pot and selecting a mug.

"That sounds good, thanks. Thanks for letting us stay here," she said, tears heavy in her eyes.

"Of course. How about something to eat?"

"Just coffee, but Nate may want something." She savored a sip of the warm coffee. "They plan to release Molly this afternoon and we'll take her home."

"I'm supposed to call Steve when you have a timeframe and he'll come back for y'all," said Becky.

Tears welled up again. "You've all been so wonderful." She gathered the mug in her hands. "I better get showered and ready so we can get back to the hospital."

"Tell Nate he's welcome to shower downstairs, to save time. I've got breakfast things ready, so if you change your mind about eating, we could make it quick."

Regi smiled through her tears. "I'll tell him."

She climbed the stairs and when she cracked the door open, he stirred. "Nate," she whispered.

"Yeah," he said in a husky voice. "I'm awake."

"I'm going to grab a shower. Becky said there's another one downstairs if you want to take a shower and she's got breakfast stuff ready if you're hungry."

"Okay, I'll take mine downstairs," he said, pulling aside the sheets. "Are you feeling any better this morning?"

"A little." She gathered her bag and disappeared into the adjoining bathroom. He heard the shower and got up and padded downstairs. Becky showed him the bathroom and promised him breakfast when he was done.

Once they were dressed and ready, Nate talked Regi into a piece of toast and he ate a huge slab of a cheesy egg dish, toast, and fruit. Becky gave them a ride back to the hospital and told them they were welcome to come back if things changed.

Nate carried both of their bags as they made their way to the elevator. Regi peeked into Molly's room, surprised to see Spence sitting in the chair, chatting with Molly. "Spence, how thoughtful of you to stop by," said Regi, moving to the side of Molly's bed.

He got up and embraced her in a long hug and whispered, "Katie called me, so I thought I'd come and check on all of you."

Regi squeezed him and then moved to sit in the chair by Molly. "How are you doing, kiddo?" Molly's right eye was swollen shut and a deep crimson color. Regi winced when she looked at her.

"I'm okay," she said. "I saw Dr. Wilson and she said things were on track. She thinks I'll be able to go home this afternoon." She gave a weak smile.

"Steve's going to come and pick us up at the marina and take us home."

"Kyle will still need a ride. Be sure and call him so he knows," said Molly.

"We talked to him last night and told him we'd call when we knew what time."

"I can give you kids a ride to the marina when you're ready," volunteered Spence.

"At least I'm on break this week, so I don't have to worry about school," said Molly.

Regi nodded, fighting back tears as she took in all the bruises in the light of day. "Dr. Wilson said you'd need to rest up this week. Do you really think you'll go back to school?"

Molly nodded. "If I don't, the creep who did this wins."

Spence patted her foot and gave Regi a look, flicking his eyes to the hallway.

"I'll be right back, Mol, okay. I just want to check on the timing of your release."

Nate sat down in Regi's chair, while she and Spence went out in the hallway.

"Thanks for bringing my mom," said Molly.

"You're welcome, sweetie. We were having dinner and watching a movie at her house. Kyle called Sam and Jeff to have them talk to your mom in person. He's a good guy."

Molly nodded and used her left hand to push the button to raise the head of the bed. She cringed when she slid up the bed and sighed when she got comfortable. "Things must be progressing with you two," she grinned, under the grazes and puffiness around her mouth.

Nate winked. "They're moving along. Your mom is a special lady and we have fun together."

"She needs someone like you. A good man who'll treat her well."

"That's a high compliment, Molly." He applied a gentle squeeze to her left hand. "Your mom is worried and upset, so she'll probably be a little overprotective with you."

"Ya think?" Molly rolled her left eye.

Nate chuckled, amazed at Molly's attitude considering what she'd been through. He only hoped her strength would continue to get her through the next few weeks and months.

Regi and Spence returned, smiling. "We talked to your nurse and she said Dr. Wilson signed the release, so they just need to get the paperwork done. We can get you dressed."

Spence and Nate excused themselves while Regi opened her bag and took out a new set of sweats Becky had packed for Molly. The police had taken her clothes and Regi was thankful someone was thinking ahead, since her mind was foggy.

Spence and Nate wandered down to the waiting room. "I'll fill you in on what I told Regi in the hallway."

Nate nodded and sat down.

"I talked with the detective in charge this morning and they'll need to interview Molly again. They'll have someone come to the island if they miss her today. She gave them a thorough description of the guy who attacked her and they've been interviewing witnesses at the party all night. It sounds like they have a line on a suspect and will probably be bringing Molly a set of photos to look at for identification."

"Looking at Molly I would guess she fought hard. Hopefully, he's got some marks on him."

Spence nodded. "There's an excellent chance of that. Plus they'll have DNA from their evidence collection here at the hospital, so it's looking good. I'll keep my nose in it and let you guys know anything I learn and can share."

"I hope she doesn't have to go through a trial."

"Me too. She's a tough cookie and if her attitude holds, she'll be fine regardless. But, if they have the evidence I think they will, they won't need a trial."

"I hope Regi can let her go back to school," said Nate. "She had just started to relax about Molly."

"She has lots of support and since Molly's feeling strong that will help. It would be worse if Molly wasn't determined to fight back."

Nate nodded. "I better give Kyle a call and let him know to come on down here, since we should be getting sprung soon. Do you have enough room for all of us?"

"Yep, no problem."

"When are you coming back for a visit?"

"Soon. I need to talk to Katie. I'm set on moving to the island, to be with her. I've loved Katie for a long time, as my best friend, but I'd like it to be more. I need to find out if she feels anything beyond friendship for me. I can't think of another woman I'd like to spend the rest of my life with, other than Katie."

"We think you're a perfect match and would be so excited to have you join our community. You'll love it."

"I'd love anywhere Katie is." He smiled with a far-off look in his eyes.

"Your advice was spot on with Regi, so I think you'll get the answer you want when you talk with Kate."

Spence's blue eyes sparkled. "Glad to hear it's working out for you two. I figured as much when Kate said you were both here."

"Yeah, Friday night Regi invited me over for dinner and told me she was ready to leave Cam in the past," Nate smiled.

"Good for you. Now wish me luck," said Spence, getting up.

Nate took out his phone to call Kyle and Spence went to check on the girls. Nate returned to the room and found Molly dressed and sitting in a wheelchair, ready to go. "Kyle's on his way here."

"We're still waiting for the discharge paperwork," said Regi, slumping into a chair. There was a knock on the door and they looked up to see a woman with a badge around her neck. "Hi, folks, I'm Detective Stewart. I was hoping to catch you before you left." She glanced over and caught Spence's eye. "Hey, Captain, good to see you."

Spence acknowledged her and then suggested they use the conference room down the hall. Nate pushed Molly and Regi asked Spence to come with them. Once they were seated, the detective pulled out her notebook and a file folder. "How are you feeling today, Molly?"

"Better, thanks."

"You remember me from last night, right?"

Molly bobbed her head.

"We've been interviewing students who attended the party you went to last night and with your description and what we've learned we've got a suspect. I was hoping you would take a look at these photos. If you recognize the person who attacked you, I need you to point him out. Okay?"

Molly nodded and said, "I understand."

The detective opened the folder to reveal a set of six photos of similar men. Molly bent over and carefully studied the collection of photos. They saw her falter when she reached the fourth photo. She scanned the next two photos and then raised her head, "It's number four."

The detective asked her to look again to make sure she had the right person.

Molly did as she was told and considered all six photos again. "I'm sure, it's number four."

"Great, Molly, thank you. I've got all of your contact information, so I'll be in touch as soon as we have news." She handed Regi a card. "Here's my contact info."

As she turned she looked back and gave Spence a slight nod. As soon as the door closed, it opened again and a cheery nurse came in with a bundle of paperwork. "I just need some signatures and then you're all free to go. There's a young man, Kyle, out in the hall waiting for you."

The nurse went over the discharge instructions, including the follow up appointment for next week and gave copies of everything to Regi. She gave her an icepack for the road. "I'll wheel you downstairs. The driver can just pull up in the loading zone and we'll get Molly out of here," she said.

Spence took them to the marina and saw them safely aboard Steve's boat. "I'll see all of you soon, maybe even next week," he said. "I'll give you a call tonight with any updates."

Steve had them back on the island in no time and they had to wake Molly up when they docked. Jeff and Sam were waiting at the marina in her SUV. They offered to transport Molly and Regi, and Murphy was in the back in her crate.

Nate dropped Kyle at his grandmother's with a hug and thanks before stopping back at Regi's to help her get Molly settled. He met Sam and Jeff coming down the walk as he was parking. "Poor Molly, her injuries look so painful," said Sam, near tears. Jeff put his arm around her and pulled her close.

"It's been a lot for Regi to handle. Molly's holding up and has been amazing. Right before we left the hospital the detective came to see Molly with photos and she picked out the man who did this to her. From the look the detective gave Spence, Molly picked the right suspect."

"I hope they lock him up and she never has to see him again," said Sam. "You let Regi know if she has to work next week, Molly could come and stay with us."

"Anything they need, just call and consider it done," added Jeff. "Murphy is in there terrorizing them now, so if she gets to be too much, I can come and get her."

"Thank you both so much. Regi said she's fortunate to have such wonderful friends to help at a time like this. Becky was great to let us stay. I'll talk to you guys later," said Nate, jogging up the pathway with their luggage.

He rang the bell, not wanting to startle them by barging in. He heard footsteps and Regi opened the door. "You didn't have to wait on the step," she said, the dark circles under her eyes taking on a purple hue.

"I wasn't sure if you wanted me to stay over and help or just get out of your hair," said Nate, pointing at his duffle.

"Could you stay tonight?" she asked, yawning. "I'm exhausted and don't trust myself to be alert enough to help her if she needs it."

"Sure, I'm happy to stay," he said, following her into the living room. "I'll just put this in your bedroom."

He heard Regi and her daughter talking and detoured to Molly's room after stashing his bag. "How's the patient?"

Molly was snuggled in her bed and Regi was sitting on the edge, running her fingers through Molly's hair. "I'm doing okay, just super tired."

"Are you girls hungry?" asked Nate.

Molly wrinkled her nose and winced. "A little."

"I could eat something," said Regi.

"I'll go get something and we have cake in the fridge for dessert. What sounds good? Pizza or Chinese or soup?"

"I think soup is probably the safest option," said Regi, and Molly nodded her agreement.

"Okay, I'll call in an order and be back in a few minutes." He called Soup D'Jour and then ran by his house for more clothes. He rang his parents, just so they knew what was going on and wouldn't worry if he wasn't home.

He returned with salads and homemade soup, plus a loaf of Ellie's fresh bread. He put together a tray for Molly and carried it down the hall to her room. Regi had fallen asleep on the pillow next to her daughter and Molly put her fingers to her lips when she saw Nate.

He tiptoed to the bed and set the tray down. "Do you need help or can you manage with your left hand?" he whispered. "I put the soup in a mug to make it easier."

"I can do it with my left hand, thanks."

He sat in the chair in the corner of the room and watched as Molly moved the mug to her mouth and tore off chunks of bread. "Mmm, yummy," she said. "I think Mom is out of it."

Nate nodded. "She didn't sleep much last night." He checked his watch and said, "You need to take a pain pill, I'll go get one for you." He crept down the hall and returned with her prescription bottle.

She finished her soup and bread and told Nate she was going to try to sleep. He collected the tray and closed her door, so they could both rest. He sat on the floor with his back against the couch and teased Murphy with one of her toys, until she got tired and collapsed in a heap on her bed.

It was getting dark and he started a fire, so the house would be cozy and warm. He turned on the television and lowered the volume. His mom had encouraged him to watch *The Inspector Lynley Mysteries* and an episode was starting. He fixed himself a dinner plate and settled in to watch the show.

As it was ending, he heard a soft knock on the door. Murphy followed him to the door and he was surprised to see Kate standing outside with a vase of flowers. "Kate, what brings you by?" He motioned her inside.

"I was just leaving the shop and Spence called to fill me in on the latest news. I thought I'd drop by and tell Regi and Molly what he shared and deliver these for Molly."

"They're both asleep in Molly's room. Have a seat and I'll put the flowers on the counter."

After sniffing Kate and getting a thorough petting, Murphy returned to her bed. Nate picked up his plate and bowl from the coffee table and offered Kate some soup. She began shaking her head and Nate said, "Come on, you haven't eaten and I need the company."

She grinned. "All right, you twisted my arm." He went in the kitchen and returned with her food and a glass of water. "I see you're a fan of this show," she said, gesturing to the television.

"I just started watching. My mom told me how great it was. PBS isn't normally my channel of choice, but I liked it. Mom was right, as usual," he grinned.

"It's one of my favorites, but I think I've seen most of them," she said, taking a spoonful of soup. "So, Spence called to let me know they arrested the man Molly identified. His name is Corey Stills. He's confident they have enough evidence to get a conviction without a trial."

Nate blew out a breath. "That would be great news. Molly is surprisingly strong, but I think a trial would be devastating for anyone who went through what she endured." He paused letting Kate finish chewing before he asked, "The detective at the hospital referred to Spence as 'Captain'. What's that about?"

Kate smiled. "Spence is a humble man. He shared he was a detective, but he retired as Captain of the Violent Crimes Division."

Nate's eyes widened with admiration. "Wow, I guess he downplayed it a bit."

"He also wants to make sure Molly talks with a counselor. He echoed what you said about her being strong, but he's afraid it's going to hit her hard later and he wants her to have all the support she needs. He said the best people for this are right at Harborview. He gave me the names of two of the finest."

"She wants to return to school after break, but I have a feeling Regi is going to balk. If she can get in with a therapist that might help Regi feel better about her going back."

"I can understand Regi's feelings. It's hard being a mother, worrying about your kids," Kate said in a quiet voice, her eyes betraying her sadness.

"How about a piece of cake?" Nate asked, hoping to bring Kate back to the present.

She blinked and focused on him. "I'll split one with you."

He returned with one plate and two forks and a slab of salted caramel chocolate cake. "I could have skipped the soup and just had dessert," smiled Kate, licking a gob of caramel from her fork.

Nate caught movement out of the corner of his eye and saw Regi. "Hey, how are you feeling?"

"Much better after some sleep, thanks. Are you two having cake?" she smiled.

"There's soup and salad in the fridge and yes, we just polished off a piece of the salted caramel."

"I'm hungry, that sounds good," she said, eyeing the fridge.

Nate jumped up. "You sit and visit with Kate and I'll fix you a plate." He gave her a hug on his way to the kitchen. "Kate brought Molly some flowers, too."

He heard Regi thank her for coming and then hushed tones of a conversation as they talked while he heated up soup and piled salad and bread on her plate. He delivered it and a glass of wine. "Would you like a glass of wine, Kate?"

She shook her head. "No, I need to get going. I just wanted to deliver the news in person." She got up and retrieved her cape from a chair. "Give me a call if you need anything."

Regi hugged Kate and thanked her for coming. "I'm sure Molly will stop by this week and see you."

"I'll look forward to it. Have a good night," she said, waving as she made her way to the door. Nate followed her out and locked up behind her.

"Good news about them arresting the creep, huh?" he asked, sitting next to Regi on the couch.

Tears pooled in her eyes. "Yeah, I'm glad that part is resolved." She took a sip of wine. "This all tastes delicious, thanks for putting it together." She tore off a chunk of bread and then gasped. "I forgot to pay Steve for his trips. I need to call him right away," she said, putting her plate down and searching for her cell phone.

Nate gripped her hands. "It's okay. Jeff told me they took care of compensating Steve for his time and fuel."

Silent teardrops cascaded down Regi's face, but she was smiling. "I've never had friends like I have here," she said. He guided her back to the couch and handed her the plate of food.

"Eat up and then we can have cake," he grinned, kissing her on the forehead.

She began eating and he tuned the television to a comedy. "Do you think I should let Molly go back to college?"

"If she wants to go, I think it's for the best. I don't know much about sexual assault, but I would think the sooner she gets back to doing her normal routine, the better off she'll be."

Regi nodded. "I'm just not sure I can let her go back there."

"With the guy in jail, she'll probably feel safer than if he was still on the loose. It's probably best to talk with one of the therapists Spence recommended."

"Yeah, he's been a great help." She ate the last of the soup and then said, "I'm really sorry our plans fell through Friday night. But, I'm so thankful you were here to help me through this." She reached up and kissed him.

"We have plenty of time to reschedule our special date. Let's just worry about getting Molly well and then you can make it up to me," he smiled, brushing his lips over hers and caressing her neck, before wrapping his arm around her and nestling her against him.

Seventeen

Early Sunday morning, a scream pierced the quiet darkness of Regi's sleep. Nate disengaged his arms that were wrapped over Regi and sprang up, running out of the bedroom. Molly's deafening shrieks made his heart pound as he hurried to her room.

In the glow of the nightlight he saw her thrashing from side to side and gently put a hand on her left arm and said, "Molly, it's okay, you're home, you're safe."

Regi rushed in and stroked her forehead. "Mol, it's Mom, wake up, honey, it's a bad dream."

Molly's eyes fluttered and opened. She was slick with sweat and breathing hard. She looked from her mom to Nate with disbelief. "Mom, oh, Mom," she cried, burying her head in Regi's shoulder.

"It's okay now. Are you in pain?" she asked. Molly nodded her head and Regi glanced at Nate.

He poured out a pain pill and held out a glass of water. "Here you go, Molly. Take one of these."

She raised her head and Regi plucked a tissue to dab her face dry, as she put the pill in her mouth and Nate brought the straw to her lips. She rested back on her pillow and let out a sigh. "Sorry, it was just so real," she trembled.

"It's okay, you're safe now," said Regi, combing Molly's hair with her fingers. "Just rest and go back to sleep." She mouthed to Nate to go back to bed, but he shook his head and held Molly's hand.

They both watched as she fell back asleep, her breathing heavy and relaxed. Nate tucked her hand inside the covers and stood up, shivering with nothing on but a pair of shorts. He moved to Regi's side and ran his hands over her shoulders. "She's asleep now," he whispered.

Regi nodded and moved a strand of hair out of Molly's face. She gripped his hand and they slipped back down the hallway. Once there they cuddled under the covers for warmth. "You better plan on taking time off this week," said Nate, hugging her close.

"I'll call today and let them know I probably won't be in all week. I need to get her in to talk to a therapist as soon as possible and she's got her follow up appointment. Linda and Max leave early Saturday morning, so I need to move my stuff over there late this week or Saturday."

He rubbed her shoulder, his fingers slipping under the strap of her silky chemise. "Don't worry about all of that. I'll move your stuff and do anything else you need." He kissed her neck and whispered, "Go to sleep for a few more hours."

* * *

The bright sunshine on Sunday morning finally woke both of them and then they heard Murphy yipping. Nate put a hand across Regi as she lifted her head from the pillow. "I'll go check."

He shuffled down the hallway and found Molly on the couch and Murphy tugging at her blanket. "Morning, Nate," she said, smiling.

"Everything okay?" he asked.

"Yeah, I feel better this morning, sore, but less groggy."

"I'll be back in a few minutes and we'll see about breakfast," said Nate, heading for the bedroom.

Regi was up, putting on her robe. "Is she okay?"

He nodded, "Molly said she's feeling better and was playing with Murphy. I thought I could go get us some breakfast after I get ready."

"I've got lots of stuff in the fridge. I'll make breakfast while you take a shower." She dashed into the bathroom on her way to the kitchen.

While Nate showered, Regi started bacon frying. She fed Murphy breakfast and took her outside. She cut off hunks of bread for cinnamon toast and by the time he was out, she had breakfast ready. Nate poured himself a cup of coffee and helped Molly to the table.

While they ate breakfast and watched in silence as Molly used her left hand to fork eggs into her mouth, Regi said, "Kate stopped by last night when you were sleeping and brought you those flowers." She pointed to the vase. "She also wanted to let us know that Spence called with an update. They arrested the man who attacked you."

Molly stopped eating. "That's great news. I'm glad." She put her fork down and munched on the cinnamon toast.

"His name is Corey Stills. He's twenty-one and a student at UW. Does that ring any bells?"

Molly shook her head. "No, I don't recognize the name. I'm pretty sure he was drunk or high." She paused and took a bite of bacon. "I'm glad he's locked up."

Regi's cell phone buzzed. She retrieved it from the charger on the counter and read a text message. "It's from Linda. She wants to make us dinner tonight and wondered if you felt like coming to her house or if she should deliver it?"

Molly turned her left side to face Regi. "Let's go to their house. I don't want to stay cooped up all week."

Regi smiled and sent a text back. "Okay, we're set for five tonight. You're coming too, Nate."

"How about we get you a shower today?" asked Regi, raising her brows at Molly.

"That sounds good, I need to wash my hair."

"I'll help you, so you don't hurt that scrape on your scalp."

"I'll take Murphy on a walk to the park while you girls get ready," said Nate, gathering the dishes from the table. "Do you need anything from the store?"

Regi shook her head. "I don't think so, but thanks." She helped Molly up and led her to the bathroom. She retrieved Molly's robe from her bedroom and ran back to the kitchen to snatch her phone and a quick kiss from Nate. She held up her phone, "Just in case."

Nate finished the dishes and then attached Murphy's bright pink leash and led her outside. They walked a few blocks before Murphy quit tugging and settled down to match Nate's rhythm. He walked in front of Harbor Coffee and Books and saw Kyle waving at him from the counter. The store was empty, so he led Murphy through the door.

"Hey, Nate, how's Molly doing?"

"Much better today." He spied Zoe's dog bed in the corner and led Murphy over to it. "Sit, Murphy, sit. Good girl," he said, as she settled into the bed.

Kyle brought him a mocha and pulled out a chair at the table nearest Murphy. "I wanted to come by and see her, but didn't want to intrude." He shook his head. "I can't believe what happened."

"We heard last night that they arrested the guy. He's a student—Corey Stills. Do you know him?"

Kyle shook his head. "No, I've never heard the name before." He looked down at the table. "I should've gone to that party with her. She asked me to go, but I didn't feel like it and wanted to relax in my room."

"You found her near the library, right?"

"Yeah, I got a call from her and could barely hear anything. I just thought she said garden by the library. So, I grabbed a flashlight and took off running. I found her on the edge of the garden area across the way from the library. I took one look at her and called 911."

"I'm glad you were able to get to her so quickly." Nate took a sip of mocha.

"All I had was my jacket to wrap her up. It was horrible waiting for them to come."

"She's lucky you were there, Kyle," said Nate. "Don't 'what if' yourself crazy."

Kyle nodded. "I know. I just wished I would've gone with her or she had walked home with a friend."

"When I get back, I'll ask her about visiting, okay?"

Kyle smiled, "That would be great. I can help her when we go back to school—with anything she needs."

"I'll let her know. We better get going, I promised Murphy she could play in the park," Nate said, reaching for the leash. He waved as they crossed the street to the park.

He let Murphy run and play catch with the ball he had stashed in his pocket. He texted Regi while they played to suggest Molly invite Kyle to go to dinner with them tonight, letting her know he was worried about her.

After almost two hours, Nate decided it was safe to venture back to the condo. He figured they would both be showered and ready. He let himself in with the spare key and deposited Murphy on her bed. He found Regi in Molly's room. Molly was on the bed, but dressed and on top of the covers.

"How was the shower?"

Molly smiled, her auburn hair shiny. "It felt good, but I'm tired."

Regi turned and said, "She's going to take a nap, so she'll be ready for dinner. She sent Kyle a text and invited him to join us tonight." She winked at Nate before turning back to Molly. "You get some rest and we'll be sure and wake you in time to get to Linda's."

Nate pulled a blanket over her and he and Regi went out in the living room. "I called work and they told me to take off whenever I need to this week. I'll call tomorrow for an appointment with the therapist," said Regi.

"If you organize what you need to take to Linda's I'll move it all after work on Friday. You're going to be tied up at her appointment Friday anyway."

"Yeah, I'm not sure what will happen Friday. If she's determined to go to school on Monday, I don't think it makes much sense for her to come to the island Friday night." She strummed her fingers on her knee. "I know I can't make her stay here, but I'm anxious about her going back to school. I feel better that the dirt bag is in jail, but I'm still worried."

"Did you call your parents and let them know?"

She shook her head. "I meant to yesterday, but forgot. I'll go do it now." She went in her bedroom and shut the door.

* * *

They had a relaxing evening at Linda's with Max grilling chicken and steaks. Kyle joined the party and spent a lot of time huddled by the fire pit with Molly. Regi saw them both laughing and it made her smile.

While Max and Linda were in the kitchen, Nate asked, "How did it go with your mom and dad?"

Regi rolled her eyes and shrugged. "They're upset and worried, but somehow my mom drove home the point that this was my fault for letting her go to college in a big city and this wouldn't have happened if she had gone to school in Ellensburg." She took a sip of wine. "I had to remind her that Molly's a grown girl and made her own choice about college and I supported her in that choice." She took another drink, "That's why I wasn't in a hurry to talk to them—my mom has a way of making me feel worse, as if I wasn't already blaming myself."

Nate took her hand in his, "It's not your fault, or Molly's, or Kyle's. He's holding himself responsible for not going to the party with Molly. It's that son of a bitch who attacked her—that's the person to blame."

Regi nodded, her eyes stinging and her throat dry. "I just want to keep her safe," she whispered.

Nate glanced out at the patio and saw Kyle engaged in a conversation, using his hands, making motions in the air, while Molly watched and laughed at the punchline. "Look out there. She's going to be okay. Her wounds will heal and the therapist will help her heal inside. You're a good mom, Regi. Stop beating yourself up—this isn't on you."

She sniffed and finished off the glass of wine. Linda came into the great room with a tray of dessert. Nate eyed the selection and said, "Let the kids choose first." Linda proceeded to the patio and was relieved of several brownies and ice cream. Max joined them in front of the fireplace and offered everyone wine, tea, or coffee. Nate took a mug of coffee and Regi let Max refill her glass.

Nate bit into a chewy chocolate chip cookie and said, "So, if Regi ends up staying in Seattle this weekend, I'll stay at the house and take care of Lucy and Murphy. I'll come over Friday after work with her things."

"That's fine with us," said Max. "I'm so sorry our trip is in the midst of all of this."

Regi shook her head. "It'll be fine. If I need to be in Seattle with Molly, Nate promised to cover your house."

Linda sipped her tea, watching Molly on the patio. "She's unwavering in her desire to return to school. She's stronger than I would be."

"I'm going to be a nervous wreck," said Regi. "I understand why she wants to go to school, but the mom in me wants to wrap her in bubble wrap and keep her locked in her room."

Max chuckled. "That's understandable. Maybe you should think about talking to a counselor. You're dealing with anxiety issues of your own." Regi nodded and he continued, "I've heard good things about a woman here in Friday Harbor. I'll get the information for you from the hospital."

They visited a bit longer and then Nate said they better get going, since he had to work in the morning. He went out to tell Molly it was time to go and Kyle rushed to her chair to help her to the car. As he made sure she got in the Jeep without bumping her arm, Regi engulfed him in a hug.

"I didn't thank you properly for rescuing my Molly. You're my hero, Kyle. If you hadn't been paying attention and got there when you did, this could have been much worse. Plus your quick action got the police looking for this jerk early. I owe you everything," she said, gripping his arm.

Kyle shook his head. "I just wish I had been with her and this wouldn't have happened."

"Let's make a pact. You don't blame yourself and I won't blame myself, okay?" she smiled.

He grinned back at her, "I'll try." He waved at Molly through the window. "I'm going back to school Saturday morning, so if she needs anything let me know."

Linda and Max waved from the driveway as Nate guided the Jeep down the road, followed by the distinctive taillights of the old Cadillac Kyle borrowed from his grandma.

"Be sure and get Regi the information on the therapist. She's going to need all the help she can get," said Linda, squeezing Max's hand.

Nate parked the Jeep and helped Molly inside. They settled Molly in her bedroom and tucked her in for the night. "You're welcome to stay the night," said Regi, when she saw Nate carrying his duffle from her bedroom.

"I was planning to go home, unless you need me tonight."

"We'll be okay, but I couldn't have done it without you." She plopped on the couch. "I'm going to turn in early, I'm worn out."

"Call me if you need anything. I've got an early morning, but we could meet up for lunch tomorrow."

"It's a date," she smiled. "I'll text you tomorrow once I figure out what we're doing. Come by for dinner, though. I've got tons of food that we need to eat this week."

"You get to bed," he kissed her on the forehead. "You need to catch up on your rest."

She clutched his hand as he reached for the duffle. "Thanks again for everything you've done for us. I'm sorry our weekend didn't work out the way we had hoped."

"I'll cash in my rain check, soon," he grinned, gripping her shoulders and kissing her hard enough to leave them both breathless.

"After Molly's settled back at school, we'll try a do-over," she smiled.

She followed him to the door, where they kissed again and she watched him get in his truck. She flicked the lock on the door and turned out the light, smiling as she wandered down the hall to her bedroom. After changing and cleansing her face, she crawled into bed, her feet creeping over to Nate's side of the bed, remembering the comfort she had felt with him beside her. She sniffed his pillow and was greeted with the lingering scent of spice and lemon. *I miss him already,* she thought, as she hugged his pillow to her chest.

Eighteen

Early Monday morning, Regi was roused from a sound sleep by Molly's screams. Her heart pounding, she raced to Molly's room and found her writhing and shouting, much as she had Sunday. She calmed her down and got her back to sleep, but Regi stayed up, drinking coffee, worrying about how Molly was going to get through this.

Regi called Monday morning and was able to get Molly an appointment on Friday with Dr. Pierce, the therapist Spence recommended. That meant she wouldn't have to go back to the city until Friday morning. She called Becky to thank her for her hospitality and ask about staying over Friday night and Saturday night, if necessary. As usual, Becky offered her house and told her she was welcome anytime. Both of Becky's children were home for a visit from college, but would be flying out Friday night, so she had plenty of room for Regi and Molly.

As soon as she disconnected from Becky, Max called with the information for the therapist in Friday Harbor. "Her name is Dr. Cummings and she has an opening today, if you want to see her." He gave her the number and she thanked him and hung up the phone.

She sipped her coffee, wavering between calling and waiting until Molly was back at college. *Crap, I'm off today, I should just go and see what she has to say. Maybe she could help me figure out how to ease Molly's nightmares.* She picked up the phone and made an appointment for two o'clock.

She peeked in on Molly, confirming she was still asleep. Regi hustled to the shower and got herself ready, so she'd be done before Molly needed the bathroom. Her stomach rumbled and she surveyed the fridge and took out the fixings for omelets, thinking the smell of breakfast would entice Molly from bed.

As the bacon finished frying and she chopped it up to add to the egg mixture, Molly slipped into a chair at the counter. "How are you?" asked Regi, pouring the eggs into a pan.

"Better today. Sorry, I woke you up again."

"Don't worry about it. Are you ready for a bacon and cheese omelet?" She looked at Molly and noticed her right eye was open. Her bruises had lost their redness and were now an inky black. "Hey, your eye looks better."

Molly nodded, "Yeah, I can see out of it." She pressed her fingers around it and said, "It's much less tender today."

"I told Nate we could meet him for lunch, but if you don't feel up to it, we don't have to go. I invited him to dinner tonight here."

"You go to lunch. I'll hang out here," said Molly, helping her butter their toast.

"I don't want to leave you alone."

"Mom," she moaned, elongating the word. "I'll be fine. I'll watch television and play with Murphy, which is what I planned to do on my break anyway."

Regi brought the plates to the counter. "Okay, I've got an appointment at two, so I'll see if he can meet at one for lunch and I'll be home after that."

After breakfast, Regi offered to help Molly shower, but she insisted on doing it herself. Regi left the door open a crack and sat on her bed, listening for a sign of distress. It took Molly longer than normal, but she emerged looking refreshed and alert, dressed in jeans and a shirt.

"I forgot to tell you, I called and you have an appointment with the therapist on Friday after your other follow up appointment, so we can take care of all of them at once. Becky said we can stay with her on Friday night."

"Okay, sounds like a plan. My roommate will be back on Saturday, so I won't be alone. I know you're worried Mom, but I'll be okay. Kyle already volunteered to walk me anywhere I need to go at night."

Regi smiled at her, swallowing her last bite. "He's a good friend. I'll do my best not to worry. Promise me, if you change your mind after you get there, you'll say so and call me. I'll come back and get you."

"I promise, but I'll be okay. They caught the creep."

Regi cleaned up the dishes while Molly fixed her hair. Murphy was trotting back and forth to the door, signaling she needed to go outside. Regi attached her leash and pocketed her cell phone, hollering out to Molly, "Be back in a minute, just taking Murphy out."

Murphy led her around the condo buildings and down the street on her quest for the perfect spot. Regi's cell phone rang while they were heading home. "Hi, Spence."

"Hey, Regi. I'm calling with some good news with regard to the suspect they have in custody. I told Detective Stewart, I'd let you know, but you can call her with any questions. Bottom line is no trial will be necessary. They have enough evidence to convict and he admitted to the attack. So, it will be up to the court system now, but Molly won't have to testify."

Regi let out a breath and felt the tension ease in her shoulders. "That's great news, Spence. Do you think we should go to the court proceeding?"

"That's up to you. Some victims need to go to see the end result and others don't want anything to do with it. Talk to Molly's therapist and you'll get a better idea. He won't be sentenced for several weeks, even months down the road. He's still in jail, by the way."

"Okay, thanks again, Spence. We'll be in the city on Friday. I got Molly in with Dr. Pierce."

"You'll like her. How about I take you two ladies to dinner Friday night?"

"We'd love it. I'll call you as soon as we're free. I'm planning to stay at Becky's Friday night, so we won't be in a rush."

"Perfect, I can pick you up, just text me."

She disconnected, thankful Murphy was paying attention and led the way home. She saw Molly was on the couch engrossed in a movie. She gave Murphy a treat, after which the puppy bounced onto the couch to nuzzle with Molly. "Make sure she's on a blanket, Mol."

She sent Nate a text to let him know about her appointment and lunch and started going through a stack of mail. He replied back and said he'd meet her for lunch at Big Tony's. She wanted to tell Molly what Spence had reported, but hated to bring up the ordeal. She decided to wait until she saw Dr. Pierce and get her advice. She busied herself rummaging through her recipe box. "What sounds good for dinner tonight?"

"Give me some choices."

"I've got chicken I need to use."

"How about stir fry teriyaki chicken?"

Regi checked the fridge and cupboards and found she had everything she needed for the dish. She did a couple loads of laundry and joined Molly to watch part of her movie marathon.

She made Molly a grilled cheese sandwich for lunch and took Murphy out before leaving to meet Nate. "Tomorrow is the day I normally go to lunch with Leon. I haven't told him anything about what happened. Think about it and let me know if you want to go to lunch with us or we could have him over. Whatever you want."

Molly nodded, engrossed in the television. "Okay, I'll think about it."

She kissed her forehead and locked the door. She elected to walk the few blocks to the harbor, soaking in the sunny day. She didn't see Nate's delivery truck outside, so went ahead and ordered the lunch buffet and got them a booth.

Nate arrived a few minutes later and slid in next to her. "I ordered, so we can go to the buffet whenever you want."

He grabbed his plate and waited for her to climb out of the booth. "It's been a busy morning," he said, filling his plate with salad and slices of warm pizza. "How's Molly?"

They reclaimed their spots in the booth and she said, "Another nightmare early this morning, but fine after that. She wanted to stay home and watch movies."

"Maybe the doctor will have a solution for the nightmares."

She nodded, pulling a string of cheese off her slice. "We have an appointment on Friday, so I thought I'd take the ferry and stay overnight at Becky's." She relayed Spence's phone call while they finished lunch.

"That's terrific news about the trial. I hope the guy rots in prison for the rest of his life."

"I'm curious to see if Molly wants to go to the sentencing or ignore it. I'm nervous to bring anything up about it until I get an expert opinion."

"I'm no help there either." He finished off his pizza and stacked their plates on the table. "Friday I'll swing by and pick up your stuff and take it to Linda's. You should be home Saturday, right?"

"Yeah, if all goes well. Molly's roommate is back Saturday and so is Kyle."

"Maybe this weekend I'll collect on that rain check," he said, wiggling his brows suggestively.

She smiled. "That could be arranged."

* * *

Regi sat in the waiting room at the hospital, a bit early for her appointment with Dr. Cummings. She was ushered into her office minutes before her scheduled time and was greeted by a woman close to her age. "Hi, Regina, I'm Dr. Cummings," she said, offering her a seat.

"Call me Regi, please," she said, choosing a comfy looking fabric chair.

Dr. Cummings took a seat across from her and began by asking her questions about what brought her to the office. She was dressed in a casual manner, but still looked professional. Rather than writing notes, she just listened to Regi.

Regi explained Molly's attack and her anxiety related to Molly's desire to return to school next week. The doctor asked more questions about Molly's father and Regi's support system, including her parents. Regi found herself baring her soul with regard to her pregnancy, the promise she and Cam made to each other, Leon, her parents, and Ronnie's death. Everything bubbled out of her like an active hot spring.

Dr. Cummings reinforced Regi's decision to move on with her life and leave Cam in the past and she was happy to learn Molly was scheduled to see Dr. Pierce. She explained that Regi was suffering from post-traumatic stress disorder, as was Molly.

"I don't believe in medications, unless absolutely necessary, so I focus on cognitive therapy, which involves talking. Dr. Pierce may talk about something called Imagery Rehearsal Therapy for Molly's nightmares. It's a way of coming up with an alternate ending for the nightmares she's experiencing and can be quite effective."

Regi nodded and asked what she thought about sharing the legal outcome of the arrest with Molly. "I would tell her. I don't think she has to make a decision right away, but let her know what's happening so she feels in control."

The doctor gave her some mental exercises along with relaxation techniques and set her up with an appointment twice a week for the next several weeks, beginning on Thursday.

She practiced some of the breathing techniques on her walk home and felt better by the time she reached the condo. When she arrived, she found Kyle visiting with Molly on the couch. He had delivered her a drink and they were watching another movie.

"Hi, Regi. I brought you a coffee and left it in the kitchen. I just got here, so it should still be warm."

"Thanks, Kyle. How are you doing, Molly?"

"Great, I feel better today."

"Okay, I'll leave you two and get to work on dinner. Can you stay for dinner, Kyle?"

"Oh, I can't tonight. I've got plans with Grandma, but thanks."

Regi sipped the coffee while she got things ready to prepare dinner. She wandered back into the living room during a commercial and decided to tell Molly about Spence's call while Kyle was here. "Spence called and has an update on the man they arrested."

Molly muted the television and turned her attention to her mother. "They have enough evidence to convict him and he confessed to the attack, so there won't be a trial. He'll be sentenced, but that could take weeks or months. So you won't have to testify."

Molly smiled and Kyle patted her knee. "That's great news. I'm relieved not to have to go to court and have to go through the whole thing again."

"I know, I'm thankful for that. Spence said we could choose to go to court for the sentencing or not, it would be up to us. We have time to think about it."

"Okay, I'll give it some thought. Right now, I'm not sure I want to, but I was mostly worried about testifying. It might be good to see him punished."

"It might. We'll see how it goes," said Regi, getting up to get back to her kitchen work. As she went to work chopping veggies, a wave of relief coursed over her. *That went well. One less thing to worry about.*

* * *

Regi decided to go to work on Tuesday and Wednesday, since Molly seemed to be doing better and was happy to veg out in front of the television. Thursday, she and Molly were having lunch with Kate at the shop and then Molly would stay there while Regi went to her appointment with Dr. Cummings.

She steeled herself for work on Tuesday morning and was thankful she hadn't been awakened by one of Molly's nightmares. She left Molly sleeping and got to work early, hoping to avoid people and questions.

With the exception of Robin and Crystal, everyone who came by Regi's office was warm and sincere in their sympathetic words. Robin and Crystal were nosy and inconsiderate, looking for fodder to feed their never-ending gossip. Regi kept things brief by saying that Molly had been attacked Friday night and the police had already caught the person responsible and she was doing well.

She was glad to have a pile of work on her desk to keep her occupied and as a convenient excuse to usher people out of her office. She texted and called Molly a few times during the day to check on her and was relieved all was well. She cancelled with Leon and lunched on leftovers from last night at her desk and by the time she left on Tuesday, she had depleted the stack of files and folders on her desk.

She had made soup in the slow cooker before she left for work, so she and Molly enjoyed it and a fresh loaf of bread from Ellie's for dinner. Nate was having dinner with his parents, but called to check on Molly before she went to bed. She called Leon and with Molly's permission gave him the highlights of the weekend.

Jeff called and told her when Steve heard she was going back to Seattle he insisted he take them over Friday morning. "He's going to be taking Kyle back on Saturday, so he can easily pick you up and bring you home. He doesn't mind and it would save you some time."

"I hate to take advantage of his kindness."

"Don't be silly. He wouldn't offer if he couldn't do it. I'll call him and tell him you'll be at the marina around ten, okay?"

"Okay, thanks, Jeff." She hung up marveling at the kindness of this community she had come to think of as her own.

The next two days saw more improvement in Molly's soreness and her bruises had faded to a hideous green color. She had fun spending time at Kate's shop Thursday afternoon and enjoyed the lunch Kate had provided from Lou's. She stayed up in Kate's office, not wanting to have to interact with or explain her injuries to any customers.

Thursday night Nate stopped by with ice cream from Shaw's and went over the items he was supposed to take to Linda's. "You're looking much better, Molly," he said, handing her a container of maple walnut ice cream.

"I feel much better today, not near as sore. I think I might be able to put some makeup on tomorrow and hide some of the bruising."

"I'm glad you're doing well." He took a bite of his rocky road and watched as Regi scooped up her strawberry.

After they finished off the frozen treats and watched some comedies, Nate got up to leave. "Jeff said he talked you into letting Steve take you over. Just call and let me know what time you'll be home Saturday." He followed Regi to the kitchen with the dishes.

"I'll know more after Friday's appointments. We're going to dinner with Spence, so when we get back, I'll call you. I don't want to keep Steve waiting, so will plan to leave as soon as he arrives with Kyle Saturday afternoon."

He brushed her hair back from her cheek and skimmed his lips over hers. "I'm looking forward to our weekend." Then he pressed her against the fridge and greedily kissed her on the mouth. "You seem like you're doing better these last couple of days."

She smiled. "Dr. Cummings is helping me with some exercises. Molly's doing better, so that helps."

"Call me if you need anything, okay?"

She nodded, giving him a quick peck. He caressed her jaws with his thumbs and with one long kiss relayed his thoughts.

"I'll walk you out," she said, as Nate gave Molly a soft pat on the head and told her goodbye.

"Thanks for staying with us, Nate. I'll see you soon," said Molly, waving as he walked to the front door.

Regi saw him out, sneaking in one more kiss before he drove away. *Saturday's going to be great,* she thought, running back to the door in her socks.

* * *

Friday morning arrived and Regi was thankful for Steve's offer of transport. Molly had a nightmare after midnight and Regi hadn't gotten back to sleep until almost five o'clock. It was a good day not to be driving, tired as she was. Regi helped Molly dab on a bit of concealer to hide the worst of the bruising on her face. Jeff picked up Murphy and wished them a safe trip.

Steve had them at the marina before lunch and they found Becky waiting. Steve told Regi he'd see her tomorrow around noon, but would be in touch to confirm. He helped load their luggage into Becky's SUV. She drove them to her house and introduced them to her son and daughter, Andy and Chloe. She had arranged for lunch on their deck overlooking Puget Sound.

"This is gorgeous, Becky. Thanks for having us here for lunch." She glanced over at Molly, engaged in a conversation with the other two college students.

"My pleasure. We're taking the kids to dinner and the airport tonight, but I'll leave you with a spare key in case you need to get in the house before we're back," Becky said, handing her a key on a pink rhinestone key ring.

Regi put it in her pocket and said, "I'm not sure when we'll finish up, but Spence offered to pick us up, so we're set. I should be out of your hair by tomorrow afternoon."

"It's fun having company. I just wish it were under happier circumstances. Sam said you'll be staying at Linda's while they're away on their honeymoon. I'm so happy for them."

"They're both so excited about the trip. I think it will be fantastic and they deserve it. They, along with Sam and Jeff, are some of the kindest people I've ever met. Molly and I couldn't have made it through this without all of you and Nate, of course."

"I saw him at the wedding. He's a cutie pie," she winked.

"He is," she smiled. "And a great guy, on top of it."

"I know you'll worry about Molly, but I plan to have her over for dinner every week and you make sure my numbers are in her cell phone. She could call and stay over with us anytime she wants to."

Regi nodded, her throat thick with emotion. She clasped Becky's hand and managed a heartfelt "Thank you, Becky," without crying.

Becky took note of the time and suggested she get them to the hospital. Andy and Chloe stayed behind to clean up the lunch mess and make sure they were packed for the trip back to college.

Becky hugged Molly and Regi goodbye when she dropped them at the entrance and told Molly she expected her for dinner next week and would be calling her to figure out the best day. "Kyle's welcome to come, if he's free," she added.

Molly hugged her back. "Thanks, I'd love to come for dinner and I'll check with Kyle tomorrow."

Regi and Molly found their way to Dr. Wilson's office and Molly went in by herself and the nurse said they'd call Regi back as soon as the doctor finished her exam. Regi flipped through a magazine while she practiced her breathing exercises. Before long, a nurse beckoned her through the patient door.

She met Molly and Dr. Wilson in her office. "Molly tells me to call you Regi," she said, motioning her to a chair.

"That's right, thank you. How's she doing?"

"Molly's healing and everything is on track. She'll start some physical therapy on her shoulder next week. Molly wanted me to share all the results of our exam with you. We did a pregnancy test and it came back negative." She glanced at Molly. "Based on the timing, there is almost no chance of a pregnancy, so that's great news."

Regi smiled at Molly, while she twisted the handle of her purse in her lap.

"She needs to finish out her antibiotics and follow up with HIV testing. The attacker was tested and was negative, but we'll follow the protocols and continue testing Molly for several months. Again, I think the chance of HIV is low."

"So, that takes care of the physical concerns. I also explained to Molly that there is a sexual abuse fund that will cover all the costs of her treatments here, including any therapy she gets, so you won't have to worry about costs. The system eventually goes after the perpetrator for reimbursement, but even if he never pays, your costs are covered."

Regi's shoulders relaxed. She hadn't even thought about costs, but was glad to hear about the program.

"Molly tells me she's set up to see Dr. Pierce today. She's a wonderful doctor who has experience with these situations. So, outside of any questions you two may have, I'll only see Molly again after her physical therapy is completed so I can check her shoulder."

Regi looked at Molly. "Any questions?"

Molly shook her head.

"I don't have any either. Thank you for taking such good care of her and taking the time to speak with us."

"You're most welcome. I'm especially glad they caught the attacker," Dr. Wilson grinned. "If you need anything, Molly, just call my office and we'll get you in." She stood and shook hands with both of them.

They checked out at the front desk and were given the name of the physical therapist and the first appointment for Monday next week. Molly entered the information in her phone before they left the office.

"Okay, kiddo. We've got a few minutes to find Dr. Pierce's office. They rode the elevator and located the office with time to spare.

As soon as they checked in Molly was led to an office and Regi said she'd be in the waiting room. The nurse told her the appointment would be at least two hours and she was welcome to leave and come back. She sat down and thumbed through her phone. She sent Spence a text and told him they'd need a ride from the hospital and she'd text back when they were done.

She saw a magazine rack on the wall and picked out a few to take to her chair. When she returned to her seat, she noticed a man in a suit sitting in the chair next to hers. As she glanced up to meet his face, she gasped, the slippery magazines slid from her hands. "Cam Foster, is that you?"

Steel blue eyes identical to Molly's stared back at her, "Regi?"

Nineteen

His dark hair was more salt than pepper and he was thin, with a drawn face, but she would have recognized his eyes and his smile anywhere. "It's me," she said, her heart pounding in her chest. "What are you doing here?"

He gave her a feeble smile. "I'm waiting for my appointment. My doctor's running late, but I don't have anywhere else to be, so I'm waiting it out."

Oh, no maybe he's ill. "Oh, I'm sorry, I didn't mean to pry. I'm just shocked to see you."

"Yeah, what's it been, like over twenty years, right?"

She nodded. *I guess he doesn't remember our little promise.*

"Are you waiting for your appointment?" he asked.

"Uh, no, I'm waiting for my daughter."

His smile brightened. "How old is she?"

"She just turned twenty-one. She's a student here."

"That's wonderful. Twenty-one, wow, you didn't waste any time did you?"

Regi shrugged. *Do the math, Cam.* "What about you, do you have kids?"

Dark clouds blurred over his eyes and his face grew slack. "Oh, Regi, it's a long story and part of the reason I'm here." He paused and cleared his throat. "I had a daughter, Isabella. She was eight years old and died in a car accident last year."

Regi brought her hand to her mouth. "Oh, Cam, I'm so very sorry."

"My wife, Elise, was driving. She never really got the whole parent thing and wanted to be Isabella's friend. She didn't want to ever make her mad, so when Isabella didn't want to wear her seatbelt, Elise let her be. Then they got in a wreck and my daughter didn't survive. She was ejected and died at the scene."

Regi took Cam's hand in hers. "I don't know what to say."

With watery eyes he looked at her, "I don't know what to do."

She held his hand for several minutes, saying nothing and then asked, "How's your wife?"

"She's gone. I lost her around Christmas. She couldn't deal with the guilt anymore and committed suicide," he said, speaking like a reporter, without emotion.

Regi sucked in a breath. "Oh, I'm sorry to have asked, Cam."

He shook his head. "Don't be. I'm here trying to figure out how to move forward and it helps to vocalize what has happened."

"Has your doctor been a help to you?"

"Yeah, he's great. I've only been coming for about three weeks, but I'm making slow progress." He released her hand. "So, what are you doing and where do you live?"

"I moved to Friday Harbor this past summer and I work at the high school and at a local coffee shop on weekends and during breaks. I've been a school secretary since I was in my mid-twenties."

"Friday Harbor, that brings back some warm memories," he said, with a faraway look in his eyes and a small smile on his lips.

"I like it there and have met some incredible friends."

"What's going on with your daughter?"

"Well, it's a long story as well. It's not easy for me to talk about yet, but Molly was attacked on campus last weekend. So, this is her first appointment to try to deal with the aftermath of being, uh, raped."

"Regi, I'm so sorry for you and Molly. How horrific for both of you. How's your husband handling it?"

"I'm not married."

"Oh, man, I'm sorry." She saw the wheels turning in his head. "You said your daughter's twenty-one?"

"Yes, that's right."

They were interrupted by a chubby nurse announcing, "Mr. Foster," at the front desk.

Cam looked at Regi and then looked at the nurse. "I, uh, I think we need to talk some more." He fumbled in his wallet and pulled out a card and wrote on the back before handing it to her. "Please call me later tonight. I'll meet you anywhere, anytime."

She took the card and looked into his eyes. "I'm leaving tomorrow, so I'm not sure if I'll have time."

"Mr. Foster," said the nurse, with an indignant tone.

Cam stepped away from Regi. "Please call me, Regi." Then he sprinted toward the nurse and disappeared behind the door.

Regi sat anchored to her seat, dumbfounded by the exchange with Cam. She knew she had to have a conversation with him eventually. She spent the next hour running through her options. She could arrange to talk with him while she was here or talk to him when she got home. She couldn't ignore him and knew she wouldn't be hard to locate, even if she tried to dodge him. *I really don't need this right now. I should probably talk to him while I'm here, since I don't want him to show up on the island. I can't tell Molly anything yet. I'll have to arrange to meet him after we get settled in at Becky's tonight.*

She was jolted from her thoughts by the same chubby nurse who paged Cam. "Ms. Brady," she bellowed. Regi piled the magazines on a table and clutched her purse as she hurried to the desk.

She led her through the door and to a conference room where she found Molly waiting for her. "Are you okay, Mom? You look super pale."

Regi did her best to mask her shock and focused on Molly. "I'm fine, just a bit tired."

Dr. Pierce came through the door and introduced herself. She wore her gray hair in a loose bun and looked more like a grandmother than a doctor. "I wanted to meet Molly's mom, since I understand you don't live here.

I've told Molly I want to see her twice a week and more often if she needs me. I wanted to assure you that what Molly is going through is perfectly normal. I've given her some techniques to try to help with the nightmares and we'll be working on some other things as we progress."

She smiled at Molly. "I think Molly's going to get through this without any lasting problems. She's smart and tough and we'll work together until she's feeling better. I suspect she'll see me for several months. There may be a time in the future where we include you in one of our meetings. Are you open to attending?"

Regi nodded. "Of course, just let me know."

"Do you have any other questions or concerns?"

"I'm mostly concerned about her returning to school. I worry about her safety. I'm trying not to and seeing a therapist in Friday Harbor."

"That's excellent, I'm glad you're talking with someone. Your feelings of anxiety and concern for her safety are perfectly normal. After spending time with Molly today, I feel she's strong enough to return to school. She has a robust support system in Kyle and her roommate, plus your friend Becky, and Captain Chandler. You couldn't ask for a better man to have on your side. I'm confident she'll do fine and if she starts to feel anxious she has tools, plus my phone number."

Regi liked Dr. Pierce. She had a matter of fact way of talking and didn't make her feel inadequate. She trusted her opinion and began to feel less apprehensive about leaving Molly at school. "Okay, I feel better hearing that."

"Rest assured, even though Molly is an adult, she's given me permission to call you if she could benefit from having you here or talking with you. So, if anything gets too tough for her to handle, I'll give you a call."

Regi nodded, "Thank you so much. If I can do anything to help, please let me know."

Dr. Pierce stood, shaking both their hands and told Molly to check in at the front desk and get her appointment schedule. Regi remained behind and Dr. Pierce provided her with a business card. "This has my cell and emergency number on it. If Molly calls you and you think she needs help, call day or night. I'm trying to rebuild her confidence and her main support will be coming from me as she gets through this, but she may gravitate to you. It's going to be hard for you to respond, especially from a distance, so feel free to call me if you feel you're in over your head."

Regi took the card. "We haven't talked about the actual attack in any detail. I've been afraid to bring it up. She's been so strong throughout all of this and I haven't wanted to risk it."

The doctor nodded, putting a hand on Regi's shoulder. "The best news is she doesn't see herself as a victim, so we're not combatting that. She fought back against this jerk and since they caught him, she's not fearful. It's mostly the nightmares and anything else that decides to crop up as she returns to her normal schedule. Not to worry, we'll get through this. She'll talk to you about it when she's ready. Right now it's easier to talk to a stranger."

Regi thanked her again and met Molly at the front desk, punching in her appointments in her phone. "Okay, ready for some dinner with Spence?"

Molly smiled. "Yep, almost done."

Regi texted Spence and told him they'd wait in the loading zone for him. They spent their time people watching. Regi sat on a bench, the encounter with Cam replaying in her head. She felt his card in her pocket, the weight of it like an anchor.

* * *

Spence treated them to a lovely dinner along the waterfront. Molly quizzed him about his children and he filled her in on their status. His oldest son was a teacher in Seattle and his middle son was very artistic and just started working at a graphic design firm. "My daughter is around your age and still in college. She lives with her mom in the Midwest."

"Does she come out to visit you on her breaks?" asked Molly.

Spence shook his head with sadness. "No, I'm afraid she hasn't been out to visit since her mom and I divorced. She's very loyal to her mother and isn't interested in a relationship with me."

"I'm sure that will change as she matures," said Regi. "She's missing out on a great guy."

Spence gave her a tentative grin. "I sure hope so."

"I spent the day with Kate on Thursday at her store. She has the coolest stuff," beamed Molly.

His blue eyes brightened. "She's a special person. I'm planning a trip to the island to visit her in the next week or so."

They finished off their meal sharing a molten lava cake and ice cream. Spence drove them to Becky's and made sure they got in safely. "I can stick around until they get home," he offered.

Regi shook her head. "We'll be fine. Thanks for everything."

He gave Molly a gentle hug. "You've got my numbers, so I expect to hear from you. You call me if you need anything."

She hugged him back. "Thanks, Spence. Maybe we could do dinner one night."

"I'd like nothing better." He waved as he got in his car.

Molly said she was tired and went upstairs to get ready for bed. Regi sat at the kitchen table and fiddled with Cam's card until the edges were frayed. He was the CEO of Foster International and he'd written his home and cell numbers on the back. It was only seven o'clock and she didn't expect Becky and Brad for a few hours. She decided she should take advantage of the quiet time and call Cam. When Spence brought them home, she had noticed a coffee shop a few blocks away and thought she could suggest meeting there.

She picked up her cell phone and punched in his cell number. He answered after the first ring.

"Cam Foster."

"Hi, it's Regi."

"Oh, I'm so glad you called me. How's Molly after her appointment?"

"She's doing well. She likes her doctor and so do I. How about you?"

"I'm okay, mostly been sitting here hoping you'd call. I think we need to talk about things."

"Yeah, we do. I was thinking maybe early tomorrow morning, like before six. I'm staying with a friend of a friend in Queen Anne. There's a coffee shop not far from her house. I could walk there and meet you."

"I'll be there. I'm in Laurelhurst about twenty or thirty minutes away. What's the name of the shop?"

"It's called the Queen Bee and it's across from the library."

"Are you sure you want to walk? I could pick you up?"

"No, I like to walk. I'll see you there about a quarter to six."

"I'm looking forward to it. Thanks, Regi. Have a good night."

"You too, Cam."

Her phone was damp with sweat and she tore off a paper towel to clean it. *I hope I'm not making a mistake.*

She helped herself to a glass of ice water and climbed the stairs to check on Molly. She was curled up in bed, a lamp on, but her eyes closed. Regi bent and kissed her forehead and clicked off the lamp.

She went back downstairs and summoned the courage to call Nate. She'd wait until she talked to Cam before telling him anything about their meeting. She hit the shortcut for Nate and he answered, "I was just thinking about you."

She smiled. "What were you thinking?"

"Hoping you were doing okay and counting the hours until you get back here," he chuckled.

She ignored the feeling of guilt pounding in her throat. "We're doing okay. Spence took us to dinner and we're at Becky's. She and Brad took their kids to the airport tonight. Molly's sleeping and I'm thinking about heading to bed."

"How were the appointments?"

"Both went well. She's starting physical therapy, but the doctor says everything is healing. Dr. Pierce was great. She's going to see Molly twice a week and gave us both her emergency number in case we need her. She gave Molly some ideas for dealing with the nightmares and told me she was optimistic that Molly would make a full recovery."

"That's great news. Are you feeling better about leaving her?"

"Yeah, I am. Becky is going to have her over and Spence is going to meet up with her for dinner soon. He said he'll be on the island in the next week or two."

"You sound much better, sweetie. I took your stuff over to Linda's tonight and took Murphy to my house."

"Don't let her sleep in your bed," she teased.

"I can't promise anything." He paused while they both laughed. "What time will you be home?"

"I'd say early afternoon. I'll take Molly to her dorm and help her get settled in. Steve thought he'd be at the marina around noon with Kyle and then we'll head home."

"I'll pick you up and I'm cooking, so don't make any plans for dinner."

"Sounds perfect," she said. "I'll see you tomorrow, Nate."

"Okay. I, uh, I, um, tell Molly hi for me. See you soon."

She disconnected, feeling like a louse for not telling him she had run into Cam, knowing she could destroy their budding relationship. *I don't want to ruin what I have with Nate, but I've got to see this through with Cam. I'm sure he's figured out Molly's his daughter and now it's going to get complicated. I'm just glad he didn't see her at the doctor's office. He'd have taken one look at her and wouldn't have been able to hide his surprise.*

Twenty

Regi left Becky a note before she turned in for the night. She told her she planned to go on an early walk and would be home by eight. She hoped she wouldn't get too curious.

She couldn't turn off the thoughts reeling through her mind, but finally succumbed to pure exhaustion and slept until her phone woke her at five o'clock. She quietly brushed her teeth, splashed water on her face, and put her hair in a ponytail. She tiptoed to Molly's room and peeked through the crack in the partially open door. She was still asleep, looking peaceful. She threw on her sweats and a t-shirt and put on a jacket before creeping downstairs and letting herself out. She took her time closing the door, not wanting to wake anyone.

Once outside, she got her bearings and headed in the direction of the library. She heard her phone ping and read a text from Cam. *Morning, Regi. I'm on my way.* She sent a reply telling him she was a few blocks away. She quickened her pace in an effort to beat him there. She wanted the advantage of getting settled and calming down before he arrived.

There were only a few cars around the coffee shop and she tried to scan inside before she opened the door to see if he was there. She couldn't see the whole place from the door so walked around the corner and not seeing Cam, claimed a secluded table in the back corner. She kept her phone on the table in case she got a text.

Within five minutes, Cam walked around the corner, all six feet four inches of him, wearing an impeccable blue suit, giving her a smile she had craved for decades. He looked older and after hearing what he'd been through she understood why. "Hey, Regi," he said, taking a seat.

"Would you like a coffee?" she asked.

"I'll get it," he said, getting up. "What would you like?"

"I'll take a mocha, thanks."

He returned a few minutes later with huge cups. "Here ya go," he said, handing her the whipped cream topped drink sprinkled with chocolate.

"So," she said. "What's on your mind?"

"Lots of things," he smiled. "I spent all night thinking about our trip to Friday Harbor and remembering the promise we made when we left the island. I can't believe I forgot it, but I did." He looked down at his cup.

"It's understandable with what you've been going through."

"Anyway, I'm sorry. I started putting it together at the doctor's office and then when I got home. Molly's my daughter, isn't she?"

Regi felt tears invade her eyes and her throat tightened. "Yes, she is." She sniffed and then added, "She doesn't know about you."

He nodded. "I wasn't sure, but figured she didn't. Why didn't you tell me you were pregnant?" The look on his face was pure defeat.

Regi took a breath. "I knew your parents didn't approve of me. They had ambitious dreams for you. You were heading back east to college and I didn't want to ruin it and make you resent me or the baby."

"What did you tell her?"

"Not much. I just told her that you left before she was born. She doesn't know your name or anything about you."

He flicked a napkin across the table. "I wish you would've told me. Honestly, I'm hurt and I feel cheated out of so much. We could have made it work." He reached for her hands and held them across the table.

She shook her head. "I thought about it, but didn't see it working out. I've lived with my regrets. I'm sorry if I hurt you."

He shook his head. "I get it, I'm just sad to think I didn't know Molly. I was thinking last night that losing Isabella was the worst pain I've ever known and now I might have a tiny chance of having another daughter."

His eyes shone with tears and he gripped her hands harder. "I'd like to meet her, Regi. I'm sorry you've been on your own with all of this for so long."

Regi nodded. "I've got to figure out how to tell her. I'm concerned because of the stress she's under right now. It may not be the best time."

"I was thinking the same thing. I don't want to create more trauma for her. But, I want to be part of her life, when she can handle the news." He let Regi's hands go and took a sip of his drink.

"She's probably going to hate me, not you, when this is done," said Regi. "I shouldn't have lied to her, but I didn't know what to do."

"You moved to Friday Harbor to be there for your fortieth birthday, didn't you?"

She barely nodded, looking everywhere but at him.

"And then I didn't show up."

She braved a look into his eyes, full of regret. "It's okay, Cam. I understand and I've moved on with my life. It wasn't a bad change for me. I like it there and want to make it my home."

"I only wish things had been different, Regi, really. I married Elise mostly because it was 'time' and yes, my parents pushed it. She was from a wealthy family they knew and it was a so-called 'perfect' match." He ran his hand over hers. "I've never loved anyone like I loved you, Regi."

She shook her head, tears threatening. "I can't go back, Cam. I just can't. I've met a wonderful man. I think we have a future and I finally gave you up a few months ago." She wiped at her eyes, as they overflowed.

"I totally understand. I'm just not sure I can walk away now," he smiled through the tears in his own eyes. "Give me a chance to redeem myself. Extend your stay for the weekend."

"I can't. I've got transportation home today. I don't have my car here."

"I'll take you back or fly you back, if need be. Please, Regi, stay until tomorrow."

She struggled with years of longing she felt tug at her and the reality of what this would do to Nate. "Oh, Cam, there's a part of me that wants to stay with you in the worst way. I just can't do this to Nate, not now."

"Does he know about me?"

She nodded. "He knows it all."

"Tell him I ran into you at the hospital and we need to figure things out about Molly." He paused, watching her think about it. "I'll take you to the ferry tomorrow. It's just one day."

Her resolve weakened, fueled by memories and dreams. "I'll call Nate and try to explain this and see how it goes."

His face blossomed into a smile, erasing the anguish of the last year and transporting Regi to the week on the island they shared so long ago. *This is so dangerous. I can't believe I'm even considering this whole idea.*

She stood and said, "I need to get back and get Molly settled at school. I'll call Nate when I get to the house and if I can make this work, without destroying what I have with him, I'll call you and we can figure out the logistics for extending my stay."

"You've made me the happiest guy in Seattle. He stood, towering over her and bent down, and without hesitating, cupped the back of her neck and kissed her.

She was surprised, but did nothing to discourage him. It was as if they'd never been apart and the feelings from so long ago washed over her, like a warm, relaxing bath. He deepened the kiss, holding her close, as she surrendered, thinking not of Nate, but only of the boy she had loved forever.

* * *

She insisted on walking back to Becky's, knowing she would need the time to clear her head and formulate the words for her conversation with Nate. She left him getting into his shiny BMW sedan and hurried back to the house.

She sat on a bench and pulled out her cell phone. Nate answered after several rings. "Hello," he said, his voice groggy with sleep.

"I'm sorry to call so early."

"Don't worry, I should be up anyway. What's up?"

"I don't know how to tell you this. Yesterday afternoon I was waiting for Molly at the hospital and I ran into Cam. He was waiting for a doctor in the same office."

"Did you say Cam? The guy from twenty years ago?"

She let out a sigh. "Yes, Cam Foster. Anyway, he asked me about my life and what I'd been doing and I told him I was waiting for my daughter. We talked and he asked how old she was and eventually he put two and two together. He called me and wanted to know if I could extend my stay so we could talk about Molly and figure out how to tell her."

Silence greeted her. "Are you there, Nate?"

"I'm here," he said. "So, you're not coming home today, I take it?"

"I wanted to talk to you about it. I'm not sure what to do, but it may be for the best. I don't want him to show up on Molly's doorstep. We need to figure out the best way to introduce her to him."

"Are you sure that's all it's about? I know how much you had your heart set on reuniting with him."

"It's about Molly and what we're going to do. I'm sorry, Nate. I know this isn't fair to you and it's ruining our plans again. I'll take the ferry home tomorrow and be there in the afternoon."

"Okay, Regi, do whatever you need to do. I'll stay at Linda's tonight and watch the dogs."

"Oh, that completely slipped my mind. I'll tell Cam we can get together some other time. He could come to Friday Harbor and we could talk there."

"No," he snapped. "Just stay there. It's fine."

"Are you sure?"

"I'm not sure of anything right now, Regi. We can talk when you get home. I'll see you Sunday."

"Thanks, Nate, for understanding." She was again met with silence, but this time, he wasn't there.

* * *

As she got ready and made sure Molly was up, she tried to put the conversation with Nate out of her mind. Disappointment and frustration had saturated his words. She put herself in his shoes and understood why he was upset. She knew it wasn't fair or kind, but she also knew she couldn't say no to Cam, not now.

Becky dropped them in front of Molly's dorm, reminding Molly she'd be calling with dinner plans. Regi elected not to tell Becky she'd be spending the day with Cam; she didn't want to tell the story one more time. She sent Steve a text and told him not to wait for her, as she was going to take the ferry tomorrow.

She helped Molly clean the dorm room and get things organized and ready for the start of school on Monday. She was in one of the modern halls and had her own private bedroom off a common area she shared with her roommate. While Molly was in her room, Regi texted Cam and told him to pick her up at the UW Visitor's Center at one o'clock. It was a short walk from the dorm, but far enough away, she wouldn't risk being seen by Molly.

Regi's head hurt and her shoulders ached. She hated the feeling of sneaking around, but didn't see any other way around it, until she was able to introduce Molly to Cam. The guilt she felt about spending time with Cam when she should have been with Nate sickened her. She was beginning to have serious doubts about her decision.

Regi suggested they take a walk while they waited for Kyle to arrive. They walked all the way to the Medical Center and back, taking in the warm day and stopping to enjoy the view of Portage Bay near the UW Police Station. Molly seemed relaxed and her bruises had waned to a golden brown, so the sympathetic looks from strangers were dwindling.

On the way back to Molly's room, they stopped at the District Market and Regi treated her to a week's worth of groceries and snacks. Kyle texted when he was on his way and they busied themselves stuffing the fridge and storage cupboard with the goodies they had purchased.

"Are you sure you're going to be okay here?" asked Regi.

"I'm fine. I like it here and I love school. I'm not going to let this ruin my life, Mom. My boss sent me an email and she said if I needed time off, I could have it. Kyle's going to be my escort at night and I'll be fine. I should have never gone to that stupid party and I should have waited and left with someone else."

"It's not your fault you were attacked."

"I know, but I need to be more careful and aware. I'll be fine and if I have a hard time I'll call Dr. Pierce. Her stuff about the nightmares has helped so far."

Kyle knocked on the door and Molly checked the peephole before opening the door. "Hey, Kyle. Mom just bought a ton of stuff at the market. You'll have to come over and help me eat it this week."

He grinned. "Hey, Regi. Steve said you're not going back with him."

Crap. "Yeah, I decided to stay in town tonight and do some shopping and go back tomorrow. So, Molly, you call me if you need anything tonight, I'll be around."

Molly crinkled her eyebrows. "Okay, but I thought you were watching Linda's place tonight."

"Nate's got it covered. I ran into an old friend who lives in the city, so I'm going to hang out and visit and I'd feel better being in the city on your first night home."

Molly smiled. "Cool, have fun shopping and I'll talk to you later." She hugged her mom and Regi held her tight.

"You call me every night, no matter what."

Molly rolled her eyes as she walked her to the door. "Yes, Mom. Love you."

Regi carted her bag out and waved goodbye with a lump in her throat and a knot in her stomach. She turned and walked by the Allen Center for Visual Arts and saw Cam leaning against his sleek car, waiting in the parking lot.

He saw her and waved, hurrying to meet her and take her bag. He gave her a long hug and led the way back to the car. He was dressed more casual in jeans and a button down shirt. He opened the door for her and ran around to the driver's side.

"Are you in the mood for lunch?" he asked.

"Sure," she said, hoping eating would settle her stomach.

He drove about a mile and pulled into The Point, rushing to open Regi's door. "This isn't far from the house and they have great food."

They were led to a cozy table near the bar. He ordered the fish tacos and she selected the sliders. "I'm so happy you decided to stay today," he said. "I thought we could go for a drive or head back to the house. Is there anything in particular you want to do?"

She shook her head as she took a drink of her iced tea. "No, I'm just trying to figure this out."

He reached for her hand. "I've been so miserable these last months, ever since Isabella died. Running into you has given me hope. I'd never thought I'd see you again and then to learn I have another daughter. It's unreal."

The waitress interrupted them delivering their meals. Regi dug into her sliders, unsure of how to respond. She hadn't eaten much at Becky's and realized she was hungry once she tasted food. She shared her fries with Cam and asked about his business while they ate.

"I took over the company from my dad a couple of years ago. We acquire properties, mainly hotels, around the world and provide many of the related travel services. We're opening a property in Italy in a few months, so that's been consuming my time."

"Sounds like an exciting career," said Regi, dipping a fry in ketchup.

"I've enjoyed it, up until the last year. Everything changed when I lost Isabella. I never forgave Elise. She was always unstable—depressed, anxious, overly emotional. She was melodramatic and was turning Isabella into the same type of drama queen. She doted on her, like a pet, more than a child. I tried to talk to her and then we'd just argue about it and I would escape to work. I gave up talking and arguing; it made me tired."

Regi nodded, nibbling another fry.

"Our marriage wasn't great before the accident and after it was positively hellish. She felt guilty and I didn't cut her any slack. I blamed her for Isabella's death and I know I'm partially responsible for Elise's suicide. She had threatened to kill herself in the past, years before the accident. I always attributed it to her constant need for attention. When she first started, I'd respond and rush to be with her, urging her to get help."

"Did she see a doctor?"

He sneered. "Oh, she saw several. She'd quit going as soon as the questions got tough or they told her what she didn't want to hear. It was a revolving door of doctors, ailments, and treatments. They were all short-lived. In the end, I'm really not sure what was wrong with her mentally, but something."

"I'm sorry, Cam."

"I should have left her long ago and then Isabella might be alive. I found her on my birthday. I came home late from the office and she was on the couch. She'd taken a ton of pills and finished it off with a bottle of vodka. She was dead when I found her."

"How horrible," said Regi, pushing her plate away. "I can't imagine the grief and stress you've endured."

"That's why I'm thrilled to know about Molly. Speaking of that, I know I owe you support for the last twenty years. I never would've shirked my responsibilities, no matter what. I'd like to pay for her college, at a minimum."

"You don't need to do that—"

"I *want* to do it. I haven't been there for either of you and I want to change that starting now. Please let me have that much. I'm sure you're working two jobs to help her."

Regi nodded, "Thank you, Cam, but it was never my intention to take your money."

"I can see that. Lots of other women would've hunted me down and taken me for everything they could get. It would make me happy to share my good fortune with Molly...and with you. I've got my lawyer working on a new will and a trust as we speak. I want to make sure Molly is provided for down the road." He took a gulp of his tea and finished the fries on her plate. "What is Molly studying?"

"She's interested in science and medical research. She's a bright girl."

He beamed with pride. "I would expect nothing less." He signaled for the check and left several bills on the table. "Shall we?" he asked, extending his arm.

Regi hooked her arm in his and they took the long way to the car, taking in the water from the walkway. "It's a gorgeous view of Union Bay," remarked Regi.

"Wait until you see the view from my house. You're going to love it."

He drove down the road and turned at the sign for Webster Point. His house sat perched on the last bit of land, before it fell away into the gorgeous water stretching out to the bay. He parked the car in the driveway, grabbed her bag and led her up the tiered steps. The house could have been designed by Frank Lloyd Wright and as she stepped through the door, she was treated to breathtaking vistas.

"Wow, I love all the windows," she said.

"It's a gorgeous spot. Wait until you see the deck." He put her bag on the floor and led her by the hand. He showed her the living area with floor to ceiling windows and the kitchen, a large sleek modern affair. She noticed a large portrait of a beautiful blonde girl hanging over the fireplace mantel. The dining room boasted panoramic views and he opened one of the doors and led her out to a patio nestled in the greenery surround the house. It overlooked the water and as she turned back she caught a glimpse of Mt. Rainier. "It's magnificent."

"It was built in the 1960's, but we've remodeled it a bit, still keeping the bones, but updating. Come on and I'll take you upstairs."

He led her to a loft area sporting a large walkway looking over the living areas below. All the bedrooms are up here. We turned the downstairs bedroom into an office. He showed her two guestrooms that shared a bathroom in between and then a beautiful pink and lavender bedroom, clearly belonging to Isabelle, with a frilly canopy bed, decorated with giant flowers on the walls and lights in the shape of fish and flowers that hung suspended from the ceiling. "This was Isabella's room," he said and hurried by the door.

"Here's the master," he said, swinging the double doors open. It was huge and took up a whole corner of the house. Windows covered two walls and the other wall held a fireplace. It also had its own intimate deck. There was room for a couch and two chairs, plus a giant bed resting against a wall covered in pictures of Isabella. Behind the wall she found a huge custom closet and master bathroom.

"What a wonderful retreat you have," said Regi.

"I loved this house from the moment I saw it. It's hard to be here now though, without them." He stared at the windows and then shook his head, as if to dispel the bad memories.

"Let's sit outside and enjoy the rest of the sunshine before it disappears," she suggested.

"I'll get your bag and you pick the guestroom you'd like to use tonight."

She had been attracted to the one done in peach tones when she saw it. "I'll take the one at the end of the hall."

He ran her things upstairs and fixed some soft drinks on his way to the deck. When he opened the refrigerator she saw only bottles of beer. She turned away and claimed a comfy chair, putting her feet up and watched the activity in the bay. He handed her a glass.

"I've been thinking about Molly and how to tell her," began Regi. "I'd like to contact Dr. Pierce and try to explain the situation and ask for her advice. I'd feel better asking her opinion than trying to figure out the right time."

He nodded. "I agree. She'd know, more than either of us, what it would do to Molly right now." He paused and looked at the water. "I'm so eager to meet her, I can't stand it. Do you have any pictures of her?"

Regi smiled. "You'll love her. I'll send you some pictures, but I've got some on my phone I'll show you." She began flicking her finger across her phone.

"I think I'll always love you, Regi."

She wiggled in her chair, concentrating on the phone. She sighed and looked at him. "I loved you for a long time Cam, but I don't think we can go back in time. Too much has happened to both of us."

He nodded his head. "I'm willing to give it a try. I could move to Friday Harbor. We could start over."

She smiled. "That's what I wanted, more than anything, for years and years. I truly had my heart set on seeing you in December and knew my fairytale would be complete. But, fairytales aren't real. Life isn't what I thought it would be when I was eighteen. We've changed. We've been changed, like those rocks along the bay. Time has worn down their edges and altered their shape. I committed to a relationship with Nate, without you in the background."

She saw a tear slide down behind his sunglasses. "There was a time years ago when I thought about leaving Elise, but then we had Isabella and she was the light of my life. I stayed because of her and the joy I got from being around her. I wish now I had summoned the courage to leave after she was born. I could have found you and we could have made a go of it with Molly and Isabella."

She put her hand on his thigh. "That's your fantasy, like you were mine. I should've contacted you when I had Molly. That would have been the time to make a go of it. I think it's just too late. What we had will always be a part of us, like Molly, but my future is with Nate. He's a wonderful guy; you'd like him."

"I'm sure if you picked him he's wonderful, but it might take me some time to actually like him," his husky voice betrayed his tears. "When I kissed you this morning, I felt like we'd never been apart."

She blushed. "Me too. Chemistry isn't our problem, Cam. It's just complicated and more people are involved now." She took a drink and then picked up her phone and showed him several shots of Molly. "I'm going to put a call into Dr. Pierce's service and ask her to call me so we can figure out the best approach."

"Molly's beautiful. She looks like a cross between you and my sister." He got up and squeezed her shoulders, resisting the urge to brush his lips over her neck and left her to make her call. She left a concise message and her number with the woman on the line.

She joined Cam back in the kitchen, checking her phone. "I emailed you all my contact information, so you'll have it, plus some photos of Molly. Dr. Pierce is supposed to call within the hour."

He nodded and excused himself to check the computer in the office. She wandered through the living areas, finding more photos of Isabella at various ages, lined up on furniture and shelves. She hadn't seen any photos of Elise yet. She perused the other side of the living room and spied a wedding picture, with both of them smiling. Elise was petite with short blond hair, and a hint of arrogance, as she posed next to Cam, tall, confident, and charming, looking more like the boy she remembered.

She then found another photo of the three of them. It looked like the first day of school, from the uniform Isabella was wearing. Cam's hair was gray, though not quite as gray as it was now, and Elise had her arms looped around Isabella, as if tethering her. Cam wasn't smiling; his face drawn and serious, not happy to be forced to pose. Isabella was the only one who looked cheerful, holding up a pink backpack and grinning. *What happened to you, Cam? Now you've got a mansion filled with nothing but sadness.*

The ring of her cell phone interrupted her thoughts about Cam's circumstances. She answered and heard Dr. Pierce on the line. She sat on the couch and explained the situation with Cam in as brief a manner as possible. She answered Dr. Pierce's questions and nodded as she listened. Cam appeared as she was thanking her and disconnecting.

He looked at her, eyes wide in anticipation. "Well?"

"She said she thinks we need to hold off on any unexpected news right now. She wants to see how Molly does in the next few weeks and then set up an appointment we can both attend and she'll help explain it to Molly. We can do it at her office."

"Whew. That's a relief. I don't want to do anything to jeopardize her recovery. I'm sure she's going to be confused and even angry."

"I know. I'm not looking forward to the conversation."

"Do you feel like going for a ride?"

"I'd like that."

He led the way to the car and headed east out of the city. "Where are we going?"

He looked over and smiled, "It's a surprise."

She sat back enjoying the scenic views, listening to oldies music. They went through Redmond and after they passed Sammamish, she grinned, thinking she knew where they were headed.

He pulled into a parking lot and as they got out of the car, they heard the thundering sounds of water. She turned and smiled at him. "I thought you were coming here. I love Snoqualmie Falls."

"I remember," he said, linking his hand in hers. They walked the short distance to the viewing platform, awed by the power and beauty of the falls. The rushing water was so loud, they couldn't hear each other. At dusk, lights came on to illuminate the majestic display.

They sat for hours on a bench, holding hands, letting the force of the cascade soothe their worries away. Regi remembered the times they had escaping their lives and driven miles to sit on this same bench. They were serious about each other and for several months she kidded herself into thinking she could have a future and a life with Cam. Then reality had set in when she overheard his parents talking about her and how it would do Cam good to get away from her and meet a proper girl. She wiped away a tear from her past, remembering he had brought her to the falls to talk when he sensed how upset she had been.

It took a few hours, but she finally told him what she had overheard. He was angry and devastated, but in his heart he knew he would be leaving and Regi would be staying. He held her as they listened to the falls and stayed, as they were tonight, until the lights illuminated the impressive display of nature.

He picked up her hand with his and brought it to his lips, kissing the smooth skin on the back of her hand. "Are you getting hungry?"

She wiggled her other hand, indicating she could eat. He got up and pulled her off the bench. He led her down the walkway and when they reached the parking lot, suggested they go to the candy store and café, just down the road.

She laughed and agreed, hopping in the car. "Let me put in a call to Molly before it gets any later."

She punched her picture and he heard Molly answer, "Hey, Mom."

"Hi, Mol. Just wanted to check on you. How's it going?"

"Fine, great. We're having dinner and watching movies. Kyle's still here and Renee's back."

"Okay, I'll talk to you tomorrow night. Send me your work schedule when you get it."

"I will. Have fun and I'll talk to you tomorrow. Love you."

"Love you, too." She poked the button to end the call.

Cam glanced over at her and squeezed her knee. He started the car and drove to the café. They feasted on greasy burgers and fries and Cam treated them to bags of saltwater taffy and homemade fudge.

It was after nine when they got back to Cam's house. Regi yawned as she made her way into the house and started upstairs. "Thanks for the trip down memory lane tonight. It was fun."

He gripped her in a hug and said, "It was the best day I've had in months." He released her and put his arm around her, climbing the stairs.

They arrived at her room and he showed her where the towels were kept and made sure she knew how to work the television and the lights. "Sweet dreams, Regi," he said, backing out and closing the door.

She flopped on the bed, dead tired, but knew she needed to touch base with Nate. Reluctant to hear the disappointment in his voice, she opted to send him a text. *Just wanted to wish you a good night. Talked to the doctor about how to discuss Cam with Molly and she gave us advice. Will be home on the 1:00 ferry tomorrow. Can't wait to see you.*

She brushed her teeth and washed her face, climbed into her nightshirt, and crawled under the covers. She tuned the television to a chick flick and heard her phone beep. *All is fine here. I'll pick you up at 1:00. How's Molly?*

She smiled, relieved his response was friendly. *She's doing great. Just talked to her a while ago…watching movies and having dinner with Kyle and her roommate. Have a good night.*

She scrunched her pillow and settled in to watch the movie until she drifted to sleep. Her phone beeped again and she saw *Sweet dreams, Regi.*

Twenty-One

As the movie ended, she realized she was thirsty and threw on her sweats to go downstairs and get a glass of water. The master bedroom doors were shut, but there was a soft light on in the kitchen. She scooted down the stairs and found a glass in the cupboard and filled it from the tap. As she turned to go back, she noticed a flickering light coming from Cam's office. She tiptoed through the living area and angled her head in the doorway. Cam was sitting in his chair, his back to her, as the giant computer screen displayed some of the pictures she had sent of Molly. She noticed a bottle of Knob Creek and a glass filled with the amber liquid on his desk. The display shifted to more photos of Isabella and as she watched the images slide across his screen, she saw his shoulders begin to shake and knew he was crying. She turned, not wanting to intrude, and shuffled back to her room.

Despite being in a strange bed, in the house that belonged to the father of her child, who she had hoped to reunite with only two months ago, Regi slept through the night. Gentle light filtering into her room woke her. She looked at the clock, saw it was almost seven, and calculated how long she had to get to the ferry.

She got up, showered, and packed up her things. When she got downstairs she found coffee already brewed and saw Cam sitting on the deck with the paper. "Good morning," she said, bringing her coffee outside. The sunshine from yesterday had been replaced with gloomy gray clouds. She shivered as a breeze rolled across the water.

"Did you sleep well?" He was alert and perky.

She studied him, watching for signs of the man she witnessed last night, but didn't see any. "Yes, I slept all night. It's very peaceful and quiet here."

"Sometimes a bit too quiet for me." He paused and noticed her holding her coffee mug to warm her hands. "It's cooler this morning."

"Yeah, we got spoiled with a perfect day yesterday."

"We need to get you to the ferry no later than eleven-thirty. I thought maybe we could drive up early and eat breakfast there."

"That sounds great. I'm ready whenever you are."

He folded his paper and drank the rest of his coffee. "Okay, let's hit the road."

He carried her bag and led her out through the garage. She noticed an enormous SUV and a red convertible in the other stalls. She also spotted the overflow of empty bottles in his recycling bin.

On the ninety minute ride, they talked more about their future together as Molly's parents. She sensed his disappointment that he'd have to wait to meet her. She suggested he plan a summer visit to the island since Molly would be spending her break there.

His attitude brightened at the suggestion. "Would you consider letting her go on a trip with me? I'll have to travel to Italy a few times and would love to take her."

"Well, Molly's an adult, so it'll be up to her, but I think she'd enjoy a trip. We haven't traveled anywhere, so it would be a new experience for her."

He held her hand across the console. "You're welcome to come with us, anytime."

"We're going to have to figure out how to do this, sort of like an ex-husband and an ex-wife. A part of me will always love you, Cam, but like I said, I'm committed to Nate."

He nodded. "I know, you told me before. I just can't help trying," he winked.

"At least I've got a beautiful daughter that I'll get to know and have in my life, I hope."

"She'll love you, Cam. Just give it some time. I think I'll be the one in the doghouse when we talk to her."

"You've been a great mother, I can tell. This will be something we can overcome, together."

They passed by field after field of colorful tulips, before arriving at the seaside town of Anacortes. They stopped at the same café they'd eaten at when they took their island vacation celebrating high school graduation. They were seated at a table for two and the waitress rattled off the breakfast specials.

They ordered omelets served with fried potatoes and homemade focaccia toast with fresh berry jam. From looking at photos on the wall, they learned that the current owner was the granddaughter of the woman they remembered from their previous trip to the island.

"Some things never change," said Regi, biting into the warm toast smothered in triple berry jam.

Cam looked into her eyes and said, "And others do."

* * *

While Regi had been reminiscing at Snoqualmie Falls, Nate had imposed upon Kate and offered to bring dinner to her house in exchange for some advice. He arrived with a bag from the Jade Garden and she steered him to the kitchen island.

He unpacked a mountain of oyster pails and she poured herself a glass of wine and offered Nate one of Spence's beers. As he shoveled food onto his plate, Kate asked, "So, what's on your mind tonight?"

"Regi," he sighed. "She was supposed to be home tonight. We had a romantic evening planned. I was cooking dinner at Linda's and planned to stay the night."

"I see," she said, looking up at him as she dished up her food. "So, what happened?"

"Cam is what happened."

She gasped, holding the spoon she was using in midair. "*The* Cam? As in Molly's father?"

He smirked. "Yep, that's the one. She ran into him at the hospital while she was waiting for Molly at her doctor's appointment."

"Wow, that had to shock the living daylights out of her."

"I'm sure it did. She extended her trip so she and Cam could talk and figure out how to tell Molly. Regi told me Molly's doctor advised them to wait and she would facilitate the conversation when she felt Molly was stronger."

"That poor girl has been through enough. They were smart to talk to her doctor."

"I spent most of the day online researching Cam. I was hoping you would call Spence with me and ask him to look into him." He retrieved a paper from his pocket and slid it to her. "This is what I found out."

"Sure, I can call him. Are you sure you want to wade into this? Why not ask Regi what you want to know?"

He shrugged. "I'm afraid I'm going to lose her. He's a bazillionaire and owns the family hotel business. I'm not wealthy and manage a delivery service. He travels the world and I've never been outside of Washington, except for Canada, and that doesn't count. She's loved him for more than half her life and has only known me for a few months. He's the father of her child and I'm…I'm…not." He had barely taken a breath during his tirade.

She put her hand on his shoulder. "Let's sit down and think this through, okay?" She pulled out the chair and handed him his beer. "Did she give you a reason to doubt her intentions with Cam?"

He shook his head. "I just know she wished for him and moved here for him. It stands to reason if they found each other, she's going to want to be with him."

"He could be married himself," she said. "Let me call Spence and see what he can find out for you." She picked up her cell and excused herself to make the call, telling Nate to eat.

She returned a few minutes later and sat at her place. "He'll call us back in a couple of hours." She finished dishing up her food and began to eat.

"I know I sound ridiculous and insecure, but I'm worried. Regi is the first woman I've had real feelings for in a long time. I told her I was falling for her and I don't know what I'll do if I lose her. How do I compete with this guy?"

"Nate, dear, I don't think it's a competition. You are you and Cam is Cam. I don't know him, but I suspect he's changed in twenty years. Remember he didn't show up like he promised or even talk to her in over twenty years. That tells me she hasn't been on his mind, like he's been on hers all these years."

Nate nodded, eating more of his food. "That's true," he mumbled.

"When is she coming home?"

"Tomorrow on the one o'clock."

"That's a positive sign. That means she took care of what she said she was going to do and she's not lingering."

"Yeah, she told me she was sorry and knew it wasn't fair to me, but she didn't know what else to do and didn't want Cam to show up and talk to Molly on his own. She offered to come home and have him come to the island to talk."

"Do you think you could be overreacting?"

He smiled and then laughed. "I could be."

They both laughed and finished their dinner. Nate asked how Kate's day had been at the shop. "It was busy. Lots of people in and out all day. Alec, the artist I met at The Haven, stopped by with several new paintings. Luckily, Leon popped in and I put him to work getting them displayed. "Would you like another beer?"

"I would, but I'm going to stop at one. I'll be driving later."

She boxed up the leftovers and tucked them in the fridge. As soon as she sat down on the couch, her cell phone chimed. "It's Spence," she said. She reached for a notebook from the table and answered.

Nate watched and listened as she talked. She scribbled notes and asked a few questions and then ended by saying, "Thanks, Spence. We'll go over all this and call you back if Nate needs anything else. I'll see you soon."

"Here's what he found out. Cam grew up rich and took over the reins of the family business a couple of years ago. He's got a house in Laurelhurst on Webster Point. It's worth about six million dollars." She paused and looked over the top of her reading glasses. "Here's where it gets a bit more interesting. Last fall his eight year old daughter was killed in a traffic accident. His wife, Elise, was driving and wasn't injured. The girl, Isabella, wasn't wearing a seat belt and was ejected and died at the scene. Last year, on Cam's birthday no less, Elise committed suicide at their home. Isabella was their only child." She stopped and put the tablet down.

"Holy shit," said Nate.

"I would imagine he's eager to meet Molly and fill the void left by the death of his daughter," said Kate.

"And his wife," said Nate, hanging his head.

"It could be, but you really need to talk to Regi when she gets back home." She took her glasses off and said, "Nate, you realize she's always going to have a connection to Cam because they have a child together. There's nothing you can do about that." She cleared her throat, "If I can be bold for a minute—at your age, you're not going to meet a woman without a past or baggage. Regi's been honest and told you her story. That's all she can do."

Nate's face was tight with worry. "I know, but I just found her and don't want to lose her."

"Speaking from my own experience, the loss of a child does terrible, irrevocable damage to the parents. I doubt Cam is the same man our Regi knew."

"Now that I know what's happened, I'm having a harder time hating him." Nate smiled, fear still lurking in his vibrant eyes. "I'm concerned she'll feel bad for him and forgive him for standing her up at Christmas. I mean, it's understandable."

"You, my friend, are borrowing a lot of trouble tonight," said, Kate. "You need a full night's rest and a long conversation with the woman you clearly love tomorrow."

He nodded his head. “Yeah, I need to get back to Linda’s and check on the dogs. Thanks for letting me barge in on you.” He stood and put on his jacket.

She took his arm and led him to the door. “You’re a good man, Nate. No matter what happens, you’re strong and you’ll get through this bump in the road. In my heart I think Regi has strong feelings for you and you need to trust her.”

He hugged her and wished her a good night. She watched him drive away and turned out her porch light. She leaned against the front door and let out a deep breath. *I hope I’m right and she deserves Nate’s trust.*

Twenty-Two

After their breakfast at the Calico Cottage, Cam drove her to the ferry landing and waited with her until it was time to board. "I'll call you as soon as I hear anything from Dr. Pierce, so we can schedule an appointment."

"Keep me posted on how Molly's doing," he said. "I'd like to know she's okay."

Regi smiled, "I will. I'll call or email."

He took both her hands in his. "I've had the best two days, thank you. I've been hanging on by a thread lately and reconnecting with you and learning about Molly, well, it's made a huge difference."

"Please take care of yourself, Cam. I don't want to worry about you. I can't pretend to know what you're going through, but don't give up. I'm glad we ran into each other and I could share Molly with you. I will always be here for you, as your friend," she said, moving to hug him.

He wrapped her in his arms and she noticed again how thin he felt. He squeezed her tight, giving her a gentle kiss on her cheek. "I'll see you soon."

She nodded and as she walked away said, "You need to take better care of yourself. When Molly meets you she's going to expect you to be around for a long time, so eat better and drink less, okay?"

He nodded and waved, his eyes misty.

She hurried up the metal walkway and did her best to hold it together until she was safely aboard. She wept for herself, but more for Cam. His life was in shambles. As much as she would like to help him, she had no desire to become ensnared in the vines that were tugging him toward a path to self-destruction. She hoped and prayed her friendship and his chance to have a relationship with Molly would be enough to keep him from the brink of despair.

The gentle motion of the ferry and the slow pace soothed her as she reflected on the last few days. It would be easy to be lured by money, a magnificent house in an exclusive neighborhood, travel, cars, and anything else she desired. She'd toyed with that idea as she snuggled in the plush sheets on the guest bed last night. But then she thought of her life on the island and of a future she could see with Nate. With Cam, she would never want for anything, but she wasn't sure she could handle the pressure, his drinking and intense sorrow, and the lifelong trauma he would endure, as would those he loved. Before Nate, she could have seen herself doing anything to be with Cam. Now, she'd do anything she could as his friend, but the longing she felt in her heart was all for Nate.

* * *

Nate tried his best to relax when he got back from Kate's. He played with the dogs and sat on the patio, enjoying the fire pit. His mind was reeling with possible conversations he'd have with Regi when she got home. He knew Kate was right—he had to talk to Regi and work through this, whatever the outcome.

He put the dogs to bed and checked all the doors, making sure the house was locked. He collapsed on the bed in the guestroom and flipped on the television for a distraction.

His phone beeped and woke him. He reached for it and squinted, surprised to see light streaming through the open blinds. The television was on, he was still in his clothes from yesterday, and he had used the bedspread to cover himself in the middle of the night. It was after nine o'clock. He saw he had a text from Regi. *On my way to the ferry. I missed you and will see you at 1:00.*

He sent a reply. *I missed you too. Lunch at Lou's?*

His phone beeped with her reply, *Yum!*

He felt better, after some sleep and the reassuring texts. He checked on the dogs, stationed in the hallway outside his door, and fed them breakfast. They didn't hide their annoyance at being fed late, ignoring Nate's attempts at nuzzling, their heads buried in their bowls. "Sorry, girls. I'll do better tomorrow," he said, scratching them on the head.

He ate a bowl of cereal and headed for the shower. He dressed in jeans and a long sleeve shirt, in a shade of blue almost the color of his eyes. He tidied the bathroom and bundled his things in the duffel. He didn't want to assume he'd be staying over tonight and if things went bad, he wanted to be able to leave without the hassle of packing.

On the other hand, if things went well, he still had everything he'd planned to cook for dinner last night and could make it work tonight. He had even picked up Regi's favorite cupcakes from Ellie—vanilla with fresh strawberry filling. He gave the house a once over and pronounced it clean.

After pacing through the house several times, he decided to head to the harbor and have a coffee while he waited for the ferry. Megan was working and fixed him a coffee and a brownie. Although cool, the day was sunny, so he elected to sit on the deck and watch for the ferry to appear.

* * *

Regi felt more upbeat as she inched closer to home. The cloud cover on the coast that had darkened not only the sky, but her mood, had been replaced by veiled rays of sunshine. She could see the harbor and made her way to the deck, so she would be one of the first to disembark. She scanned the landing for Nate and on her second pass, saw him, his bright shirt catching her eye.

The ferry thumped as it made contact with the dock. As soon as the apron was level and the chain removed, she was the first one to sprint across the landing. She waved and saw Nate smile as he made his way to her.

She dropped her bag on the ground and put both arms around him, hugging him close. "I'm so glad to be home," she said. She released her grip and met his eyes, noting the strain around them and detecting apprehension percolating below the surface. He picked up her bag and she slipped her arm in his.

They walked to Lou's and sat on the deck. "Are you going to be warm enough?" he asked.

She burrowed into the cardigan she was wearing. "Yeah, it feels good out here and is shaping up to be a lovely day. It was really cloudy in the city."

They ordered lunch and Nate asked, "Molly got settled and is doing okay, huh?"

She nodded, taking a sip of her tea. "She seems to be doing well. I think Kyle's going to be her designated guardian angel for the foreseeable future."

"That's not a bad thing," he said, smiling.

She set her glass on the table. "So, I know I disappointed you and ruined our evening last night. I'm truly sorry—the timing was horrible, but I'm glad I ran into Cam. I needed to talk to him…for a long time, but fear held me back."

"Was he surprised to learn about Molly?"

Her eyes widened and her brows peaked. "Oh, yeah. The whole encounter was surreal. He was sitting in the chair next to mine when I turned around to sit down. I thought it was him and then he recognized me too. We talked about what we had both been doing and I told him I had moved to Friday Harbor. He obviously didn't remember the pact we made. Later, he figured it out. We only talked for a few minutes and when he learned I had a twenty-one year old daughter, I could see he was putting it together."

She paused while the waitress delivered their plates. "He had to go to his appointment, which is another whole story, and gave me his card, asking me to call so we could talk more. So, I called him and set up a time to meet after I got Molly settled on Saturday afternoon."

She took a bite of the lobster mac and cheese they were sharing. "As it turns out, Cam had an eight-year old daughter, Isabella, who was killed in a car wreck last fall. Then to top it off, his wife, who he blamed and who blamed herself for the death of their daughter, killed herself on his birthday."

Nate feigned surprise, "What a horrible ordeal. That's a worst nightmare sort of scenario."

She nodded. "I know. After he told me this, I understood why he looked so much older and almost deflated. He's a tall guy, very gray, and scary thin. He eventually remembered the promise we made and our time on Friday Harbor, but obviously that wasn't his priority this past Christmas."

"Did you stay at his place last night?" Nate asked, while looking down at his plate.

She reached out and put her hand over his, forcing him to look at her, drilling her eyes into his. "Yes, I stayed at his huge house on Webster Point. I slept in the guestroom and never saw him until this morning. He kissed me once, earlier when we first met, not at the house." Resentment and a hint of anger flashed in his eyes.

She gripped his hand, "Before I told him that I'm committed to you. I told him he'd always have a special place in my heart and a connection through Molly, but I wasn't interested in picking up where we left off two decades ago."

"You're sure?" he asked.

She nodded. "I love it here and I see us having a future together. I think if I hadn't met you I would've been tempted to rekindle our relationship and try to make my imagined life a reality. But, I realized I've changed and he's changed and we can't go back. Cam's miserable. It sounds like his marriage wasn't good before and after the loss of his daughter, it totally deteriorated. He feels guilty about his wife and his house is basically a shrine to Isabella, with photos of her everywhere. I know he's drinking and not eating well—nothing like the boy I fell in love with so long ago."

"I feel for the guy. I'm not sure I could handle what he's been through any better. It may take me longer to actually like him, but I certainly sympathize with him." He paused and took a gulp of tea. "I realize he'll always be part of your life, but I need to know what part I have. I love you, Regi."

She blinked away the tears in her eyes and smiled. "I haven't loved a man for so long it's hard to know what I feel. This trip clarified it for me though, I thought about you, missed you, worried about what I was doing to whatever it is we have going, and to answer your question—you're the leading man in my life."

He grinned, leaning into her and touching her forehead with his. "I love you, more than you think. What we have going is serious." He kissed her with determination, leaving no doubt as to his feelings for her. He felt her hands dig into his shoulders and she returned his kiss with equal force. He broke away, slightly out of breath. "I hope this means I'm staying the night," he whispered, eyes full of mischief.

"I'm counting on it," she said, her gray eyes wide with anticipation.

* * *

While Nate paid the tab, Regi went in to see if she could speak with Leon. Lou sent him out to the alcove near the kitchen. "Hey, Regi, how's Molly?" he asked when he saw her.

"Much better, thanks. I took her back to Seattle and got her settled at school. She's determined not to let this ordeal define her as a victim. She's going to a therapist and starts classes tomorrow. I just wanted you to know she was doing better."

"Kate told me they arrested the son of a bitch who did this to her. What a sick creep."

"His arrest helped her feel safer and she won't have to testify, which is a huge relief. How are you doing?"

"Things are great. I'm busy here and am helping Kate when she needs it. I'll have the car next week and still need to figure out housing, but I'll find something."

She heard Lou hollering for him. "You better go. I just wanted to catch you up on Molly." She waved as he hurried back through the swinging door.

She found Nate waiting for her on the street below, holding her bag. They walked hand in hand to his pickup and he drove them away from town. He parked in Linda's driveway and when they opened the door, Murphy bounced to Regi and greeted her with licks. She knelt down and gave her a thorough rubbing, while Lucy poked her nose in to get some pets.

Nate was holding her bag along with his duffle. "I slept in the blue guestroom last night."

"That's the one I always use. Why did you take your duffle bag?"

"I honestly wasn't sure if I'd be staying here. I had lots of crazy thoughts running through my head this weekend."

She opened his hand and let the bags fall, intertwining their fingers. "I'm so sorry, Nate. I knew this was going to be hard on you when I decided to stay in the city. I thought you may tell me to hit the road." She smiled and then said, "Thanks for your trust and understanding."

He tossed his head back. "Okay, we're being totally honest, right?" She nodded.

"Then I need to tell you something. I was a wreck Saturday, so I took Chinese over to Kate's and told her what was going on and asked her to call Spence and have him check out Cam. I was worried about you and wanted to know what kind of guy he was. I know it was sneaky and probably seems like I didn't trust you, but I couldn't stand not knowing." He finally took a breath and then said, "I'm sorry."

She was still holding his hands. "That was resourceful and a little sneaky, but I understand. I put you in an impossible situation. You listened to me talk about Cam for months and then I tell you I'm going to spend the weekend with the man I loved and the father of my child. I get it." She sighed. "Thanks for being honest with me."

"Since we're being honest and all, did you enjoy Cam's kiss?"

She sucked in a breath. "At the time, yes. It made me feel eighteen again and like we'd never been apart. It was my fairytale ending, but then I was jolted back to reality seconds later." She moved within inches of his face, noticing the tiny white strands in his brilliant eyes. "You're the only one I want kissing me."

He closed the gap between them and met her lips. It sent a spark of excitement down her body and elicited a gasp. When he pulled away he said, "I'm known for my deliveries," he joked.

"How long do you need to cook dinner?" she asked.

"Since we ate lunch late, I probably don't need to start cooking for about three hours."

"I think we have time for you to redeem your rain check," she smiled. He picked up their bags and she reached behind her, seized the fabric of his shirt, and led him to the guestroom.

* * *

It was almost seven when they finished cooking dinner. Along with tender steaks, Nate layered potatoes, onions, garlic, and butter in a foil packet on the grill. He topped it with cheddar cheese and let it melt before removing it from the heat. She made a tossed salad and sliced some fruit. He poured Regi a glass of red wine and snatched a cold beer out of the fridge. Dressed in their robes, they huddled around the fire pit and devoured the tasty meal he had planned. They gazed across the water, watching the sun slip into the sea, until the last whisper of light was silenced.

When it was dark, they went inside and he unveiled the beautiful cupcakes he had stashed for their special night. "Ah, my favorite, you remembered," she said, taking a lick of the cream cheese frosting. Although stuffed, they managed to share one cupcake and stored the rest.

After cleaning up the dishes, Nate started a fire and powered on Max's television. They snuggled on the couch, under a soft afghan, as the dogs dozed on Lucy's bed, warmed by the flicker of the fire. "This has been a perfect evening. Thanks for delaying it one night," she said, kissing his cheek.

"It was worth the wait," he said, pulling her even closer.

"I could get used to this," she murmured, wrapping her arm around his waist. Her cell phone rang and she tossed the afghan aside and scurried to the kitchen, where she'd left it in her purse.

She saw Molly's picture on the screen. "Hi, Mol."

"Hi, Mom. Just calling to check in and see what you're doing."

"Nate and I just had dinner and are watching television. How was your day?"

"I got all my laundry done and clothes ready for the week. I decided to take this week off from the library. I've got physical therapy, plus Dr. Pierce, so I want to see how that works, before I add in work."

"That's smart. Don't push yourself too hard."

"Give Murphy a kiss for me and tell Nate hi," said Molly, before she disconnected.

She poked her phone and put it back in her purse and returned to her position next to Nate. As she tugged on the afghan to get comfortable, his head lolled back and his eyes were closed. She tucked herself beside him and whispered, "I think I love you too, Nate."

Twenty-Three

Monday morning was hectic. Regi and Nate overslept, having moved to the bedroom sometime during the night after they fell asleep on the couch. Being in a new place, Regi felt disorganized. Nate volunteered to use the other guest bathroom and she hopped from the bed to the shower.

She hadn't taken the time to organize her things last night when she got home and was digging through her suitcase and the plastic bins she had Nate move. Nate was ready in minutes and took care of the dogs. He poked his head into the bedroom, watching Regi rummage through the clothes hanging in the closet. Dressed in only her bra and panties, her hair wet, dripping over her soft curves, she bent to retrieve her shoes. He walked up behind her and slipped his arms around her waist, and she let out a yelp.

"I didn't mean to scare you, but you're hard to resist," his hands gliding up her body, resting on the silky fabric covering her breasts, his lips exploring her neck.

She giggled, "I'm going to be late, Nate. And so are you,"

"I know the boss and I'll write you a note for school," he grinned, turning her around and grazing her lips. He kissed her as he positioned her against the wall, wanting more.

She shuddered as the charge of his touch traveled through her. She put her hands to his chest and pushed. "As much as I'd enjoy staying here this morning, I've got to get to work. I'm way behind from last week. I haven't even packed my lunch yet."

His eyes flashed with amusement. "I like seeing you all flustered."

She feigned irritation and stepped to the side and under his arm. "I've got to get dressed, you goof."

He held up his hands in surrender. "Okay, okay. I'll bring you lunch today, since I've delayed you."

She pulled on her pants and began buttoning her blouse. "That's a fair trade."

He stepped closer and began unbuttoning her blouse. He smacked his hands away, laughing. "Nate Martin, I'm shocked at your adolescent behavior."

He grinned and laughed. "I'll wait for you in the kitchen. Do you want something to eat?"

She looked at her watch. "No, I need to fix my hair and get going. It's a longer drive to school from here and you'll have to run me to the condo to get my Jeep. I should have gotten my stuff organized last night."

He rubbed his hands over her shoulders and arms, "We were otherwise occupied last night and it was a lot more fun than organizing your closet." He kissed her quick and then said, "Are you okay if I stay tonight?"

She felt the heat rise in her cheeks. "I'd be hurt if you didn't," she smiled.

"I'll need to go get some more clothes, but I'll be here around five-thirty. I already took care of the dogs, so you don't need to worry about them and I picked up your Jeep yesterday, with Jeff's help. It's in the empty stall of the garage."

"Oh, thanks." She sighed and said, "That will save me a few minutes this morning."

He turned around and wiggled his eyebrows at her, "So, we have a few more minutes," he joked.

"You're incorrigible," she said, shutting the bathroom door and turning on the blow dryer.

After a bowl of cereal, he made sure the doors were locked and opened the garage door and pulled her Jeep outside. When he came in, she was ready, slinging her purse on her shoulder.

"Your Jeep's outside, ready to go. You have the keys to lock the front door when we leave?"

She jingled them in her hand and bent to pet the dogs. "We'll be back soon. You girls be good."

Nate kissed her once more before getting in his pickup and following her down the driveway. He waved when she turned to follow the road that led to the high school and he sped away to his office.

Regi's desk was covered with files and paperwork and she spent several hours sorting it so she could prioritize her day. The principal and several of the secretaries stopped in to check on her and make sure Molly was doing well. Before she knew it, Nate had arrived with deliveries and takeout for lunch.

She spied the bag from Dottie's and her stomach rumbled. "Oh, yummy. I got so busy, I didn't eat any breakfast this morning. I'm famished," she said, opening the bag and clearing a spot on her desk for Nate.

After polishing off sandwiches and fresh potato salad, Nate grabbed his drink. "I gotta run, sweetie. I'll see you tonight." He leaned across the desk and gave her a long and thorough kiss.

"Wow," she said. "You might have to bring me lunch more often."

"That should give Robin and Crystal something to chat about today," he laughed, glancing out in the hallway.

"I think we have plenty of leftovers from last night for dinner, if that's okay?"

"Perfect. That will give us more time to pursue other activities," he winked as he walked out her door.

She shook her head, grinning, and went back to plucking out files and papers that needed to be dealt with before the end of the day. She glanced out her window and saw Nate wave at her as he started his truck.

Before she went home, she checked her email one last time and saw one from Linda and one from Cam. Linda was checking in from New York. She wanted to make sure Molly was doing well and things were okay at the house. She filled her in on their activities in New York and said she'd email again when they arrived in Ireland later in the week.

Cam wanted to know how Molly was doing and thanked her again for meeting him and spending time with him. He sounded lonely.

She typed out a quick reply giving Linda an update and wishing them a safe trip. She answered Cam, reported that Molly was doing well and as soon as she heard from Dr. Pierce she'd let him know. She asked if he had a preference on dates in the coming month for a meeting. She also asked about his sister, since she hadn't done that in person. She was hoping she was still close to him emotionally and geographically. "Cam needs some friends so he does something besides dwell on his daughter. I think he should consider selling his house, so he's not bumbling around that empty place alone, reminded of everything he's lost," she muttered as her fingers flew over the keyboard. She continued typing asking about activities, hoping to prompt him into doing something.

She surveyed her desk, wishing she had gotten more accomplished, but turned off her computer and gathered her purse. She was the last one to the leave the office and hurried to her Jeep to get home and have dinner ready for Nate. She knew he'd be tired from a long day and didn't want him feeling like he had to work in the kitchen.

She used the garage remote when she arrived and pulled her Jeep into the stall. "I bet you could get used to living in a garage, huh, Jo." When she had first purchased the Jeep, used of course, she named it Josephine and had shortened it to Jo, in honor of the character in *Little Women.*

She collected the mail and put it on the dining room table and then nuzzled the dogs and gathered their food bowls. The dogs were watching her every move as she scooped the kibble. "Okay, girls, dinner time."

By the time Nate arrived, she had organized her things in the bathroom, put all her clothes away, and stuck some garlic bread in the oven to bake. "Smells yummy," he said, coming through the door with a suitcase and several hangers of clothes.

The dogs followed him to the bedroom while he put away his things. He changed into jeans and a t-shirt and flicked on the television before finding Regi in the kitchen. She was pulling out leftovers from the fridge and he moved in behind her, encircling her with his arms, burying his head in her hair, and kissing the back of her neck.

A snicker escaped and she wriggled, "That tickles."

He laughed. "How was the rest of your day?"

"Busy. I stayed late and am still behind," she popped the dishes in the microwave to reheat.

He unearthed the salad and retrieved dinner plates. "Shall we eat outside?" he asked.

She looked out the windows and said, "Sure, it looks like a pleasant evening."

After turning on the fire pit, he poured her a glass of wine and grabbed the iced tea, taking the salad and bread outside. She followed with the meat and potatoes. They ate while watching the last streaks of light dance across the water.

"Linda emailed today and said they're having a great time and they'd get in touch at the end of the week when they arrived in Ireland. I also got an email from Cam asking about Molly. I think it's best that I tell you when I talk to him, so you know about our interactions."

He put his fork down and reached for her hand. "I appreciate that. I trust you, Regi, but I admit I feel, I don't know, I guess vulnerable, when it comes to you and Cam. I wanted to ask if you would let me come with you when you get your appointment to tell Molly about Cam? I'd like to be there for you and I'd like to meet him."

Regi smiled. "Of course, I'd like you there. Can you take the time off work?"

He held up both of his arms, "I'm the boss. I can do whatever I want…sort of," he said with a grin.

"Well, then, that's easy. As soon as I get a date, I'll let you know." She took a sip of her wine. "When I replied to Cam I asked about his sister and mentioned some activities, like boating, that he always liked, hoping to prompt him to connect with someone. I think if he got out and did things, he'd feel better."

"Sounds like he's withdrawn, with the drinking and house full of reminders."

She nodded. "Yeah, that's what's worrisome. He needs to interact with people. I think he buries himself in work and obviously self medicates when he's home." She finished the last bite on her plate. "I forgot to tell you, he asked about taking Molly on a trip to Italy this summer. He's opening a new hotel."

Nate began picking up the plates, "What do you think?"

"I think she'd love to see Italy and it would give them a chance to bond. She'll have to decide, but I don't really have a problem. I'll never be able to give her exotic trips and it would be great for her to experience another country."

"Maybe you guys did run into each other for a reason. Molly could be just what he needs to refocus on something besides the death of his family."

"I hope so. I'm nervous about telling her. I think she'll be angry; I probably would be. I just hope she gets over it soon."

"She's pretty level headed. She probably has a better chance of understanding at her age, than she would've years ago. It seems like teenage girls are overly dramatic—at least what I remember about my sisters."

Regi laughed. "I hope you're right." She helped him gather the remaining items and take them inside. "Cam also wants to pay for Molly's college. He feels bad that he never contributed to her support and wants to do it now."

"That would be a big load off of you, wouldn't it?"

She nodded, "Yeah. That's why Molly didn't go right after high school. I never had enough to put aside money for college, so we had to save up before she could go. I could probably cut back on some of my work at the coffee shop."

While they were cleaning up, Molly called. Regi sat in the great room and visited with her for a few minutes.

She came back to help Nate and said, "Molly sounds great. She had physical therapy and her appointment with Dr. Pierce. She said everything went well with her classes today."

"I'm glad she's doing well," he said. "We're done in here."

He brewed some coffee and they took it outside to enjoy the blush and purple hues along the blue horizon, as the light of day disappeared. A soft quilt draped the rocking bench stationed by the fire pit, perfect for gazing at the night sky and snuggling.

In the midst of several passionate kisses, Regi felt her blouse slip off her shoulders, replaced by Nate's warm hands. His lips moved from her mouth and down the side of her neck to the swell of her chest. His mouth tugged on the sheer fabric and with a flick of his thumb, the delicate material fell away. She gasped as the cool air met her bare skin.

She felt his caress and then his lips as they moved to capture her mouth. She heard herself moan as the kiss deepened. When he finally pulled away, he whispered, "I've been waiting to get you out of these clothes all day."

She laughed, seeing the flames from the fire reflected in his eyes. "How about we take this inside?"

He grabbed the quilt, tucking it around her. "I'll turn off the fire and meet you in the bedroom," he said, taking her arm and pulling her off the bench.

She held the quilt and hurried inside. The dogs were sacked out on their bed and she scurried down the hall to the bedroom.

Nate picked up her clothes from where they had fallen on the patio, locked the doors and doused the lights. He followed the hallway to the bedroom, lit only by a string of lights in a vase of flowers on the dresser. He detected a slight lump in the bed and shed his clothes in a pile on the floor, before sliding across the crisp cool sheets.

He felt only Regi's smooth skin, reaching out and touching her bare thigh. "Thought I'd save you the time of messing with all those pesky buttons and zippers," she said, laughing as she put her arms around him.

* * *

Over the next week, Regi and Nate kept to the same routine. She worked late several nights, catching up from her time away. The coming Easter weekend would be followed by Regi's break from school and her goal was to be caught up so she could enjoy her vacation. She wasn't working at the coffee shop and Nate suggested he take some time off and they travel around the islands. In the evenings he worked at his shop to ready the boat and kayak in anticipation of an outing.

Friday night Regi left work with a happy smile and a clean desk. When she got home, Nate suggested they celebrate the end of the week and the start of vacation with dinner out. "How about we invite Kate to join us? I've missed seeing her." suggested Regi.

Nate agreed and dialed her cell phone while Regi played with Murphy and Lucy. "She said she'll meet us at Lou's in an hour."

"I'm going to throw a load of laundry in," said Regi. "Do you have anything?"

He showed her his basket and she added it to hers and when she returned from the laundry room, he had iced teas waiting on the patio. "I love this house," he said, gazing out at the water.

"I know. It's gorgeous," she said, guzzling half her glass of tea. "Whew, it's warmer than I thought."

"It's supposed to be sunny this whole week. It should be perfect on the water."

"What shall we do for Easter Sunday? Do you have plans with your parents?"

He shook his head. "No, they're going to my sister's in California. We could cook something or go out, it doesn't matter to me."

"I always make Molly an Easter basket, even as old as she is now. I ordered one online and sent it to her. She called me today when it arrived."

"I bet that made her happy."

"Yeah, she said she was going to miss being home Sunday, so she was excited to get all her favorite treats. She's going to Easter brunch with a group of friends and Becky is having her for dinner next week." Regi's cell phone rang and she frowned when she looked at the screen.

Nate heard her say, "Oh, yes, Dr. Pierce, I'm fine." He went and put the laundry in the dryer and rejoined Regi. She listened and nodded her head and then said, "Okay, Friday works and I'll get in touch with Cam. If there's a problem, I'll phone you."

Nate tilted his head to the side and raised his eyebrows at her.

"So, Dr. Pierce thinks next Friday will work to talk with Molly. She has her scheduled for an early appointment that morning. Since we're both off, that works out, right?" Her leg bounced as she spoke and she twisted the ring she wore on her finger.

"That's great for me. We could go over Thursday and stay the night. I'm sure we could get Sam and Jeff to take the dogs for one night." She bit her bottom lip, thinking. "Regi, sweetie, did you hear me?" he asked, touching her hand.

"Oh, yeah. Sorry, just thinking. Dr. Pierce said she'd let Molly know I'd be joining them for part of the Friday appointment and she would set the stage for me to tell her about her dad. Then she'd have Cam come in, provided Molly's agreeable."

Nate sandwiched her hands between his. "It's going to be okay. Dr. Pierce will be there and she knows how to handle tough situations."

She nodded. "I know. I better call Cam right now." She picked up the cell and scrolled to his name. Nate started to get up and she pulled his hand and mouthed for him to stay.

He answered and she said, "Hi Cam. I just heard from Dr. Pierce and she wants us to be there next Friday at nine for Molly's appointment." She went through the plan as the doctor had outlined it. Nate watched her nod and then she said, "Nate and I are going to come over on Thursday and stay the night, so we'll be there on time." She shook her head, "No, Cam, thanks, but we have a place to stay. We appreciate the offer, though." She paused and said, "Uh, let me see what Nate has planned and I'll get back with you." She talked for a few more minutes and then disconnected.

"He offered to let us stay at his house. He also invited us to go to dinner Thursday, so we could all get a chance to meet before the appointment with Molly. What do you think?"

Nate shrugged, "I don't think it's a bad idea. I'd rather meet him at dinner than in the waiting room at Molly's appointment."

"Okay, I'll let him know. Do you want to stay at Becky's?" she asked, getting up, since it was time to leave for dinner.

He got up and swung his arm around her as she passed by him. "No, I'll take care of getting us a hotel. That way I can have you all to myself," he smiled and leaned in to kiss her. "We'll make a mini getaway out of it, my treat."

She gave him a quick kiss. "I'm one lucky woman," she said. "Let's get going."

On the way to town, she called Sam and confirmed Jeff could watch the dogs Thursday and Friday, until they returned. While she was on the line, Sam invited them to celebrate Easter with them at their house. Sam told her she planned to ask Kate to join them and Regi volunteered to extend the invitation.

When they arrived at Lou's they found Kate in a booth and were surprised to see Spence sitting next to her. He stood and hugged Regi and gave Nate a firm handshake while he gripped his shoulder.

"What a great surprise," said Regi.

Kate smiled, looking radiant in a geranium pink shell blouse and silky scarf. "He walked in right after I hung up from you. I didn't know he was coming," she said, bumping her shoulder into his.

Spence grinned. "It was a spur of the moment decision." He paused and rested his blue eyes on Kate's face. "She's fun to surprise."

Lou stopped by the table to greet them and take their orders. After he left, Regi said, "Before I forget, I just talked to Sam and she invited us to Easter dinner and wanted me to ask you, since we were seeing you tonight."

"Sounds terrific," she said, turning to Spence. "I don't have any plans. Do you have anything else up your sleeve?"

"No plans here," he said, raising his hands off the table.

"We'd love to go. I'll give her a call and see if we can bring anything."

"Since you're both here, Regi and I talked about her situation with Cam and she knows I enlisted your help to find out more about him. I didn't want either of you to feel awkward and I apologize for putting you in that position," said Nate.

"No need to apologize, but I'm thrilled you two talked it through," said Kate. Her eyes twinkled as she looked first at Nate and then at Regi.

Regi put her hand over Nate's, slipping her fingers between his. "I've assured Nate that Cam is firmly in my past. It's more complex because he's Molly's dad, but Nate's my present," she paused to look at him. "And my future, I hope."

"Wonderful news," said Spence. "You make a lovely couple."

"Thanks, Spence," said Regi, giving him a wink and tiny nod toward Kate, when she wasn't looking. "Thanks too for recommending Dr. Pierce. She's wonderful and Molly likes her."

Nate added, "We're going to Seattle on Thursday and Regi's going to meet with Molly and her doctor to explain about Cam on Friday. He'll be there to meet Molly."

Kate noticed Regi bite her bottom lip and saw the concern wash over her face. "It will be a good thing to talk to Molly about Cam and for them to meet. Plus, with her doctor there, it's a safe environment for you to have what could be a difficult conversation."

Spence nodded, "It'll be a huge relief when it's over. Sometimes the anticipation of a challenging or painful situation is worse than the actual event. Plus, Nate will be there for you."

Regi smiled, but her eyes betrayed her fears. "I'm so thankful he's coming. It worked out on a good week. I'm on break from school and Nate had already decided to take the week off so we could go out on the boat. I'm excited and nervous and downright scared, but I know it's for the best."

Their food arrived and they enjoyed Lou's famous crab cakes and several other dishes they all shared. While they ate Nate suggested they all go out on the boat and asked if there was a day that worked for Kate.

"When Spence showed up, I decided to close for the weekend, so probably tomorrow would be the best day." She pushed her plate away and said, "Your mom's off this week, so I've got to work the week."

"She'll be back by the weekend."

"I'm going to see if I can talk her into working two days a week. She's terrific with the customers and I need the time away," Kate said.

Lou brought the bill and Nate swiped it off the table as Spence reached for it. "My treat tonight. I owe you both for putting up with me last week."

As they left, they strolled around the harbor area discussing tomorrow's boat excursion. Regi volunteered to pack lunch for everyone and Nate had the boat ready to go, already in the slip at the marina. Nate assured Spence he had plenty of fishing gear for both of them. They decided to meet at the Front Street Café for breakfast before heading to the marina.

Spence treated them to ice cream at Shaw's on their circle around the harbor and they parted ways back at Lou's. Kate hugged both of them and confirmed they'd see each other in the morning.

* * *

Regi savored a few relaxing days, starting with the boat trip on Saturday with Spence and Kate. When Spence and Nate weren't landing fish, they were telling fish stories and laughing. Regi and Kate lounged and took in the scenic views as they meandered around the island.

While they were sipping iced teas, Regi asked, "Did you ever spend time in Italy on one of your buying trips?"

Kate nodded. "I have spent time there. I'd love to go back and do more exploring in the countryside. Why do you ask?"

"Cam told me he'd like to take Molly on a trip there this summer. His company is opening a new hotel there."

"That would give them time together, so they could get to know each other."

"I think so too. I hope she'll consider going." Regi paused and stared at the water along the coast. "I keep rehearsing what I'm going to say when I see her on Friday and nothing sounds right."

"Just tell her the truth. There was nothing sinister in what you did. You made the best decision at the time." Kate paused and then asked, "Have you talked to your parents about Cam?"

Regi shook her head, hiding behind her sunglasses. "No, I'm not looking forward to telling them anything. My mom has a way of making me feel like a total loser no matter what I do and I'm sure she'll have an opinion about this. She always wanted me to go after money to support Molly and she's been disappointed with me ever since I ended up pregnant and showed no interest in finding a husband. I don't think Dad is as critical, but he never bucks Mom. He's silent and lets Mom do all the talking."

Kate nodded and took another sip of her drink. "I can imagine your brother's death and Leon's involvement was difficult for them."

"They were devastated when Ronnie was killed, but neither of them seemed to affix blame to Leon. Instead they seemed to dote on him." She shook her head. "They helped me a lot when Molly was born and as she grew up. It's just their help always came with a free lecture and a stamp of disapproval. When I decided to move here, they weren't happy either."

"Maybe they just miss you," suggested Kate.

"I'm sure they miss us, but Mom also misses controlling things and knowing everything going on in my life."

Spence hollered, "Are you girls ready for some lunch?"

Kate laughed and shouted back, "We can be. Give us a few minutes." She helped Regi retrieve the giant sandwiches she had made this morning, along with chips, fruit, and some cookies, courtesy of Sweet Treats.

After lunch, they stowed the fishing gear and Nate steered them around some of the smaller islands and pointed out landmarks along the way. They didn't dock at the marina until late afternoon.

"For not doing a thing, I'm pooped," said Regi.

"What a wonderful day," said Spence, smiling. Kate stepped from the boat, using his hand to steady herself.

"It was a perfect day. Maybe we could go again one day this week. Are you going to be here all week?" Nate asked Spence.

"I'll be around. If you feel like going out, give me a ring."

They traipsed to their cars, Regi and Kate discussing Easter, and Spence and Nate making a plan for another day of fishing. They waved goodbye, with Kate and Spence thanking them for a wonderful time.

Before they drove home, Regi hurried to Sweet Treats to pick up the bread she promised to bring for Easter dinner. She also stopped in the market and picked up a few bottles of wine. When Regi and Nate got home they put everything away and flopped on the couch, both tired from the day in the sun.

As the week progressed, Regi became more anxious about Friday. She spent most of Wednesday night staring at the ceiling while she should have been asleep. Her mind on overdrive, running through the words she would use when she explained Cam to Molly. She knew she needed to sleep for the trip tomorrow, but her brain wouldn't shut off. *I'm so thankful for Nate. There is no way I could do this alone. I've got to try and relax so we can at least enjoy our day in the city tomorrow.* She practiced the techniques Dr. Cummings had given her and finally fell asleep with Nate's arm wrapped around her waist.

Twenty-Four

Regi did her best to focus on Nate and their time together, shelving her anxiety about Friday. They took the Jeep and after getting off the ferry he drove to Pike's Place Market. They wandered through the shops and had a late lunch at a deli. Nate had made reservations at a boutique hotel downtown and they were able to check in early.

Their room was on an upper floor and afforded them a beautiful view of the city. They walked to Chihuly Garden and Glass and took in the breathtaking exhibits before meeting Cam at a waterfront restaurant. He was already seated when they arrived.

Cam stood and shook Nate's hand and kissed Regi on the cheek. "I'm so glad you could come tonight," he said, waiting for Regi to sit down.

Nate took in Cam's expensive suit and couldn't help but feel underdressed in his khakis. "So, are you ready for tomorrow, Cam?" asked Regi.

He grinned. "I'm excited to meet Molly, but I'm nervous about the whole situation. How about you?"

She nodded. "I'm nervous. Nate kept me busy sightseeing today, thank goodness." She leaned into Nate and he put his arm around her.

Cam asked about Nate's family and what he did on the island. Nate talked about his parents and sisters and the delivery business he had managed for the last fifteen years.

They talked about Molly and Nate commented, "I'm amazed at how strong she has been through this ordeal. She's remarkable."

"I'm so glad they caught the guy," said Cam. "It makes me want to find him and beat him senseless."

"There'd be a line of people standing with you," said Nate. "She's a sweetheart."

"She's got a close group of friends and loves her job at the library. One of her best friends is Kyle, who also works at the coffee shop on the island. His grandmother lives in Friday Harbor." Regi took a sip of her drink and added, "She's lucky to have a strong support system. We have a couple of friends who live in Seattle and they're available if she needs them."

"I hope, after tomorrow, I'll be part of her support system," smiled Cam. "How do you think it's going to work at the doctor?"

Regi explained about the plan for Dr. Pierce to break the ice and then call Regi in to explain about Cam. "Once that's done, it'll be Molly's choice if she wants to invite you to join the session."

They declined dessert and as dinner came to an end, Nate said, "Cam, I wanted you to know how sorry I am for the recent loss of Isabella and your wife. Regi explained what happened and you have my sincerest sympathies."

Cam nodded. "I appreciate that, thanks. It's been a horrible few months, but I finally feel a glimmer of hope." He turned his eyes upon Regi and Nate saw the admiration, mixed with a hint of sadness. "Letting Regi go is my biggest regret, but knowing I have a beautiful daughter in Molly will be my greatest joy."

Regi felt her lip begin to quiver and Nate reached for her hand.

Cam paid the check and insisted on giving them a ride back to their hotel. "Thanks for dinner, Cam," said Nate, as he helped Regi out of back of the car. "Good luck tomorrow," he said, shaking his hand.

"It was a pleasure to meet you Nate. I knew you'd be a great guy, as Regi's choice, but I honestly like you. You've got a great woman—she deserves true happiness," said Cam, clapping Nate across the back.

Regi was waiting on the sidewalk and watched the interaction. She waved at Cam as he got back in his car. "See you in the morning," she said.

Nate put his hand on the small of Regi's back and guided her through the door. "What did Cam say to you?" she asked.

He smiled. "He told me he liked me and wants to make sure I make you happy."

She grinned. "What did you think of him?"

"I liked him too. I'd probably like him better without the fancy car, his pricey suit, and mansion on the bay, but he's nice and very personable."

He opened their door and held it for her. "Now we just have to wait and see what Molly thinks of him," she said, as she tossed her things on the chair.

* * *

After a quick breakfast at a bakery, Regi and Nate arrived at the doctor's office. Molly was already in with Dr. Pierce and Cam arrived a few minutes after they were seated. Regi fidgeted in her seat, shuffling magazines around on her lap, crossing and uncrossing her legs. She fiddled with her necklace and twisted the ring on her finger until the skin was chafed.

Nate gripped her hand and placed it on his knee, covering it with his. "It's going to be okay. Think of the positive possibilities, instead of worrying about the negative."

She nodded and turned to smile at Cam, sitting on the other side of Nate. The surly nurse who had called Cam back when they met, came out to retrieve Regi. She stood, gripping her purse like she was holding a rope dangling from a cliff.

Both Nate and Cam murmured assurances as she walked away and was led through the door. "Poor Regi. This is so hard on her," said Cam.

They waited for over an hour in relative silence, interspersed with a few questions from Nate on the topic of Cam's new hotel in Italy. "I told Regi I think your offer to take Molly this summer is terrific. That would give you guys some time together."

"I hope she'll go. It's a beautiful area near Chianti. The hotel is a large villa among the vineyards."

"Sounds like a perfect place," said Nate.

"I've been giving some thought to spending more time there. It's peaceful and calming. I don't have anything to keep me here, except Molly now." He sucked in his breath. "I'd do anything for her."

They heard the brusque voice call out, "Mr. Foster."

"Well, I guess I'm up," said Cam, standing and straightening his tie.

"I'll be here," said Nate. "Good luck."

The nurse tapped her toe, holding her clipboard against her side with the other hand on her ample hip. "This way, Mr. Foster."

* * *

Dr. Pierce met Cam in a conference room. She introduced herself and then got down to business. "Regi has shared her story with Molly and your daughter wants to meet you. She's angry right now at her mother for lying to her and keeping her in the dark." She paused and added, "Regi is feeling guilty."

"So, what do you suggest I do?"

"Molly's interested in meeting you. Regi shared the loss of your daughter and wife with her, so she's very sympathetic toward you and irritated with her mother."

"That's what Regi was afraid would happen."

She nodded. "It's understandable and a rather normal reaction. I think she'll get over it, especially if you're supportive of Regi. It's important not to feed into blaming her for the decision to keep your identity a secret."

"What's done is done. We really can't go back, so I'm going to do my best to build a future with Molly and Regi. I missed my chance with Regi and I don't want to mess things up with Molly."

She smiled. "I think you'll do just fine. Molly's a lovely girl and quite mature. She and Regi are very close, so this will probably be much harder on Regi. She'll be brooding about it long after Molly moves on, I'm afraid."

He nodded. "Okay, I guess I'll go meet my daughter," he said, with a huge smile.

Dr. Pierce led the way to her office, where he walked in to find Molly waiting. Regi was waiting in another room to give them some time together. "Molly, this is your father, Cam Foster," said Dr. Pierce. "If you need me, I'll be right across the hall." She nodded to Cam and closed the door.

He looked into her eyes, red and puffy from crying, but he saw in the midst the same steel blue eyes that stared at him every day in the mirror. The look on her face was a mix of sternness and fear.

Molly's frown disappeared and she popped up from the chair and rushed to Cam. "Wow, I can't believe I'm really here with you." She extended her hand and he moved to hug her. He enfolded her in his arms and squeezed and heard her sob.

"I'm so thankful to meet you, Molly. I can't tell you how happy I've been these past weeks, looking forward to this day." He kept his arms clasped around her and let her collect herself.

She gulped and a squeak escaped. "I can't believe Mom didn't tell me the truth all these years." She shrugged, "I mean I understand when I was young, but she could have told me before today." She sat down on the couch and he sat next to her.

Placing a hand on her knee, he said, "I understand your feelings, but your mom was doing what she thought best. We made a promise to each other over twenty years ago and I didn't keep up my end of the promise. She moved to Friday Harbor based on our pact to reunite this past year. I think as the years went by she pinned her hopes on our getting together and thought that would solve everything. When I didn't show, it threw a wrench in her plan. I know she's a good mom and I also know she made the best decisions she could for you."

Molly wiped tears from her eyes. "It's just so unfair to keep me from knowing my dad. We could have done stuff together."

"I think she was afraid, Molly. Our situations when you were born were very different. My family didn't really approve of our relationship. I was on the east coast, wrapped up in college and my life. Then I married my wife and was focused on running the family business. Quite frankly if she had found me even when you were a teenager, I wouldn't have been available for her, and I'm not sure how things would've worked out. My wife wasn't the most understanding woman and Isabella was young. I wish we could have been together before today, but I'm going to focus on how wonderful it is to connect now." He shook his head as he felt tears gather. "You know about my daughter and wife. I've been devastated, to say the least. So, I think I met you at the exact moment I was supposed to. You're my second chance."

Molly grinned through her tears. She wiped her eyes and after a heavy sigh said, "I have your eyes."

"Yes, you do and you're a cross between my sister, Harper, and your mom—both beautiful and stunning, like you."

She beamed and said, "So what do we do now?"

"I'd like to spend some time with you and get to know you. I'm not far from the campus, maybe we could do something this weekend, unless you have plans."

She shook her head. "Just studying, no plans."

"If you're up to it, I could pick you up tomorrow morning."

"Sure, that works for me. I've got to get myself pulled together. I have a class and work this afternoon," she sniffed and brushed her hair out of her face.

"Everything's going to be okay, Molly. I told Regi I was going to see if you'd like to go to Italy with me this summer. She thought it sounded like something you would enjoy."

Her eyes sparkled. "Italy? I'd love to go to Italy. That would be so cool."

He smiled, enjoying the delight in her expression. As she pulled her long shiny hair out of her face, he was again reminded of his sister; they both had hair the color of a new penny. "I would love to have you along. I'll probably need to be there for about a month, is that doable?"

Her eyes widened. "Wow, a whole month. Yeah, I was just going to spend the summer with Mom. I'm so mad at her right now, I can't imagine spending much time with her."

"I know you're upset, but give it a little time and try to see it from her point of view. It's not easy being a parent."

She nodded, but kept a firm scowl on her face, while a storm brewed in her eyes.

"Shall I go get your mom?"

She shook her head. "No. I told her I needed some time and didn't want to talk to her right now. I'm too mad."

"What time is your class?"

"I need to be there at one o'clock."

He glanced at his watch. "How about we grab lunch and figure out our weekend plan?"

She smiled and nodded. "I need to use the restroom and then I'll be set." She gathered her things and he held the door.

Dr. Pierce saw them in the hallway and hurried to them. "How are you two doing?"

Molly answered, "Great, I'm just going to find the restroom and then we're going to lunch." She continued down the hallway. "I'll meet you in the waiting room."

Cam added, "She's upset with Regi and doesn't want to talk to her. I wasn't sure what to do, so I suggested lunch. I was hoping we could all go."

"Regi's in a room down the hall with Nate. Poke your head in and tell her."

He opened the door and saw Nate and Regi at a table littered with soiled tissues. Nate had his arm around Regi, her entire face pink and raw from crying. Nate asked, "How'd it go?"

"Not bad," said Cam. "She's upset right now, but I'm going to take her to lunch and see how it goes. We're going to get together this weekend. I wanted all of us to go, but Molly's got a stubborn streak. She says she's too mad right now to talk to Regi. I'm so sorry."

Regi nodded. "It's like I expected. I knew she'd blame me."

Nate patted her arm. "Could you give Regi a call later and let her know how it's going? I think we'll head back home today."

Regi nodded. "I'd appreciate a call, just so I know."

Cam said, "Of course, I'll call tonight and keep you posted throughout the weekend. I think she'll come around and I'll do my best to explain things again. I tried now, but she's too upset to listen."

Regi thanked him and she and Nate waited for a few minutes to make sure Cam and Molly had time to leave the building. "How about we just head up to the ferry and get home, unless you want to have lunch somewhere?"

"I can't eat, so let's go." She collected her purse and they walked in silence to the Jeep. On the drive to the ferry, Regi fell asleep. Once they were parked, Nate woke her; amazed she could sleep through all the clanking and banging of the loading process.

"Regi, sweetie," he said, shaking her shoulder. "Let's go sit down."

He carried their jackets and led her to the deck outside. He held her hand and said nothing, just rubbed his thumb across the back of her hand. The calm motion of the ferry lulled them into a trance while they watched the lush green islands float by the railing.

"I hope she'll forgive me. I've made such a mess of things." She coughed out a laugh. "I spent twenty years wishing for Cam and now I wish I'd never found him."

"Give it a few days. Molly will get it together and everything will work out," said Nate, moving to massage the back of her neck and nestle her closer.

She stared across the water, fixated on the horizon. "I hope you're right." She rested her head on his shoulder for the rest of the journey home.

Nate tried to interest Regi in lunch, but she said she wasn't hungry. He phoned in an order to Dottie's and picked it up on their way to Linda's. When they walked in, Regi went straight to the bedroom.

Nate ate and checked on Regi, who was sleeping. He left her a note that he was going to pick up the dogs from Sam and Jeff. When he pulled up, he heard barking from the backyard and joined Jeff and Sam on the deck.

"Hey, Nate, how was the trip?" asked Jeff. He was playing fetch with all four dogs and they were sitting, watching him, while their tails wagged in anticipation of his next throw.

"We had a fun day Thursday, but the meeting Regi had with Molly to explain finding Cam didn't go well. Molly's peeved at her mom and won't talk to her right now. She's accepting of Cam and they're actually spending some time together this weekend, but Regi is on the outs."

Jeff went back to his game with the dogs, listening to the conversation as he played. "Oh, that's going to be hard for her. They've been so close," said Sam, delivering a glass of lemonade to Nate.

He thanked her and took a sip. "She's down in the dumps. I told her to give it a few days. It's a lot for Molly to process."

"Where is she now?" asked Sam.

"At Linda's, sleeping. I don't think she slept last night worrying and the whole day has been nothing but stress. She won't eat and barely talks."

"I wonder if her parents would be of any help?"

He shook his head. "I don't think so. I get the impression Regi doesn't share much with them. I think her mom is hypercritical and Regi avoids conversations like this one."

Sam nodded. "Yeah, I got the same feeling when she talked about them."

"She seems to look up to Kate, maybe she could talk to her," said Nate. "Murphy might cheer her up. I should probably get going with the dogs."

He thanked Jeff and Sam for watching the dogs and loaded them in his pickup for the quick ride to the house. When he walked in the dogs ran around the house, excited to be home. Regi was still ensconced in the bedroom and when he glanced in he saw her on the bed, asleep.

He busied himself doing his laundry and playing with the dogs. As he was tiptoeing down the hall, intending to wake her for dinner, he heard her cell phone ring. He crept back to the great room and turned on the television. Several minutes later she emerged from the hall, her clothes wrinkled and her face pale, devoid of expression.

"Hey, sweetie, do you feel better after your nap?"

"A little," she shrugged. "Cam just called and told me lunch with Molly went well. They have plans tomorrow and he's going to introduce her to his sister, Harper. She's very excited to meet Molly. He said Molly's still upset with me, but he's trying to sway her to my side." She plopped on the couch next to him.

"What sounds good for dinner?" he asked.

She shrugged. "Nothing, whatever you want is fine."

He kissed the top of her head and left her with Murphy and Lucy while he went to forage for food. He returned with grilled cheese sandwiches. While they were eating in front of the television, Regi's cell phone rang.

Regi glanced at the screen and answered, "Hi, Kate."

She talked for a few minutes and then said, "Sure, I could help you for a couple of hours. I'll see you in the morning."

Nate raised his brows in question. "What was that about?"

She sighed. "Kate needs some help tomorrow and since I'm off this weekend, she thought I might be available."

"It'll be good for you to get out and do something. It'll take your mind off Molly for a couple of hours."

She nodded. "Yeah, I know. I just want to curl up in bed until this is over and Molly and I are back to being best friends."

He took their empty plates and put them on the coffee table, but when Murphy's tongue found its way to the remains of the sandwiches, he put them in kitchen. "I'm no expert on mother-daughter relationships, but don't you think it's normal for college girls to pull away from their mothers at some point, especially when there's a disagreement?"

"I'm a perfect example of that and I guess that's what makes me afraid. I don't have a strong relationship with my mom. It ended when I got pregnant. She always took care of me and Molly, but not graciously. I was a burden and a disappointment and I still am."

"Is there any chance Molly would call your parents and tell them about Cam?"

New fear etched her face as she raised both hands to her cheeks. "I hadn't even thought of that." She got up and paced around the area rug. "She probably talks to my mom more than I do. Crap, crap, crap."

"Why don't you just call your parents and get them up to speed? That way it will be over. They're going to find out sooner or later anyway."

"I know. I know. I'm just tired of all of this."

Nate peeked at the clock on the wall. "Do you want me to stay with you tonight?"

"I'll be lousy company. I think I'd rather just be alone. After I call my parents, I'm sure I'll be even crankier." She stomped down the hall with her phone and he heard the bang of the bedroom door.

Twenty-Five

Saturday morning Regi pulled up to Kate's shop as she was unlocking the front door. "Good morning, Regi. Thanks so much for coming today."

"You're welcome. I could use the distraction." She juggled her coffee cup and her purse as she came through the door.

"Things didn't go too well with Molly yesterday?"

Regi shook her head, "Not really."

"I'm sorry to hear that. As soon as I get rid of Alec this morning, we'll talk it through, okay?"

Regi nodded, wishing her own mother could be half as supportive as Kate. "I'd like that, thanks." She moved to the register and Kate showed her how to ring things up and where she could find bags and ribbons.

Alec came through the door as soon as Regi had stashed her purse under the counter. "Ladies, what a lovely morning." He gave Kate an air kiss and then started to do the same with Regi, but she turned to straighten the tissue shelf.

"Regi's going to man the register while we work on your display. It looks like you brought quite a few today," said Kate, eyeing his stack of bubble wrapped paintings.

"Shall we take a peek?" he asked, raising a brow. "I did several new ones over the past week or so."

She led him to a blank display wall. "Let's spread them out on this table."

Regi wandered the shop while Alec and Kate chose paintings for the large display wall. She chatted with customers as they browsed the shop and sold a few small items.

Nate stopped in around noon, with a bag from the Jade Garden and a quick kiss for Regi. "I'm glad you stopped by. I meant to call you this morning. I need to apologize for being so rude last night," she said in a soft voice.

"It's okay, I know you're stressed out."

She shook her head. "It's not okay. You've been nothing but kind and helpful, so I'm sorry I took out my frustration on you."

"Apology accepted," he said with a smile. "I'll put lunch in the back. Are you almost done?"

She glanced over at Kate and Alec and saw he was gathering a few paintings and his pouches. "Looks like they're about done. I'll go see if she wants to eat with us."

Kate saw Regi and said, "What do you think? Aren't these lovely?" She waved her hand across the paintings that filled the table.

Regi nodded. "Yes, they're beautiful."

Alec put his pouches under his arm and kissed the back of Kate's hand. "Belle dame," he said, winking as he turned for the door. "Salut," he said, waving.

Regi asked, "Is he French?"

Kate laughed. "I'm not sure, but I think he believes it impresses people and makes him seem mysterious."

Nate added, "I think he's obnoxious."

Kate laughed. "He's an artist—some of them live in a different world." She looked at Nate peeking out from the back of the shop. "I smell lunch."

"Nate brought Chinese," said Regi, leading the way to the backroom.

When they finished lunch Nate said, "I've got to get back to my chores at home. I'll see you ladies later." He took Regi by the hand and kissed her.

She whispered, "Please stay tonight. I promise I'll be better behaved. I'll even cook us dinner."

He smiled and kissed her again. "Deal, I'll see you later this afternoon."

Kate and Regi spent the next few hours visiting in between customers. Regi rehashed her day with Molly and over several cups of tea, Kate assured her the situation would improve.

"I called my parents last night and it was the nightmare I knew it would be. Dad answered, but after saying hi he passed the phone to Mom. She, of course, berated me for upsetting Molly and gave me the 'what was I thinking' line about twenty times."

"I'm holding out hope that Molly will calm down and you two will return to the same close relationship, but your mom is another story. It sounds like your mom is upset that you left, so she's taking every opportunity to remind you of the failures she perceives are yours. I'm not sure how to bridge that gap."

Regi nodded. "I know. I've come to accept that our relationship is probably always going to be damaged. I've been less stressed being away from her—that is until now with Molly."

They continued talking until closing time, both surprised that the afternoon had disappeared. "Oh, I need to run to the market to get some things for dinner. Would you like to join us?" asked Regi.

"Are you sure you want company tonight?"

"Yes, this is the best I've felt since before this all happened with Molly. You're better than the therapist I'm seeing," smiled Regi.

Kate grinned and pulled her into a warm hug. "You and Molly are going to get through this. Give it some time and give her space." She released her and held her by the shoulders, "As for dinner, it sounds terrific. I'll stop by in about an hour when I'm done here."

Kate locked the door behind Regi and rang out the day, heading to her office to finish her work. She put in a call to Leon to see if he could come by and hang the new paintings for Alec's display and finished some correspondence.

She decided to take one of the new paintings, a gorgeous landscape of the island featuring a vivid sunset, home. She had the perfect spot for it in her bedroom.

* * *

Nate talked Regi into going out on the boat on Sunday. She did her best to set aside the struggle with Molly and could tell talking to Kate had helped. They had enjoyed a simple dinner on the patio and all three stayed up late talking around the fire pit. Sunday night her phone rang and she saw it was Cam. She sat on the patio talking while Nate finished putting together their dinner.

Regi had finished the call by the time Nate carried their meal outside. He saw Regi flipping through things on her phone and smiling. "What are you looking at?" he asked.

"Oh, Cam sent me some photos from the weekend. He and Molly went to the zoo and they had Harper and her husband over for dinner. He wanted me to see the shots he took of Molly and Harper. They could be sisters." She showed him the screen with both of them smiling and posing for the camera. Both wore their cinnamon hair in almost the same style, their arms around each other, laughing.

There were also some great photos of Molly and Cam sitting together on his patio and at the zoo. She flicked through all of them so Nate could see the photos. "Did he say how Molly was doing?"

She looked up and sighed. "Sounds like she's doing fine, except not budging on her feelings for me at the moment. Cam said she's seeing Dr. Pierce tomorrow again, so he's hopeful things may change after she talks to her."

"Looks like they had a good weekend, huh?"

Regi smiled. "Yeah, I'm glad she's taken to him so easily. She needs to have someone she can count on right now."

He motioned to the salmon salad and said, "Come on, let's eat."

She took a few bites and then pushed the rest of the salad around on her plate. "I was convinced she'd call me today, after her weekend with Cam. Kate tells me I need to give her space and be patient, but it's so hard."

"Let's just take one day at a time and see what happens. You need to eat more than that," he said, pointing at her plate with his fork.

She forked another bite into her mouth. "Cam told Molly he's going to pay for her college. Sounds like her anger slipped for a minute because she told him that would help me since I work two jobs to pay her way."

"See there's a tiny crack in her shell of anger. That's a positive sign. I actually think she's hurt more than angry."

"You're probably right. I want to call her so bad, but I'm trying to give her time and I don't want to risk the rejection right now." She took a slice of bread and started ripping it apart. "He said she's excited to go to Italy and it sounds like Harper may join them. Molly will love her. She's full of life and funny. Cam's parents are old money, stuffy, and arrogant, but those are traits they didn't pass to their children. Harper's about five years younger than Cam. She works with him at the family company."

"What about his parents?"

She shook her head. "They're in Europe for several months, so she hasn't met them. That could be interesting to see how they react."

"I think it's neat that Molly has an aunt. It'll be great for her to have some relatives and get to know them. I have fun spending time with my nieces and nephews."

"Yeah, she hasn't had much of an opportunity to have those relationships. With Ronnie being killed so young and Leon being a total loser most of his life, it's been just the two of us."

"You're not alone anymore, you know that don't you?" His eyes locked on hers.

She stared into the penetrating blue depths. "I know." Then she leaned her head and met his lips.

* * *

Each day of the following weeks Regi woke up hoping she'd hear from Molly, but when the third Saturday came and she still hadn't heard from her beloved daughter, her heart sank. Through Cam's regular communications she knew he and Molly were spending some time together during the weekends.

Nate was fishing with his dad this weekend and she had a short shift at the coffee shop. She crawled out of bed and got ready for the day. After feeding the dogs she stepped out on the patio and took a deep breath. "I should walk you guys and take advantage of this gorgeous view," she said, petting both their heads. She had been consumed with worry and fear about Molly and felt like a robot. She got up each morning hopeful and went to bed each night weighted down by misery.

Last week when she went to lunch with Leon she told him about Cam and the situation with Molly. He was surprised and sympathetic, even sending Regi a small bouquet at work. Nate did his best to distract her, but she knew her anguish was wearing on him. She was glad he was doing something he enjoyed this weekend, instead of trying to coax her into activities meant to divert her from the constant bleak thoughts that occupied her mind.

Max and Linda would be home in a week and she felt as if she hadn't even enjoyed her time in their home. As she stared into the mirror, doing her best to hide the telltale signs of worry and insomnia carved in her face, she vowed to stop obsessing. *I know Molly's safe. Cam's not going to let anything happen to her. This is just a rough patch we're going through. It's not going to be like my relationship with Mom. It can't be like that.*

She grabbed the keys to her Jeep and hurried to the coffee shop. Once there, she distracted herself with drink orders and chatter with her regular customers. Although the tourist season wouldn't be in full swing for another month, there had been a noticeable increase in visitors, especially on weekends. She kept busy for the entire shift, only having time to nibble on a pastry for breakfast.

When she was relieved by Megan around noon, she decided to stop at Alexander's and see Kate. Her shop was busier than usual with several tourists milling about the display areas. She spied Kate at the register, ringing up a sale and waved.

Once she was done, Regi slid onto a stool behind the counter. "How are you today, Kate?"

She smiled, "I'm busy, which makes me happy." She plopped onto another stool. "What brings you by?"

"Just got done at work and didn't feel like going home. I thought I'd buy Molly a card and send it to her, just so she knows I'm thinking of her."

"Still no word, huh?"

Regi shook her head, trying to keep her lips from quivering.

A customer stepped to the register and Regi wandered over to a rack of cards featuring Ryan's photographs of the island. She found one with a breathtaking view at sunset, almost as if it had been taken from Sam's deck. She took it and another one that featured the bench at the park near the harbor. She thought she'd send that to Cam to thank him for his help with Molly.

Kate rang up her cards and asked, "Is Nate gone for the whole weekend?"

Regi nodded. "Yeah, he and his dad have been planning this trip. He was really excited about it. He only wished Spence was on the island so he could go too."

"He'll be sorry he missed it. He's been busy with some work, so I'm not sure when he'll make it back here." Kate's eyes danced and she said, "But, my son is coming for Mother's Day. I can't wait to see him."

"Oh, how exciting for you. I know you've been looking forward to seeing him."

"It's been too long. He's only going to be able to stay for a few days, but I'll take whatever I can get."

The phone rang as Kate was about to sit down and she picked it up and reached for a notepad. She scribbled notes and double checked the address and credit card information. "Thank you so much and I'll get this shipped out on Monday for you."

"Now you're selling things by phone?" asked Regi.

"It's weird. I've had a few calls recently about Alec's work. He must be doing some advertising, but this will make six of his landscapes I've sold and shipped." She prepared an invoice and added the overnight shipping to the order and then ran the credit card. Once it cleared, she plucked the two small paintings from the display wall and began wrapping them for shipment.

"Maybe he's more famous than you thought," suggested Regi.

"I'm not sure. He's got a website, but it's pretty bare and I never heard of him until I met him at The Haven. His work is appealing and he captures the feel of the island, but I'm surprised at the interest from the east coast. It would make more sense if customers were from the Pacific Northwest, but all of them have been in the New York and New Jersey areas."

She finished applying the label to the box and put it on the counter. "Do you want me to run that down the street? That will save you an errand on Monday?"

"Sure, that would be great. Just have Kim put it on my account," said Kate, handing Regi the box. "Could I interest you in watching a movie tonight?"

Regi's face brightened. "That sounds fun. How about you come to Linda's? I'll take care of dinner and you bring a movie. Or we could use Max's fancy television to download one?"

"Perfect, I'll see you about six when I get out of here."

Regi dropped the shipment and stopped by the market to gather a few items for dinner. She wasn't a great chef, but teriyaki chicken was something she did well and it sounded tasty. She dropped by Ellie's on the way home and picked up some dessert. "I don't know how you keep up," said Regi, staring at the case full of deliciousness.

Ellie laughed and put the dog treats in a separate bag from the human box of desserts. "Well, when you don't have a life, it's pretty easy. I get in here by three in the morning and then when my day is over, I basically go home, eat, and go to bed so I can do it all over again."

"That doesn't leave you much time for yourself or your family."

"It's just me and my dog. It's probably a good thing I'm not married or even dating anyone. I don't have a spare minute. Sometimes I feel bad for Oreo, she's my dog."

"Cute name," laughed Regi.

"She's the reason I started to carry dog treats. She's a sweet border collie and luckily I have some acreage for her to roam when I'm at work. I've been in the process of training a helper. I'd like to be able to take some time off and she's a quick learner, so starting next month, I should have more free time."

"How long have you owned the bakery?"

"It's been in my family for decades. Let's see, I'm thirty-five now, so I've been running it on my own for five years. My parents moved off the island and I stayed. I immersed myself in work to get over a bad break-up and here I am," she flipped her hands over in front of her.

"I know what it's like to work all the time—exhausting. You deserve some time to yourself."

"That's my plan—stay tuned to see if it works. If you come in early in the morning you'll meet Nicole. She's going to be my early girl at least four mornings a week."

Regi clutched the pink box to her side and carried the bag of dog treats with her purse. "Good luck, Ellie, I'll see you soon," she said, waving as she went through the door.

She ran by the condo to collect the mail and check on things and then sped away from town. When she got home, the dogs were delighted to see the bag from Sweet Treats and of course, Regi. She gave them a treat and sat on the patio to enjoy the rest of the afternoon.

She penned the card to Cam and addressed the envelope. She stared at the other card, hesitating as her pen hovered above the empty white space. *I don't want to say the wrong thing.* She inhaled as she gazed at the water, concentrating to hear the soft lap of the waves against the beach.

She took another breath and the black ink of the pen began to flow over the snowy paper. She filled the card and turned it over, writing on the back before signing it. She addressed another envelope and decided to drive into town and mail them before she lost her nerve. She put both dogs in the Jeep for the excursion.

When she returned she started dinner and in the midst of cooking, Kate arrived. They visited while they finished preparing the meal and watched a movie. When Kate was leaving, Regi hugged her and said, "I always feel better after spending time with you. Thanks for coming over."

Kate grinned and kissed her on the cheek. "Anytime, my dear. I've never had many girlfriends, but I do enjoy our time together. Keep me posted on Molly."

As Regi climbed into bed that night she got a text from Nate. *Just thinking about you. Wanted to wish you a good night. Wish I was there to snuggle with you. Love, Nate.*

She sent a reply and slipped under the cool sheets. For the first time in weeks, her head wasn't whirling with negative thoughts. Part of it was the wine she had consumed, but the other part was due to talking with Kate and having the support of a wonderful man like Nate.

Twenty-Six

When Regi pulled into the parking lot of Cooper Hardware Sunday morning, she saw a couple of police cars in front of Alexander's. She glanced at her watch and saw she had enough time to pop by on her way to open Harbor Coffee and Books. The front door was open and she saw Kate speaking with a police officer.

"Kate, are you okay?" asked Regi, unable to disguise the fear in her voice.

"I'm fine. We just had a break-in early this morning. I'm trying to figure out what's missing."

"Oh, no. How did they get in?"

"Through the back. It was fast because the alarm company notified the police and they were here within ten minutes. It sounds like they think the thief planned it and timed it to escape on the first ferry of the morning."

"What did they take?"

"From what I can tell, most of the missing items are paintings. Alec's paintings."

Regi's brow furrowed. "They're not very valuable are they?"

Kate shook her head. "Not compared to some of the other items in the store. I've got to do an inventory, but most of the pricier items haven't been touched. Maybe the thief was interrupted."

"I'd stay and help, but I need to open the coffee shop. I'll call and see if someone can come in and I'll be back as soon as I can. Did you call Spence?"

"Yes, I called him as soon as I got down here. After making sure I was okay, he rattled something off about the ferry schedule and surveillance cameras and told me he had to run and he'd call me later."

Regi gave Kate a hug and hurried to the coffee shop. She opened and served the first wave of customers and then called Sam. She and Jeff arrived within thirty minutes and Sam stayed and worked while Jeff and Regi checked in with Kate.

The police had left and Kate was busy with her printouts and a pencil checking off items. She was still wearing her pajamas under a coat. "We can take over if you want to go home and get changed," offered Regi.

"Oh, that would be a huge help. I don't want to leave it unattended until I can get the back door repaired."

Jeff strode into the backroom and announced he'd go to the hardware store and get everything he needed to fix it. Kate showed Regi her system and left her with the inventory lists.

Jeff had the door repaired when Kate returned. She and Regi worked to finish the inventory and confirmed the only missing items were Alec's collection of paintings. He had not replenished the ones Kate had sold, so only twelve were left in the store and all of them had been taken.

Kate consulted her records and dialed Alec's number. She got a recording that the person she was calling wasn't accepting calls. She tried again with the same result. She called The Haven next. When she hung up from talking to Sherrie she said, "Sherrie said Alec's not in his room and must have left early this morning. His phone isn't working."

Regi and Kate both stared at each other. "I think there's more to this story than we know," said Kate. "This is too much of a coincidence."

"Did he have a car?"

"Sherrie said he drove a rental car and it wasn't there. I'll call the police and let them know what we found out on the inventory and tell them I can't locate Alec. I need to let Spence know as well."

Regi's shift was almost over, but she offered to work the afternoon since she had missed the morning. Sam told her not to worry about it and enjoy the rest of her day off. She bought two drinks and some snacks and carried them back to Alexander's.

"Oh, great. I missed my coffee this morning," said Kate, taking the cup.

"So, did the police say anything?"

Kate shook her head as she took another sip. "No, just thanked me and said they'd be in touch when they knew more. Spence asked me for the information on the shipments I made for Alec's sales. He was excited about that and said he'd be in touch."

Regi helped her clean up the shop and reposition items to fill the void left from the stolen paintings. They dusted and vacuumed and had the shop restored back to normal by late afternoon.

As they were taking one last look around, they heard the front door chimes. "Spence, what are you doing here?" asked Kate, eyes wide in surprise.

"Nice to see you too," he said with a wink. "Hi, Regi."

Kate laughed. "Sorry, I just didn't expect you here. It sounded like you were busy when I talked with you this morning."

"Well, your burglary helped me close the case on the art theft ring I've been working. We found Alec, whose real name is Robert Jones, at the airport. He was on his way to the east coast. He's singing like a little birdie as we speak."

"Well, we need more information than that, Captain Chandler," teased Kate.

"How about I take all of us to dinner and I'll tell you the whole story? Where's Nate?"

Regi answered, "He should be back soon. He and his dad had a fishing weekend. I'll give him a call right now."

When she returned from talking to Nate she found Kate and Spence upstairs on the couch. "I'm going to run home and let Spence check out the only painting I have left from Alec's collection. I bought one for my bedroom. He says he suspects he can show us rather than tell us what's going on."

"Okay, Nate was on his way home when I called. He said he'll be ready within an hour. I'll run home and change and we'll meet you at your house to see the demonstration before dinner."

When Regi and Nate arrived the small painting was resting on several newspapers and old cloths on top of Kate's island, while the two of them sipped iced teas. "Okay, Spence, they're here. Now you can show us," said Kate, rushing to the island.

Spence retrieved a bottle of liquid and a rag and began dabbing some on the corner of the painting. "The art guys gave me this to use. I'm not sure what it is, but it works like magic." As he applied it, the rag became saturated with blue from the image of the water in the painting. He kept rubbing and then stepped back so they could all see. What remained below wasn't a canvas, but another painting. "What is that?" asked Nate.

"I'm afraid it's not good news for Kate," he looked over his reading glasses at her. "We'll have to take this painting as part of the evidence and eventually return it to its rightful owner."

"So, Alec, was stealing valuable paintings and then repainting them to launder them?" asked Kate.

"Exactly, except he wasn't doing it alone. He's providing the police with his accomplices. He didn't steal the paintings, just painted over them and found places to move them."

"So the buyers who called Kate from the east coast were in on it. Did you get them?"

"They're tracking them down. The paintings were stolen from all across the country, so the FBI is also involved. It's a huge case."

"What a bunch of excitement for our sleepy little harbor town," said Nate.

"I hope I don't have to turn over the money from those sales. I haven't given Alec his consignment check yet either," said Kate, studying the painting. "It's such a shame, I really liked this one."

"He won't need his consignment check in prison and I doubt you'll have to give anything back, just your records. You'll probably have to testify if it goes to trial," warned Spence.

"Oh, I hope not. I don't want anything to do with it," she said. "Go ahead and take the painting and let's get to dinner."

Spence drove everyone and on the way Nate asked, "So, now that the art heist is solved, when are you coming back to fish?"

"I thought you'd never ask," said Spence, with a smile stretching across his face.

* * *

The next day Nate and Regi both worked late and she grabbed a pizza for dinner on the way home. When she walked in the dogs didn't greet her as they usually did. She put the pizza in the kitchen and opened the sliding doors to the patio. She heard the dogs and saw they were in the dog run.

She went outside and saw the doggy door had been locked. "That's weird. How'd you two manage to lock yourselves out?" she asked, as they hightailed it through the door and into the house.

As soon as she dished up their food, Nate walked in. "Regi, I'm home," he said doing his best imitation of Desi Arnaz. "I'm going to change and I'll be right there."

He came back a few minutes later and said, "Where's the television from the bedroom?"

"What? I don't know. I didn't do anything with it," she said, as she was opening the pizza lid.

Nate went into the great room and then she heard him running down the hall to the master suite. He was back in a flash and said, "Regi, we've been robbed. All the televisions are missing and so is the computer equipment from their offices."

"Oh, no." She ran through the house looking for anything else she could identify as missing. "That's why the dogs were locked outside."

"I'll call the police," said Nate, picking up the phone.

Regi returned, her face leached of color. "I'm not sure what sort of jewelry they had, but the box in their closet is empty."

"They're on their way," said Nate. "They said not to touch anything."

She shook her head and through clenched jaws said, "Leon."

Twenty-Seven

The next morning, Regi woke early exhausted from the responsibility she felt for the robbery. She had sent an email to Linda and Max and told them what had happened and asked them to call when they could. She hated to phone them in the middle of the night in Ireland.

She had tried contacting Leon and his phone went straight to voicemail. Jeremy confirmed Leon wasn't in the cabin and his Suburban was gone. It was his day off, so he hadn't been expected at work. The police put out a bulletin on Leon and his car and were going through the footage on the ferry to pinpoint when he left the island.

When the police questioned Lou he told them Leon had stopped by earlier in the day for lunch, which was unusual. He then checked his petty cash box and discovered it empty. The police had also found the point of entry. They kept calling the person "a suspect", but Regi knew in her heart it was Leon. He had used a glass cutter to access the lock on a set of doors to the patio. She hadn't noticed them, because they weren't used often and a curtain covered the hole.

All of these thoughts swirled through her mind and her stomach churned at the thought of talking to Linda and Max. She let out a sigh.

Nate cuddled closer to Regi. "I think you should call in sick today and get some rest."

"I think I need to move. I knew he'd never change and now he's hurt the people closest to me again," she retorted.

"Come on now, you're not responsible for him and you know that. You warned everyone in town and did all you could. He's the bad guy here, not you."

"I'm not sure how much more of this I can handle. I'm barely hanging on as it is and now he's got to pull another one of his famous stunts."

"You've got your appointment with Dr. Cummings today, right?" She nodded. "Just take the day. Linda and Max are probably going to call this morning, and you don't need to deal with that at work."

She glanced at the clock and used her phone to send an email to her boss, since it was still too early to call him. "I've got to call my parents and let them know in case he shows up there." She flung the covers off and sat up, putting her head on her knees. "I'm done with my brother. This is the last time he's going to screw with me." A tear trickled down her face and she sniffed. "Shame on me for buying his line about changing and staying on the straight path."

Her phone bleeped and she scrolled to an email from Max. He told her to contact his insurance company and that they would call her at seven in the morning her time.

Nate followed her to the bathroom door. "I'm going to call Trevor to cover my route today and I'll stick around here with you."

"I'm okay, you don't need to do that."

He closed the gap between them and seized her in a hug. He kissed the top of her head and whispered, "I know, but I want to. I love you, Regi."

He felt her tears dampen his chest. "I'm not sure I deserve you, Nate, but I love you."

He held her tight, until he felt her relax in his arms. "You don't have to figure everything out by yourself." He kissed her and said, "I'm going to feed the dogs and fix us something to eat."

She started the shower and he checked the fridge for the makings of breakfast. When she returned, dressed with damp hair, he had cheese omelets and toast ready. "Let's try to enjoy the morning and eat on the patio," he suggested.

As she took the first bite of the warm cheesy eggs, she was reminded of her hunger and the dinner she had skipped last night. Sunlight bounced off the water and the day was shaping up to be gorgeous. As they finished breakfast, her phone rang.

She showed Nate the screen and he gave her hand a squeeze when she said, "Hi, Max."

"Hi, Regi. Are you okay?"

"I'm fine, just so very embarrassed and sorry. I didn't trust Leon when he moved here, but over the last four months he had been doing well, so I had just started to believe he'd really changed. I'm just sick about your stuff, Max."

"Don't worry, Regi. As long as you're okay and the dogs didn't get hurt, we can replace our stuff. Did you find the insurance information in my file?"

She nodded. "Yes, I'll call them first thing this morning and get them a copy of the police report. You'll have to follow up when you get back, but I think it's your electronics and whatever jewelry was in the closet. I'm not sure of anything else or if you want me to check anything."

"We kept a small amount of cash in the house. It's in my office in the bookcase, in a fake set of books." He went on to describe them and she ran into the house to check while he was on the line.

She pulled down the books and opened it to find a stack of cash. "It looks undisturbed to me. I can count it, if you hold on."

"No, don't bother. I'm sure it would all be gone if he'd found it."

"What about the stuff on your computers?"

"We talked about it this morning and Linda said her records are all backed up in a cloud service. I don't have anything valuable on my system, just my lecture notes and papers, but Linda backed those up before we left, just in case we had a power bump or something fried the hard drive, so I think we'll be fine."

Regi let out a breath. "That's a relief. I haven't talked to the police today, but I'll stop by this morning and see if they've had any luck locating

Leon. I'm sure he's hooked up with some of his deadbeat friends already. I've got to call my parents this morning so they know what's happened."

"Please try not to stress too much. Our insurance will cover the stolen items and we'll go from there."

"I'll pay your deductible, whatever it is," she said with her heart pounding. "I should have never brought him to your home."

"You don't need to pay anything. We can discuss it more when we get home. This call probably costs more than my deductible anyway," he laughed. "By the way, Linda wants to say hi."

Linda came on the line and she did her best to assuage Regi's feelings of guilt. She reiterated the fact that their insurance would replace the items and distracted Regi by asking about Lucy and Murphy.

Regi ended the call by saying, "I'll email you any updates from the police and we'll see you in about a week."

Nate had cleared the plates and tidied the kitchen while she had been on the phone. "Feel better?" he asked when she hung up.

"Maybe. They're both so understanding. It just frosts me that Leon violated their home and trust." She looked at her phone seeing a missed call that had come in when she had been on the phone. It was from her mother.

Regi rolled her eyes and said, "Mom tried to call me. I better call her back."

"I'm going to go get showered and then we can work on the police and insurance. Hopefully, we can get that glass panel replaced soon."

"Jeff said he went ahead and had the glass guy order it, so it could get fixed quickly. He's sure the insurance will pay and like he said, it's got to be repaired regardless."

Nate nodded as he padded down the hall. "I'll be ready in a few minutes."

She braced herself as she hit the button to call her mother. "Hey, Mom, I missed your call a few minutes ago."

"I can't believe you didn't call me sooner to let me know the police suspect poor Leon of burglary. They said you implicated him. How could you do that to your own brother?"

"Because he did it, Mom. The house I'm staying in was robbed. Leon is nowhere to be found. The place he worked at is missing cash. He won't answer his cell phone and he's disappeared. Come on, Mom. You need to quit sticking up for him."

"Did you ever stop to think maybe he's hurt or something happened to him? You always just want to believe the worst about him," she screamed.

Regi pressed her fingers to her temple. "Mom, I'm not going to have this conversation again. Leon is bad news. He's the reason Ronnie's dead and he's done nothing but cause trouble his whole life. He went to prison, Mom."

"He just got in with the wrong crowd. He's a good boy."

Regi took a deep breath, trying to steady her voice. "Have you heard from him in the last few days?"

"No."

"Have you tried calling his cell phone?"

"Yes, but there's no answer."

"If you hear from him, you need to contact the police. They need to talk to him."

"Yes, the surly officers they sent over here to terrorize us said the same thing. You know Leon never would have gone to that godforsaken island if you hadn't have moved there. He needs his family."

"Don't start, Mom. You're the one who told Leon to come and visit me. He could have stayed at your house when he got out of prison." She paused and then continued, "You know what? It doesn't even matter. You're never going to admit that Leon's a mess. I get pregnant and you've never forgiven me, but Leon has been a complete loser since high school, gets Ronnie killed, goes to prison, and then continues his life of crime and drug abuse, and he's the golden boy. I'm done, Mom. I can't keep doing this." She poked the red button to end the call and sat at the counter, her hands shaking.

Nate walked up behind her. "I'm sorry, sweetie. That sounded horrible." He rubbed her shoulders, feeling the knots in her muscles. She sat with her eyes closed, her head hanging down, as he tried to massage away the pain.

"I'll never understand my mom," she said in a soft voice. "She always finds a way to blame me." She reached for his hand. "Thanks, my neck feels better."

Nate drove them to town and parked in front of the police department. They met with the officer in charge, John, who Nate knew from high school. "So, we looked through the camera footage from the ferries and found Leon's Suburban boarding here and departing in Anacortes. We talked to Skagit County and they were able to follow him until he turned off the main highway. They, along with neighboring counties, are actively looking for him, but he was ahead of them by several hours."

Regi asked about getting a copy of the report to take to the insurance office and he provided her with several copies and his business card. "I called my parents today and Mom told me that some officers had come to the house asking about Leon."

John nodded, "Yes, we alerted Kittitas County as well and they paid a visit to your parents' house to see if he'd been there or had called. We found his cell phone in a trash bin on the ferry he rode out of here."

"My mom is convinced he hasn't done anything wrong, so I'm not sure how cooperative she'll be. She's a bit naïve when it comes to Leon."

The officer's eyebrows rose. "Looking at your brother's record, he hasn't been an angel. He's been in and out of the system since he was a teenager." He shook his head. "Sometimes parents don't always see the truth when it comes to their kids."

"Thanks for your time and help. If you get any news, please let us know, so I can keep Max and Linda informed," said Regi.

"Will do. Don't expect too much. We're running down his recent calls to see if that could help us pinpoint him or if there's anyone he knew in prison he may try to contact. Do you know any of his friends?"

She shook her head. "I haven't talked to him in years and was surprised when he showed up here. I don't know anything about his recent life. He was into drugs and drinking, which always seemed to lead to theft. He was supposedly going to AA meetings here, but I'm not sure of that either."

"Okay, we'll let you know if we get anything." He stood and shook both their hands. "Take care."

"Thanks, John," said Nate, putting his hand on the small of Regi's back to lead her outside.

They drove to the insurance agent's office and explained the situation and turned over the police report. She promised to get the claim processed immediately and Nate emailed her the pictures he had taken of the damaged patio door. Regi gave her Max's contact information and told her he'd be available by email for the rest of their trip.

They stopped by the hardware store and talked to Jeff about the new glass. "It should be here on Thursday and they'll install it Friday. I can let them in, since you'll be at work," he offered.

While Regi went to her therapy appointment, Nate stopped at Alexander's, hoping Spence might be there. When he walked in, Kate was at the register. "Good morning, Nate. Spence is up in my office."

He waved and continued through the store to the stairs. Spence was sitting on the couch, reading a book, but looked up when the stair creaked. "Nate, what brings you by?"

"Regi's gone to see Dr. Cummings and I thought I'd fill you in on the latest drama."

Nate handed Spence the police report and waited for him to finish reading it. He shoved his reading glasses down his nose. "What a mess for Regi. I'm sure she feels responsible, right?"

"I see why you're a great detective," smiled Nate. "Yeah, she's upset and then she talked to her mom and it got worse. I've never met her, but she must be a real doozy. She twists things around and in her mind this is all Regi's fault and poor Leon hasn't done anything wrong." He shook his head. "Regi's on overload right now. First Molly's attacked, then she finds Cam, then has to tell Molly, and now Leon."

"Let me make a couple of calls and see if I can learn anything from my contacts in the city," said Spence, taking out his cell phone.

Kate joined them while Spence was on the phone and Nate filled her in on the crisis of the day. When he finished Kate said, "I'd like to get my hands on Regi's mother and slap the living snot out of her."

Nate grinned. "You'd have to wait in line behind me. The thought of her as my mother-in-law is the only thing that could keep me from asking Regi to marry me."

Kate squealed and put her hand to her mouth. "Oh, don't let her deter you. I'm so pleased to hear you say that."

He lowered his voice. "I've loved her from the moment I met her, but I've been waiting to make sure I didn't scare her off. I keep thinking when things calm down, I'll get up my nerve. I was really hoping Molly would contact her and patch things up, but we're working on almost a month now."

She patted his hand. "Have you considered talking to Molly?"

"I've toyed with the idea, but hate to get in the middle of everything and I don't want to make it worse."

"If you marry Regi, you're going to be in the middle of all it," smiled Kate.

He head bobbed in agreement. "Regi's working this weekend, maybe I'll take a trip and see Molly."

"Spence is going back home Friday night. Maybe you could go with him and do some fishing. That would give you an excuse to be in the city."

"You're a wise woman, Kate."

She grinned and batted her eyelashes, "I've been told that a time or two."

Twenty-Eight

Friday evening Spence and Nate took the ferry and Nate's plan to talk some sense into Molly began to take shape. He knew from Regi's conversations with Cam during the week that Molly was working Saturday afternoon, so he decided to show up at her dorm on Saturday morning. He was hoping for a productive conversation that would leave him time for fishing with Spence before he returned to Friday Harbor on Sunday.

Kate vowed to keep Nate's secret and he bunked on Spence's couch. It was late when they got to Spence's place. He mulled over the points he wanted to make as he fluffed his pillow and pulled the blankets around him. He hated to see Regi upset and was hoping he could appeal to Molly in person.

Spence dropped Nate in front of Molly's dorm. "Just call or shoot me a text when you want me to pick you up."

Nate had enlisted Kyle's help to make certain that Molly would be home when he got there. Kyle was going to be at Molly's to pick her up for breakfast at the same time Nate would arrive. As he made his way upstairs his phone beeped with a text from Kyle letting him know he had arrived.

He knocked on her door and when she opened it, she let out a gasp and threw her arms around him. "Nate, what are you doing here?"

"I was in the neighborhood and was hoping to talk with you."

"Come in," she said, opening the door wide and motioning him inside. "Kyle just got here. We're going out for breakfast. Do you want to come with us?"

"We can go another time—" began Kyle.

"Sure, let's all go and it's my treat," said Nate. *Having Kyle there could help.*

They walked to a café a few blocks away and took a table outside on the patio. After they ordered, Nate began the conversation. "I'm here because I'm worried about you and your mom. She's been miserable for weeks not hearing from you. She feels horrible about the whole situation, but you two aren't going to resolve anything if you don't communicate."

Molly pursed her lips, but nodded her head.

"Another reason I'm here is I want to talk to you about marrying your mom."

Her eyes widened and she brought her hands to her cheeks. "I was hoping you would ask her someday. I was rooting for you even when she thought she wasn't dating you."

Nate smiled. "Thank you for that."

"That's great news," said Kyle. "You guys make a cute couple."

"I got a card and note from her last week. I should have called her, but I'm still mad."

"She knows your upset with her and she understands, but you've got to forgive her and move forward. Think about your life together. She made this mistake that was very damaging to you, but she didn't do it to hurt you. None of this has been easy on her. She made her own way and from what I can see has taken excellent care of you, working nonstop to make sure you had everything possible. She knew Cam could have paid for everything and didn't try to squeeze him for money. She wanted him to come back to Friday Harbor. She had this whole fairy tale written in her mind and she lived her whole life waiting for her fortieth birthday. That's a long time. Think about it."

He paused and took a sip of his orange juice. "When she was your age, you were two. She had to take care of you, work, and she went to college. Granted your grandparents helped take care of you, but she made sure she provided for you. She didn't date anyone for twenty years, waiting for Cam."

"When he didn't show up, her world fell apart, but she had to keep it together for you. She gave up hope of ever seeing him again and then bam, she runs into him at the doctor's office. Then she had to face the task of telling you about your dad, in the midst of you healing from being attacked. Don't make her wait any longer, Molly. She loves you and needs you in her life."

The waitress delivered huge plates heaped with fresh food. When Nate looked back at Molly, he saw tears trickling down her face. He felt bad, but he wasn't letting up. "This past week, Leon broke into Max's house and stole a bunch of stuff, plus took cash from Lou's and disappeared. Now she has to deal with that. Your grandmother is blaming her for Leon's actions and is convinced he's innocent. She doesn't have a good relationship with your grandma and her greatest fear is to lose you."

The trickle turned into a flood and Molly used her napkin to cover her face. Kyle put his hand on her shoulder. "It's okay, Molly. Just talk to your mom. Everything's going to work out. I know a little about how you feel. My mom never told me about my dad either."

She nodded. "And you forgave her," she said, gulping through her sobs.

"I did. I was upset with her, but I understood why she did what she did. I lucked out because now I have Sam in my life. I've always been close to my mom and now I'm getting to know my dad and the bonus is Sam." Kyle stabbed a forkful of his scramble and added, "It's weird at first, but now I'm used to it."

"You've been spending time with your dad and obviously he adores you," said Nate.

She nodded and smiled through the tears. "Yeah, he's great and we have fun together. I really like Aunt Harper. It's been lots of fun spending time with both of them."

Nate took her hand. "You know your mom isn't going to do anything to stop you from spending time with them or loving them. She wants you to have them in your life. She wants you to be happy."

She bobbed her head. "I know. I'm not sure why I've been so mean. I think I just wanted to punish her."

"Mission accomplished," said Nate, narrowing his eyes. "She doesn't deserve to be punished. She loves you and from what I can see has lived her life doing her best for you."

Molly's eyes softened. "I know she didn't mean to hurt me and she hasn't had it easy. My dad told me he made the worst mistake of his life when he left her and went to college."

"I'm not about to lose her. That's why I'm here. I want to ask her to marry me and I know she won't say yes until you guys are back on solid footing. So, will you please consider talking to her and patching things up?"

She wiped her eyes again and nodded. "Yes, I'll do it. I've wanted to. I've been scared and it's easier to ignore it than talk about it." She picked up her fork and took a bite of fruit. "I'm going to go to Italy with Cam, I mean Dad, as soon as school is out in May. Maybe I could come to the island for Mother's Day next weekend."

Nate let out the breath he had been holding and smiled. "That would be wonderful."

"I'll send her a text tonight and tell her I'll be there to spend the weekend so we can talk."

"That will mean the world to her, Molly." He finished his last bite. "I take it I have your blessing to marry your mom?"

"Of course you do. She's happiest when you're around. You'll be my bonus," she winked at Kyle.

* * *

Regi called Nate on Saturday night after she received Molly's text and he could tell she was thrilled to have heard from her daughter. When he stepped off the ferry he saw her. She greeted him with a bright smile, waving her hands above her head so he'd spot her.

He put his duffle bag on the ground and captured her in his arms, lifting her off the ground. "You are beautiful and I've missed your smile."

"I can't wait until she gets here. Part of me is nervous, but her texts were encouraging. I'm trying not to contact her and let her be the one to initiate."

"How about we grab pizza, I'm starving," he said, putting his arm around her and gathering his bag.

Regi rambled on about her weekend as they walked along the harbor. She had gone to see Lou and tried to give him the two hundred dollars Leon had stolen, but he wouldn't take it. "At least Leon didn't screw Jeremy out of any money."

"The silver lining is he probably won't be returning to the island."

"Another reason to stay here," she said, squeezing his hand. "Can you believe it's our last night at the house? They'll be home tomorrow night."

"I've enjoyed spending time there. It's secluded and I love the outdoor living spaces," he said, opening the door to Big Tony's.

"I know. Someday I'd love to have a house with a view."

They mowed down a pizza and he told her about fishing with Spence. "He told me his lease runs out in January. I think he's planning to move here."

"That would be great for Kate…and us. Even though they're old enough to be my parents, I really enjoy spending time with them." She sipped her iced tea. "That reminds me, Kate's son is coming for Mother's Day."

Nate nodded as he swallowed the rest of his drink. "It's going to be a busy weekend."

When they got home they spent their last night cuddled together on the rocking bench, warmed by the fire, watching as stars filled the indigo sky.

* * *

As Regi was leaving work Monday, Spence called to let her know he had heard from a colleague that Leon had been picked up on the Oregon-Washington border, outside of Vancouver. He was in jail and charged with the burglaries, plus driving under the influence of both alcohol and drugs. None of the stolen items were recovered, but he did have several hundred dollars in cash.

She sent Nate a text to update him and stopped by Buds and Blooms to pick up some flowers for the house. She made a trip to the market to stock their fridge and picked up a special dessert. When she got to the house, she did one more walk through to make sure they had collected all their belongings and everything was clean. She collected Murphy and hugged Lucy goodbye and left the card she had written them next to the flowers on the island.

When she got back to the condo, she put away the bag of groceries she had bought for herself and played ball with Murphy to distract her from the loss of her dog buddy. She watched television while she ate a salad and started making a list for the weekend and Molly's visit.

Nate showed up as she took her first bite. He met her with a kiss when she opened the door. "Do you do that at all your delivery stops?" she joked.

He chuckled. "No, it's an added service just for you." He kissed her again, and she led him inside. She talked him into a salad and bread.

"I stopped by and talked to John at the police department. He said the same thing Spence told you. Leon's denying the burglaries, but when they searched the car they found Linda's tablet under one of the seats. They don't think they'll recover the stolen items, since he most likely traded them for drugs or sold them."

"Did they call my parents?"

He nodded, stuffing a piece of Ellie's crusty bread in his mouth. "Yeah, John talked to your mom. He said she wanted to know where he was in jail so she could go get him. She's convinced he's innocent and it must all be a misunderstanding."

She shook her head. "Unbelievable."

"John said Leon will most likely go back to prison, since he was on parole. He hadn't checked in with his parole officer since he'd been here and your mom wouldn't divulge his location, so he was in trouble before he even robbed the house."

"See what I've had to put up with all these years? I'm so done with Leon and I don't want to talk to my mom anytime soon."

They finished dinner and Nate wrestled with Murphy while she cleaned up the kitchen. "I know you only have to work half a day Friday. How would you feel about getting away for a few hours with me? We could have lunch on the beach and be back here in time for the evening ferry and Molly."

She smiled and said, "I can't think of a better way to spend an afternoon." She kissed him and rested her forehead against his. "I'm so glad I moved here."

"Me too." His blue eyes flickered with mischief as he seized her and rolled her onto the couch.

* * *

She met Max and Linda for coffee early Friday morning. Max and Linda were all smiles when Regi slipped into a chair at their table. Sam was working the counter with Hayley and delivered their drinks with an invitation to a Mother's Day brunch at their house on Sunday.

"Jeff's family will be there and I invited Kate and she said she'd bring her son and Spence, so you make sure to bring Molly and Nate."

"That sounds fun. What shall I bring?" asked Regi.

"Yeah, we'll bring something too," offered Linda.

"I've got it under control. Ellie's coming and she's going to do a couple of desserts. I can't think of anything else I need. Just come and enjoy yourselves."

Linda took a sip of her hot chai. "Thanks so much for the flowers and stocking us up with groceries. We've been lounging around all week, tired from all the travel."

Regi apologized again for Leon's actions. Max gripped her hand. "Regi, please let's forget about it. I already ordered new televisions and computers. Our insurance covered it and you took care of getting the glass replaced. It's all fine."

Linda caught herself yawning. "I can't seem to shake this jet lag." She smiled at Regi. "Max was thrilled because he learned there's a newer model of his ginormous television."

Regi grinned as she saw the delight on Max's face. "Nate said the police recovered your tablet in Leon's car. So you'll probably get that back eventually."

"Not to worry. It's just stuff. Now if he had hurt my Lucy girl, there would've been hell to pay, but we can buy new stuff."

She felt the sting of tears in her eyes. "You're both wonderful. I couldn't ask for better friends than I've found here." She finished her drink and they hugged as Regi left in a hurry to get to work.

* * *

Like most shortened days, Regi's morning was chaotic and she spent all her time dealing with a variety of teenaged crises. When the bell rang for dismissal, she was shocked and double checked her watch. She hurried to her office, dismayed by the stack of work on her desk, but shut down her computer.

The teachers had to stay for a meeting, but she went racing out of the parking lot, looking forward to unwinding with Nate. The forecast called for warm temperatures and sunny skies, so she braved shorts, vowing to get some color on her pale legs.

She threw in a jacket and a pair of yoga pants in case it got cooler on the water. She put her hair in a ponytail and stuck it through the back of her old Mariners hat. Nate was taking care of lunch, so she just threw in a towel and sunscreen, and tucked her sunglasses in her beach bag.

Nate arrived and drove to the marina. His boat was ready to go and after helping Regi board, he guided them out of the slip into the open water. They traveled south and he steered them into a secluded cove on the southern part of Griffin Bay. As they got closer, she saw pebbles lined up on the beach. He took them in as far as he dared and shut off the engine.

She looked again at the beach and saw the pebbles spelled out *I love you Regi. Will you marry me?* She gasped and covered her mouth with her hands. "When did you do this?" she asked.

"This morning," he grinned, putting his arm around her as she continued to stare at the beach. He slipped a velvet box out of the pocket of his shorts and flipped open the lid. "So, will you be my wife, Regi?"

A smile filled her face and she flung her arms around his neck. "Yes, I will, Nate. I love you."

He kissed her and put the ring he had chosen on her finger. The large cushion cut diamond glittered in the sun. "Oh, my gosh, Nate, it's gorgeous."

"I had a little help from my mom and Kate. She found it for me through one of her contacts in the city."

Tears streaked Regi's face. "I'm so surprised. I can't believe you did this." She held her hand out admiring the sparkle. "I'm sort of a mess, if you haven't noticed. Are you sure?"

He answered her by drawing her close and covering her lips with a kiss that sent a sizzle traveling through both of their bodies. His touch sparked a longing for more and soon they forgot about the lunch he had put so much thought into packing. After making love, they talked and dozed on a soft blanket, their limbs tangled together, lulled by the soft sway of the boat and the warmth of the sun on their skin.

The slap of water against the boat jarred them from the brink of sleep. "We should probably get up and eat some lunch before we head back," said Nate, rubbing her shoulder.

He put on his shirt and unpacked the cooler. They feasted on cheese and bread, pasta salad, fresh fruit, and moist vanilla and strawberry cupcakes, smothered in cream cheese frosting. "Delicious," pronounced Regi, as she popped the last bite of her cupcake in her mouth.

They stored everything in the cooler and repacked the blanket before starting back to the marina. As he maneuvered through the bay she stood behind him and put her arms around his chest. "Thank you for the best day I can remember."

"How do you feel about a December wedding? I'd like you to have something wonderful to remember this Christmas."

She smiled, the wind flowing through her loose hair, the ponytail long undone. "It sounds terrific. I'd have the bonus of a couple of weeks off and that would give us time to plan a wedding."

"If my mom hasn't already got it done. She's so excited about the possibility. I'm the oldest and the last to marry. I think she thought I'd be single forever."

"Speaking of old," she said, sitting down. "You realize I'm too old to have another baby? I mean, it's probably possible with a lot of procedures and money, but I think it's almost too late for the natural route."

He nodded and looked at her. "I know, sweetie. I'm marrying you because I love you, not because I'm looking for a baby. If we decide to have one, we can check out the options or adopt. Besides, we'll always have Molly."

"Do you want to have a child?"

He shrugged. "It would be fine if we did, but it's not something that's a priority for me." He looked at her. "How about you?"

"I haven't thought about it recently. Long ago I thought it would've been fun to have a sibling for Molly, but they're a lot of work."

"Let's not get hung up on worrying about it. I love you and want to spend the rest of my life with you."

She reached for his hand. "I love you, Nate. I only wish I'd met you sooner."

Twenty-Nine

Nate met Regi and Molly for breakfast on Saturday morning. He and Regi agreed it would be best if Regi and Molly spent Friday evening alone, talking through the events that had damaged their relationship.

He was seated at an outdoor table at the Front Street Café when they walked up, both looking happier than he could remember. "Good morning, ladies," he said, standing and kissing Regi. "How are you two?"

"We're great," said Regi, glancing at Molly.

"Everything's okay, Nate," said Molly. "Mom showed me her ring." She rushed to him and hugged him. "I'm so happy for you guys."

"Thanks, Molly. Did your mom tell you we're thinking about a Christmas wedding?"

"She did. That would be perfect. I told her last night I'm going to Italy in a couple of weeks and I've decided to study one semester abroad, so I won't be back until December."

"Wow, that's exciting news," said Nate, as the waitress appeared with menus. "How are you handling that, Mom?"

Regi patted Molly's hand. "I'll miss her, but it sounds like a wonderful opportunity. Cam's going to stay in Italy, so she won't be without help if she needs it."

"Plus I'll get to travel and see some other countries while I'm there." They ordered breakfast and Regi was given a complimentary mimosa in honor of Mother's Day.

"So, we checked the calendar last night and December twentieth looks like the best day for the wedding. I'll be back early that week and could help with anything you need done," offered Molly.

"It seems we have a couple of wedding planners on the job," laughed Nate. "My mom can't stop talking about it. She wants us to stop by today so she can see you and talk about the wedding. If you add in Linda and Jen, they'll have this thing all planned by Monday."

"I haven't talked to my parents," said Regi, looking down at her napkin. "I need to do that today."

"Later," said Nate. "I thought I'd take you girls for a spin on the water."

Molly's eyes brightened. "Sounds perfect to me." Regi slipped her hand under the overhang of the tablecloth and onto Nate's lap. He squeezed it tight and gave her a wink.

* * *

They arrived at Sam's house on Sunday morning with sparkling cider, wine, and champagne, and as they were walking to the front door saw Spence's SUV coming down the driveway. Jack and Lulu were following in their car.

Kate introduced them to her son, Mitch, who was carrying a huge vase of flowers. "Great to meet you, Mitch. Your mom was so excited you were coming to visit," said Regi.

"I meant to be here before now, but my work has been crazy. I work at the Washington State Legislature. We wrapped up our session in March, but I haven't been able to get any time off until now."

"Kate said you could only stay for a few days. If you were here longer, we could do some fishing. Spence and I are planning to go at the end of the week," said Nate.

Mitch smiled. "I wasn't sure I could get the time, so I didn't want to disappoint Mom, but I'm here for about ten days, so fishing sounds great."

Nate introduced Molly to his parents and Lulu hugged her, "What a beauty and we heard all about your travel plans to visit Italy. How exciting," she rambled, as she linked her arm in Molly's and followed the path to the front door.

Jeff opened the door to welcome them and by thc time they were seated on the deck, Jeff and Max had agreed to join the fishing expedition. Jeff made sure everyone was introduced to Mitch and Max helped deliver drinks.

Once all the food had been brought out, Max asked all the mothers to gather at the end of the deck. He raised a glass and toasted all of them ending with, "No matter how old we are, we always need the wisdom and comfort of our mothers. Today we celebrate all of you. We love you."

Mitch squeezed his arm tight around Kate, knowing she was thinking of Karen today. Jeff linked his hand in Sam's as she brushed a tear from her cheek, remembering her mom, Sophia. After all the moms received hugs from their kids and grandkids, Nate whispered to Regi and she nodded.

He cleared his throat and said, "Before we start, Regi and I have some news to share." The chatter stopped as everyone looked upon them.

"I asked Regi to marry me Friday and she said yes," he shouted. "You're all invited to our wedding on December twentieth."

Applause and squeals of delight erupted, along with barks from all the dogs giving their stamp of approval to the engagement. Linda and Sam rushed to see the ring and hug Regi. Plates were heaped with food, glasses were filled, silverware clinked, and the steady hum of female voices planning a wedding filled the air.

* * *

After brunch, Nate and Regi took Molly to the ferry. Molly sat on a bench between the two of them as they waited for the boarding call. Regi tried to hold back the tears, but in the end they were both crying. She hugged Molly and said, "I can't believe I'm not going to see you for six months."

"It'll go by fast and we can video chat with each other. Dad does it all the time for work and said we could set up a time with you each week."

Regi nodded, smiling, as tears streamed down her face. "I'll miss you." She hugged her again. "Thank you for coming this weekend and for forgiving me."

Molly sobbed, "I should have never been so mean to you. I'm sorry, Mom. I love you."

The announcement to board squawked over the loudspeaker. "I love you, Molly. Be careful and keep in touch."

Molly hugged Nate. "Bye, Nate. Take care of my Mom, okay?"

Nate smiled. "I will. Be sure and call her often," he whispered, as he hugged her close.

They stood waving as Molly boarded and made her way to the deck outside. They waved at each other until they couldn't see her anymore and the ferry became only a bump on the sea of blue.

After the emotional sendoff, Nate took Regi for an ice cream cone and then drove to his house. She decided to call her mom before it got any later. While she was on the phone, Nate took Murphy outside to play ball.

"Happy Mother's Day, Mom," she said.

"Thank you. I wondered when you were going to call."

"Molly came to visit this weekend and we were at brunch. She just left on the ferry to go back to school."

Her mother harrumphed. "Have you talked to Leon?"

"No, Mom, I have no plans to talk to him."

"Well that's no way—"

Regi cut her off. "I called to wish you a happy day and tell you some exciting news. I've been dating a wonderful man here in Friday Harbor. His name is Nate Martin. He's asked me to marry him."

She was met with silence from the other end of the phone.

"Mom, are you still there?"

"I'm here. When are you getting married?"

"December twentieth. Molly helped us pick the date. She's going to be spending the next few months in Italy with Cam and will be back in December."

"That's a terrible time for a wedding. Your father and I will have to handle that horrible drive in winter and then take one of those awful ferries over and it's Christmas."

"Yes, Mom, I know. It's the best time for us, so that's when we're doing it. I thought if you had this much notice, you could work it out."

"I'll talk to your father and we'll see."

"Did you do anything fun this weekend?" Regi asked, trying to keep the conversation light.

"We visited Leon today. You know they put him back in prison while he's awaiting his court hearing. Something about violating his parole."

Regi rolled her eyes and said, "No, I didn't know. Molly's doing great. Her arm is almost back to normal."

"And now you're going to let her go traipsing off to Italy. God only knows what will happen to her there." Her mother's words were heavy with disapproval.

Regi resisted the urge to scream. She took a deep breath and said, "She'll be with Cam most of the time. I'm sure he'll take good care of her and it'll be a wonderful experience for her."

"I need to go," said her mother and the line went dead.

She hit the disconnect button on her phone and Nate handed her a glass of wine. "I'm sure you could use this," he smiled.

* * *

The months following their engagement rushed by in a blur. Memorial Day was highlighted by the arrival of hordes of tourists and the moving dedication of Cooper Gardens. Linda had done a stellar job of designing a peaceful environment and Jeff and Sam delivered a wonderful welcome speech.

The end of the school year was always a hectic time and summer brought more visitors to the tiny community. Regi stayed busy working a few days a week at Harbor Coffee and Books and spent her free time planning the wedding. She and Nate both wanted to find a house that offered privacy, a large shop for Nate's toys, and as much of a water view as they could afford. They had found a stunning home not far from Max's, but there was no way they could afford it. Jack promised to keep looking for the right house and the right price. To save money, she moved out of the condo and into Nate's house in June.

Sam, Linda, Jen, and Kate took Regi on a weekend visit to the city where they met Becky for another trip to Rose's Bridal Boutique. Maureen was delighted to meet Regi and helped her find the perfect dress. Since it was a winter wedding, she chose a dress with three quarter lace sleeves. The bodice was a simple scoop neck, but was encrusted with beads and crystals. The skirt was full and made of layers of organza. After twirling around to let them admire it one more time, she said, "We need to find a bridesmaid dress for my daughter and one for my maid of honor." She glanced at the group of women she cherished, sitting on the couch, sipping champagne. "Kate, would you be willing?"

Kate gasped and put her glass down. "Me, you want me? But, I'm old," she said, surprise written on her face.

Regi smiled. "You're not old and yes, I would be grateful if you would accept. I'm so lucky to have you in my life and I can't think of anyone I admire or look up to more than you."

Tears rolled down Kate's face as she got up. "I'd hug you, but I don't want to mess up your dress." She gripped her hand instead and squeezed it. "It would be my pleasure, Regi."

Maureen whisked Kate into a dressing room and selected a few dresses for her to try. The wedding would be silver and white with touches of black and red. Maureen chose a variety of dresses, representing each of the colors. Kate looked great in everything she tried on, but the showstopper was an elegant floor length dress, decorated with silvery sequins and pearl colored beads. It had a high slit up the side and showed off her shapely legs.

When she came out in it and stood next to Regi, the chatter stopped and all of them shrieked in delight. "That's the one," shouted Becky. "Don't y'all think it's spectacular?"

They all spoke at once saying it was perfect and it matched the bodice of Regi's gown. Linda snapped a picture of the two of them. "Do you have anything that would go with it for my daughter, Molly?" asked Regi.

Maureen dashed off to the racks and returned with a shorter version of the dress in the same fabric, but a more youthful style. They all nodded their approval and Regi discussed Molly's size with Maureen. Ultimately she decided to ship two sizes to her in Italy and let her get it fitted there, since she wouldn't have time for a fitting in Seattle. Maureen provided a label for return of the other dress.

Once the bride and Kate were dressed in their own clothes, Sam insisted on treating everyone to lunch. As they walked to a nearby restaurant, Sam took Regi's arm in hers. "I'm sorry your mom isn't here. I called her and invited her and even offered to arrange transportation."

Regi shrugged. "It's okay, Sam. I appreciate the effort you made. I've finally accepted that she isn't interested in being part of my life unless she's controlling it. So, until she makes an attempt, I'm afraid it's going to be like this."

They spent the rest of the day shopping and Spence joined them for a barbeque at Becky's. The women drove Brad nuts, giggling and talking until the wee hours of the morning.

The next morning they sat outside on the deck as the ferry plodded toward the island. Regi smiled as she considered her circle of friends. She'd never had many girlfriends, but was now blessed to be surrounded by a group that felt more like sisters. She may have moved to Friday Harbor to fulfill a youthful promise, but had gained so much more than she ever hoped.

Thirty

Kate threw Regi an elegant and fun shower at her house the week after Thanksgiving. Between the normal holiday chaos and the wedding preparations, there was no time for relaxing. Nate worked late almost every night between Thanksgiving and the wedding. They attended a few holiday parties, most notably the annual party Nate's parents hosted the first week of December. They were able to squeeze in one date night, which consisted of a romantic dinner at the Cliff House followed by an evening of holiday music at the Community Theatre.

Soon it was the week before the wedding and Molly was due to arrive. Regi had heard from her dad and he confirmed he would be at the wedding to walk her down the aisle, but he wasn't sure about her mom. Becky helped Nate take care of the details of getting Mr. Brady fitted for a tux and making sure it was on the island the day before the wedding.

When Regi met Molly at the ferry, she was surprised to see her in the back of Cam's car along with a woman she didn't recognize in the passenger seat. He parked on the street and Molly leapt out before he stopped. She ran to Regi and clasped her arms around her. "Mom, I've missed you," she said.

"I'm so glad you're here," said Regi. "And your dad came?"

"Yeah, he wanted to surprise you. Wait until you meet his girlfriend, Gianna. She's gorgeous and owns one of the vineyards by the villa."

Regi felt an unexpected twinge of sorrow at the thought of Cam with a new woman. "How wonderful," she said, knowing she should be happy he had moved on with his life. She held Molly by the shoulders and admired her hair, pinned into a loose chignon. "I like your hair—you look so grown up."

"Gianna helped me with it."

Cam helped Gianna out of the car and draped his arm around her waist to lead her to the sidewalk. "Regi, I'd like you to meet my friend, Gianna."

Regi extended her hand. "Lovely to meet you. Molly tells me you own a vineyard."

Gianna smiled, her gorgeous dark hair swirled into a similar style as Molly's. "I'm so pleased to meet Molly's mother. She and Cam have told me so many wonderful things about you, Regina. And, I hope you'll make room for us at your wedding. Molly insisted we come."

"Of course," said Regi with a smile, hearing the sincerity in Gianna's heavily accented voice. "We have plenty of room and would love to have you."

"I'd love to take us all to dinner tonight. Are you and Nate free?" asked Cam.

"Sure, that would be fun. He's been working late, so we probably need to make it around seven."

"Sounds terrific. We're staying at The Haven, but we'll meet you at seven. What sounds good?"

"How about Lou's? It's casual, but one of the best spots on the island and it will be easy to get a table," suggested Regi, knowing Nate would be more comfortable at Lou's than a fancy place.

Cam hugged Regi goodbye and she gave him directions to the bed and breakfast.

She and Molly linked arms and threw her suitcases into the back of the Jeep. They stopped for a coffee and Molly got a chance to visit with Kyle, who was working there on his winter break. Regi texted Nate with the dinner plans and called Lou to reserve a table.

After a walk around the harbor, and stopping to see Kate, Ellie, and Linda, they didn't have much time to get to Nate's to pick him up for dinner. Nate was in the shower when they walked in and Regi helped

Molly get settled in the extra bedroom. Murphy stuck to Molly like honey on a spoon.

Regi changed into a fresh turtleneck and added some jewelry, feeling frumpy next to the glamorous Gianna. When she came out she found Nate and Molly gabbing on the couch. "Ready to hit the road?" she asked.

They slipped on their coats and Nate drove the Jeep into town. As soon as Lou seated them at one of the tables in the back, Molly saw Cam walk through the door. She ran to lead him to the table.

Nate put his arm around Regi and gave her a kiss. "So, in less than a week I can call you Mrs. Martin."

She grinned, "I like the sound of that." She took his hand, "I hope it snows for the wedding. Linda and I were laughing about that. She was praying for sunshine on her day at Lakeside and I'm hoping for snow. I think it would make for some cool pictures," she said.

"They said there's a chance of snow this weekend, so it might happen." He kissed her again. "I don't care if it's sunny or snowy or rainy, I just want to marry you Saturday."

Molly cleared her throat. "Nate, this is Gianna," she said, as she put her hand on Gianna's arm.

Nate stood and shook her hand. "A pleasure to meet you." He also shook Cam's hand. "Nice to see you again, Cam. Molly's been telling me what a great time she had in Italy."

They listened to Molly ramble about all the fun she had touring Italy and her trips to France, Switzerland, and Austria. She had a new group of friends from school there and was sad to be leaving them behind.

They made some recommendations and placed their order with Lou, who Nate introduced to Cam and Gianna. He returned with some complimentary appetizers for the table.

Cam shared how he had come to love Italy and was planning to spend most of the year there, with Seattle serving as his second home. He had sold his house and would stay in the hotel his company owned when he was in the city.

Molly added, "Dad says I can stay every summer with him and I'm thinking about doing another semester abroad next year."

As they finished their meals, Cam said, "I've got a gift for your wedding I'd like to give you now. I don't want you to argue about accepting it, Regi. I've given this a lot of thought and I owe you more than I'll ever be able to repay. I want you, both of you, to have this as you start your new lives together." He handed a large manila envelope to Regi.

She frowned and looked at Nate and shrugged. When she opened it she saw a beautiful wedding card and inside was a picture of a house and a bunch of legal documents. She gasped when she realized what it was. "Nate, this is the house we wanted to buy."

"Oh, Cam, that's way too generous," said Nate.

"I insist you take it with my gratitude and best wishes. Regi could have pressed the issue of support all these years and she didn't. She raised our beautiful daughter on her own and did a wonderful job. Believe me, this gift is a drop in the bucket, compared to what I owe her. Learning about Molly and having the opportunity to have her in my life has made me a different person. I was on the brink of disaster the day I ran into Regi and giving you both something special would mean the world to me."

"It's not like he can't afford it," said Molly, earning disapproving looks from Nate and Regi. "You deserve a new start, Mom."

"Think of it as the support you're due for the last twenty years or so, plus interest. It's like finding a savings account you forgot about," smiled Cam.

Gianna added, "Please, Regina and Nate, accept his gift. He's been so excited and happy to be able to give you something as you start your new life. It would break his heart if you refused."

Nate shook his head. "I just can't believe it."

"Talk about it and consider it, please. Don't say no until you think it through," said Cam, as he took the check and handed his credit card to Lou. "It's the perfect house for you, plus it has plenty of room for Molly and any guests that come to visit you," he winked.

"We'll discuss it, but I'm not promising anything," said Regi.

* * *

Molly spent the rest of the week helping Linda prepare the flowers for the wedding and visiting with Ellie while she put together the wedding cake. She spent the evenings visiting with Kyle or Megan, leaving Nate and Regi time to discuss the gift.

They consulted with Nate's parents and sought advice from their close friends, including Spence and Kate. Jack confirmed the legality of the sale and the accuracy of the deed of trust. He had sold Cam the property, but wasn't allowed to divulge his intentions until he had presented the gift. Although all their friends prefaced their guidance by telling them they had to make their own decision, they all thought they should accept the house. Thursday night before the wedding they had dinner at Kate's.

"I think this is part of Cam's healing process. He's doing his best to make up for what he views you lost when he left for college and then again when he didn't meet you last year. You both feel guilt, I know," said Kate.

Spence added, "If you logically analyze it, his gift isn't too far off the mark of the twenty years of support you would've been due and awarded by the courts. He's worth billions and your monthly support would have been enormous. He's trying to give you what he feels he should have provided decades ago. It's a grand gesture, but I think he'd be devastated if you refused it."

On the way home Nate held Regi's hand and said, "I think we should agree to the house. I know it seems weird, but Kate and Spence made sense tonight. I do think it could damage your relationship with him and make it tougher on Molly. Spence was right about the math, so I know it sounds greedy and materialistic, but we love it and he loves the idea of giving it to us."

"Yeah, I came to the same conclusion tonight. Refusing it would be mean, when he's trying so hard to do the right and kind thing. I thought I'd invite him and Gianna to the dinner party tomorrow and we can announce it there."

"Perfect idea," he said turning into his driveway. "He's a remarkable person to care enough to do this."

"He seems so much better than when I saw him that first day while I was waiting for Molly. His color is better and the tension around his eyes isn't there anymore. I'm happy he sold the house and is moving to Italy." She paused, "I hate to admit it, but when I saw Gianna I felt a bit jealous. She's gorgeous and so sophisticated, but I can see the kindness in her. I think they're good for each other."

He brought her hand to his lips and kissed it, then turned off the engine. "You're gorgeous and I love you."

* * *

Saturday morning when Regi woke up she rushed to open the heavy drapes and check for snow. Her shoulders slumped when she looked out and saw only heavy clouds and a dreary sky. As part of the wedding package, she and Molly were staying in the honeymoon suite at the Lakeside Resort. Molly would be spending the night with Megan tonight and the newlyweds would be making use of the suite.

Seeing Molly curled up in bed, she let her sleep while she showered. They had appointments at Jen's for a full morning of beauty, so they needed to get moving. After she finished in the bathroom, she shook Molly to wake her and guided her into the bathroom.

While Molly got ready, she took advantage of room service and sipped her coffee and nibbled on a warm croissant while nestled in a chair overlooking the deck. Last night had been a wonderful evening. Cam had been so pleased when they accepted the house. He cried when she thanked him and hugged Nate.

Her dad had enjoyed himself, visiting with her friends and Nate's family. Her mother had decided not to make the trip, since it was her weekend to visit Leon in prison. She couldn't remember ever seeing her dad without her mom. He was like a butterfly emerging from a cocoon. He danced with his sister, who had come with him, and with several other women. Without her mother to dictate his every move, he was relaxed and talkative. During a break from dancing, he sat with Regi. "I'm sorry about your mom. She's a stubborn woman." He sighed and continued, "I'm not sure I can stay with her any longer. She's getting worse as the years go by—almost mean. Life's too short to be miserable." She felt a tear slide down her cheek.

That had been the only dim spot in an otherwise fun-filled evening. Max toasted the happy couple and Spence and Kate danced with each other, looking more like a couple than friends. Kate's son Mitch was visiting for Christmas and he and Ellie spent much of the evening visiting with each other by the fireplace.

She fingered the new necklace Nate had given her last night. It was a beautiful pearl and diamond necklace and came with a matching pair of earrings. She knew it would look gorgeous with her dress and he admitted Kate helped him pick them out.

As soon as Molly was ready they took off for town and their bridal makeovers. Nate and Brett, his best man, were in their suite at the resort. Brett was Nate's best friend from high school and the husband of his sister. Nate had asked Spence and Max to serve as ushers and they, along with Mr. Brady would all be using the suite to dress for the wedding.

Jack and Lulu attended Jeff's church and Pastor Mark had agreed to perform the ceremony. He was stationed at the front of the large room in the lodge. Jeff tapped on the suite door to alert the groom that it was time. He and Brett headed to the main lodge.

The honeymoon suite was filled with the bustle of women as they helped Regi get ready and made sure Kate and Molly were zipped and fastened. Jen double checked hair, adjusting the pearl and crystal hair comb she had used on the bride.

Jeff knocked on the door and let them know it was time. Sam, Linda, Jen, and Megan rushed out to get their seats, while Kate and Molly remained with Regi. "You look gorgeous, Mom."

Ryan's assistant took a few more photos of the three of them, before Molly and Kate left to get in line. Regi met her dad in the hallway outside the main lodge. "Oh, you are so beautiful, Regina."

"Thanks, Dad. I'm so happy you're here." She put her arm through his and steadied herself for the walk down the aisle. She peeked around the corner and watched as Kate and Molly stood, holding their gorgeous red rose glamelia bouquets Linda had designed. They were so simple, but stunning against the shimmery pearl dresses.

As the first notes of the" Butterfly Waltz" began, she heard the audience stand and she and her dad began their walk together. She swept her eyes over the crowd and saw Molly and Kate, both smiling, and then her eyes locked on Nate's. His brows arched and his vivid eyes went wide when he took in her silhouette and grinned.

She clutched her creamy white bouquet of peonies, roses, and ranunculus, with silvery sprigs of dusty miller tucked between the romantic blossoms. As she neared the front, she saw Nate's family, Lulu with tears in her eyes, and all her dear friends looking on as she floated by on her way to the man she loved.

As Nate took her arm, she glanced at the floor to ceiling window and sucked in her breath when she saw the large flakes of snow falling from the sky. He squeezed her arm and her gray eyes sparkled with amusement. At their request, Pastor Mark kept the ceremony short. At the end of the ceremony Nate took her in his arms and kissed her, for what seemed like five minutes. The crowd cheered and he did it again. Amid laughter and hoots, they were introduced as Mr. and Mrs. Nathan Martin.

As "My Wish" began to play, they started down the aisle, amid hugs and well wishes from their guests. Kate loaned the bride a luxurious white fur stole to wear and the photographer led them outside for a few shots in the fresh snow. Nate put his arms around her as they stood under a snow covered branch, flakes swirling around them. "You got your wish for snow today," he teased, kissing her. "You're the most beautiful woman I've ever seen," he said, tilting her chin up with his fingers.

"I got more than my wish—I got you," she smiled, looking into his eyes. Ryan directed them into a few more poses and finished the outdoor photos. They made their way to the ballroom for dinner and dancing, detouring only to steal a few kisses alone, before they were surrounded by their guests.

As soon as they were done eating, Nate led her to the dance floor for their first dance. He had selected "Amazed" and the band began playing the familiar melody. He took her in his arms and led her in a romantic slow dance. As she looked around the room and saw the candles flickering on the tables, twinkling lights decorating the beams, and the festive Christmas trees throughout the room, she felt like a snow princess.

The band leader invited everyone to the dance floor for the next song and she saw Spence take Kate's hand. She glanced over and saw Cam dancing with Molly and he looked across the room and met her eyes. Regi smiled back, content in the knowledge that their best days were ahead of them and that the promise she had made so long ago had eventually led her home.

Thank you for reading the third book in the Hometown Harbor Series. If you enjoyed it and want to continue the series, follow the links below to my other books. I'd love to send you my exclusive interview with the canine companions in the Hometown Harbor Series as a thank-you for joining my mailing list. Instructions for signing up for my mailing list are included below. Be sure and download the free novella, HOMETOWN HARBOR: THE BEGINNING. It's a prequel to FINDING HOME that I know you'll enjoy.

All of Tammy's books below are available at Amazon

Cooper Harrington Detective Novels

Killer Music

Hometown Harbor Series

Hometown Harbor: The Beginning (FREE Prequel Novella)

Finding Home

Home Blooms

A Promise of Home

Pieces of Home

I would love to connect with readers on social media. Remember to subscribe to my mailing list for another freebie, only available to readers on my mailing list. Visit my webpage at http://www.tammylgrace.com/contact-tammy.html and provide your email address and I'll send you the exclusive interview I did with all the canine characters in my books. I encourage you to follow me on Facebook at https://www.facebook.com/tammylgrace.books/, by liking my page. You may also follow me on Amazon, by using the follow button under my photo. Thanks again for reading my work and if you enjoy my novels, *I would be grateful if you would leave a positive review on Amazon.* Authors need reviews to help showcase their work and market it across other platforms.

If you enjoyed my books,
please consider leaving a review on Amazon

Hometown Harbor: The Beginning (FREE Prequel Novella)

Finding Home (Book 1)

Home Blooms (Book 2)

A Promise of Home (Book 3)

Pieces of Home (Book 4)

Killer Music: A Cooper Harrington Detective Novel (Book 1)

Praise for Tammy L. Grace, author of The Hometown Harbor Series and the Cooper Harrington Detective Novels

"This book was just as enchanting as the others. Hardships with the love of a special group of friends. I recommend the 4 part series as a must read. I loved every exciting moment. A new author for me. She's Fabulous."

— *MAGGIE!, review of Pieces of Home: A Hometown Harbor Novel (Book 4)*

"Killer Music is a clever and well-crafted whodunit. The vivid and colorful characters shine as the author gradually reveals their hidden secrets—an absorbing page-turning read."

— *Jason Deas, bestselling author of Pushed and Birdsongs*

"I could not put this book down! It was so well written & a suspenseful read! This is definitely a 5 star story! I'm hoping there will be a sequel!"

—*Colleen, review of Killer Music*

"Tammy is an amazing author, she reminds me of Debbie Macomber… Delightful, heartwarming...just down to earth."

— *Plee, review of A Promise of Home: A Hometown Harbor Novel (Book 3)*

"This was an entertaining and relaxing novel. Tammy Grace has a simple yet compelling way of drawing the reader into the lives of her characters. It was a pleasure to read a story that didn't rely on theatrical tricks, unrealistic events or steamy sex scenes to fill up the pages. Her characters and plot were strong enough to hold the reader's interest."

—*MrsQ125, review of Finding Home: A Hometown Harbor Novel (Book 1)*

"I thoroughly enjoyed this book. I would love for this story to continue. Highly recommended to anyone that likes to lose themselves in a heartwarming good story."

—*Linda, review of Pieces of Home: A Hometown Harbor Novel (Book 4)*

Made in United States
Troutdale, OR
02/05/2024